ACCLAIM FOR ROBIN

"In *I'll Be Seeing You*, Robin Lee Hatcher has created a dual-time novel that pulled me through its pages. Each story is complete and engaging. Put them together and this is a book that I couldn't put down with its themes of family and love. I highly recommend it!"

—CARA PUTMAN, AWARD-WINNING AUTHOR OF *FLIGHT RISK* AND *LETHAL INTENT*

"Set against the backdrop of the first days through the end of America's involvement in World War II, Hatcher's latest is a poignant look at one family's experience of hearth and home during the height of the conflict. When one mistake changes everything for sisters Lillian and Daisy, they must dig deep in order to forgive each other . . . and themselves. *I'll Be Seeing You* is a powerful journey through the testing of faith, the sometimes broken bonds of sisterhood, and how forgiveness for yesterday can become the hope that binds our tomorrows."

— KRISTY CAMBRON, CHRISTY AWARD–WINNING AUTHOR OF *THE PARIS DRESSMAKER* AND THE HIDDEN MASTERPIECE SERIES

"When Brianna's college history assignment forces her to interview her great-grandmother about life during World War II, she soon learns the truth about Daisy's past. *I'll Be Seeing You* proficiently explores love, heartbreak, family, mistakes, and consequences, and Hatcher highlights that God's grace and mercy is with us even when we're certain we don't deserve it. I was hooked in chapter one and devoured this beautiful story in two sittings!"

—AMY CLIPSTON, BESTSELLING AUTHOR OF *THE VIEW FROM CORAL COVE*

"Robin Lee Hatcher is at her best in this beautifully written double-feature romance. With one storyline in the present and one during World War II, readers are treated to two memorable heroines and their search for love, along with two true heroes. This touching story shines light on the difference between romantic passion and true love. A sigh-worthy read."

—Lynn Austin, Christy Award–winning author, on *I'll Be Seeing You*

"I love this book, and I read it in a day! Heartbreaking yet heartwarming, tender and touching—these characters came alive to me. Robin Lee Hatcher is one of my favorite novelists, and *I'll Be Seeing You* is one of her finest works!"

—Tricia Goyer, *USA TODAY* bestselling novelist of over 80 books, including *A Secret Courage*

"Robin Lee Hatcher never disappoints! I loved both eras of this dual timeline story, each with characters you will grow to genuinely care for. The beautiful overarching umbrella for both generations' stories is redemption from the pain of past betrayals. Another keeper from one of my favorite authors!"

—Deborah Raney, author of *Bridges* and the Chandler Sisters Novels series, on *Make You Feel My Love*

"What a delight to step back in time with the charming community of Chickadee Creek! Robin Lee Hatcher is one of my favorite storytellers, and I loved both the past and present threads in her latest novel as the main characters partnered together to overcome their difficult pasts and find genuine hope in God. With endearing characters and elements of suspense, this heartwarming romance was pure joy to read."

—Melanie Dobson, award-winning author of *The Curator's Daughter* and *Catching the Wind*, on *Make You Feel My Love*

"More than a century apart, two young women flee home, determined to forge new lives in remote Chickadee Creek, where they pray their abusers will never find them. Robin Lee Hatcher weaves together two generational love stories of the Chandler family, both rich in the courage required to relinquish fear and to discover the freedom in trusting God beyond the pain of betrayal. *Make You Feel My Love* blossoms as a novel of faith, love, and hope amidst the brave and sometimes faltering steps of newly found faith. An uplifting read with great characters, Hatcher's fans will love this."

—Cathy Gohlke, Christy Award–winning author of *Night Bird Calling* and *The Medallion*

"Robin Lee Hatcher tells the story of two people dealing with addiction in their lives in *Cross My Heart* . . . This is a good romance that deals with some very tough issues that happen all the time now."

—*Parkersburg News & Sentinel*

"Hatcher continues her Legacy of Faith series (*Who I Am with You*) with the story of Ben, Jessica's cousin, using alternating chapters to tell of Ben's great-great-grandfather through his family Bible during World War II, and how his struggles then mirror some of Ben's challenges now. Ben's faith is more solid than Ashley's to begin with, but Hatcher shows the growing process, and even in her portrayal of addiction is matter-of-fact, leaving readers to find their own truths . . . As usual, Hatcher is an auto-buy for all library collections."

—*Library Journal* on *Cross My Heart*

"Hatcher (*Who I Am with You*) continues her chronicle of the Henning family in the powerful second installment of her Legacy of Faith series . . . This touching story of forgiveness and redemption will appeal to fans of Colleen Coble."

—*Publishers Weekly* on *Cross My Heart*

"In *Cross My Heart*, book two of her Legacy of Faith series, author Robin Lee Hatcher continues to delve into the powerful influence of a spiritual family heritage. She weaves together two touching stories that examine life choices and their consequences. Utilizing a dual-time plot set against World War II and present day, Hatcher writes with realism and compassion about how hope and healing can grow from our deepest wounds."

—Beth K. Vogt, Christy–award winning author

"In this seamless time-slip novel, Hatcher provides inspiration in each character's growing relationship with the Lord and prompts readers to reflect on their own journey. This story of loss and redemption is sure to win the hearts of contemporary and historic romance fans alike."

—*Hope by the Book* on *Who I Am with You*

"This [is] a lovely story of love and loss and forgiveness."

—*Parkersburg News & Sentinel* on *Who I Am with You*

"Best-selling inspirational romance star Hatcher weaves a story of love and identity lost and found . . . The characters are authentic, the butterflies of anticipation are persistent, and the protagonists' deferred attraction is thrillingly palpable; you cannot help but hold your breath until they realize it too."

—*Booklist RAVE* review on *Who I Am with You*

"Hatcher's moving novel is rich in healing and hope, and realistically portrays the tough introspection that sometimes comes with being hurt."

—*Publishers Weekly* on *Who I Am with You*

"Tender and heartwarming, Robin Lee Hatcher's *Who I Am with You* is a faith-filled story about the power of forgiveness, second chances, and unconditional love. A true delight for lovers of romantic inspirational fiction, this story will not only make you swoon, it will remind you of God's goodness and grace."

—Courtney Walsh, *New York Times* and *USA TODAY* bestselling author

"Whenever I want to fall in love again, I pick up a Robin Lee Hatcher novel."

—Francine Rivers, *New York Times* bestselling author

"Hatcher's richly layered novels pull me in like a warm embrace, and I never want to leave. I own and love every one of this master storyteller's novels. Highly recommended!"

—Colleen Coble, *USA TODAY* bestselling author

"Engaging and humorous, Hatcher's storytelling will warm readers' hearts . . . A wonderfully delightful read."

—*RT Book Reviews*, 4 stars, on *You're Gonna Love Me*

"Hatcher has written a contemporary romance novel that is a heartwarming story about love, faith, regret, and second chances."

—*CBA Market* on *You're Gonna Love Me*

"Hatcher (*Another Chance to Love You*) creates a joyous, faith-infused tale of recovery and reconciliation."

—*Publishers Weekly* on *You're Gonna Love Me*

"*You're Gonna Love Me* is a gentle romance that offers hope for second chances. Author Robin Lee Hatcher has a gift for welcoming readers into fictional, close-knit communities fortified with love and trust. With each turn of the page, I relaxed into the quiet rhythm of Hatcher's storytelling, where she deftly examines the heart's desires of her characters set against the richly detailed Idaho setting."

—Beth K. Vogt, Christy Award–winning author

"*You're Gonna Love Me* nourished my spirit as I read about a hero and heroine with realistic struggles, human responses, and honest growth. Robin Lee Hatcher makes me truly want to drive to Idaho and mingle with the locals."

—Hannah Alexander, author of *The Wedding Kiss*

"I didn't think *You'll Think of Me*, the first book in Robin Lee Hatcher's Thunder Creek series, could be beat. But she did it again . . . This second chance story will melt your heart and serve as a parable for finding redemption through life's lessons and God's grace. Thunder Creek will always hold a special place in my heart."

—Lenora Worth, author of *Her Lakeside Family*, on *You're Gonna Love Me*

"With two strong, genuine characters that readers will feel compassion for and a heartwarming modern-day plot that inspires, Hatcher's romance is a wonderfully satisfying read."

—*RT Book Reviews*, 4 stars, on *You'll Think of Me*

"A heart-warming story of love, acceptance, and challenge. Highly recommended."

—*CBA Market* on *You'll Think of Me*

"*You'll Think of Me* is like a vacation to small town Idaho where the present collides with the past, and it's not clear which will win. The shadows of the past threaten to trap Brooklyn in the past. Can she break free into the freedom to love and find love? The story kept me coming back for just one more page. A perfect read for those who love a romance that is much more as it explores important themes."

—Cara Putman, award-winning author of *Flight Risk* and *Lethal Intent*

I'll Be Seeing You

Also by Robin Lee Hatcher

Make You Feel My Love

The Heart's Pursuit

A Promise Kept

A Bride for All Seasons

Heart of Gold

Loving Libby

Return to Me

The Perfect Life

Wagered Heart

Whispers from Yesterday

The Forgiving Hour

The Shepherd's Voice

Legacy of Faith Series

Who I Am with You

Cross My Heart

How Sweet It Is

Thunder Creek Series

You're Gonna Love Me

You'll Think of Me

Kings Meadow Romance Series

Love Without End

Whenever You Come Around

Keeper of the Stars

Where the Heart Lives Series

Belonging

Betrayal

Beloved

The Sisters of Bethlehem Springs Series

A Vote of Confidence

Fit to Be Tied

A Matter of Character

Coming to America Series

Dear Lady

Patterns of Love

In His Arms

Promised to Me

Stories

I Hope You Dance, included in *Kiss the Bride* and *How to Make a Wedding*

Autumn's Angel, included in *A Bride for All Seasons*

Love Letter to the Editor, included in *Four Weddings and a Kiss*

I'll Be Seeing You

A NOVEL

ROBIN LEE HATCHER

THOMAS NELSON
Since 1798

I'll Be Seeing You

Published in Nashville, Tennessee, by Thomas Nelson. Thomas Nelson is a registered trademark of HarperCollins Christian Publishing, Inc.

Thomas Nelson titles may be purchased in bulk for educational, business, fundraising, or sales promotional use. For information, please e-mail SpecialMarkets@ThomasNelson.com.

Scripture quotations in historical scenes are from the American Standard Version. Public domain.

The quote in chapter 70 is from the movie *Chariots of Fire* (1981).

Library of Congress Cataloging-in-Publication Data

Names: Hatcher, Robin Lee, author.
Title: I'll be seeing you : a novel / Robin Lee Hatcher.
Description: Nashville, Tennessee : Thomas Nelson, [2022] | Summary: "In a captivating split-time romance from beloved author Robin Lee Hatcher, will one family's biggest secret haunt the generations to come or will God's grace be free to shine?"-- Provided by publisher.
Identifiers: LCCN 2021056846 (print) | LCCN 2021056847 (ebook) | ISBN 9780785241416 (paperback) | ISBN 9780785241423 (epub) | ISBN 9780785241430
Subjects: LCGFT: Novels.
Classification: LCC PS3558.A73574 I45 2022 (print) | LCC PS3558.A73574 (ebook) | DDC 813/.54--dc23/eng/20211119
LC record available at https://lccn.loc.gov/2021056846
LC ebook record available at https://lccn.loc.gov/2021056847

Printed in the United States of America

22 23 24 25 26 LSC 10 9 8 7 6 5 4 3 2 1

To the One who brings beauty from ashes.

Chapter 1

PRESENT DAY—JANUARY

Brianna Hastings slipped into the rear of the classroom, choosing the corner with the poorest lighting. Perhaps she wouldn't be noticed by the professor back here. She'd registered for this class because, first, it would fulfill one of her requirements. Second, her mom had badgered her into it.

"History is interesting. Give it a chance. You'll love it."

Right. Fascinating. Sure.

She sank onto the chair and pulled her laptop from her bag, setting it on the table in front of her. After connecting to the college Wi-Fi, she clicked to open her messaging app. Quickly, she typed a text.

Meet for lunch at Dairy Queen?

She watched the moving bubbles indicate her best friend, Hannah Smith, was reading the message. Seconds later, the reply came.

👍 12:30

Other students continued to file into the classroom. Lots of them. Apparently this was a popular course. Maybe it was an easy A. She shook her head. Probably not. But an easy C would make her happy.

"Hey, Brianna." Adam Wentworth, one of her best friends since childhood, slid onto the chair to her right. "How's it going?"

"Okay."

Some girls in the row ahead of them turned, smiled, and greeted Adam, then Brianna, before facing forward again.

Adam leaned toward Brianna. "I've heard great things about Professor Meyer. This should be a good semester."

Adam was one of those guys everybody liked. He was average looking but had a smile that made friends in an instant. He was smart too. But what made him stand out was how nice he was. He was the sort of guy who stood up for the weird kid getting bullied in school. He was the guy who would set aside something he wanted to do in order to help someone in need. She'd seen all of that for herself ever since they'd become friends in elementary school.

She slid down in her chair. "I've never cared much for history."

"Really? But it's fascinating to learn how people used to live, used to think. Dad likes to say that the more things change, the more they stay the same. That's what I've seen when I study history. We've got things to learn from both the bad and the good of other times, other cultures."

He might have gone on, but he fell quiet, along with the rest of the room, when a man with glasses and salt-and-pepper hair stepped to the front. Professor Joseph Meyer, Brianna presumed. As soon as he began to welcome the students to his class, she zoned out. All of her professors had basically said the same thing for her past three semesters. She didn't expect Professor Meyer to break the pattern.

She opened her email app. Her friends rarely communicated that way, but the college did, so she'd learned to check at least once a day during the term. Nothing of importance showed up in her in-box. She closed the app and was about to open her browser when the professor's words caught her attention.

"This assignment will count for 50 percent of your grade and will have several parts."

Brianna glanced at Adam. "What assignment?"

He gave her one of those looks that said, *You should have paid attention*, before turning his eyes toward the front again.

"You'll find more information about it on page five of your syllabus, and more detailed instructions will be included in the weekly modules you'll find online."

Something told her she could say bye-bye to an easy A, B, or C.

Later that afternoon, Brianna sat at the kitchen counter, slicing carrots, while her mom peeled potatoes opposite her.

"At least you don't have to wonder who you'll interview," her mom said. "The oldest member of our family is GeeGee. Interviewing her will be a delight."

"A delight?" Brianna loved her great-grandmother, but spending hours listening to a ninety-eight-year-old woman talk about the past didn't sound like much fun to her.

If only she could have gone away to a university in another city like several of her friends. They got to do what they wanted, go where they wanted, study when they wanted. If only she wasn't stuck living at home with her parents, Mrs. Thrifty and Mr. Practicality.

Her mom took the prepared potatoes and placed them into the pot on the stove. "Would you like me to call Grandma? Set up a time for you to meet? This doesn't sound like a project you can put off. An early start will serve you well."

"Fine."

The look her mom sent her wasn't all that dissimilar to the one

Adam had given her that morning, and it made her want to grind her teeth. Who were they to judge her? She had a right to her opinions, to her likes and dislikes.

It's not fair. None of it.

It would serve her parents right if she failed everything. All that tuition, all those fees and textbooks, wasted. She could bail on her classes and just hang with friends until another semester was over. Only, all of her friends were in college or had jobs. Nobody would be free to hang with her. And she didn't *really* want to flunk her classes. Nor did she want to disappoint her parents, especially not her dad.

Life wasn't fair. That's what Dad would tell her if he knew her thoughts. Hadn't he said it a million times to her already? And that wasn't all he liked to say. *"You have it easy, Brianna. You don't know what* hard *is. Your parents aren't rich, but you've never spent a winter's night without heat. You've never known real hunger. You've never had to do without any real need and not very many wants either. I love you to death, Brianna, but I'm afraid you and your whole generation have been spoiled."*

"If you keep frowning like that," her mom said, intruding on her thoughts, "you're going to get a horrid crease in the middle of your forehead."

She sighed. "I can't do anything right."

"Oh, sweetheart. What a thing to say."

Brianna got up from the kitchen stool. "I'll call GeeGee. I might as well get started. Like you said."

Her mom smiled as she returned to chopping more vegetables for the stew.

Chapter 2

SATURDAY, DECEMBER 6, 1941

"Come on, Daisy. I swear, you're slow as molasses."

Daisy Abbott turned her attention from the downtown department-store window to her older sister, who'd stopped near the entrance.

Lillian gave her an impatient look. "Are you coming or not?"

"I'm coming."

Lillian pushed open the door and stepped inside. Daisy followed right behind her. She was thankful for the warmth awaiting them after the bitter cold of outdoors and paused long enough to enjoy it.

The store was busy on this first Saturday in December. Other Christmas shoppers moved about the aisles, and the air was richly scented with perfume from a display to their right.

Daisy sneezed into her gloved hand. "Let's get away from here." She sneezed again.

Her sister released a sound of exasperation. Lillian loved perfume, but she had to know Daisy wouldn't stop sneezing until they were well away from the fragrance counter. With a slight toss of her head, she hurried down an aisle.

"Why are we here?" Daisy asked as she trailed behind. "We bought everything on your list already."

"Not everything. I still have to get Brandan's gift."

As usual, Daisy's heart skipped a beat at the sound of Brandan's name. He was coming home on leave for Christmas, but of course he wasn't coming home to see her. Brandan Gallagher was Lillian's boyfriend. Still, Daisy would get to see him when he came to their house.

Lillian stopped at the display of men's watches. "Father prefers a gold watch, but I think silver looks better on Brandan." She looked down through the glass. "Don't you?"

Perhaps it's his blue-gray eyes. I love his eyes.

"Daisy, are you listening to me?"

"Yes, I'm listening."

"I asked if you think a silver watch is better than gold for Brandan."

"Yes. You should get the silver."

Daisy knew it didn't matter how she answered. Lillian didn't want her opinion. She wanted an audience. All her life, Lillian had enjoyed being the center of attention. She was the beautiful Abbott sister. She was the sister who could walk down the street and stop a man in his tracks.

The same way she'd stopped Brandan in his tracks when she was sixteen.

Jealousy coiled in Daisy's stomach. Speaking softly, she said, "You think he's going to propose when he's home for Christmas. Don't you?"

"Of course he's going to propose. Why wouldn't he?" Lillian met her gaze and smiled. "We're in love. He's got his college degree, and soon he'll finish his aviation training. Marriage is the natural next step for us."

"He hasn't seen you in months. Maybe he found a new girl in Louisiana."

For a moment, Lillian's smile faltered. Daisy didn't feel like smiling either. It was bad enough that Brandan loved her sister and barely knew Daisy was alive. It would be even worse if he fell for someone so far from home. What if she never saw him again?

Lillian tilted her chin. "I know Brandan. He would never betray me. Never. He's devoted to me. By summer, he'll be a pilot in the US Army Air Corps. A second lieutenant. That's what he's worked toward all these years, and I've waited as he asked me to. Now the waiting is almost over. Wherever he's posted next year, he'll want me with him."

Daisy wondered if her sister was as confident as she sounded.

A salesclerk stepped to the opposite side of the display case. "May I help you, miss?"

Lillian turned her gaze on the man. "Yes, thank you. I would like to see that watch." She looked down and pointed at the item beneath the glass.

"Of course."

Daisy leaned close and whispered, "Lillian, how can you afford that?"

"I've saved for it."

"Maybe Brandan doesn't need a new watch. If his watch still works, he won't want to replace it."

"What do you know about what Brandan wants?"

The words stung. Daisy knew a lot about Brandan. Much more than Lillian would ever guess. She knew he liked the attention that other girls gave him. She knew that he was ambitious and meant to follow his plans to achieve success with continued resolve. She knew he didn't mind going without something now if it meant having more later. She knew he was smart, sometimes caring, and sometimes careless. And she knew he wouldn't want a new watch if his old one worked.

Lillian looked at the salesclerk and all but batted her eyelashes at him. "My fiancé will want this watch, won't he?"

"Yes, miss. It's the best model we offer." He draped the band over his fingers and began to detail the watch's features.

After the dishes were washed and dried that night, Daisy took Jupiter, the family dog, for a walk. It was dark and cold outside, but she didn't care. She needed some time to herself.

Lillian had gone on and on about Brandan during dinner. He was scheduled to return to Boise in a week, and Lillian had made plans for nearly every minute of his leave. Daisy hoped her sister remembered that Brandan had a mom, a dad, and a couple of brothers who wanted to see him too.

And me. I want to see him.

She wiped away a tear with the back of her knitted glove.

Like it was yesterday, Daisy remembered the first time she'd seen Brandan Gallagher. She'd been not quite fifteen, a sophomore in high school, and hideous looking, her mousy brown hair too curly and her nose too long. Brandan was eighteen, a freshman at Boise Junior College, and as tall and handsome as a Greek god. He hadn't noticed her at the time. Why would he? She'd been just another kid in the crowd at a football game.

"Years later, and he still doesn't notice me," she said to Jupiter.

Somehow, before Daisy had had a chance to change from a girl into a woman and learn to tame her hair and apply makeup, her own sister had set her cap for Brandan, and he'd fallen hard for her. They'd been a couple ever since. Everyone—especially Lillian—believed they would get married soon.

Even Daisy believed it. "If only I didn't."

"Daisy? Is that you?" Todd Kinnear, the Abbotts' next-door neighbor, appeared in the light from his front porch.

She stopped and answered in a loud voice. "Yes. It's me."

Daisy didn't remember a time when the Kinnears hadn't lived next door. The two families had been close while Todd's parents were still living, everyone going back and forth between yards. Todd had been more like a big brother than a neighbor. More than once she'd gone to him with a problem she hadn't felt ready to share with Lillian or their mom. Six years her senior, Todd had seemed wise and steady. She still thought of him that way, although he didn't joke with her the way he had when she was younger. He was much more serious now, perhaps because he'd been managing Kinnear Canning ever since his father's death. At sixteen, he'd started helping his mom run the business, then had become the owner after she passed away when he was twenty-one.

"Cold night for a walk," he said.

"Yes." She pulled up the collar of her coat. "Jupiter needed some exercise."

"How's your family?"

"Everyone's well."

"Ready for Christmas?"

She thought of Brandan coming home on leave. Home to Lillian. "Yes, we're ready."

"Good. That's good." Todd cleared his throat. "Well, I won't keep you out here freezing. Good night."

"Good night, Todd."

He turned and went inside, and she and Jupiter continued on their way.

Daisy entered the back door of the house a few minutes later. The dog ran on ahead of her while she removed her gloves and stuck them into her pockets, then took off her coat and hat and hung them on the coatrack in the corner. By the time she reached the living room, Jupiter was lying on the rug in front of the fireplace. Her father sat near a lamp, reading a newspaper while smoking his pipe, and her mother was on the sofa, knitting a scarf.

"Did you have a nice walk?" Her mother's needles paused midair as she waited for an answer.

"Jupiter liked it." Daisy sank onto the sofa beside her. "Where's Lillian?"

"In her room. She said she had gifts to wrap and some cards to write. I've never seen her this excited for Christmas. Not even as a child." She resumed knitting. "I suppose it all has to do with Brandan, not Christmas itself. She is so head over heels for him. I hope she doesn't get her heart broken."

"He's a sensible young man." Her father turned a page in his newspaper. "Brandan knows it's important to stay focused on his studies until he graduates. Priorities. A man with his priorities straight will do well. He'll make a fine officer, and he'll make Lillian a good husband when the time is right."

Poor Brandan. It must be hard to stay focused with Lillian doing her darnedest to distract him.

A log tumbled in the fireplace, sending up red and orange sparks. Jupiter groaned as he shifted position on the rug. Her mother's knitting needles clicked at a steady pace.

It was a winter evening like so many other winter evenings gone before, and Daisy suddenly felt stir-crazy. Would her life go on like this forever? The family finances didn't allow for college. Not that it mattered. Most girls got married and stayed at home, whether or not they'd continued their education. After graduating from high school the previous spring, Daisy had found a job in a drugstore three blocks from the house. She worked there five days a week from nine to four. The money wasn't great, but she couldn't complain. Not after others had been out of work for years because of the Depression. What she could complain about was the sameness of the job. Nothing about it challenged her. Nothing occupied her mind. It was simply the same dull work, day after day after day.

As for boys and the possibility of marriage . . . Well, that was another problem, wasn't it? She wasn't interested in boys her own age. She wanted a man. Someone with something interesting to say. Someone who would sweep her off her feet. She wanted a man like Brandan Gallagher.

But there isn't anybody else like Brandan.

"Daisy, dear," her mother said, intruding on her thoughts. "Is something wrong?"

She shook her head. "No."

"Well, do stop frowning. If you don't, you'll have a crease on the bridge of your nose before you're thirty."

Who would notice?

She pushed up from the sofa. "I think I'll go to my room." She stepped to her mother and kissed her forehead. "Good night." She repeated the action and words with her father, then made her way up the stairs.

She stopped at the door to Lillian's room, intending to knock. After a moment's hesitation, she instead moved on to her own bedroom.

Daisy couldn't remember a time when she hadn't tagged along everywhere with her older sister. They'd shared a bedroom for a while. They'd played with dolls and taught school to their teddy bears. They'd been as close as two peas in a pod—until Daisy fell for Brandan. If only Daisy had told her sister how she felt about him, way back at the beginning, maybe Lillian wouldn't have felt the same. Then again, would Lillian have taken her seriously? Who cared about the romantic crush of a fourteen-year-old except for the fourteen-year-old herself? And besides, Lillian did tend to get what she wanted. And she'd wanted Brandan.

Daisy flopped onto the bed and stared at the ceiling. "I have to stop thinking about him. He doesn't see me except as Lillian's little sister. He'll never see me the way I want him to. Give up. Give up. Give up."

Tears welled again. They trickled over her temples and into her hair.

"Why can't he love me instead?"

She knew all the reasons, of course. Lillian was the beauty in the family. Lillian had a sparkling, irresistible personality. Men were drawn to her like bees were to honey.

And Brandan was drawn to Lillian. He would never belong to Daisy.

Todd Kinnear settled into the comfortable chair beside the fireplace and picked up his book. But he didn't open it. Instead, he listened to the silence filling the house. Most of the time, the stillness didn't bother him. He was used to it. But tonight it did. Maybe he should have asked to join Daisy and Jupiter and gone with them to the Abbott home. He was always welcome there.

Todd had a vague memory of the day he and his parents had moved into this two-bedroom house on Eastman Street. He'd been four and a half at the time. After that, he couldn't think of a time when the Kinnears and the Abbotts hadn't moved freely back and forth through the gate that joined their backyards. The men helped each other with home repairs. The women shared recipes. When Lillian and Daisy were sick with the mumps, Todd's mother had made a huge pot of chicken soup for them. When Todd had the accident that left him with a bum leg and less-than-perfect hearing, Nancy Abbott had taken turns with his own mom, sitting next to his hospital bed, reading to him, comforting him.

Todd had been sixteen when his father died from a heart attack, and Carl Abbott had been there to advise Todd as he struggled with finishing high school while trying to help his mom make sure the cannery didn't fail. Carl and Nancy Abbott had been there for Todd again when he buried his mom three years later.

As for the little Abbott girls . . .

He closed his eyes and rested his head against the chair back.

The Abbott girls weren't little anymore. Lillian was twenty and hoping to get married soon, and Daisy was eighteen. Or was she nineteen by now? No, still eighteen.

He smiled as he pictured the younger sister. Daisy wasn't the natural beauty that Lillian was, but she had a sweetness of spirit that he'd always found far more attractive. Lillian's beauty seemed only skin deep. Todd had caught more than a few glimpses over the years of her self-centeredness. Any man who took the time to really look would see the difference between the two sisters.

If it were me, I'd choose—

He broke off the thought before it could fully form. Daisy would never be interested in a guy like him. Not as anything more than a surrogate big brother, the way she'd always seen him. And he couldn't blame her. She was special and deserved somebody special. Not an ordinary working stiff like Todd.

Annoyed at the direction of his thoughts, he straightened and set the unread book on the nearby end table. Then he turned the knob on the Philco. Music came through the speaker, chasing silence into the corners of the small living room.

Chapter 3

PRESENT DAY–JANUARY

Daisy was nodding off to sleep when she heard the doorbell ring. For a moment, she expected to open her eyes and find herself in the living room of the house that had been her home for more than seventy years. But, of course, she didn't find herself there. These days she lived with her daughter, Elizabeth, and had for the past six years. *Six, already? Yes, six.*

Glory. How the years could blend together in her mind.

"Look who's here, Mama." Elizabeth led the way into Daisy's spacious bedroom.

"Hi, GeeGee." Brianna crossed to Daisy's recliner and gave her a kiss on the cheek. "Thanks for agreeing to talk to me."

"And why wouldn't I? There's nothing I like more than spending time with my family. Since most of them are scattered from here and gone, I welcome your company all the more." She reached up and patted the girl's cheek. "You're doing me a favor just being here."

"Can I get anything for you, Brianna?" Elizabeth asked.

"No thanks, Aunt Liz. I'm good."

"Mom?"

Daisy shook her head. "Thank you, dear. No."

Before settling onto a second chair, Brianna took her ever-present phone from the back pocket of her jeans and set it on the small table between the two chairs. "I'm supposed to record the interviews. Hope that's okay."

"Of course. Of course it's okay. At my age, it's nice if anybody wants to hear what I have to say. Let alone record it for a history class."

"GeeGee, that's not true."

Daisy smiled rather than attempt to correct the girl. Brianna wouldn't understand. She was so young, so fresh and innocent. Even in this age of the internet and the constant bombardment of information, even in a time of confusion and conflicting ideals, those of her great-granddaughter's age could never completely understand. That took living and experiencing. It took disappointments and heartaches. It seemed to Daisy, in some ways, that the young of today were even more . . . not innocent but . . . What was the word she wanted? Oh, yes. *Unprepared*. Unprepared for the realities of life. Entitled, she'd heard young people called. Perhaps it was true.

Lord God, let Brianna have more joy than sorrow in her life. Help her make good choices. Protect her from the temptations of the Deceiver.

She drew a deep breath and folded her hands over the soft flesh of her belly. "So, where do we begin?"

Brianna checked something on her phone, then pressed the screen and set it down again. "First, let's talk about what it was like to live in Boise when you were my age. Not in general but for you specifically."

"Remind me how old you are."

"I'll be twenty on my next birthday."

Daisy squinted as she searched her memory. "A few weeks from now. Right?"

"Yes, February the thirteenth."

"Twenty. So young. So very young."

"It's not all *that* young, GeeGee. You were married before you were twenty. Right?"

"Yes. I was."

"At least you got to do what you wanted to do. You were lucky."

Daisy heard something in Brianna's tone that reminded her of her sister, Lillian. Dear Lillian. Lillian, the girl who'd wanted what she wanted when she wanted it.

But was I so very different from Lillian back then? I wanted what I couldn't have. Or at least what I shouldn't have.

"GeeGee?"

She blinked. "I'm sorry, dear. I got lost in thought. Where were we?"

"Tell me what Boise was like when you were my age. Or what the country was like."

"Boise was all I knew. In a way, it *was* my country. I'd never traveled more than a hundred miles beyond its limits." Daisy leaned her head against the chair, her eyes looking not at the wall above Brianna's head but at the past. "I was a little younger than you as the Great Depression came to an end. My father was one of the fortunate ones. He didn't lose his employment during those lean years, but it was still very hard. Everyone learned to do without, including the Abbott family. Mother's garden helped keep us from going hungry, and there always seemed to be enough food for her to share when someone came to our back door, asking for help." She smiled wistfully. "Very few girls went to college back in those days, and my family certainly didn't have the money for it. It wasn't like today. Girls grew up expecting to find some nice young man and get married."

"What would you have studied in college, if you'd been able to go? Was there something you wanted to be?"

Daisy laughed. "Women didn't have as many choices back then as you have now. Remember, we'd had the vote only twenty years by the time I graduated from high school."

"Wow. I hadn't thought of that."

"But if I'd been able to go to college, I suppose I would have chosen to be a teacher because it would have meant I could encourage others to embrace learning." She leaned forward in her chair to look directly into Brianna's eyes. "Never stop learning, dear. And never be satisfied with the easy answer. Go deeper. Look closely at everything. Even what your college professors tell you shouldn't be enough to satisfy you."

Her great-granddaughter nodded.

"But I have wandered off the subject again, haven't I?" Daisy laughed at herself. "I suspect that will happen often. Don't be afraid to interrupt me if I go off too far."

"Okay."

"So let's see. What was Boise like back then? In the spring of 1941, when I graduated, I suppose the population was a little over twenty-five or twenty-six thousand. The airport had moved from near the river out to its current location. Which back then seemed way out in the desert. Boise State was still a junior college, and the only high school was Boise High."

In her mind she pictured many of her old school friends. She'd outlived most, if not all, of them. The downside to longevity, she'd learned, was losing people she'd known and shared memories with.

"In many ways I wasn't so different from you when I graduated from high school. Despite the Great Depression, I had dreams. My world was smaller, but my hopes weren't. The same was true for my friends." She released a sigh. "Europe was already at war, of course, but we were all so sure that we would stay out of it. Isolationism, it was called. America was determined not to become involved in a problem we didn't think was ours. How very, very wrong we were."

Chapter 4

SUNDAY, DECEMBER 7, 1941

The news of the attack on Pearl Harbor reached Brandan Gallagher as he walked toward his barracks at Barksdale Field, Louisiana. The next hours passed in a blur—listening to the radio reports, listening to fellow cadets guessing what would happen next, listening to the cacophony of thoughts in his head.

War.

The United States was at war. Not declared yet by Congress, but it was true all the same.

Brandan hadn't joined the Army Air Corps to go to war, although he'd known it could happen. After all, Germany had invaded Poland in 1939, and by the time Brandan started his training, most of Europe had become embroiled in the hostilities. Still, his sole reason for enlisting had been to become the best pilot possible, and that's what he'd told Lillian last spring after making his decision to enlist.

"Lill, aviation is the future. Before long, trains will be the transportation of the past. People will fly all around the world. You'll see. I want to be ready for it. The Army Air Corps is the best place for me to do that."

He hadn't mentioned the war in Europe at the time. Neither had she. His omission had been intentional. But Lillian? He wasn't sure she ever thought about what was happening overseas. Her world was much smaller than that. She cared about clothes and music and the movies. And marriage. She cared about marriage a lot, beginning with an elaborate wedding. No one had to tell him she was hoping for a proposal soon.

Brandan loved Lillian. He did. And he wasn't opposed to marriage. Just not this soon. He didn't want to be rushed. And it felt like she was rushing him. After all, he'd gone off to university before entering the military. He and Lillian had been apart more than they'd been together. They needed to take their time. Especially now.

He frowned, imagining the arguments they would have when he went back to Idaho. He was good at making her see things his way, but it would be unpleasant at first. Lillian liked to get her way.

Maybe they'll cancel our leaves because of the war.

He should be so lucky.

Daisy wasn't a fool. She knew that a war had been happening on the opposite side of the Atlantic for over two years. But she'd felt untouched by it in her quiet Idaho town.

She didn't feel untouched any longer.

Her father's face was grim as he listened to the radio. "We won't get the whole truth yet," he'd said a short while before. "The government will edit what's reported so we don't accidentally give important information to our enemies during the crisis."

"Our enemies."

The words continued to shiver through her. There were enemies out there. Enemies who wanted to kill and destroy, to conquer her country. Innocent people who'd been going about their lives on a beautiful Sunday were dead or dying. Not only sailors and airmen. Nurses and wives, mothers and little children. Babies, even.

She looked toward the windows of the living room and wondered if those same Japanese airplanes could fly to America's mainland. Could they even fly this far inland?

A knock sounded at the door, startling her. "I'll get it," she told her parents.

Her friend, Martha Neville, waited on the front porch. "Isn't it awful?"

"Yes." Daisy grabbed her coat and stepped outside. Better to be cold than listen to the news drone on.

Martha seemed to understand. "My brother says he's going to enlist tomorrow."

"I suppose a lot of men will do the same."

"Boys we went to school with."

Brandan won't have to enlist. He's already in it. She'd tried not to think of him, of what war meant to someone already in the armed services. She couldn't ignore the thoughts now.

"My dad remembers the last war," Martha continued. "He still talks about how many people died before it was over. Civilians and soldiers alike."

Daisy pulled her coat closer about her.

Martha's voice lowered. "Do you think this war will last for as many years as the last one?"

A different sort of chill passed through Daisy. Years? Years of war. She remembered from history classes that the Civil War had lasted four years. The Great War had lasted four years too. The current war in Europe had already raged for more than two years, and only the Germans seemed to be winning.

Martha sank onto a chair on the porch. "Why did they do it? What did we ever do to the Japanese to make them want to attack us?"

"I don't know." She wondered if her father understood the why of it. Or did it even matter why?

"I'm scared, Daisy."

"I'm scared too."

They fell into silence then, listening to a cold wind blowing through the leafless limbs of the trees, the faint drone of the radio reaching them through the closed front door.

Chapter 5

PRESENT DAY–JANUARY

Brianna closed her laptop, then crossed her arms on top of it and rested her forehead on her wrists. Facts and dates swirled in her head until she couldn't think straight.

"Are you doing homework or taking a nap?"

She lifted her head and watched Hannah Smith sink onto the chair opposite her.

Her friend pointed at the book near Brianna's right elbow. "History?"

"World War Two."

Hannah wrinkled her nose.

"You can't believe how much work this is. I mean, it's cool talking to my great-grandmother. I've always liked spending time with her. And the genealogy aspect of the assignment is interesting. It's kinda fun learning more about my family tree. But all of this other stuff the professor wants us to do? There's a lot to it. I'm wishing my oldest family member wasn't ninety-eight. Maybe another era would be easier. My mom was born in the seventies, so it was the nineties when she was my age. At least she probably had a cell phone."

Even as the words left her mouth, Brianna knew she wasn't

speaking the whole truth. The assignment wasn't easy, for sure, but she'd found it far more interesting than expected. Even when she wasn't working on it, her thoughts often returned to World War II and the stories her great-grandmother had shared already.

"I doubt the nineties would be easier," Hannah replied. "Sounds like your prof wants you to have to work for your grade. What're the students without older relatives doing?"

"Professor Meyer is connecting them with someone to interview. I'm glad that didn't happen to me. GeeGee is sweet. I'd hate to have to talk to a stranger a bunch of times."

Hannah reached for Brianna's book and pulled it toward her. "So what're you reading this for?"

"I'm researching the attack on Pearl Harbor and what led up to it. Trying to answer why it caught America by surprise. GeeGee said nobody expected it. Not regular people anyway. Maybe a few in government thought it could happen, but nobody else."

"Come on." Hannah pushed back her chair. "Let's get out of here. You're starting to sound like a textbook."

"That's mean." Brianna grabbed both book and laptop and got up.

Outside, they were met with a blast of cold air that tried to drive them back into the building.

"My car's over here," Hannah said above the whistle of the wind.

Brianna followed her friend, pulling up the hood of her coat to avoid the stinging cold. When they reached the vehicle, she put her laptop bag and library book on the back seat and then got in the front, releasing a huge sigh as she closed the door.

"Let's go see a movie." Hannah put the key into the ignition. "That new Liam Hemsworth film is supposed to be good."

Guilt niggled at Brianna. "I should go home and study."

"A couple of hours isn't going to make any difference."

Maybe it wouldn't make a difference for Hannah. Like their mutual friend Adam Wentworth, Hannah was one of those students who seemed to know and understand without a lot of late nights hitting the books. But Brianna had to work for everything. It wasn't just the history class that had proved difficult. Everything seemed to come harder for her.

"Never stop learning, dear. And never be satisfied with the easy answer. Go deeper."

GeeGee's words of advice had returned to her often in the days since their first interview. And recalling them now made up Brianna's mind for her. "You'd better drop me at home or let me out at the stop to catch the bus."

"Seriously? No time for Liam?"

"I can't. I've got to turn in some notes by Sunday night, and I'm not even close to having them ready."

"All work and no play makes a guy dull. Mom says something like that to Dad all the time."

"Gee, thanks. You think I'm dull." Brianna turned her gaze out the passenger window, starting to wish she'd stayed in the library.

"I'm sorry. That wasn't nice of me, and I didn't mean it that way. You aren't dull."

"Thanks again."

"Okay. No movie. I'll drive you home. I don't want you freezing to death at the bus stop."

"I appreciate it." She knew her tone belied her words.

Hannah waited until she was driving down the main thoroughfare. Then she turned on the radio, flooding the car with music instead of silence. It wasn't until the car stopped in front of Brianna's house that either of them spoke again.

Hannah lowered the volume on the radio. "Do you have classes tomorrow?"

"A couple online." Brianna got out and retrieved her things from the back seat.

"Want a ride on Friday?"

"Sure." She started to close the door, then said, "Thanks for the ride home."

"Glad to do it." Hannah's smile said she'd forgiven Brianna for her earlier surliness.

As soon as the car pulled away from the curb, Brianna hurried inside. The house was quiet. Normal for a Wednesday. Her dad was at work, and her mom volunteered at the senior center on this day every week. That was one of the reasons Brianna needed a ride to and from the campus with a friend or had to take the bus. She couldn't borrow her mom's car on Wednesdays, and Brianna's car, bought with her own hard-earned money when she was seventeen, had died toward the end of last semester, only a few days after Thanksgiving.

Pepper, the family dog, came to greet her. "Hey, girl." She set her bag and book on the kitchen counter and leaned down to ruffle Pepper's ears. "Want a treat?"

The dog turned three quick circles, body language for, *"Yes!"*

Her spirits improving, Brianna laughed, and she reached for the plastic jug of dog biscuits. If it weren't so cold and windy, she would take Pepper for a walk, but she supposed it was just as well she couldn't. She truly did need to work on her history assignment.

Sighing, she removed her coat and hung it over the back of a tall chair. Then she took her laptop from its bag and carried it and the book to the kitchen table.

Chapter 6

THURSDAY, DECEMBER 11, 1941

Todd pushed up from the chair behind his desk and walked to the window of his second-floor office. A dusting of snow lingered in the shadows of other buildings. The sky was clear, yet everything felt gray and gloomy to him.

It was official. The United States was at war not only with Japan but with Italy and Germany as well.

Some of his employees, men around Todd's age, had enlisted over the past four days. Many who hadn't done so yet would do so in the days and weeks to come. Todd wanted to be among them, but he doubted the armed forces would take him. The boyhood accident that had left him with 60 percent hearing loss in his right ear and a persistent weakness in his left leg would make him less than perfect in the military's eyes, he feared.

For a moment, he was thirteen again and messing around with the firecrackers a friend's dad had brought back from a business trip. Each of the boys had taken a turn, lighting a fuse and running for cover. But when it was Todd's turn, he'd tripped and fallen only a few steps away from the explosive. The blast had been deafening.

Literally, as it turned out. And the clumsy fall had broken a bone in his leg that never healed right. A stupid accident that had changed his life.

Of course, neither of those handicaps kept him from running a business or helping out a neighbor or walking long distances or accomplishing difficult tasks. He went hunting every fall and was a great shot with a rifle. He could certainly kill an enemy soldier without perfect hearing or a smooth gait. He could run fast enough when he had to, and he'd been told more than once that he was strong as an ox. He was ready and willing to serve. Believing the armed forces would reject him didn't mean he wasn't going to try to enlist. He wouldn't wait for a draft notice. Tomorrow he planned to go to the recruitment office first thing. There was a chance they would take him. After all, as of today the country was fighting wars on two fronts. They would need men. Many men. Even men who weren't physically perfect.

A knock came at the office door.

"Yes?" He turned as it opened, revealing a young clerk.

"Mr. Kinnear, sir. You're needed in Mr. Jamison's office."

Todd arched an eyebrow, expecting more information. Instead, the clerk backed into the hallway and disappeared. That told Todd all he needed to know. He strode out of his office and down the hall.

Roy Jamison, the accountant for Kinnear Canning, was slumped over his desk when Todd entered. An almost empty bottle of whiskey sat just beyond reach of an outstretched arm.

"Roy." Todd closed the door firmly behind him. "Mr. Jamison?"

The man muttered something, shook his head, and finally straightened.

Todd moved across the office. "You needed me for something?"

"I didn't."

"I must have been misinformed." Casually, Todd took the bottle from the edge of the desk and moved it to the table against the wall.

Then he returned and settled onto a chair opposite Roy. "Are you all right?"

"Perfectly all right." Roy spoke slowly, not so much slurring the words as trying to make sure what he said made sense. "He joined up, the young fool." He picked up the empty glass and put it to his lips. Finding not even a drop of liquor left inside, he slammed it back onto the desk. "I told him to wait."

Todd nodded, understanding this drinking spell was about Roy's son, Harry. Not that Roy Jamison needed much of an excuse. He'd been drinking more and more in recent months. Lately, it was a rare day when he didn't drink at his desk. Only a few in the company knew about the problem. Still, Todd didn't think it could be hidden for much longer. He didn't want to let the man go. Roy was good at his job. Besides, Todd liked him. But he might not have a choice about firing him. Who could trust the figures he came up with when he was drinking?

"Harry's of age." Todd stood.

Roy covered his face with both hands. He said something, but the words were muffled.

"What did you say?" Todd touched the other man's shoulder.

Roy lowered his hands. "I might have kept him out of it."

"Not many will be kept out of this one."

Roy shook his head.

"You should go home. It's nearly the end of the day. Nothing to keep you here." He motioned with his head. "Come on. I'll take you. I'm done for the day."

"Young fool," Roy muttered.

Todd assumed he meant Harry, although that wasn't guaranteed. Roy might have meant Todd. The older employees hadn't liked it when Todd became their boss. He'd been only nineteen when he took over the reins from his mom, and many had seen him as a kid, still wet behind the ears. They'd been right. He'd had a lot to learn. But somehow he'd muddled through. Despite the lingering effects of the Depression, the company had grown stronger under his leadership. Resistance to his authority didn't happen often these days, but he wasn't surprised when it did.

Roy stood and took an uncertain step away from the chair. Todd went to his side and grasped his arm. "We'll go out the back way." They moved toward the door. "I'll have you home in no time at all."

Roy stopped and looked at Todd, eyes bleary. "*You* won't go to war. You've got more sense than that."

I'll go if I can, Todd thought but chose not to say it aloud.

Roy's feet shuffled, and his upper body wobbled to and fro, but Todd managed to get him to the end of the hall, down the back stairs, and out to the parking lot. He helped the man into the passenger seat of his car, then went around to the driver side and started the engine.

It took less than ten minutes to drive from the factory near the river to the Jamison home on Warm Springs Avenue. It was an impressive house made of brick and sandstone. Certainly not the sort of place that an ordinary accountant could buy. But Roy Jamison hadn't bought it. He'd married Theresa Bellingham, the daughter of a wealthy cattleman. The house had been a wedding gift to the young couple. Or so local gossip said.

Leaving Roy in the car, Todd went to the front door. Not long after, with the butler on one side and Roy's son on the other, the intoxicated man was helped up the walkway and into the house. Todd watched from the sidewalk until they disappeared, then turned to open the car door. Harry came outside again before Todd could get into the vehicle.

"Thanks," the younger man said.

"This is because you enlisted?"

"Yeah. Father's taking it hard." Harry glanced over his shoulder, then back again. "He lost three brothers in the last war."

"Ah."

"He's been afraid of this ever since Germany invaded Poland." Harry rubbed his forehead. "I guess that's when the drinking started. I was still away at school, and Mother didn't tell me until I got back and could see for myself. It used to be just at night, but I guess that isn't so lately. I guess . . ." With a shake of his head, he let the words trail into silence.

Todd knew Harry Jamison had been sent to a fancy boarding school for four years rather than attend the local high school. His father's drinking explained why Harry hadn't left Boise for the next phase of his education this fall. He'd been needed at home.

"But I couldn't stay home after what they did to Pearl Harbor," Harry continued. "I couldn't."

"I understand the feeling."

"I told Mother I was going to enlist. She said I needed to make my own choices." He met Todd's gaze. "Maybe I was wrong." Uncertainty edged his voice. "But it's done now."

"'It's done now.'" Todd wished he could do more than echo the boy's words. And at eighteen, maybe nineteen, he *was* still a boy, even if he didn't know it.

"Mr. Kinnear, would you look after my dad once I'm gone? Like you did today."

Todd wasn't sure how to answer. Hadn't he just wished he could do more? Now Harry was asking him to do more. He swallowed hard, then said, "If I'm still around, I'll do my best to look after your father. I promise." *If I'm still around*, he repeated silently.

Chapter 7

SATURDAY, DECEMBER 13, 1941

Lillian didn't budge from the living room window for over an hour, knowing that Brandan could pull up to the curb at any moment. His leave hadn't been cancelled because of the war and neither had his travel plans. Unlike civilians, he could get a seat on a transport plane, and he'd arrived in Idaho hours ago. But he'd had to go home to his parents and brothers first.

But he didn't have to stay there so long. Did he? Why isn't he here by now?

The sky had turned from blue to gray as dusk settled over the earth. Soon it would be dark. She hated winter. She hated when it got dark before the day was even over.

"Maybe Mrs. Gallagher kept him at home," Daisy said.

Lillian looked over her shoulder. "He'll come tonight. He'll want to."

"You know how Mom would be if either of us was away for months. She'd keep us at home and within her sight. Especially if we were going to be sent off to war soon."

Lillian didn't want to think about the war. "He'll come tonight.

He's been away from me just as long as he's been away from his mom."

Daisy gave her a strange look, then turned and disappeared into the kitchen.

Lillian resumed watching out the window. It shouldn't surprise her that Daisy didn't understand. After all, her sister didn't know what it was like to be in love and to be loved in return. Daisy was probably jealous of what Lillian had. And why wouldn't she be? Daisy would never find a guy as wonderful as Brandan.

Lights flashed at the end of the block, and a car drove in her direction.

Let it be him. Let it be him. Oh, please, let it be him.

The automobile slowed and pulled to the curb in front of her house. She left the window, grabbing her coat from the rack and hurrying onto the porch before Brandan had a chance to get out of the car. There was still enough light for her to see his grin.

"Brandan." She went down the porch steps.

He met her halfway along the sidewalk and took her in his arms, lifted her feet off the ground, and twirled her around as he kissed her. Oh, how he kissed her.

"I was afraid you weren't going to come," she whispered when their lips parted. It was a confession she hadn't made to her sister but could say now that Brandan was with her.

"Not see my girl? Impossible." He kissed her again.

When they came up for air, Lillian said, "It's been the worst week of my life." She turned, hooking her arm through his, and drew him toward the house.

"The worst week for every loyal American."

His words and grave tone sent a shiver through her.

"How are your parents?" he asked. "How's Daisy?"

"Daisy's okay. Dad's glued to the radio when he's at home. Mom's trying to pretend none of it's happening."

"Nobody can do that now. It's happened. It's real."

They climbed the steps and went inside. As Brandan closed the door, Daisy reappeared from the kitchen.

"Hi, Brandan."

"Hi, Daisy. Good to see you."

"You too."

A moment later, both of her parents entered the living room.

"Brandan," her father said, walking forward with a hand outstretched. "Glad to see you home again. I don't know that any of us are ready to say Merry Christmas this year."

"No, sir."

They shook hands.

"Sit down. Sit down." Her dad motioned toward the sofa. "Tell us about your training. Will it be shortened now that we're at war?"

Lillian's heart nearly stopped at the question. Why would they shorten his training? Did her dad mean that Brandan could be sent to fight right away? Surely not. She looked at Brandan, frightened what his answer would be.

"No, sir. Not that I've been told. I should graduate in the summer. They're going to need plenty of well-trained pilots."

Relieved, Lillian sank onto the sofa, and Brandan sat beside her.

"Brandan," her mother said. "We haven't eaten yet. Would you like to join us?"

"I'd like to, ma'am, but I can't. I promised Mom I'd be home for dinner. I can't stay long." He looked at Lillian. "But I needed to see Lill for at least a little while."

Tears welled in her eyes. She tried to blink them away, wanting to see him clearly instead of through a blur.

Her father cleared his throat as he stood. "Well, then. Why don't we leave you two to yourselves?" He glanced at his wife. "I'm sure we'll see you before you return to Louisiana."

"Yes, sir. I'm sure you will. I don't go back until after Christmas."

"I'm glad. Say hello to your parents for me."

"Will do."

Lillian waited until her mother and father disappeared into the den and Daisy went up the stairs. Then she snuggled close to Brandan's side. "Your leave isn't nearly long enough. It will go by so fast."

"I'm lucky I got to come home at all with what's happened. But I'm here now. I'm with my girl." He kissed her on the forehead.

"Brandan, you . . . you know that I love you. Don't you?"

He drew back and cupped her face with one hand. "Yes." His eyes were filled with tenderness. "And I love you."

"I'll be glad when you're home for good. After you graduate, you—"

"It won't be for good, Lill. I'll be sent overseas. I don't know where. Maybe to the Pacific."

"The war could be over by summer. Lots of people say so."

"It won't be."

"But some say it will."

"There are people who have said that about every war back through history. It rarely happens. Maybe it never does. This one definitely won't."

She felt cold all over. "Must you go? Maybe you could train other pilots. You're—"

"I'll have to go. This is what I've been trained to do."

"But not until you graduate."

"Not until then."

Lillian took hold of his hand. "Let's get married, Brandan."

"What?"

"You said you love me. You know I love you. Let's get married. Let's get married next week. Before Christmas. Before you have to go back to Louisiana."

"Lillian, be reasonable."

Brandan almost never called her Lillian. It was usually "Lill" with him. His use of her proper name told her how serious he was.

"There's no way I can get married now. I'm going to war."

"Other men have enlisted, but lots of them will marry their sweethearts before they leave. I know a couple of girls who plan to get married before the new year."

"Are you listening to yourself?" He got up and stepped toward the fireplace. "We're not getting married. Not as things are."

She fought back tears. This wasn't going as she'd imagined. If only she hadn't blurted it out like that. She hadn't meant to. She'd wanted getting married to be his idea. It would have been, if only she hadn't felt that rush of panic. A week ago it had seemed reasonable. Almost certain.

But a week ago America hadn't been at war, and the man she loved hadn't been destined to go fight in it.

Brandan ran a hand over his hair. "Look, Lill. I'm sorry. I didn't mean to upset you. I don't want to hurt you."

Part of him wanted to go to her, hold her, comfort her. But he knew what would happen if he did. He'd end up kissing her, and she'd end up trying to convince him that it was time they got married. And marriage wasn't in the picture for him. Not any time soon. He'd told her that he loved her, and he meant it. He did love her. But he wouldn't marry her yet. Later, when the war was over, if he made it back alive and in one piece.

Even without a war, he wouldn't have been ready to marry, not even by next June. Without a war, he'd planned to serve out his time in the military as a pilot. Later, once he was discharged, there would have been a future with TWA. Then he would have been ready to marry. He could have given Lillian a home in a nice neighborhood, and they could have had children together.

But there *was* a war, and before this time next year, he would be flying bombers somewhere far away, like he'd been trained to do.

Lillian dried her eyes with a handkerchief. "I thought . . . I thought you . . ." She let the words drift into silence, her gaze pleading.

"I know." He returned to the sofa and sat beside her. "I know what you thought. But sweetheart, it isn't the time."

She pressed her face against his shirt. "But—"

"Lill, I don't want to leave you a war widow." It was a good excuse, although not the whole truth. He wasn't ready to settle down with a wife. He wasn't ready for a family. He liked things the way they were now. He liked the camaraderie he'd found in the air corps. He liked flying bombers. He wasn't ready to go home to the little lady and, in time, a kid or two. Not yet.

She pulled away, sucking in a breath. "Take it back. Don't say such a thing. It's bad luck. I wouldn't be a war widow."

"It's a fact that it could happen. Saying it aloud doesn't bring bad luck."

She choked back a small sob.

It made him wish he could change his mind about getting married, but he couldn't. And wouldn't. "Let's take it one day at a time. Okay? Let's enjoy my visit while I'm home. Nobody knows what tomorrow will bring."

"It isn't fair," she said, her voice almost inaudible.

He agreed. It wasn't fair. Brandan had had plenty of plans of his own. War hadn't played into any of it, even though it had been a possibility. He kissed the top of Lillian's head again before saying, "I've got to get home. Mom'll have dinner on the table soon."

"Will I see you tomorrow?"

"Tomorrow morning. I'll be at church with the family."

"Church, of course. But what about afterward? Will you come for Sunday dinner? Mom will want you to come."

He touched her cheek with his fingertips. "I'd better see what my folks have planned before I commit. Maybe you can come have Sunday dinner with us."

She stuck out her lower lip in a pout but didn't argue. He was thankful for that small mercy. Lillian had a way of manipulating him. Even when he recognized that's what she was doing, he had a hard time resisting her charms.

When he stood again, he drew her up with him, pulled her into his arms, and kissed her thoroughly. Holding her felt so good, so right. She belonged in his arms, as if she'd been made for him. Right from their first date he'd known it would be this way between them. He wanted to be her husband, to lie with her in bed, to make love to her at night and wake up with her beside him in the morning. Just not yet. One of them had to think clearly, and it was obvious that someone was him.

Chapter 8

PRESENT DAY–JANUARY

Daisy looked at her great-granddaughter, seated on the floor of the family room, a notebook in hand, her computer nearby. How many years had it been since Daisy could get down like that? Longer than she cared to remember. Her mother used to tell her that youth was wasted on the young. She hadn't known how true that was at the time, of course. Young people couldn't comprehend what it meant to be old until they got there themselves.

"Brianna, what is it you want to do when you graduate?"

"I haven't decided. Something that will make me a lot of money. I'm sick and tired of doing without."

"Doing without?"

"Yeah. Like a car. The car I bought a few years ago died and can't be fixed without a ton of money. Way more than it's worth. And Mom and Dad won't buy me a better one. It doesn't matter that I need it. They just say they can't afford it right now."

Daisy wondered if the girl heard herself. Did she have any idea what it was truly like to make do or do without? She might not have a car of her own at the moment, but she went to college, she had good clothes, she had a mobile phone and a laptop.

Entitled. The word came to her again. A word that could be applied to a number of recent generations, she supposed. Brianna's generation was labeled something like Generation X or Y. Her own had been called the Greatest Generation. Her children had been born into the Silent Generation. And then had come the Baby Boomers. After that, she didn't know.

She shook her head. What did it matter? Were such labels important? There was nothing new under the sun, no matter how you changed labels. And God knew every person of every generation. He knew them by name, and He cared about a person's heart alone, not the label the world gave them.

"Your mother and father are kind and sensible people, my dear. You can be sure that they're trying to do what is best for you."

Brianna rolled her eyes.

Daisy suspected she hadn't been meant to see it, but she did. "A good plan will serve you well, and a college education is of great importance these days, so I'm told. So what is your plan?"

"Like I said, I haven't decided. I don't like science. I'm okay with math. I guess some sort of business degree."

"Don't you have to declare a major?"

"I went with liberal arts since I couldn't decide what else I wanted. But I'll probably change. I've got two more semesters before I transfer to Boise State. Maybe I'll switch to media arts or marketing. Those might be interesting." She released a long sigh. "I just wish it was over already so I could leave home and get a real life."

"'Get a real life,'" Daisy whispered.

"You're probably going to say something like Mom does."

"And what's that?"

"Oh, like my life is real already. Something lame like that."

Daisy smiled at her great-granddaughter. "Can you argue with her?" She was met with another dramatic sigh. "My sister was impatient to get on with life. She knew what she wanted and was determined to get it. But it didn't turn out the way she thought it would. Life rarely does."

"Did yours, GeeGee?"

She smiled tenderly at the girl. "No. But my steps were guided by God, and when I went astray, the Lord was still able to turn all things to good when I returned to Him in faith and trust."

"Nobody thinks like that anymore. I mean, I'm a believer but . . ." Brianna let the words trail into silence.

"You're wrong, Brianna. God will always have a remnant who think like that, even in an age like this one. And remember, the Lord doesn't have grandchildren. Only children. Your generation is no different from mine or any other in that regard. We must each come to Him in our own faith, not the faith of our mothers or fathers."

"Plenty of kids I know have never been to church. Most of them, maybe."

Her great-granddaughter's words caused a wave of sadness to wash over Daisy. It left her feeling that she'd lived too long. She was a dinosaur living in an age of handheld devices, a time of calling good "evil" and evil "good." "Even so, come, Lord Jesus," she whispered.

"What?"

Drawing a breath, she focused on the girl on the floor. "Tell me, Brianna. What have you learned so far about the nineteen forties? About the war?"

"Not a lot yet. I'm reading a book the librarian suggested and did some research online. I know Japan hated us. Like some other countries hate us today. I guess that never changes. People don't seem to like Americans much."

Nothing new under the sun, Daisy reminded herself.

"Sometimes I don't blame them," Brianna added.

Here was one of the greatest differences between their generations. Daisy and her sister and their neighbors had been raised to be proud of their country. Patriotism had been the norm, not the exception. Lately, it seemed that Americans found more reasons to hate the country of their birth than reasons to love it. What a shame when the ideals that had birthed the nation were still so good, even while the people were imperfect.

She leaned her head against the back of the chair. "After Pearl Harbor was attacked, most all of the young men I knew enlisted in the military in those early weeks and months. Lillian's beau was already in the Army Air Corps. That's what they called the air force back then. And men who didn't fight because of age or health—men like my father—most of them found other ways to serve. Women and girls too. We were galvanized as a nation. We'd been tried by the Great Depression and then, it seemed, we were refined by the Second World War."

Chapter 9

SUNDAY, DECEMBER 14, 1941

Church on that Sunday morning, the first following the attack on Pearl Harbor, was a solemn affair. Across the nation, it was a day to pray for the mercy of God. It was a day to ask the Lord for a swift conclusion to the war.

Seated in a back pew, Todd looked at the families clustered together in the sanctuary. He saw the fear on the faces of the fathers and mothers, especially those with sons. He saw grim understanding on faces of the older men who'd served in the Great War. And he saw uncertainty wherever he looked, even here among people of faith.

Several pews ahead of him and on the opposite side of the aisle sat the Abbott family. He watched as Lillian leaned to her right and whispered something to her boyfriend. Todd knew Brandan had joined the air corps last summer and would be completing his training in the coming months. How soon would he join the fight overseas? Would he be sent across the Atlantic or the Pacific? And how soon would he come back? Lillian and Brandan had to be wondering those things, along with so many others in this sanctuary.

People stood for the closing hymn, pulling Todd from his wandering thoughts. He quickly joined them.

As the final note of the hymn faded and the service was over, the congregation left the sanctuary, some heading out into the cold to their automobiles, others following the hallway to the fellowship hall. With nothing awaiting him at home except leftovers in the refrigerator, he went with the latter group. He filled a cup with coffee, and when he turned around, he saw both the Gallagher and the Abbott families enter the hall. Carl Abbott broke away from the group and headed toward the coffee.

"How are you, Todd?" The older man filled a cup with the hot brew.

"Doing all right, all things considered."

"All things considered." Carl's gaze moved to his family. "Troubled times ahead of us."

"Yes."

"It might sound terrible, but I thank God I have daughters. I won't have to send either one of them off to war."

"I understand, sir."

Several years before, Carl had encouraged Todd to stop calling him "sir" or "Mr. Abbott" and to use his given name. He still found that hard to do, try as he might. Carl Abbott was more surrogate father to him than a friend.

Daisy and another girl hurried across the hall toward them. Daisy gave Todd a quick smile. "Good morning."

"Good morning, Daisy."

She turned to her father. "Dad, Martha's invited me to have dinner with her family. You don't care if I miss Sunday dinner at home, do you?"

"No. You go on with Martha."

"Thanks." She stood on tiptoe to kiss her dad's cheek, then she and Martha hurried off again.

Carl looked at Todd. "Seems we have an empty chair at our table. Would you care to join us?"

"I wouldn't want to intrude."

"I apologize for my lousy invitation. I don't need you to 'fill a chair.' I want you there. You know we enjoy having you with us. And this isn't a day for anyone to be alone."

Todd nodded in agreement. He'd felt the silence at home more than usual this past week. After his dad died, Todd and his mother had been made welcome in the Abbott home on countless occasions for countless meals. On Thanksgivings and Christmas Eves. On Easter Sundays. For summer barbecues. And after Todd's mom passed away, the invitations had continued. The Abbotts were good neighbors, kind neighbors. Todd felt lucky to have them in his life.

"Well?" Carl prompted. "There's a roast in the oven even as we speak."

"I'm too smart to turn down one of Mrs. Abbott's roasts."

"Good. That's good. And with Daisy gone and Brandan coming to dinner, for once the men will outnumber the women at the table. A welcome change."

"The dinner was wonderful, Mrs. Neville." Daisy lifted a stack of dirty plates from the table. "Thanks for having me."

"We love having you, dear."

Daisy followed Martha into the kitchen, and the two of them quickly washed the dishes. Then they escaped up the stairs to Martha's bedroom.

"What is up with you?" her friend asked as she pulled a record from its sleeve and set it on the player. "You hardly said two words the whole time we ate."

Glenn Miller's "In the Mood" came through the speaker.

Daisy sank onto the floor. "Sorry. I guess I was lost in thought."

"Thinking about the same boy you always think about?"

A shiver of alarm raced through Daisy. "What boy?"

"The one you've mooned over for ages."

"I don't know who you mean."

Martha laughed as she plopped onto her back on the bed. "Right." She rolled onto her stomach, feet up in the air, her eyes locked on Daisy. "Someday you'll tell me who he is. Or maybe you'll finally meet somebody who'll like you in return. Somebody super nice, like my brother." Her friend's smile evaporated. "Greg leaves right after New Year's."

"Does he know where he'll go for training?"

"Not that he's told me." Martha closed her eyes. "I really hate the thought of him going. Most of my life I thought he was a pain-in-the-neck big brother and couldn't wait until he moved out. Now I miss him before he's even gone."

Would Daisy miss Lillian if she moved out of their parents' house? Of course. But if Lillian moved out, it wouldn't be to go to war. It would be because she got married. Married to Brandan.

At least Brandan hadn't proposed yet. Daisy knew that for certain. If he'd proposed, Lillian would have told her in a heartbeat. She wouldn't keep it a secret. She'd want it announced from the pulpit and in the newspaper before he could change his mind.

Daisy felt a flutter of hope in her chest. Was there any chance Brandan would change his mind about loving Lillian? If he hadn't proposed when he'd first gotten to Boise, maybe he wouldn't ever propose. Maybe he didn't want to marry Lillian. Maybe—

"Who is he, Daisy? The guy you can't forget. You can tell me."

She met Martha's curious gaze. "Somebody who doesn't even know I exist."

"I don't believe that." Martha got up and went to the record player.

"It's true. He likes somebody else. Somebody older. Somebody beautiful."

Bing Crosby began to croon "Only Forever," and the lyrics made Daisy want to cry.

"You're pretty, and you're smart." Martha returned to her bed and sat on the edge. "Any guy would be crazy not to fall for you."

Daisy pictured Brandan sitting beside Lillian at church that morning. "It's a lot easier than you think." She drew in a deep breath and released it slowly. "What about you and Frank Martin?"

"He's sweet, but it isn't serious between us."

"Never?"

Martha shrugged. "Maybe. Someday."

"Will he enlist?"

"I don't think so. He says he'll wait to be drafted."

Daisy twirled a strand of hair around a finger. "Maybe the war will be over before that happens."

"Maybe. I hope so. It will get dreadfully boring around here once everybody's gone."

Daisy drew back in surprise. How selfish Martha sounded. Didn't she realize many of their former school friends could die in this war? Boredom should be the least of their worries.

"What about Brandan Gallagher?" her friend asked. "He's already in the service. He'll be one of the first to be sent overseas. Your sister will die if anything happens to him."

"Yes. She will." *And so will I.* Daisy got to her feet. "I'd better get home."

And she hoped she wasn't too late to see Brandan.

Chapter 10

WEDNESDAY, DECEMBER 24, 1941

Lillian sat before her dressing table, staring at her reflection in the mirror. In a short while the family would leave for the Christmas Eve service at church. She would rather not go. All the joy had gone out of Christmas because there wouldn't be an announcement of her engagement before Brandan returned to Barksdale Field. He'd finally made her understand that. He refused to get engaged right now. He refused to think about a wedding next summer.

"Too much is unsettled, Lill. I won't do it. I love you, but I won't do it."

How many times had he said those or similar words to her over the past ten days? She'd tried reasoning. She'd tried pleading. She'd tried tears. She'd tried anger. But nothing had made any difference. Brandan was bullheaded, plain and simple.

"Maybe I won't give him his Christmas gift. He doesn't deserve a new watch." She heard the pettiness in her voice and knew she should feel ashamed. But she didn't. She felt angry, disappointed, hurt, rejected, confused, and lonely.

Lonely.

Brandan was still in Boise for a couple more days, but he'd made her feel as lonely as if he'd never come home at all. She'd spent time with him every single day. Still . . .

"I love him. He loves me. Why isn't that enough?"

Her image in the mirror blurred.

"Lillian?" Her sister's voice came to her through the closed door. "Are you ready?"

She dabbed her eyes with a handkerchief. "Nearly. Tell Dad I'll be down in two shakes."

"Okay."

Lillian released a breath, glad Daisy hadn't caught her crying. Her sister would have pressed for the reason, and Lillian wasn't willing to tell her what was wrong. She wouldn't ever be ready. She would have to put on a brave face before others while she waited for Brandan to realize she was right about getting engaged, about getting married, and he was wrong. The war shouldn't change that. He loved her. She knew he did, without a doubt.

Not true. She had some doubt. Because if he truly loved her, wouldn't he be as eager to marry as she was? Wouldn't he want to be with her, as man and wife, before he was sent away? Wouldn't he want something more than kisses when they were together and letters when they were apart?

Drawing a quick breath, she stood and grabbed her small pocketbook before heading for the bedroom door. Her parents and sister waited for her downstairs, all of them wearing their coats and hats.

"Come on, slowpoke," her father said with a tolerant smile.

The family joke was that Lillian had been running late ever since she was born, an event that happened almost three weeks past the due date. She tolerated the teasing, often laughing right along with them. She didn't feel like laughing tonight.

A short while later, Lillian and Daisy huddled close together in the back seat of their dad's 1938 Dodge sedan, shivering. They would arrive at the church before the car's heater got warm enough to make a difference to them.

Christmas lights twinkled in some windows as they drove through the neighborhood. The sight usually delighted Lillian. This year, the colored lights made her feel sad. As if something was sifting through her fingers, about to be lost forever. Not Christmas itself. Christmas would always be celebrated. Perhaps it was her childish delight in the holiday that was slipping away.

It wasn't a lengthy drive from the Abbott home in the north end to their church located in downtown Boise. At this hour of night, the streets were mostly empty, but the parking lot behind the church was more than half full when they arrived.

Lillian couldn't remember a Christmas Eve when the Abbotts hadn't attended the eleven o'clock service, and it was a tradition she normally loved. Poinsettias in red and white were everywhere in the sanctuary. White tapered candles flickered in gold candelabras. Red and white fabric draped the pews. A choir, also wearing red and white, filled the chancel beyond the pulpit.

Her dad guided the family into one of the pews. As soon as she was settled, Lillian looked for the Gallaghers. She didn't see them at first, and a wave of disappointment flowed over her. But then she caught sight of Mrs. Gallagher's red hat, the same one she wore to every Christmas Eve service. Lillian smiled, hope surging, but only for a moment. Only until she realized Brandan wasn't with his parents and younger brothers. Where was he? She tried not to be obvious as she looked around, searching for him.

Chords from the organ filled the air, and the congregation rose to sing "O Come, All Ye Faithful." Lillian held the hymnal in front of her, but she didn't see the words on the page. They were all a jumble. Stupid tears. She needed to stop this before someone saw her. Before Daisy saw her. Others wouldn't guess the reason. Daisy would. Lillian had bragged to her sister about her certainty of getting engaged over Christmas.

"Hey, beautiful."

She drew in a breath as Brandan stepped to her side. With his right hand, he took hold of the hymnal, supporting it between them. He smiled, then looked forward and added his voice to the song of celebration.

Hope. Wasn't that partly what Christmas was about? Lillian allowed herself to hope again as she, too, began to sing.

Chapter 11

PRESENT DAY–JANUARY

As soon as Brianna entered the church that Sunday, she parted from her parents and went looking for Hannah. She found her best friend in the sanctuary, talking with three other girls and two guys. She knew all but one of them. They'd come up through youth group together.

"Hey, Brianna. I'm so glad you're here." Hannah sounded as if they hadn't seen each other in ages. "Have you met Greg Truman?" Her friend looked toward the tall, dark-haired guy to her left.

Brianna's heart skipped a beat or two. A common reaction, she supposed, to his incredible good looks. "No. I don't think so."

"Greg, this is Brianna Hastings."

He stuck out his hand. "Nice to meet you."

His hand was large and warm as it enveloped hers, and his smile made her melt like butter on a hot skillet. She blinked, trying to make her mind focus, trying to come up with something intelligent to say. Something like "Hello."

Hannah's voice interrupted the lengthening silence. "Greg moved to Boise right before Christmas. His family came here a couple of years ago, and he finally decided to join them. He transferred to Boise State this semester."

No one was as good as Hannah at gleaning information from people she'd just met. She was a one-girl welcoming committee who loved God with a passion and loved serving Him by serving people.

"I guess you like it here, then?" Brianna asked Greg.

"Yeah, I do. It's perfect for somebody like me. I love the outdoors. Biking, hiking, and camping especially."

She had a sudden desire to take up all three hobbies that very day.

The worship team moved to their positions on the platform, and Hannah motioned for Brianna, Greg, and the others to move into the same row of chairs as the music began. Wouldn't you know it? Greg Truman had a voice that put the worship leader to shame, and Brianna stopped singing so she could listen to him. He turned his head, caught her watching him, and grinned without missing a beat.

Brianna wasn't a complete neophyte when it came to boys. Yes, her parents were conservative and hadn't allowed her to date until she was sixteen. But the guys she knew, the ones she'd spent time with—like Adam—were friends, and that was all. Romantic movies had seemed more silly to her than anything . . . until about five minutes ago.

Chapter 12

FRIDAY, DECEMBER 26, 1941

On the day after Christmas Brandan stood next to his car, the engine running. Lillian stood before him, looking up, eyes beseeching. He could feel her sadness wrapping around his heart, like the tendrils of a vine.

She touched his cheek with her fingertips. "I can't bear to let you go."

"The army doesn't give a guy a choice."

"It'll be months before I see you again."

"I'll write often. As often as I can. Like usual."

Lillian lowered her hand and pressed her forehead against his coat. "I don't know how I'll bear it."

He feared the coming months would bring far worse things to endure than the two of them being separated by 325 miles. Swallowing that reply, he kissed the top of her head instead.

She drew back. "You'll call me when you get there?"

"I'll call you Sunday after you're home from church."

"You want me to wait two whole days to know you got to Barksdale okay?"

The toll on long-distance calls was sky-high. Lillian knew that, yet still she asked as though it cost nothing. Sometimes he wondered if she understood anything about the real world, about income and expenses, about budgets. When they did get married, would she be able to manage their home without putting them into the poorhouse? Only a couple of years separated them in age, but she seemed child-like at times.

"Please," she persisted.

He shook his head and gave her a firm look. "I'll call Sunday when the rates are down."

She played the pout card, but Brandan wasn't inclined to give in to it. Not this time. In fact, he thought her adorable with her lower lip poked out. It made him chuckle.

She tapped his chest with her mittened hand. "What's funny?"

"You are. Now, I've wasted way too much gas while I said good-bye. I've got to go. Dad's waiting to take me to the base. I've got a plane to catch." He kissed her on the lips but didn't let himself linger. "I love you, Lill, and I'll talk to you on Sunday." He turned and got into the car. After putting it in gear, he glanced out the window and waved, then pulled away from the curb.

He smiled as he drove through the quiet neighborhood toward State Street. Lillian would be mad at him for a while. Probably for the rest of the day. But she would get over it.

If only she would understand why we can't get married yet.

The thought made his smile fade. Lillian's persistence regarding an engagement now and a wedding in June had taken some of the shine off of his leave. He'd spent as much time as possible with her without making his mom feel neglected. It hadn't been enough for Lillian. Nothing had been enough. She'd counted on that engagement ring as one of her Christmas gifts, and he hadn't given it to her.

Was he wrong to think she would understand in time? Or would she decide he wasn't worth it? If the war lasted for years, would she still wait for him?

For a moment Brandan was tempted to turn the car around, to go back, to sweep her into his arms and propose. But only for a moment. It was better this way. By the end of next summer, he could be flying bombers in a war zone. The idea excited him. He'd trained for it. He was good at it. As much as he cared for his girl, he wasn't about to alter the path he was on.

Chapter 13

SATURDAY, AUGUST 8, 1942

Todd carried a tray of condiments and hamburger buns through the open gate that separated his backyard from his neighbor's. Smoke billowed above the grill as Carl Abbott flipped burgers.

"Need help?" Todd called as he set the tray on a folding table between two picnic tables.

"Got it covered, thanks. Might see if Nancy could use a hand."

"Will do." He headed for the back door, stopping to knock on the jamb before entering. "Anybody need help in here?"

"Oh, Todd." Nancy Abbott flashed him a harried smile. "Yes. Could you take those salads outside? The girls are welcoming our other guests at the front door."

"I've got these. And just so you know, it looked to me like the burgers are about ready."

He picked up two bowls—one filled with tossed greens, the other filled with Jell-O and fruit—and carried them toward the back door. Outside, he set them next to the condiments and buns on the food table. By the time he turned around, other people were stepping onto the porch.

Brandan Gallagher, looking self-assured in his uniform, came down the steps with Lillian clinging to his arm. Behind the young couple followed Brandan's younger brothers. Todd didn't remember their names. Next came Daisy, and finally Elenore and Andrew Gallagher and their hostess, Nancy Abbott.

After saying hello to everyone, Todd's attention was drawn back to Brandan and Lillian. In July, Brandan had completed his flight training at the top of his class, but neither Carl nor Nancy had mentioned what his assignment would be. Perhaps they didn't know. Wherever Brandan was sent, Todd would be jealous. His own efforts to enlist had been rebuffed, as he'd feared they would be. Classified 4-F. There were other ways he could serve his country, other ways he could make a difference for the war efforts besides fighting on the front lines. But it stung all the same, being called unqualified for military service, especially at his age. He had a good, sound mind, even if he couldn't run a marathon. Couldn't a guy like him be put to use in one of the armed services? There had to be something he could—

"Come and get it!" Carl called, intruding on Todd's troubled thoughts.

Everyone milled around, filling their plates, laughing with the person to their right or left. Jupiter, the Abbotts' Brittany spaniel, stayed close by, vigilant in case food fell to the ground. Feeling a bit of pity, Todd tossed the dog a chunk of cheese.

"I saw that," Daisy said, her voice raised enough for him to hear clearly.

He looked across the table at her. "Couldn't help it. I'm a sucker for doleful brown eyes."

"Oh, really? I didn't know that about you."

Todd felt an odd reaction in his chest as he looked at her. Daisy's eyes were brown. Were they doleful? Was he a sucker for her brown eyes? Yeah. If he was honest, he was. But she wouldn't return the feelings, even if she guessed he had them. He was the guy next door, a fixture in the Abbott family. And Daisy? Daisy was the odd little duckling who'd blossomed into a swan.

Uncomfortable with his unexpected thoughts, he stood. "Excuse me. I need to get something to drink." He cleared his throat. "Do you need anything?" He pointed to the empty place before her where a beverage should be.

"Yes, please. Lemonade would be lovely."

Daisy Abbott wasn't a child, he reminded himself. She'd graduated from high school a year ago. She was an adult. But she'd been more like a little sister to him for years. Right up until a few moments ago when he'd let himself admit his attraction to her.

Todd filled two glasses with lemonade and carried them back to the table. By then, Daisy was deep in conversation with Elenore Gallagher. He put the glass on the table near her plate, then sat and reached for his burger. Jupiter appeared out of nowhere to sit near his left knee. Todd slipped the dog another small square of cheese before he picked up the burger and took his first bite. Lettuce crunched, and the sweet taste of tomato burst in his mouth, followed by other flavors that spoke of warm summer days and Sunday afternoons spent in the company of friends.

Raised voices from the other table drew his attention. It sounded like the Gallagher brothers were having a heated discussion about baseball.

"I'm tellin' you," the youngest of the brothers said. "Too many of the players are joining up or getting drafted. Major League Baseball is over for the duration."

"Ah, you're crackers," the middle brother said. "Roosevelt says baseball needs to keep going. You know. Keep up the morale at home."

Brandan leaned toward his brothers. "But that wasn't my question. I want to know who's the best. Ted Williams or Ernie Lombardi?"

Listening to them, Todd wondered if the war *would* put an end to the games before long. No matter how much the president wanted baseball to keep going. Men from the ages of twenty-one to thirty-six were subject to the draft, and those were prime years for professional baseball players, in both the major and minor leagues. So who would be left to play? Guys like him who'd been classified 4-F? That thought made him want to laugh out loud.

"Todd," Daisy said.

He met her gaze across the table, turning his head so that his good ear was toward her.

"Did you hear I'm thinking of trying to join the new Women's Army Auxiliary Corps?"

"What?" He hadn't considered that even Daisy might be able to serve when he couldn't.

She repeated her words in a somewhat louder voice.

He realized she thought he hadn't heard her, not that he couldn't believe her. "Didn't the paper say they already had far more applicants than positions?"

"If the war keeps going the way it is, they'll need more of us. They're bound to open up applications again."

He leaned forward, lowering his voice slightly. "What do your folks think of that idea?"

"Oh, Mom's not too happy. If I got in, I'd have to go off to Fort Des Moines for training, and then it's hard telling where I could be posted. It's all new, so there are a lot of unknowns."

"Aren't you a bit young?"

She stiffened. "There are boys younger than me fighting already."

"True."

"And if I can't join the WAACs, then maybe I can get a job at Gowen Field. They're hiring civilian employees."

"Your mom and dad would like that idea better."

Daisy looked as if she would say more but was interrupted by another voice.

"Can I have your attention?"

Everyone looked in Brandan's direction. He stood at the end of the other table, waiting for silence.

"I've got an announcement to make."

Todd wondered if Brandan and Lillian were engaged at last, but when he glanced at Lillian, he saw neither joy nor excitement. She seemed no more informed about what Brandan would say than anyone else.

Dread snaked through Daisy. Was this it? Had it happened? Had Lillian managed to change Brandan's mind after all? Her sister hadn't said a thing to her. *Look at her, sitting there, acting like nothing—*

"When my leave is over, I'll fly to Fort Dix and then to Grenier Field. We're preparing for deployment." He glanced at Lillian. "I can't tell you our final destination. Not yet."

With a sound of protest, Lillian hopped up and ran into the house. Daisy hesitated a moment before hurrying after her. She found her sister in the living room, seated on the sofa, her face hidden in her hands as she wept.

Daisy sank down beside her, wrapping an arm around her back. "It's okay, Lillian. He'll be fine."

"Why did he do it? Why did he enlist last summer? He didn't have to." Lillian lowered her hands. "We weren't at war. He didn't have to learn to fly. He says he loves me, but now he's going away without . . . without—"

"He does love you." The words left a bad taste on Daisy's tongue.

"Does he?"

"Yes," Brandan answered from the dining room doorway. "He does."

He gave Daisy a pointed look, and reluctantly she removed her arm from around Lillian's shoulders and stood. Then, eyes downcast, she scurried from the living room. She managed not to pause in the kitchen, despite how much she wanted to linger to hear what they said to each other.

But she did stop when she reached the back porch. A quick glance around the picnic tables told her that Andrew Gallagher was proud of his eldest son, even though it came with concern. Elenore Gallagher's expression said she was terrified of what might happen to him. And Brandan's younger brothers still seemed more concerned about baseball than a brother headed off to war. As for her own parents, they were anxious for Lillian, judging by the way both of them kept glancing toward the back door.

Finally, her gaze went to their next-door neighbor. Unlike her parents, Todd looked right at Daisy, a question in his eyes. She gave a slight shrug before going down the steps to join him at the table. He half rose until she was seated on the opposite bench.

"I have a feeling I should go home," he said as he settled again.

"Why?"

He glanced at the two sets of parents. "Brandan's leave is almost over. I imagine there are things to be said before he goes. Private things."

"Don't be silly. You're like a member of the family. Lillian won't mind you being here."

He was silent a short while before saying, "But I'm not *actual* family."

It surprised Daisy to hear him say that. He'd always seemed more brother than neighbor to her, and she knew he loved the Abbott family, especially her dad. Had one of them made him feel unwelcome?

His gaze shifted to beyond her shoulder. Judging by his expression, Brandan and Lillian must have come out of the house. Had they resolved their differences? She wanted to hope they had, for her sister's sake. But how could she hope it? How would she bear it if they got married? Lots of young couples had quick weddings before a GI shipped out. If they married now, Daisy might never—

She twisted on the bench in time to see them descend the steps. Lillian's arm was looped through Brandan's, and she pressed it tight against her side, as if to make sure he couldn't escape.

Does he stay because he loves her or because he can't get away?

The thought shamed Daisy and reminded her that it was way past time she got over her girlhood crush. It was time to be realistic. Even if Brandan stopped loving Lillian, even if he broke it off with her, that didn't mean he would start loving Daisy. He thought of her as his girlfriend's kid sister. If he wasn't with Lillian, he wouldn't be around at all.

She looked at Brandan. So tall and handsome. Like a young Gary Cooper is what she'd always thought. Except for his black hair.

He's going off to fight. He might not come back.

She looked at her sister. Pretty enough to get any guy she wanted. And the one she wanted was Brandan Gallagher.

And we might both lose him forever.

Chapter 14

PRESENT DAY—FEBRUARY

"Mother?"

Daisy looked up from the papers spread across her bed.

Elizabeth stepped through the open bedroom doorway. "What are you doing?"

"Going through old letters."

"Who are they from?"

"Lots of people. Lillian. Brandan. A few old classmates. My grandchildren when they were young enough to think it was fun to write to Grandma and before they got those newfangled devices."

Her daughter laughed softly. "You try to sound like you hate the electronics, but you love your iPad."

"Well, I wouldn't say I love it, but it does have its uses. Even for an old-timer like me." She lifted a bundle of letters tied with a blue ribbon. "Still, there is something about paper and ink that is so much more . . . personal and satisfying."

Pressing the letters from her sister to her chest, she closed her eyes. Oh, how beautiful Lillian had been. Daisy remembered well the way men had stopped whatever they were doing when Lillian

Abbott walked into a room. For many years Daisy had envied her sister her beauty, but eventually she'd come to understand that no one passed through life without heartache, whether they were plain or beautiful.

"Look how far these go back."

Daisy opened her eyes and watched as Elizabeth set down one envelope on the bed and picked up another.

"I can't believe you've kept them all these years," her daughter added.

"I'm a product of the Great Depression and World War Two. Things were not as disposable in my day. We used them up, wore them out, and made them do. Your generation didn't invent recycling, you know. All sorts of things were reused during the war, even fat from the cookstove."

"Do you mean bacon grease and such? What was it used for?"

"Ammunition. One slogan said something like, 'One tablespoonful of kitchen grease fires five bullets.'"

"If I ever learned that in school, I've forgotten." Elizabeth sat on a chair on the opposite side of the bed.

"Why would you remember? The war was almost over by the time you were born, and life was very different in the years that followed its end."

"For the better?"

Daisy smiled at her daughter. "In many ways. Not all, but most, I suppose." She sighed. "My grandmother once told me that as she grew older the past seemed more real to her than the present. I didn't believe that could be true, but I was wrong. It is true. Sometimes when I open my eyes, I expect to see your father coming through the door at the end of the day or to see your brother playing in the middle of the living-room floor with that set of blocks he loved so much when he was little."

"Talking to Brianna has stirred up a lot of memories, hasn't it?"

"Yes. But I like to remember. The memories are precious and should be shared with those we love."

"I agree." Elizabeth rose from the chair. "But don't overdo. Okay?"

"I won't, dear."

She watched her daughter leave the bedroom.

It was a strange time of life, when the child became the guardian of an elderly parent. Telling them what to do. Trying to shelter and protect. In most ways Daisy didn't mind. Without her daughter, she would be dependent upon strangers. She wouldn't care for that at all. For a woman of her advanced years, she was in good health, but she wouldn't be able to live alone.

She gave her head a slow shake, then untied the ribbon on the bundle of her sister's letters and drew a piece of blue-colored stationery from the first envelope. Lillian's penmanship was lovely, and just looking at the writing brought back the memory of her sister seated at the desk in her bedroom, light from the window falling over her. As a young woman, Lillian had spent hours at that desk, writing love letters to Brandan while he was away at the university, then later in flight school and finally overseas.

I wonder what happened to all those letters she sent him.

It was a question that couldn't be answered. Both her sister and Brandan had shuffled off this mortal coil. She frowned, wondering who had coined that particular idiom for death. Shakespeare? Most likely Shakespeare. Even people completely ignorant of the Bard quoted him without knowing they did so.

She shook off the thought and closed her eyes again, envisioning Lillian as she'd been many, many decades before. As girls, Daisy had followed her sister around like a puppy follows its master. In some ways Lillian had expected Daisy's adoration—welcomed it, encouraged it, anticipated it. Perhaps it would always have been thus between them if not for Brandan Gallagher.

Chapter 15

MONDAY, AUGUST 10, 1942

Brandan had hoped dinner and a movie would improve matters between him and Lillian. But choosing *Mrs. Miniver,* a film released in the states only a few days earlier, had been a mistake. All he'd known going in was that it starred Greer Garson and Walter Pidgeon and that people were saying how good it was. He supposed he'd heard the mention of war. But wasn't talk about the war everywhere? Films. Radio. Newspaper. Chatting with a neighbor over the back fence. He hadn't known the movie was about bombs dropping on English homes and killing innocent civilians.

He glanced at Lillian, seated beside him as he drove along a quiet street after leaving the theater. Her hands were clenched in her lap, her gaze glued to the road ahead. Even at dinner before the movie, she'd chosen to nod or shake her head rather than say much of anything. He wasn't sure if her silence was meant to punish him or if she was too emotional to trust herself to speak.

He slowed and turned the car at the next cross street. He sensed Lillian look over at him and knew she wondered where they were going if not to her home. But she didn't ask. Again, silence.

Only when he followed the road up into the foothills did she ask, "Where are we going?"

"Some place where we can talk."

Leaving the city and neighborhoods behind, Brandan steered the car along a dirt road. The ruts jerked the vehicle this way and that. He could see his destination as twilight settled over the valley. "Almost there."

Minutes later he pulled off the road onto a level outlook. When he cut the engine, a hush blanketed them. The city below was mostly dark. Although some thought it unnecessary for a city hundreds of miles from the coast, most homes in Boise employed blackout curtains at night. Between the silence and the darkness, it almost seemed Brandan and Lillian were the only two people remaining on earth.

He twisted on the seat. "Lill, please. Can we talk?" He couldn't see her face, couldn't try to read her expression.

"What is there left to say? You're going away. I'm staying behind."

"I have to go."

A soft sob escaped her.

"I don't have a choice."

"You had a choice last summer before your enlisted. You could have gotten a job instead. You had your degree. You didn't have to put yourself in danger."

He drew a slow breath and released it. "Even if I didn't enlist then, I would have enlisted after Pearl Harbor. Why should I be the one who isn't in danger? Others are risking their lives right now. Why not me?"

"Because I love you," she whispered. "Because I don't want to lose you."

Brandan was pretty sure she silently added, *Because we were supposed to get married.*

He faced forward on the seat again. Maybe coming up here had been a stupid decision. What more could he say to her or her to him?

Nothing would change. He would leave Idaho next week, and by September he could be flying bombing raids somewhere.

"Brandan, I don't want it to be like this between us."

"Neither do I."

"Did you know that Lois Rutherford got married last week?"

He felt his jaw tighten. "No, I didn't know."

"She met her husband less than six weeks ago. He's leaving for the navy soon, so they decided not to wait."

See? Nothing would change. Lillian had only the same things to say to him. She had one thing on her mind. Just one.

"You and I started dating your first year of college," she went on. "That's almost five years ago."

"I've been away a lot of that time. First at the university, then in flight training."

"But it isn't like we don't know each other. I know how you like your coffee. I know the kind of books you like to read. I know your favorite type of movies. I know your favorite baseball players and your best friends. We aren't strangers, Brandan. My parents like you. Your parents like me. What—"

"Don't, Lill. Please don't. We've argued about it enough. I'm going off to war. Could you make my last week at home pleasant instead of one long fight?"

Maybe he couldn't see well in the darkness, but he knew she didn't like what he'd said. She might be hurt. She might be mad. Probably a combination of both.

"Maybe I should take you home," he said.

"Yes. Maybe you should."

He tried to think of something else to say. No. Better to call it a night. He would only make it worse. He started the engine and backed the car onto the single-lane dirt road.

Hopefully, Lillian would forgive him before he left for Florida.

Chapter 16

WEDNESDAY, AUGUST 12, 1942

Todd looked through the glass toward the factory floor below. A year ago, Kinnear Canning had employed a predominately male workforce. Now, about 85 percent of his employees were women. He didn't mind the difference, but it still seemed strange when he looked down and saw so many heads covered with kerchiefs.

"Mr. Kinnear, the country needs your help."

Without turning to look at the two other men in the room, Todd asked, "Isn't canned produce important to the war effort?"

"Yes. It is. But what you make here remains primarily in this region. Most housewives can do their own canning. But they can't help us make compasses in their homes. You have the factory and the personnel who can."

Todd turned at last. "It isn't that I don't want to help, but I've got produce unloading on my docks even as we speak. I can't just—"

"We don't expect you to stop production immediately," the taller of the two men, who'd done all the talking, answered. "Modifications will have to be made. Your workers will need to be trained. Materials will have to be shipped to you. It will take some time for the transition. But we have seen industries pivot into war production with surprising speed this year. We have no doubt that your company will be able to do the same."

"Then my answer is yes."

"You won't be sorry, Mr. Kinnear."

"The only thing I'm sorry for, sir, is that I wasn't allowed to enlist when the war began. I want to help in the best way possible. I want to do my part."

"Then you'll be doing that. Why not give us a full tour and we can discuss specifics."

More than an hour later, Todd stood in the parking lot, watching as the two government agents got into their automobile. He waved as they pulled onto the street, then returned to his office and sat at his desk, his thoughts racing. He would need to contact all of his suppliers as well as his customers. The plums and nectarines that had arrived this very morning could be processed and sold, but it looked like peaches, pears, grapes, and apples would have to go elsewhere in the autumn. Kinnear Canning should be producing compasses for the fighting forces by the time those fruits were ready for harvest.

A soft rap drew his gaze to the office doorway. He expected to see one of his employees but instead found his neighbor stepping into the room.

"Am I disturbing you?" Carl Abbott removed his hat.

"No, sir." Todd stood. "Not at all. You're always welcome. What can I do for you?"

Carl lowered his gaze to the hat, now held between his hands. "I . . . uh . . . I feel strange coming to you."

"What's wrong?" Todd's thoughts flashed to Daisy, then to Lillian and their mother.

The older man looked up again. "My firm is closing its doors. I . . . I've lost my job."

Throughout the Great Depression, Carl Abbott had remained

employed and able to provide for his wife and two daughters, and the shock of his job loss now showed on his face. It seemed to have aged him a good ten years.

"I've been looking for work, but I've come up empty." Shame had joined shock in Carl's expression. "I wasn't ready to go home yet. I'm not ready to tell Nancy how grim things look. With the war and rationing, she's already worried about too much. I was driving past your factory, and I just . . . I turned into the lot without thinking. I don't know why I came to see you. I don't know . . ." His voice trailed into silence as he looked down at his hat once more.

Todd took a step around the edge of his desk. "Mr. Abbott, you couldn't have come to my office at a better time. I'm in need of a floor manager."

Carl looked up. At first he appeared confused. Then surprised.

"In a few weeks, Kinnear Canning is going to be producing compasses for the military. It's just been arranged."

"Son, I never meant—"

"I need you, sir. I need a man of your experience with people and with business matters." He thought of Roy Jamison, whose work had been less than exemplary since his son's enlistment, and he had no doubt Carl could prove helpful in that regard as well. "Don't refuse me. You'll be doing me a favor."

"But I don't know anything about manufacturing compasses."

"None of us do. We'll all be learning. It's your business- and people-sense I need. If you weren't around to offer advice after Mom passed, I'm not sure we'd be standing in this factory today."

A spark of hope entered Carl's eyes. "If you're sure."

"I'm more than sure." Todd offered his hand, hoping to silently communicate how much he loved and respected this man. "Can you start tomorrow?"

Carl took his hand and shook it. "Yes. But only if you stop with that 'sir' and 'Mr. Abbott' business once and for all. You'll be my boss. Can't have the other employees thinking it's the other way around."

Todd smiled. "See, it's that kind of thinking I need." He shook the other man's hand once more, then released it. "Carl."

Chapter 17

PRESENT DAY—FEBRUARY

Brianna arrived at the coffee shop early. After getting her favorite latte, she sat at a table in the corner and watched the door, her heart hammering with excitement.

She hadn't believed it when she got Greg Truman's text, asking her to meet him here. She hadn't even considered refusing the invitation. Professor Meyer and his facts and dates would have to get along without her for a day. As long as he didn't spring a pop quiz on the class, it wouldn't matter if she missed. She could ask Adam to share his notes. Adam always took good notes, and he would be willing to help. As any BFF would.

The door opened, and she caught her breath when Greg stepped into view. He was every bit as gorgeous as she'd remembered. Last night, she'd even dreamed about him. That had never happened before. She'd liked a few guys, but she'd never felt anything like this. And she didn't even *know* him. Not really. Not like she knew Adam. Not even the way she knew some of the guys who'd been part of the youth group at church.

Greg's eyes found her. His grin seemed to brighten the entire coffee shop. He pointed at her coffee, then at himself. Understanding, she nodded. She just hoped the barista would hurry with whatever he ordered.

Her phone pinged, and she checked the message. It was from Adam.

Don't see you in class. You sick?

She glanced toward the back of the shop, where Greg still waited for his order, then replied.

Not feeling myself. Can I see your notes later?

A twinge of guilt accompanied the *ping* sound as the text left her phone. She'd just lied to Adam. Why had she done it? She could have said she had something else to do. That would have been enough. Adam wouldn't ever lie to her. Not even a little white lie.

Sure. Take care. We'll talk later.

She put the phone facedown as Greg walked toward her, coffee in hand.

"Thanks for meeting me," he said, settling onto the chair across from her.

"Sure." She fought the blush that tried to rise in her cheeks.

"I didn't have a class today, and I'm sick of the library."

"I get that."

"So." He leaned back on the chair. "Have you always gone to church at Trinity Community?"

She nodded.

Greg looked completely relaxed, but Brianna felt like her insides were tied in knots. If she didn't get over it, he would wonder why he'd bothered to ask her to meet him.

A smile tipped one corner of his mouth. Had he guessed what she was thinking? "Your friend Hannah's nice. In fact, everybody I met on Sunday was nice. I plan to go back."

"That's good," she managed to say. "You'll feel at home in no time. We've got a great bunch who came up through youth group together. Everybody really likes the pastor too."

Greg sipped his coffee before answering. "Yeah. He preached a good sermon."

As old-fashioned as it seemed—even to some of her Christian friends and even to Brianna herself—she'd never been able to ignore her mother's advice against going out with guys who didn't share her faith. That made the dating pool shallow at best. But here sat a gorgeous hunk of a guy who was a Christian and also seemed to like her. How perfect was that?

She held her coffee between both hands but didn't drink any. "What's your major?"

"Business. If I'm lucky, I'll be running my own company by the time I'm thirty."

"What sort of company?"

"Not sure yet." He shrugged. "But something will catch my interest. What about you?"

"Liberal arts for now. I'm still trying to decide what I'll do when I graduate. I'll have to make up my mind soon."

"You like it? School, I mean."

"Yes. I'm not happy that I have to go to a local community college. I wanted to go someplace out of state."

He chuckled. "Leave home, you mean. Get away from your parents."

"Yes." It pleased her that he understood without any explanation.

"Do you plan to transfer to BSU after you get your associate's?"

"Yes. That's the plan."

Funny, wasn't it? She'd complained and cajoled and done

everything possible to convince her parents to let her go to a university out of state. And now she could hardly wait to attend one right in her hometown. All that mattered to her fluttering heart was that Greg Truman was there.

Chapter 18

FRIDAY, AUGUST 14, 1942

Brandan stared at the telephone, feeling anger boil up inside. For the past four days, Lillian had avoided him. They'd spoken on the phone a few times, but she'd always had something else to do when he suggested they go out or spend time together.

Well, guess what? Two could play at that game. He wouldn't call her today. He wouldn't ask her out. He had only a few more days left at home. If his girlfriend didn't want to spend time with him, he would hang out with some of the guys he'd gone to school with. The few who hadn't joined up yet.

"Mom." He reached for his car keys on the table near the door. "I'm going to meet Jack and George. Not sure what they've got planned. Not sure what time I'll be home. Don't wait up. Could be late."

His mother stepped into the kitchen doorway. "You're not going to see Lillian?"

"Afraid she doesn't want to see me."

"Oh, honey. I'm sorry."

"She'll get over it." He hoped he was right. Then again, maybe he didn't care. He was tired of being manipulated. "I guess we need time to cool off, the both of us."

His mom offered a tight smile.

"I'm right about not getting married before I ship out. You think so, too, don't you?"

She was silent a moment before answering, "Yes, son. Since you aren't married already, you shouldn't do it. You'll have enough on your mind once you're . . . Once you're overseas." Tears glittered in her eyes, and she turned away, wiping them with the hem of her apron.

"Don't cry, Mom. I'm a good pilot. I'll be okay." He put his hands on her shoulders and placed a kiss above her ear.

She patted his left hand with her right one but kept her back to him. "Go on. Shoo. Go be with your friends. You deserve a night out."

He decided to obey her before a real crying jag began. His dad had said there was nothing that made him feel as helpless as when a woman cried. Brandan felt the same way. Especially if the woman was his mom. Besides, the idea of an evening out with his friends was growing on him by the minute. Brandan and Jack Foreman had been good friends since the fifth grade. George Peterson had made them a threesome during their senior year of high school. Brandan liked them both, although Jack had a bit of a wild streak that got him into trouble on a regular basis. Whenever Jack got drafted, heaven help the army.

Jack and George were waiting for Brandan on the curb in front of Jack's apartment.

"Where to?" Brandan asked as they climbed into his car, Jack in the front seat and George in the back.

"The Starlite," Jack answered. "We're gonna flirt with all the girls we dance with, and maybe we'll get a little drunk." He pulled a flask from his pocket. With a wink, he added, "George's got one too."

While Brandan drank an occasional beer—mostly so other guys wouldn't call him a wimp—he didn't care much for liquor. He didn't like the taste of it, and he preferred being in full control of his thought processes. Still, he might be in the mood to partake tonight.

The Starlite had been in business since the early thirties, but it hadn't amounted to much until the spring of 1941 when the first full company of soldiers, the 253rd Quartermaster Company, arrived at Gowen Field from Fort Douglas. After that, the dance hall had become *the* place for GIs to go on an evening off. Its popularity had exploded after the base became a combat-crew training school for the B-24 Liberator.

When the three friends entered the Starlite, the place was hopping. It was packed with men, most of them in uniform, and women in colorful dresses, their hair swept up and their lips painted bright red.

"The girls really go for you flyboys," Jack said above the music. "You'll have a partner for every dance if you want one. George and I won't have it so easy. We're only civilians, slaving away on the home front."

It had been more than four years since Brandan had danced with anybody other than Lillian. Even when he'd enjoyed a night out with buddies while in training, he'd watched from a table while others danced. But he wasn't sure what he would do tonight. If Lillian didn't want to spend time with him, maybe he shouldn't want to spend time with her either. And what harm was there in a few dances? He wasn't engaged, and there was no ring on his finger. His orders were sending him overseas. He deserved a good time. Who knew when he would be back again? Maybe not for years. Maybe not ever.

"Come on." Jack moved deeper into the building. "We'll find a table, and then I'm off to find a girl willing to dance with a civilian."

Faces seemed to blur around Brandan as he followed his friends. With each step, his anger increased. If Lillian wasn't so selfish, she would be here with him. But she was selfish. She was punishing him, trying to bring him to heel. Well, he wouldn't be manipulated that easy. He could be selfish too.

As he sank onto a chair, he said, "Jack, let me have your flask."

His old friend laughed as he complied.

The Starlite sparkled with lights hanging around the ceiling and walls. The orchestra was good, and the dance floor was packed with couples. Daisy had danced with over a dozen different servicemen, who'd each told her how much they liked Boise. "The girls here are so pretty," more than one of them had added while smiling at her, as if to say, *And you're the prettiest*. Even in her wildest dreams she wouldn't have believed them.

"It's all good for a girl's ego," she told Martha with a laugh as the two of them squeezed through the crowd on their way to the ladies' room. But Daisy stopped dead still when she saw Brandan dancing with a woman in a red dress. A woman who looked nothing like Lillian.

The music ended at that moment, and Brandan turned in her direction, his hand under the elbow of his dance partner. His gaze met hers. At first he didn't seem to recognize her. Then he grinned. Not his normal debonair smile. No, there was something odd about this one.

"Daisy." He left the woman he'd danced with and approached her. "It's great to see you."

Was he drunk? Brandan Gallagher, drunk? No, that couldn't be. But when he got close enough, she smelled the whiskey on his breath, and she drew back. "Where's Lillian?"

"Good question. Not here. Not with me."

His words weren't slurred, exactly, but she could tell his mind was muddled.

"Daisy?" Martha appeared back through the crowd. "I lost you." Then she saw who Daisy was with. "Oh. Hi, Brandan."

"Martha, I think Brandan could use some fresh air. You go on without me. I'm going to take Brandan outside. I'll find you later."

"Are you—"

"I'm sure." She took hold of Brandan's arm and started to draw him toward the main entrance.

"Jack's here," he said as the orchestra began to play "Chattanooga Choo Choo." "So's George."

"We'll find them later." Somehow she managed to guide him through the crush of people and out into the warm August night. "Did you drive your car or come in Jack's?"

"I've got mine." He looked around, frowning, and she guessed he didn't remember where he'd parked it.

"Come on. We'll find a place to sit down."

They moved from the entrance of the Starlite, out of the way of the couples and groups of servicemen who were arriving. Daisy didn't have a destination in mind. A bench somewhere. But then she saw what looked like Brandan's Pontiac. In a sea of black automobiles, the light-brown convertible stood out, even at night.

"Is that your car?" She tightened her arm around his and drew him toward the automobile.

"Yeah. That's her." He patted the car door. "She doesn't fail me. She's here when I want her. She doesn't try to twist me in knots or manipulate me. She's dependable."

That must've been some fight you two had.

He turned toward Daisy. "You don't fail me either. Do you? You're special that way." He touched her cheek with his fingertips.

A frisson of hope swept through her. A yearning for something she couldn't define. Shouldn't define.

"You've never once tried to tell me what to do."

She cleared her throat. "Why don't you give me your keys, and I'll drive you home."

"I can drive."

"Please let me do it, Brandan."

"See?" He leaned closer. "That's what I mean." He lightly brushed her lips with his.

Her heart fluttered like the wings of a captured bird while something strange coiled in her belly. Something strange and beautiful and dangerous and wonderful and forbidden.

He took the keys from the pocket of his uniform and placed them in her hand. "You drive, but let's not go home. Let's go up Eighth Street. The night's warm, and the top's down." He went around to the passenger side, weaving a little on his way. "Your sister *hates* to drive with the top down. She hates to have the wind mess her hair. You don't care, do you?"

Daisy got in and put the key in the ignition before sliding the seat forward so she could reach the pedals. Forced to pull his knees close to his chest, Brandan laughed.

Common sense told her to take him straight to his parents' house. But she didn't want to do the sensible thing. Brandan Gallagher had kissed her. True, it hadn't been long or even particularly romantic. If she'd turned her head only a smidgeon, he would have missed her mouth altogether. But it was still a kiss. She'd wanted him to kiss her from the moment she first saw him. She couldn't take him home now. Not yet.

What about Lillian?

To drown out the voice of her conscience, she started the engine and backed out of the parking space. Then, as requested, she made her way to Eighth Street and up into the foothills.

With the city left behind them, she said, "You'll have to tell me where we're going."

"I brought Lill up here the other night. All we did was fight. I thought it'd be romantic. But no. She wanted her own way."

Daisy set her mouth. She didn't want him to talk about her sister.

"I think it might be over between us."

Her pulse quickened. "Really?"

"Pull over there." He pointed. "That's my favorite spot."

Yours and Lillian's?

She obeyed his directions. When she turned the key, she felt the silence as much as she noticed the absence of sound.

"Can you slide the seat back?" Brandan asked. "My legs're gonna cramp."

She did as he asked.

"Thanks." He leaned his head on the top of the seat back, his face pointing toward the starry heavens. After a lengthy silence, he said, "I love to fly, Daisy. It's the most amazing feeling in the world. And I don't just mean being up in a plane. I mean being at the controls. When I enlisted, I wasn't thinking about fighting in the war. I was thinking about becoming a pilot. There were still plenty of men saying we wouldn't enter the war, and I guess I believed it because I wanted to believe it. But since I have to fight, in the air is where I want to do it."

Daisy's mouth and throat went dry, and she was barely able to draw a breath. She didn't want to talk about the war any more than she wanted to talk about Lillian.

"I'm not a fool. I know what the odds are that I'll make it through to the end, and they aren't great."

"Don't talk like that, Brandan."

"Why not? It's the truth." He drew a breath and let it out. "Lillian acts like she doesn't care if I live or die."

Daisy couldn't help but reach out and touch his shoulder. "I care. I care a lot."

He lifted his head and stared in her direction. She couldn't read his eyes in the dark, but she felt him watching her all the same. The night seemed to grow even more still.

And then, somehow, he'd drawn her to him. She was in his arms and he was kissing her. Kissing her as she'd never been kissed in her life. Cold and heat rushed over her, through her.

I love you, Brandan. I've always loved you. I always will. Love me back. Please love me back.

His kiss deepened, and Daisy moaned, ignoring the alarm bells trying to be heard in her head.

Chapter 19

PRESENT DAY–FEBRUARY

Snow fell on that Saturday morning, a lacy curtain of white. The flakes were large and drifted slowly to the ground, but experience told Daisy that wouldn't last long. The forecast called for up to six inches of snow. That meant the snowstorm would get serious before long.

"Hi, GeeGee." Brianna entered the family room with bright-pink cheeks and an even brighter smile.

"I thought you might change your mind because of the snow. The roads could get bad."

"I'm not worried. I've got a warm coat and good boots." She glanced down at her stockinged feet. "I left them at the door."

"Gracious. You walked over?"

"Sure. It's not *that* far, GeeGee."

"No. I suppose not. When I was your age, I walked everywhere. During the war, gas was rationed and tires weren't to be found, so driving anywhere was rare."

Brianna crossed the room and sat cross-legged on the sofa, facing Daisy, her phone on the cushion before her.

"Tell me, dear. How are your studies going?"

"Okay." The girl shrugged.

"And what about this history class?"

"It's taking a lot more time than my other classes. That's for sure. I watched about four hours' worth of videos last night. I mean, if all I had to do was this interview with you, that'd be a lot. But there's tons more besides."

Once again, Daisy caught a glimpse of her sister in this girl. Restless. Perhaps a little spoiled.

"But," Brianna continued, "I'm liking it more than I thought I would. I expected it would be boring, but it hasn't been. Especially learning how it was for you back then."

Releasing a soft breath, Daisy reached for the envelopes on the table beside her. "Then I think you might like what I have for you. I went through some old letters the other day. I thought you might like to read a few." She held them toward Brianna.

Her great-granddaughter took the letters. "Are these from the war?"

"Yes. From the last year of the war. They aren't very detailed. People were very careful what we put in letters at the time. 'Loose lips sink ships.'" She gave Brianna a quick smile. "But I think the letters will give you a glimpse of what life was like at the time. Perhaps they'll bring up some questions you might like to ask me."

"GeeGee." Brianna set the letters on the sofa cushion beside her. "I have a question, but it isn't about the war."

Daisy smiled again in invitation. "And what is that?"

"You've been in love. Right?"

Laughter bubbled up inside Daisy and spilled over.

"Sorry. Dumb question, huh?"

"Not dumb." She shook her head. "I suppose not everyone experiences romantic love, which I assume is what you meant."

Brianna nodded.

"And the answer is yes, I've been in love. In fact, it would be fair to say I've been in love more than once and have loved in different ways." She leaned forward in her chair, peering at the girl. "Perhaps you should answer that same question."

"One more question first," Brianna countered. "Do you believe in love at first sight?"

"Oh." Daisy leaned back again. "That is a more difficult question to answer. I have the benefit of hindsight."

Brianna released a soft sound of exasperation.

"I believe that deep love—lasting love—comes with time, with living. Love is often a decision we make on individual days for a lifetime. For some, that first attraction becomes a love that lasts a lifetime. For others, it can lead to disappointment and heartache." She closed her eyes, memories pressing in. "The world loves to tell us to follow our hearts. But Scripture makes it clear that the heart cannot always be trusted. Jeremiah wrote, 'The heart is more deceitful than all else.'" She looked at Brianna again and turned the question back to her. "Do *you* believe in love at first sight?"

"I didn't used to. But then I met this guy." The dreamy look in her eyes said far more than her words.

"And does he have a name?"

"Greg. Greg Truman."

"Where did you meet?"

"At church. He's new to Boise, but his parents have lived here a couple of years. He's going to BSU. A business major."

Her great-granddaughter's words sounded like a list to be checked off. Facts but nothing more. "What sort of young man is he?"

"He's really cute, and he's really nice."

"No, Brianna. What sort of man is he? What is his character? Who is he at his core?"

"He's nice," Brianna repeated.

Daisy sighed. "I was younger than you when I gave my heart to a boy for the first time. For several years I carried a torch for him.

I thought I knew him, but I didn't. Not really. So much of what I thought I knew was imagined."

"Are you saying your heart deceived you? Like that Jeremiah passage?"

It was as if Daisy could hear the orchestra playing "Don't Sit Under the Apple Tree (With Anyone Else but Me)." In the air she caught the scent of women's perfume mingled with the smell of warm bodies on the dance floor. She felt the crush of people, girls wearing bright-red lipstick and men in uniform.

Yes, my heart deceived me, Brianna. Be ever so careful that it doesn't happen to you.

Perhaps, if she closed her eyes, she would discover that she was eighteen again, and she would remember the sound advice of others. Maybe then she would make a different choice.

Chapter 20

SATURDAY, AUGUST 15, 1942

Lillian lay awake as twilight blanketed the earth. The night had been long and her sleep fitful. She'd never felt so miserable in her life. Brandan hadn't called her the previous day, not even to give her another chance to say no to him. She'd waited, hoping that finally he would realize getting married was what they should do. There were only a few days left before he went back to his base, before he left for God knew where. And now . . .

Did I go too far? Did I push too much?

Sounds from the bathroom told her that Daisy was up earlier than usual. A surprise since she'd gone out with Martha Neville last night. Lillian had been in bed before her sister came home. Part of her wanted to go knock on Daisy's door and pour out her troubles. Another part—the larger part—wanted to keep her heartbreak to herself. Besides, Brandan would come around. Brandan always came around. He wanted to make her happy. When they were together, he loved to spoil her.

She pulled the pillow over her face.

Could she still believe that after the past eight months? He'd stubbornly refused her wishes in December. He'd ignored the pleas in her letters and in their brief phone calls in the months that followed. And since his return in August, he'd continued to refuse her.

Voice muffled, she confessed, "He really isn't going to marry me before he leaves for war."

What should I do? Should I call him or wait for him to call me? How early should I call him? I don't want to alarm his family. I don't want anybody to know we've been fighting. What should I do?

She heard a creak, then a click, as Daisy's bedroom door closed.

Go talk to her.

But what could her little sister say that would make Lillian feel better? Daisy knew nothing about being in love. At least not the way Lillian loved Brandan. The kind of love that lasted for years, forever and always. But maybe it wasn't forever and always. Maybe Brandan was tired of her. Should she care? Maybe not. Maybe she should tell him to go to the devil. Punish him for hurting her.

She tossed the pillow aside and sat up. Her hair tumbled over her face, and she pushed it back as her gaze went to her door. Daisy was awake now. If Lillian waited, she might fall back to sleep.

Go talk to her.

She reached for her summer robe and donned it over her nightgown. Then, on bare feet, she left her room and crossed the hall. She tapped lightly on the door. "Daisy? Can I come in?"

There was no answer. Had she fallen back to sleep already?

"Daisy?" Her voice was louder this time.

"Come in."

When Lillian opened the door, she was surprised to see the dress Daisy had worn last night in a puddle of fabric on the floor near the dresser. That was unlike her sister. Daisy was particular about her things, and she kept her room as tidy as a pin. Lillian stopped to pick up the dress and draped it over the chintz-covered chair nearby. Daisy watched her from the bed, a sheet pulled up to her chin, looking as if she wanted to pull it over her head.

"I heard you in the bathroom," Lillian said. "I hoped we could talk."

"Now?" The word came out almost a squeak.

"Please."

Daisy sighed. "All right."

"It's about Brandan."

"Of course it is."

"I think . . . I think he's mad at me. Really mad. He didn't call me yesterday. He's called every day this week until yesterday. I didn't mean to . . . I don't know what to do about it."

Daisy sat up. "You could support him in his decision. You could do whatever you need to do to make him happy before he goes off to war."

Lillian drew back, surprised by the anger in her sister's words.

"Don't you get it, Lillian. Brandan could *die*, and all you can think about is getting a ring on your finger. Why don't you love him the way he is? Why aren't you willing to forget what you want for a few days? You could have spent every single day of his leave with him, but instead you refused to see him because he didn't give you your way. Because he thinks it better *not* to get married before he ships out."

Lillian dropped onto the chair where she'd draped the dress a short while before. She shook her head. Why did Daisy sound even more angry than Brandan had the last time they spoke? Was everyone turning against her? She covered her face with her hands, hopelessness washing over her, and began to cry.

Only a moment or two passed before she felt Daisy's arms wrap around her from behind the chair. "Don't cry, sis. I didn't mean to . . . to be so harsh." Daisy's cheek rested on the top of Lillian's head. "I'm sorry. I . . . I . . . Please forgive me."

Daisy fought back her own tears, shame washing over her in waves.

Please forgive me. Please forgive me.

How could she have betrayed her sister like that? No matter how Daisy felt about Brandan, she knew the difference between right and wrong. She should have driven him to his parents' home from the dance hall. She should have said no when he'd kissed her. She could have stopped him when he—

She squeezed her eyes shut, stopping the direction of her thoughts at the same time. Finally, she gave her sister a squeeze and straightened. "I'm sorry."

"It's okay." Lillian sniffed. "I know you didn't say what you did to hurt me."

Daisy's words weren't the problem. Her words weren't why she was sorry. But Lillian could never know. Never.

She swallowed the lump in her throat as she remembered the way Brandan had turned away from her, giving her privacy in the darkness of the car. She remembered his words of apology, his pleading for forgiveness. She remembered her own realization that he hadn't really made love to her. In his alcohol-altered brain, he'd thought of Lillian the whole time. And when the effects of alcohol had worn off some time in the wee hours of the morning, all he'd felt was disgust. Maybe for himself. Definitely for Daisy.

I wish I'd die.

She returned to her bed and sat on the edge, her gaze cast downward. Her anger of a short while ago had dissipated, and all that remained was guilt. Painful, mind-numbing guilt. At some point, Lillian would see the emotion on her face. And then what? What could she tell her sister when Lillian asked what was wrong? Would Daisy lie or tell the truth?

No, she couldn't ever tell the truth.

"You're right." Lillian rose from the chair. "I've been unfair to him. I've been wrong. I'm going to tell him so. I'm going to tell him right away." She came to the bed and hugged Daisy, then hurried out of the room.

Daisy lay down again and pulled the sheet over herself, then curled into a fetal position and wept. Despite washing in the bathroom after sneaking into the house, she felt dirty. A lifetime of Sunday-school lessons about the consequences of sin replayed in her head.

O God, I'm sorry. Please forgive me.

How desperately she wanted her simple prayer to take away the shameful feelings. But it didn't. It wouldn't. It couldn't. What was it the reverend taught? True repentance was making a 180-degree turn and going in the other direction.

"I won't ever do it again," she whispered. "I'll be good. I promise."

She rolled onto her other side.

What must I do now?

How would she face her mom and dad? How would she face Lillian again?

Or Brandan.

She felt warmth spread up her neck and into her cheeks. She didn't want to face Brandan. Not today. Not ever. Maybe she wouldn't have to. Maybe he and Lillian would break up, and he would never come to their house again.

She thought of the way Brandan hadn't looked at her when he let her out of his car in the alley behind the Abbott house. The promise of dawn had provided enough light for her to see him, but he'd kept his eyes focused straight ahead. Neither of them had said a word.

He still loved Lillian. He'd lain with Daisy in the back of his Pontiac convertible, but he still loved her sister.

"I'm a fool. O God, what have I done?"

It was early on Saturday morning when Todd carried some gardening tools from the garage out to the backyard. His mother had loved gardening. She'd found joy in taking care of the rose bushes and peonies and other flowers in this yard. She'd never allowed a weed to last more than a day before it was plucked from the soil.

Todd wished he took pleasure in the task, but he didn't. It was just another chore that had to be done to keep his property looking respectable, and he hoped his mom couldn't look down from heaven and see what a poor job he did of it.

He was about to kneel when he heard a door slam closed. A moment later, he saw Daisy hurry down the porch steps and out to the swing that hung from a tree next to the detached garage. Even from across the hedge that separated their yards, he recognized her distress.

Should he let her know he was there? That he'd seen her? No, probably better to let it be. No doubt it was boyfriend trouble, and he wouldn't have any advice to give her. She was young and pretty and smart. It would work out.

He knelt on the lawn and began to work the soil with the spade, digging up crabgrass and other annoying weeds that didn't belong in his mother's garden.

Some of the older men at church kept telling him that he needed to find a girl and get married. "There's a surplus of eligible girls these days," one of them had told him last week. He'd heard what hadn't been said: *with all the other men off to war.* It made him feel as if he couldn't find a girl to love him unless he was one of the few still not in the military.

Todd wasn't what anybody could call a ladies' man. He was too quiet natured for that. Still, he didn't think he was bad looking. No Clark Gable. He knew that. Maybe more like Jimmy Stewart with an aw-shucks appeal.

He shook his head, amused by the direction of his thoughts.

Maybe he *should* get married. He was tired of his own cooking, and it would be nice to have someone to sit with in the evenings. But he'd never met a girl who made him think, *She's the one*. Worse yet, he'd never gone out with a girl who looked at him the way Lillian Abbott looked at Brandan Gallagher. Call him stupid, but he'd like someone to look at him like that. As if he'd hung the moon and the stars.

Todd had been fifteen when his father told him that romantic love was fun but the steady, everyday commitment love was the kind that made life worth living. Todd could see his dad's point, but he would still like to fall head over heels for a girl and have her do the same for him.

Chapter 21

PRESENT DAY—FEBRUARY

Brianna stood with her usual circle of friends near the front of the sanctuary, but her eyes were glued to the main entry doors. Behind her, she heard the sounds of the worship team taking to the stage. The service was about to start, and there was still no sign of Greg Truman.

Disappointment sluiced through her. She should have texted him last night or this morning. After her talk with GeeGee yesterday, she'd decided to let Greg make the next move. But her meeting with him at the coffee shop on Friday had been at his invitation, so maybe she should have asked him to go to lunch after church. That would have made certain he was there this morning. He'd said he planned to return to Trinity. So why hadn't he come? She hoped he was all right. She hoped his family was all right. He didn't know her well enough to tell her if something was wrong. She didn't know him well, either, but it would only be friendly to make sure he was okay. Right? After all, he was new to Boise.

I should text him. She reached for the phone, her pulse quickening as she did so.

Then the music started, and as usual, Hannah led the way into the row of chairs. Brianna released the phone, letting it slide back into her pocket. She managed to sing along for the entire first worship song before glancing over her shoulder toward the entrance. Not that she could see much of anything. The lights had been dimmed, and most of the congregation stood during worship.

The next ninety minutes felt interminable.

"What's up with you?" Hannah whispered at the close of the service.

"What do you mean?"

"Your head was someplace else all morning."

"No, it wasn't."

Hannah gave her a hard look. "You were like a two-year-old, fidgeting through the sermon."

Brianna was about to object again but then thought better of it. There was truth in what her friend said.

"So . . ." Hannah gave her another one of those looks. "What's up?"

"I was hoping Greg would come to church again. That's all."

"Greg? The guy who was here last week?"

She nodded.

Hannah grinned. "He got to you, did he?"

"No." She felt the heat in her cheeks. "But I thought he was nice."

"Doesn't hurt that he looks like Liam Hemsworth."

"I didn't notice."

"Sure you didn't." This time Hannah laughed. "Are you coming out to lunch?"

"If I can get a ride home."

"You got it."

"I'll tell Mom. Meet you outside the front door."

Brianna was in the large fellowship hall, looking for her parents, when she caught sight of Greg. And he was talking to her mom and dad. As she approached, he looked her way and smiled. A now-familiar melting sensation flowed through her.

"Hey," she said as she drew closer. "I didn't think you were here this morning."

"I was late, so I sat in the back. And I just met your parents. Small world, huh?"

She glanced at her dad, who wore an approving look on his face. Good. That meant he liked Greg already. She looked up at him again. "A bunch of us are going out to lunch. Would you like to come along?" *Please say yes. Please say yes.*

"Sure. That would be great."

Releasing a quick breath, she turned to her mom. "Hannah said she'll give me a ride home."

"Okay. Have fun. It was nice to meet you, Greg."

"You, too, Mrs. Hastings. Mr. Hastings."

Brianna turned toward the main doors of the church and led the way outside. Snow still covered the ground, and an icy wind buffeted them.

"Where is it we're going?" Greg asked.

She told him the name of the restaurant and how to get there.

"Why don't you ride with me?"

Her pulse quickened. "Sure. But I've got to wait for Hannah and the others. I told her I'd meet them here."

Brianna didn't mind the frigid temperature or the wind that pushed at her back. Not while she stood beside Greg Truman for all the world to see. Part of her wanted to slip her arm through his, a silent way to declare that he was her guy. Not that he was. He seemed to like her, but this was only the third time they'd met.

"What sort of man is he?" GeeGee's voice whispered in her memory. *"What is his character?"*

Her heart wanted to answer that Greg was wonderful. Anybody with eyes could see that. And he liked her. What more did she need to know for now? The rest would come with time. Right?

The glass doors opened, and Hannah came out, followed by four other friends. When she saw Greg, she smiled. "Look who's here." She stuck out a mittened hand. "Good to see you again."

"You too. Hannah, right?"

Brianna said, "I invited Greg to join us for lunch."

"Great. Well, let's go before the restaurant gets too full."

"I'm going to ride with Greg. In case he gets separated."

Hannah's look said she doubted that was the real reason. And her friend was right. It wasn't. Riding with Greg would make it feel like they were truly together.

"What sort of man is he?"

Brianna couldn't answer her great-grandmother's question, but she meant to do everything she could to find out.

Chapter 22

SATURDAY, AUGUST 15, 1942

Brandan didn't go home after leaving Daisy in the alley behind her house. Despite the government's directions that pleasure driving should be something of the past, he drove up Highway 55 and didn't stop until he reached McCall. He parked the car, made his way to a sandy beach, and sat on a large rock, watching as the water lapped against the shore. As the morning air warmed, families arrived at the beach. Moms and dads stood with their feet in the water, watching as their kids played in the shallow edges of the lake.

He watched it all, but inside, nothing registered. His thoughts remained down in Boise. His thoughts remained on what had happened between him and Daisy. He wanted to blame the whiskey for making him lose control. He and Lillian had managed to avoid going too far in their times alone together. It hadn't been easy, but they'd never crossed the line. But last night . . . with Daisy . . .

He'd known, of course. He'd known that Daisy had a schoolgirl crush on him. He'd never paid it much heed. He'd been sure she would get over it in time. After all, Lillian was his girl. Daisy's sister was the one he planned to marry, when the time was right.

But Lillian hadn't been with him last night. Lillian had refused to talk to him, and he'd been angry and fed up and . . . and looking for a little revenge, he supposed. Then Daisy had appeared, looking at him with trust and . . . and something more. She'd come into his arms with ease, and he'd—

He groaned, drawing the gaze of a woman holding the hand of a toddler. Could she tell with one look that he wasn't a man to be trusted? That he was the sort who would betray the woman he loved and the moral code of his parents? That he was so depraved he would take advantage of an innocent girl, using her the way he'd used Daisy? Selfishly, with no regard for what their night together could mean for her. No, he hadn't raped her. She'd been more than willing. She hadn't protested, not even once. But that didn't relieve him of responsibility.

How was he supposed to make things right? If he could turn back the clock, he would. He wouldn't go to the Starlite. He wouldn't dance with any of those other girls. He wouldn't swallow even a sip of Jack's whiskey. And if he saw Daisy, he would smile and walk away. Because he loved Lillian. Because despite not being ready to marry her yet, he did want to marry her eventually.

But he couldn't turn back time. He couldn't undo what was done.

So what am I supposed to do?

Perhaps it was for the best that he was leaving Idaho in less than forty-eight hours. Perhaps it was best that Lillian was too mad to speak to him. He wouldn't have to face either her or Daisy. He only had to get through tomorrow, and then he would be gone.

He stared over the lake where sunlight glittered across the surface of the waves.

Life had always come easily to Brandan. He'd done well in school and college without hours upon hours of study. He caught on fast when learning anything new, like driving a car or flying a plane. He was good at sports. Guys and girls both liked him. He fit into all sorts of crowds. When he'd gotten into scrapes as a kid, he'd been able to charm his way out of trouble, and that knack had continued into adulthood.

But he couldn't charm his way out of this. Lillian couldn't know what he'd done. She wouldn't forgive him. Would Daisy keep it a secret, or would she want to see him punished?

Brandan lowered his head and closed his eyes. *I didn't mean to do what I did. Help me out of this mess, God. Please.*

He rose from the rock and left the beach, but instead of getting into his car, he walked through the small resort town. Up one side of the main street and down the other. Waiting. Hoping for an answer to his dilemma to suddenly come to mind. Hoping for a way out that would protect him from others knowing what he'd done. Hoping for deliverance from the mess he'd made.

As he got closer to where he'd parked his car, he remembered the many Sundays since leaving his parents' home when he'd skipped church, both while at university and then during flight training. There'd been so many other things to do—studying, hanging out with friends, catching up on sleep. And when was the last time he'd opened the Bible his parents had given him for his sixteenth birthday? He couldn't recall. As for prayer . . .

His dad's voice rang in his memory: *"Even people who don't believe in God cry out for His help when their lives are in danger."* The words pierced Brandan like an arrow. Was he the same as that unbeliever his dad referred to, turning to God only when he was in trouble? He feared it was true.

He got into his Pontiac, then paused to look up at the clear-blue sky. "Help me out of this mess, and I'll try to change." He started the engine and pointed the convertible south toward Boise.

"I'm sorry, Lillian," Brandan's mother said. "I haven't seen him all day. He must have left before the sun was up. Perhaps he's with Jack Foreman again." She stepped back, opening the door wider. "Would you like to come in? I have no idea when he'll return, but you're more than welcome to wait here."

Afraid she might burst into tears, Lillian shook her head. "No. Thank you, Mrs. Gallagher. Just tell him I came by and to call me when he can."

"I will, dear."

She turned and descended the front porch steps. The August sun beat down upon the valley, but thankfully there were tall trees shading the sidewalks as she headed toward home. Up ahead, she saw children playing in a sprinkler in the front yard of a home on the next corner. Their squeals of joy and carefree laughter reached her, and envy surged through her. She would like to be a child again, unaware of a world at war, unafraid of what tomorrow might bring, and convinced that life was as it should be.

She was so lost in thought that she almost didn't see the approach of Brandan's car. When she did, she stopped still on the sidewalk, her heart seeming to do the same as he pulled the convertible to the curb. It seemed forever before he opened the door and got out. He didn't smile when their eyes met. He looked . . . miserable. As miserable as she felt.

"I . . . I was coming from your house," she said.

He nodded but didn't speak.

"I was afraid . . ." Her voice trailed off, the lump in her throat making it impossible to say more. What more was needed? She was afraid. She didn't need to explain why.

Brandan reached out and cupped her cheek. The touch was light and tender. She leaned into the palm of his hand, closing her eyes, waiting for him to tell her he loved her and that he was sorry he'd been stubborn. Waiting for him to make everything all right.

"Come on." He withdrew his hand. "I'll drive you home."

She wanted him to take her in his arms. Instead, he turned and walked to his car, opening the passenger door for her. Wordlessly, she followed and got in.

The drive to her house was torture. Brandan kept his gaze locked on the road. His mouth was set in a firm line. The space between them felt a million miles wide. A distance impossible for her to cross. She straightened and looked down the street as well.

When Brandan stopped the car in front of her house, he spoke at last. "I've been gone all day. I'd better get home. I've got some things to do since I fly out Monday morning."

As if she wasn't aware of when he would leave.

He added, "I'll see you at church in the morning."

"Yes. At church." She reached for the door handle.

"Lill?"

She looked over her shoulder.

"I *do* love you."

She wanted to throw herself into his arms, but something about the way he looked warned her to stay back. "I love you too."

He looked out the windshield as if he couldn't bear to meet her gaze for long. His reluctance seemed at odds with his words.

Close to tears again, she got out of the car and hurried up to the front porch. By the time she turned to look back, he'd started the engine and was pulling away from the curb.

Lillian moved to the porch swing and sank onto it. She didn't try to stop the tears from falling. Brandan was gone. No one would see her crying. In fact, maybe she should have let him see her cry. Maybe he didn't understand how truly sorry she was for the way she'd behaved over the past week.

It will be all right. She sniffed and dried her eyes with a handkerchief. *He said he loves me, so it has to be all right*. She drew a long, deep breath and released it slowly. *When I see him in church tomorrow, I'll tell him I'll wait for him. I'll let him know it's okay between us*. She drew another breath. *I'll make him want me more than he's ever wanted me before*.

"Lillian?"

She looked toward the front door. Her mother stood on the porch, watching her with a worried expression.

"Are you all right, sweetheart?"

"I'm okay, Mom."

Her mother moved toward her. "Are you worried about Brandan?"

She nodded, the lump returning to her throat.

"I was a little younger than you when our boys marched off to the Great War." Her mother settled onto the swing beside Lillian. "I'm forever thankful that your father was never sent overseas. He was in training when the war ended. We married a year later."

Lillian placed her head on her mom's shoulder.

"Commit yourself to pray for Brandan until he is stateside again. For his safety. For his well-being. For him to trust in God and listen for His voice. And pray those things for yourself as well. You'll need God's guidance in the months to come."

"What will I do if I lose him?" she asked softly. *What if I've lost him already? What if I've lost him before he ever goes to war?*

"Oh, Lillian." Her mother kissed her head. "I hope you don't have to discover the answer to that question. But one thing I can tell you without a doubt: God doesn't leave us alone in times of despair. He will see us through whatever we must face in life, if we invite Him in."

How does a good God allow so much evil to happen? Lillian wanted to voice the question aloud, but the words seemed blasphemous. Would God punish her for doubting Him?

Her mother patted Lillian's upper arm. "Come inside. I need to get back to dinner preparations."

"Where's Daisy?" she asked.

"She was called into work. One of the other girls is sick. But she'll be home in time for dinner."

Maybe it's time to look for another job, Lillian thought as she followed her mom inside. After finishing high school, she'd worked as a file clerk for an insurance salesman. Then Pearl Harbor had happened.

Her boss had enlisted and closed his office. Holding onto hope that Brandan would change his mind and marry her, Lillian hadn't sought other employment. Other girls her age were working in shipyards and airplane factories. Countless women of all ages were working for the war effort in one way or another. Daisy had talked about the Women's Army Auxiliary Corps, saying she thought it would be exciting to be a part of something like that, but they weren't enlisting more women yet.

"Are they still hiring civilians to work at Gowen Field?" she asked as her mother stirred something in a pot on the stove.

"I believe so. Mrs. Masterson at church works out there. Why?" Her mom turned to look at her. "Do you want to apply for a job?"

Lillian nodded.

"I think that's a good decision. Too much time on your hands is never helpful."

She thought of Brandan, leaving to fly bombers over hostile territory. She would definitely need something to keep her mind busy so she wouldn't have all that time to think about the danger he was in. Or the fact that he'd left her behind without a proposal and a ring.

Chapter 23

PRESENT DAY—FEBRUARY

"Hey, Brianna." Adam Wentworth slid onto the chair opposite her and set his backpack on the table between them. "How's it going?"

"Okay."

"Are you feeling better?"

"Yes. Thanks for asking. I hated to miss class." It bothered her, not telling Adam she'd skipped class in order to have coffee with Greg. But why should she tell him? Adam didn't know Greg. On the other hand, Adam was one of her dearest friends. Why not tell him the truth? Why did she feel the need to keep her interest in Greg a secret?

"Do you still want the notes I took?"

"That would be great. Thanks."

Adam opened his laptop, then clicked a few keys. "Okay. I've got them. Want me to AirDrop them to you?"

"Sure." She opened her laptop. A few seconds later, she heard the *ping* and accepted the file. Her downloads folder bounced. "I'll look at it later." She closed her laptop again.

Adam stared at his computer screen for a few moments, more keys clicking. Then he looked at her again. "Who're you interviewing for Meyer's paper?"

"My great-grandmother."

"GeeGee? I remember meeting her at a barbecue at your house. How old is she?"

"She turned ninety-eight last October, so mostly we're talking about World War Two."

"She must have some great stories to tell you."

Brianna nodded. "She has. Although sometimes, when we're talking, she sort of drifts off into her own little world, and I'm not sure I get the point of what she's saying." She gave him a wry smile. "And sometimes she seems to want me to do even more studying than Professor Meyer does. I'll ask her a question, and she makes it something for me to research before the next time we get together."

"Sounds perfect to me."

"You would think that. Who're you interviewing?"

"My grandpa Ryan. He's not much of a storyteller. I've got to drag stuff out of him."

"Hey, Brianna." Hannah pulled out the chair on Brianna's right. "Hey, Adam. Gads, what a morning. We had to watch some horrible movie for my film class. So glad *that's* over."

"I thought you loved your film class."

"I do. But not what we saw this morning." Hannah released a dramatic sigh, then turned one of those searching looks on Brianna. "So, what happened after you and Greg left the restaurant yesterday?"

From the corner of her eye, Brianna saw Adam straighten as if in surprise. What? Did he think she couldn't get a date? Although that wasn't what it had been. Just friends eating together after church.

"Come on," Hannah continued. "Tell."

"There's nothing to tell. He drove me home afterward. That's all." That . . . and a kiss on the cheek before she got out of his car.

Hannah sucked in a breath. "You're blushing."

"I am not." But when she put her fingers on her cheeks, her skin felt warm to the touch.

"What did he do?"

"Nothing."

"Who's Greg?" Adam asked.

Hannah answered, "A new guy at church. Brianna likes him."

"We barely know each other, Hannah."

"But you like him anyway."

Adam looked back and forth between the two girls, settling at last on Brianna. "Maybe I should meet him. Make sure I approve."

Brianna drew back, ready to tell him what she thought of that. Then she caught the laughter in his eyes and relaxed.

"Seriously," Adam said, "maybe we could all go to a movie or something."

"Just not the one I had to watch in film class." Hannah stuck out her tongue.

Adam and Brianna laughed. Then Adam checked his phone and hopped to his feet. "Time I got to my next class. Let me know if you decide on a movie." He stuffed his laptop into his backpack, pulled one strap over his shoulder, and took off.

"He looked upset," Hannah said in a low voice.

"Did he? No, I don't think so. Why would he be?"

"Maybe because he *likes* you."

"Adam likes everybody. He's just that way."

"You know it's more than that."

Yes, Brianna *did* know. But she preferred things the way they were. She liked having Adam for a best friend, along with Hannah. What if she let the friendship become something more with Adam, and then it didn't work out between them? Could they go back to being good friends again? Even she knew that rarely worked. No, it was better to pretend she didn't know what Adam wanted. Better by far. Besides, now there was Greg. Greg, who made her pulse quicken just thinking about him.

"I knew it. I knew you knew." Now it was Hannah's turn to check the time on her phone. "But I've gotta run. Math class." She hurried off in the opposite direction from Adam.

Brianna watched the flow of students pass by her table, some going one way, some another. The decibel level rose for several minutes, but as students either left the building or entered classrooms, quiet began to descend over this area again. With a sigh, she opened her laptop a second time. She might as well look through the notes that Adam had shared with her.

But first . . .

She picked up her phone and sent a text to Greg, asking if he would like to join her and a couple of friends for a movie on Friday. It seemed to take forever before his reply came.

It's a date. Send details.

Her heart trilled in her chest, and it took a good five minutes before she could actually concentrate on the document open on her screen.

Chapter 24

SUNDAY, AUGUST 16, 1942

Brandan slept badly and awakened late on Sunday morning. He told his parents to go to church without him and he would catch up. Perhaps that was a good thing, he thought after they left. He might want to leave church early. He wasn't sure what he would do or what he would say when he saw Lillian and Daisy together.

But as it happened, he didn't see them together. Daisy wasn't in church that morning, and he felt a wave of relief combined with guilt when he realized it. The coward in him wanted to turn and leave or join his parents in their pew. But Lillian was looking at him, and her uncertain smile pulled him in her direction. "Sorry I'm late." He sank onto the pew beside her.

The choir chose that moment to rise and begin to sing the opening hymn. Reprieved from saying more, he plucked the hymnal from the back of the pew and opened it. He moved his lips, following the words on the page without actually giving voice to them.

Was he a hypocrite to even enter the church after what he'd done? But he'd asked God for forgiveness. He'd asked God to help him change. What more could he do? Besides, he wasn't a bad person. He'd made a mistake. He would get over it. Daisy would get over it.

Things would work out. It might not feel good right now, but it would get better. Time healed all wounds, right?

The service passed in a kind of blur for Brandan. As much as he tried to listen to the reading of Scripture and to the reverend's message, he kept thinking about the Abbott sisters. He'd fallen for Lillian when they first met. She was so incredibly beautiful. Who could have eyes for anybody else when she was in the room? As for Daisy, he hadn't given her much notice. She was the little sister. A nice kid. Sweet and caring. Pretty enough, but not his type.

Of all the girls dancing at the Starlite on Friday night, why had he chosen to take Daisy up into the foothills? If he'd wanted sex, he'd had other options. But that hadn't been his plan when they left the dance hall. There'd been no plan at all. He'd been too intoxicated to make a plan.

But not so drunk I didn't know what I did was wrong.

He gave Lillian a sideways glance. Would they be okay? Sure they would. She was still his girl. She loved him, and she was still the one he wanted to marry someday.

When the service ended, Lillian took Brandan's hand as they left the pew. It wasn't a possessive gesture, as it often seemed to him. Her hold was more tentative, uncertain. Very unlike her. Lillian had an abundance of self-confidence. Which was why, much of the time, he was putty in her hands.

Outside in the bright sunlight, the day already warm, Lillian's mother asked, "Brandan, will you join us for Sunday dinner?"

"I'm sorry, Mrs. Abbott, but this is my last day in town. I've promised to spend it with my parents."

"Of course you have." Lillian's mother glanced at her daughter. "We understand."

But Lillian looked near tears. At the beginning of his leave, she'd come over to eat at his house several times. He knew his mom would be okay with it if he asked her to join his family today. But he couldn't. The more they were together, the more likely she was to guess the truth.

"But you'll come over this evening," she said softly. "Right?"

He tightened his hold on her hand. "Yes."

The instant the word was out of his mouth, he regretted it. He loved her, but there was a big, ugly secret between them now. A secret he didn't know how to handle. But how could he not see her one more time before he left?

Shame washed over him again. Could Carl Abbott look at him and know what he'd done to Daisy? If so, the man would want to kill him, not let him sit with Lillian on the front porch swing.

"I'd better go." His voice felt scratchy in his throat. He leaned down and kissed Lillian on the cheek, then spun on his heel and strode toward the church parking lot.

If he got shot down on a mission, it would be his own fault. He deserved whatever bad came his way.

Daisy was still in bed when she heard her family return from church. It wasn't long before there was a rap on her door, followed by her mother's soft voice.

"Daisy, are you awake?"

She considered not answering but said, "I'm awake."

The door cracked open, enough for her mother to look inside. "How are you feeling?"

"A little better." It wasn't true. She doubted she would ever feel better than she did right then. But her mother thought she was ill, not guilt ridden, and so it seemed the right answer.

"Do you feel able to come downstairs for Sunday dinner?"

Daisy shook her head. "No."

"Some soup and toast? Here in your room?"

"Yes. That would be fine." She wasn't hungry. She doubted she could swallow even a few sips of soup. But it would make her mom happy if she tried.

"I'll be up with it in a while."

"Okay." She turned away from the door and closed her eyes, fighting back a fresh wave of tears.

Another knock sounded. It was too soon to be her mother returning. She said nothing, hoping to be left alone. It wasn't to be. The door opened.

"Hey, sis. How are you? I'm sorry you're sick."

Go away, Lillian. Leave me alone.

"Mom said you were a little better."

She released a sigh and rolled over, looking at her sister, who still wore her Sunday best. "A little."

"Brandan was at church. He couldn't come to eat with us, but he said he'll come over tonight."

Daisy felt truly sick at the idea of seeing him. Pretending wasn't required.

"I hope you're well enough to say goodbye. He leaves in the morning."

"Maybe I will. I'll try."

"It's hard to know when he might be back."

"I know, but it isn't me he'll come to see. It's you." Oh, how that truth hurt.

"You're right. And we don't want him to catch whatever you've got. It wouldn't do for him to get sick just as he's leaving for overseas."

"No." Daisy closed her eyes, hoping Lillian would take the hint and leave.

"Okay. I'm going to change my clothes. Feel better."

"Thanks."

The door closed with a *click*.

Daisy opened her eyes again, thankful to be alone. Thankful that

Brandan would leave Boise in the morning so that she wouldn't have to worry about seeing him. Not seeing him this soon after . . . after what had happened between them. By the time he returned from the war, she would have come to terms with . . . everything. She would be different. He would be different.

But he's coming over tonight. He's coming to say goodbye to Lillian. He won't care if he doesn't see me. He'd rather not see me. I'm nothing to him. Worse than nothing.

She covered her face with her hands as she recalled for the hundredth time the way Brandan had whispered Lillian's name in the wee hours of the night when she'd thought him asleep beside her. She'd looked up at the stars above her, tiny white dots on an inky black canvas, hating herself, hating him, hating her sister.

"Trials are not forever," her mother liked to say.

But this felt as if it would last forever.

Get up! her mind screamed at her. *Do something. Do anything.*

"Tomorrow," she whispered. "I'll get up tomorrow."

Chapter 25

PRESENT DAY–FEBRUARY

Leaning on her walker, Daisy shuffled toward the piano on that quiet Sunday afternoon. She leaned on the walker in the very way that nice young man at the rehab facility had told her she shouldn't. Although that advice had been given more than fifteen years ago, she thought of it often as she traversed the house or on one of her rare outings. She tried to remember to walk upright with her eyes forward instead of on the ground, but when one's body didn't have the strength it used to, it wasn't easy to comply.

Old age was such a bother, she thought as she sat on the piano bench. She often wondered what use she was, why God allowed her to remain when so many she'd known and loved had passed on to their reward. Then she remembered that God had a purpose for every life, even the very old ones. Even hers. She simply had to look for those moments when He wished to use her.

She played a few notes on the piano. Then, like a child at her lessons, she ran through the scales. Not as fast as she would have played years ago. Her fingers weren't as agile as they'd once been. But fast enough to please her. And without errors, which also pleased her. When she finished, she lifted her fingers off the piano keys and stared at her hands. So wrinkled, the skin like parchment. When had that happened? It didn't seem any time at all since her hands had been young and smooth. She remembered her mother's hands at the end of her life. Mother's fingers had been gnarled by arthritis, and she'd only been in her seventies.

Only in her seventies.

Daisy shook her head, remembering back to when she was a girl. She'd been about ten years old, she supposed. Todd's father, a neighbor to the Abbotts, had passed away. He was a man in his early forties—she remembered because her mother had made special note of it at the dinner table—and Daisy had later said to a friend, *"At least he lived a long life."* Now, when she thought of her own mother dying at the age of seventy-eight, her reaction was, *Mother was so young.*

"Perspective," she whispered—and smiled.

"Hi, GeeGee."

Daisy twisted toward the family-room entrance. "Brianna. I didn't know I would see you today. Did I forget something?"

"No. I just thought I'd drop by."

"Well, that's nice of you."

Brianna crossed the room and sat on the end of the bench, facing the opposite direction.

"How was church this morning?"

"Good. What about yours?"

"Mine was good too. I don't attend in person very often. I simply don't have the strength for it. But with the internet, I'm able to still feel a part of my home church. I'm so very grateful for that. It wasn't that long ago people like me didn't have such an option. There were televised services, of course, but it wasn't a person's local church body."

"Seems funny to think of that. I mean, not having YouTube and Facebook and other websites where you can watch."

"When I was your age, not only did we not have the internet, we didn't have a television either. TVs weren't around until the fifties. But every home had a radio in the nineteen thirties and forties. My dad never missed listening to the news, and he had several favorite programs that he faithfully followed. And the newspaper. Gracious. Dad couldn't have managed without his daily paper. He would have thought the world was at an end if someone told him people would one day read news on their phones." She laughed softly as she shook her head.

Brianna laughed, too, before saying, "Last night I watched one of the documentaries from my history professor's list for the forties. It was mostly filmed during the war, up in the bombers flying over Europe, but they've added interviews with survivors who flew those planes or were gunners and navigators and jobs like that." The girl twisted to look into Daisy's eyes. "GeeGee, they were all so young—I mean, twenty or twenty-one or twenty-two—and they were flying bombers through flak and being shot up by fighter planes. Lots of them were dying. Thousands died in the Eighth Air Force alone. It said that those guys had less than a 25 percent chance of making it to twenty-five missions. It's really awful to think about."

Brandan's face flashed in Daisy's memory. Second Lieutenant Brandan Gallagher. So young and so brave. So handsome in his uniform. Off to fight in a war not of his own making, but a war that had to be fought.

So many who never came home.

Brianna said, "One of the things mentioned is that some people call World War Two the Good War. Do you think a war can be good?"

More images came to mind. Images of the dead and dying in nations around the world. Pictures of the survivors of concentration camps and prisoners of war camps and the London Blitz. Names of servicemen killed listed in the newspapers and etched on memorials.

"No, Brianna. I don't believe war itself is ever good. It brings death and so many other horrible things. But I do believe some wars have to be fought. If the men I knew, and others like them—Americans, Canadians, Australians, the British, and many other nationalities—if they hadn't gone off to fight Hitler and the other tyrants, you wouldn't live in a free country today. Of that I am sure."

Brianna nodded, her expression thoughtful. "Would you tell me again about the day the Japanese attacked Pearl Harbor? I'd like to understand better what you felt when you heard the news. I don't think I understood at first how awful it must have been. How scary."

"Of course, dear." She reached for her walker. "But let's get comfortable. You know I am prone to ramble."

Chapter 26

FRIDAY, SEPTEMBER 25, 1942

Todd and Carl left the factory a little after six o'clock on that Friday evening. In the weeks since Carl had come to work for Kinnear Canning—a misnomer now that they were manufacturing compasses for the military—the two men had fallen into the habit of walking to and from work together. Although rationing of gasoline hadn't started yet, the sale of rubber tires was severely restricted, and most people left their automobiles at home whenever possible. The bonus from walking to and from work was that the two men had that time to talk and exchange ideas.

The transition from canning fruits to making precision instruments had involved long hours every day but Sundays. It had required intensive training, the hiring of more employees, and countless unexpected decisions. Todd remembered to thank God in his prayers every day for sending Carl to the factory back in mid-August. He couldn't imagine going through all this without him. Carl was a steadying presence on the production floor and in the business offices on the second floor of the factory. Even Roy Jamison seemed to be doing better, drinking less and focusing more on his work.

"Has Lillian found a new job yet?" Todd asked when they turned the corner onto Eastman Street.

"No. Nothing yet. But she got a letter from Brandan yesterday, so she's in much better spirits. She didn't let us read the letter, of course. Private words between young people in love. But she did say he was stationed in England. I don't know how temporary that is. I guess it depends how things continue to go in North Africa."

Todd nodded. Most of the news this year had centered on the war in the Pacific, and too much of it had been bad news. As for the other side of the Atlantic, everyone he talked to anticipated that American troops would join the British in the North Africa campaign before anything could be done to stop the Nazis in Europe.

"What I wouldn't give to fight like Brandan," he said beneath his breath.

Apparently, Carl heard him. "You are fighting. Just in a different way."

"Doesn't feel like it."

"No. I don't suppose it does. But what you've done at the factory is important to the war effort."

Todd continued as if Carl hadn't spoken. "I get asked a lot when I'm going to enlist. I'm twenty-four, and I look healthy. Why wouldn't they wonder about me? Some people think I'm a coward. I'm not, but that's what they think. But I hate to tell them I'm classified 4-F. That seems almost as bad as being a coward. It makes me feel . . . worthless."

Carl stopped walking, forcing Todd to do the same. "Son. Don't let others do that to you. You know who you are. You know who God says you are. Live up to that, and it doesn't matter what others think or say."

His throat tight, Todd nodded. But he wasn't sure he agreed. It did matter what others thought or said. At least to him it did.

After a moment they started walking again, silent this time until their houses came into view.

Carl asked, "Want to join us for dinner?"

"No, but thanks. Give Nancy and the girls my best."

"Will do."

Todd stopped at his front walk and watched until Carl reached his own. Then he waved at the other man and headed inside. After closing the front door behind him, he paused to look around. He hadn't changed a thing since his mom passed away. In almost five years, he hadn't moved any of her knickknacks or hung any new pictures. He hadn't rearranged the furniture. The canisters remained in the same place on the kitchen counter, and he always used the same burner for the coffeepot. It was all familiar to him.

And tonight it felt . . . too empty.

Chapter 27

SATURDAY, SEPTEMBER 26, 1942

Daisy,

I'm sending this letter to Jack and asking him to get it to you. I don't want to take a chance on anybody else seeing it.

I'm not sure what to write to you except to say I'm sorry for what happened before I left Boise. It was never my intent to do what I did. I'm not blaming you. I'm to blame. But it's Lillian I love. God knows if or when I'll make it home again. But if I do, whenever that is, I'm hoping Lillian will still want to marry me. She's the only girl for me. I realize that even more now than I did before.

I'm asking you to forgive me, Daisy. I hope you can. You're a sweet girl. And like I said, I'm sorry. Please don't tell Lillian what we did. Please, for all our sakes. And again, forgive me.

Brandan

Closed in the upstairs bathroom, Daisy read the letter from Brandan for the umpteenth time since Jack Foreman had delivered it to her on Thursday. But no matter how many times she read it, the words remained the same. Brandan hadn't wanted her when he'd kissed her or when he'd made love to her. She'd been only a substitute for the woman he truly loved. A substitute for Lillian.

Daisy had known, of course, how he felt. She'd known it on the night it happened. She'd known it the next day and the next. But somehow, she'd continued to hope that maybe, just maybe, he might care for her. At least a little.

Bile rose again in her throat, and she dropped to her knees to empty her stomach into the toilet. Her eyes watered and her nose ran as she continued to heave, even when nothing remained. If it was only the letter that troubled her, that would be enough to make her sick. But it was worse than Brandan's rejection. Much worse.

It can't be. It can't.

When the world seemed to settle, she wiped her mouth with some toilet paper, then lay down on the cool tiles, letting her tears fall.

Dear God, don't let it be true. It was one mistake.

In her mind she counted again the weeks since she'd gone dancing at the Starlite, the weeks since she'd driven Brandan's car into the foothills and—

Six weeks. Six weeks that would change her life forever. One time. One moment of weakness. It couldn't be true but it was. Her period was late. Several weeks late. And her periods were like clockwork. Never late. Always on time.

She was going to have a baby.

She was going to have Brandan's baby.

A girl Daisy knew in school had gotten pregnant out of wedlock the previous summer. Her parents had shipped her off to an aunt to have the baby and give it away. It was all supposed to be hush-hush, but Daisy had heard about it through Martha. She imagined her own mother, hanging her head in shame, unable to meet the stares of other women at church or at the market. She imagined her father telling her they'd arranged for her to stay in that maternity hospital for unwed mothers. She could almost hear the whispers as word got out, and a chill passed through her, colder than the bathroom floor.

A knock made the door shudder. "Hey, Daisy," Lillian said, irritation in her voice. "Are you going to stay in there forever?"

She swallowed and sat up. "Sorry. I won't be much longer."

She stood, flushed the toilet, then ran water in the sink. She washed her face and rinsed her mouth. The water removed the bad taste but did nothing to stop the pain in her heart.

What am I going to do?

She could never tell Lillian who'd fathered her baby. She couldn't tell her parents either. She would have to keep it a secret, no matter what came. Daisy looked at her reflection in the mirror.

I could go away so they never know what I've done.

Her sister knocked again, harder this time. "Come on, Daisy. You aren't the only one who lives in this house. I need to shower. I've got plans today."

"Okay. Okay." She dried her face with a towel, stuffed the letter into the pocket of her bathrobe, and opened the door. "Sorry."

Lillian hardly gave her a glance as they exchanged places. Just as well, Daisy thought. She didn't want her sister to guess that she was sick or upset. Lillian might insist on knowing what was wrong, and Daisy had never been a good liar.

"I'd better get better at it," she said as she closed her bedroom door.

She walked to the large window that overlooked the Kinnear house. Although still early, Todd was pushing a mower around his backyard. Seconds later, Jupiter ran up to the gate and barked at him. Todd stopped and walked over to greet the dog. She could see his mouth moving as he talked to Jupiter. Then he slipped his hand through the slats and patted the dog's head before he stood and returned to the mower.

She smiled sadly, the moment seeming poignant for some reason. Perhaps because it felt as if everything familiar was about to slip away.

Determined not to let her mood descend further into despair, Daisy dressed and went downstairs. The scent of fried sausage hung in the air, and her stomach roiled for the second time. Hoping to avoid being sick again, she hurried through the kitchen and out onto the back porch, where she filled her lungs with clean air.

"Aren't you going to have breakfast?" her mother called after her.

"In a little bit. I feel like a walk."

"The eggs will be cold by the time you get back."

"I'm not hungry yet." Before her mom could say more or ask any questions, Daisy bolted down the steps and out the back gate to the alley. She paused for a moment or two, gulping in some more air, forcing back the queasiness, then finally set off with no destination in mind.

Her hair still damp from the shower, Lillian strolled into the kitchen. "Mom, where's Daisy? She's not in her room."

Her mother answered, "She went for a walk."

"With Jupiter?"

"I guess not. I heard him barking a minute ago."

Lillian took a plate from the cupboard and spooned scrambled eggs onto it. A couple of sausage patties followed, along with a slice of buttered toast. Orange juice awaited her on the table.

"What about Dad?"

"He ate early. Reverend Rubart asked him to help a woman and her children move into an apartment. Her husband is in the navy, and the house she'd rented has been sold."

"Dad never slows down. He ought to rest. Let somebody else help them."

Her mother sat opposite Lillian. "Your father's happiest when he's serving others."

Lillian nodded, then began to eat. This afternoon, she planned to meet a friend at the Granada to see the movie *Holiday Inn*. She'd considered asking Daisy to go along with them, but her younger sister had been in a strange mood for weeks. Definitely not much fun to be around. And after the way she'd hogged the bathroom this morning, it would serve her right to be left behind.

"I'm going to make jam next week," Mom said. "Is there a day you could help me with that?"

Lillian hated it when her mom put up preserves, jams, and jellies. The kitchen got hot, and the steam messed with her hair. It was so much easier to buy a jar at the store. "I've got a couple of job interviews next week, but I'm not sure of the days and times. Let me check my calendar when I go upstairs."

"All right, dear, but don't forget."

Lillian took her empty plate and juice glass to the kitchen sink and left them there. "I'm going to get ready to meet Patty."

"So early?"

"We're going to do some window shopping before the matinee." She hurried up the stairs.

In her room, she went to the desk she'd used throughout her school years. She flipped the pages on the calendar and wrote down the days and times of her job interviews to give to her mom. She wasn't interested in either of them, but it would be nice to earn money again. And if she got a job, she wouldn't be asked to help out around the house as much. That would be a bonus.

As she closed the calendar, her gaze fell on Brandan's letter. She picked it up and read it again, her feelings conflicted.

Dearest Lill,

Sorry it's taken so long for me to write this letter. I can't tell you anything about our journey here. Only that it had some tense moments. But we made it, and my group is settled on a base where we should be stationed for a while. Can't tell you its name or location. Just somewhere in England. But we're getting to know a lot of the British flyers from the RAF. They're good blokes, as they call each other. I'm not sure how long we'll be stationed here. Maybe for the duration. Maybe not.

I hope you'll write soon. Letters from home mean a lot to all the guys, but letters from you will mean the most to me. I always loved getting them while I was in training. I know I'm not the best correspondent, but I'll keep your letters and read them again and again. I'm hoping you'll write often.

I'm sorry we had a bad time during my leave. I wish I could do things over. Do them different. But I can't. What I can do is tell you how much I love you, and I hope you'll forgive me. I messed up. I hurt you, and I never meant to do that. I love you, Lill. I think of you all the time. You're in my dreams at night.

Please write and let me know things are okay between us.

Brandan

She'd been so happy to get his letter after weeks of silence, but something had kept her from writing a reply. Part of her wanted to make him wait, the same way she'd had to wait. She'd regretted her behavior his last week at home. So why did his declaration of love and his need to hear from her stir up anger and a desire to punish him? If they were married, she wouldn't feel that way. Would she?

She drew a breath as she pulled out the chair and sat down. From the drawer, she took a sheet of cream-colored stationery.

Dear Brandan,

Thank you for your letter. With the passing of so many weeks, I wasn't sure if you would write to me. It helped when your mother told me she hadn't received a letter yet. But then that made us wonder if something happened during your transport overseas, so then we worried. Both of us.

I'm sorry you and I didn't spend more time together when you were home, and I forgive you. You know that I love you too.

I've started looking for work again. I don't want anything like Daisy's boring job at the drugstore. She hasn't mentioned the WAAC lately, but I'm sure she's still thinking about it and hoping to get accepted when she can apply. In the meantime we both applied for civilian work at Gowen Field. Todd Kinnear suggested we could work at his factory. They're doing war work now. I guess I shouldn't say more about what they're making. Loose lips sink ships, as they say. Did you know Dad's working for Todd? I can't remember if that happened before or after you left. Even if it was before, I don't think you knew about it. But it does seem odd. Todd's only a couple of years older than you, and now he's my dad's boss. Dad seems okay with it. I'm not sure I would be.

I will write to you, Brandan, as often as possible. And I'll pray that you stay safe and that you'll come home to me soon.

Love,

Lillian

She set down the fountain pen and stared at the brief letter. It wasn't romantic like most of the letters she'd written when he was away at college or while in Louisiana. But maybe that was just as well for now. Maybe now he would realize how truly devastated she'd been by his refusal to marry her before he went overseas.

Chapter 28

PRESENT DAY–FEBRUARY

Brianna listened to her great-grandmother talk about that Sunday in 1941 and tried to imagine what it must have been like. The first time GeeGee had related the story, Brianna hadn't truly understood the fear that permeated the house as the news came over the radio. But this time it all felt more real to her. While she wasn't ready to admit as much to Adam, she'd discovered that the study of history wasn't as dry and boring as she'd once thought it. It wasn't about just facts and dates. History was about people. People like her great-grandmother. People like her.

"Hey, you two." Great-Aunt Elizabeth stepped into the family room. "I hate to interrupt, but I'm about to start dinner. Brianna, would you like to stay and eat with us?"

To her own surprise, she wasn't ready to cut this visit short. "If you don't mind, I'd love to." She glanced between the two women.

GeeGee reached over and patted the back of Brianna's hand. "Of course we don't mind. It's wonderful to have you here. And besides, we've talked a lot about me. I still need to hear about you. The last time you came over, you mentioned a young man?"

Elizabeth gave a little wave of her hand. "I'll get started with dinner." Then she disappeared again from view.

"I believe his name was Greg," GeeGee said, as if there hadn't been an interruption.

Brianna smiled. "Yes. Greg."

"From the look on your face, you still like him."

"Yes." She felt her cheeks grow warm. "I do. We went to see a movie on Friday night."

"Just the two of you?"

"No. With a couple of my friends."

Remembering Greg, remembering the way he'd looked at her, remembering the fluttery sensations in her stomach that had made it impossible to pay attention to the film, made her smile and go all warm on the inside. Maybe GeeGee was right about love at first sight, but what Brianna felt for Greg Truman had to be something close to it.

Disappointingly, he hadn't been at church this morning. But at least he'd sent her a text, letting her know he had a family thing and he would call her later. "Later" hadn't happened yet, which was one of the reasons Brianna had come to see GeeGee. Anything to take her mind off the passage of time.

"What more can you tell me about him?" her great-grandmother asked, intruding on her thoughts.

Brianna shared the few things that she'd learned on Friday. It wasn't a whole lot. Greg didn't seem to like to talk about himself or his family. It wasn't that he was shy. He exuded self-confidence. He was also interested in others, judging by the questions he asked. He knew much more about Brianna and her family than she knew about him.

"Perhaps," GeeGee said with a nod, "you could bring him over. I would love to meet him."

"Sure. I'll do that sometime."

Chapter 29

TUESDAY, SEPTEMBER 29, 1942

Daisy carried a cardboard box of Bayer aspirin down the drugstore aisle and set it on the floor when she reached her destination. Leaning down, she opened the lid, then began placing the small bottles on a shelf at eye level. The work didn't take much in the way of concentration. A bad thing for Daisy. It left her mind free to worry and fret, to replay her mistakes, to imagine the disasters that awaited her.

Somehow, a baby's cry managed to break through the cacophony in her head, and she turned to look toward the sound. A young mother, not much older than Daisy herself, stood at the end of the aisle, bouncing the screaming baby in her arms while searching the shelves with her eyes.

For an instant, Daisy pictured herself in the same predicament, and the image sent a chill shooting through her as she stepped toward the mother and baby. "May I help you find something?"

Looking as if she might start to cry right along with her baby, the mother answered, "She's teething. A friend said to try chamomile. I don't know what that is."

"It's an herb." At least Daisy had an answer. "My mother likes to drink a cup of chamomile tea before bed."

"Do you know where I can find it? How do I use it for teething?" Tears welled up and fell down the mother's cheeks.

"I don't know, but maybe Mr. Armstrong can help you. Let me get him."

As Daisy hurried toward the back of the store, she wasn't sure if she was rushing to get the woman help or to escape the screams of the baby that seemed to pursue her. A short while later, the druggist stood with the young mother. As if understanding his advice would provide relief, the baby ceased wailing, instead making a soft hiccupping sound every ten seconds or so.

After telling the woman where she could purchase the chamomile herbs, Mr. Armstrong said, "Just brew a cup as you would any tea. Allow it to cool completely. Then dip a corner of a clean cloth in the brew. Put the cloth in the freezer for a time and then offer the frozen end for your baby to chew."

"Will that work?"

"The chamomile has anti-inflammatory and calming properties. It'll ease your baby's pain. The cold helps as well."

Daisy took more bottles of aspirin from the box and set them on the shelves, a new fear rising within her. She wouldn't know what to do when it came to teething. How did a new mother learn about such things? How would Daisy know what to do?

The answer was simple. She wouldn't know what to do.

Maybe she should go away to have the baby. Maybe she should let someone else raise it. She could give it up for adoption. Adoption wasn't a bad thing. There were people who wanted babies who couldn't have them. If she gave up the baby, she could start over, fresh. No one need ever know. But where would she go in the meantime? How would she get there? She didn't want her parents to know what she'd done. Whether or not she kept the baby, she would have to go away if she was to save them from the shame.

I should write to Brandan.

Even as the idea went through her head, she knew she didn't want to tell him. What could he do from England to help her? He couldn't marry her. And even if he could, he would hate her. Hate her for destroying any hope of his happiness with Lillian. And while that might serve him right, she couldn't do it to him. She was as much to blame as he was for the mess she was in. He might be older. Maybe he was even wiser. But she wasn't a fool. She could have stopped him. He wouldn't have forced himself on her.

But she hadn't wanted to stop him. She'd given her heart to Brandan when she was only fourteen, and she'd longed for him to love her in return. Had she believed giving him her body would make him love her? If so, she'd been a fool.

Tears welled in her eyes at the thought.

"Miss Abbott?"

She turned to look at the druggist.

"Are you feeling all right?"

"I'm fine, Mr. Armstrong."

He gave her a hard look. "Well, why don't you call it a day?"

"Are you sure? I—"

"I'm sure. It's near enough to closing time, and you've finished everything I asked you to do."

She didn't hesitate longer. "All right. I'll see you tomorrow."

"Have a good evening. Give my best to your parents."

"I will, sir."

In the back room, she removed her work apron and retrieved her sweater from the locker, then exited the building through the door to the alley. Soft light from the late-afternoon sun accompanied her as she walked home. It wasn't long before she thought again about the mother with the crying baby. That could be her in another seven months or so. She could be the young mother wondering how to help her baby.

"What will Mom and Dad do when—if—I tell them?"

Some parents would kick their daughter out, refusing to even see her. She'd heard of that happening. But she couldn't imagine either of her parents reacting that way. They would be sad and dismayed, but they wouldn't reject her. Would they? Then again, maybe their sadness would be worse than rejection. She'd never liked disappointing them. She'd always tried her best to please them. If they learned what she'd done, their pride in her would be shattered forever.

How soon? How soon would she have to tell them, if she chose not to go away? How many weeks before she started to show? Her stomach was as flat as ever now. When would that change? Could she not say anything until it became obvious to everyone? Or was it better to come clean at the start?

Her vision blurred, and she stopped walking.

"Hey, Daisy!"

She stiffened at the sound of Todd Kinnear's voice. He and her dad always walked home together from the factory. She didn't want them to catch her crying. Especially not her dad. He would insist on knowing what was wrong. Hastily, she wiped beneath her eyes with her fingertips, then pasted on a smile before turning.

But she didn't see her dad. Only Todd. Relief helped for a moment, but then the tears came again. Falling this time.

"Daisy?" Todd stopped before her. "What is it?"

She shook her head.

"Let's get you home."

"I can't go home." She shook her head again.

"Why not?"

"I don't . . . I don't want . . . I just can't."

"Come on." He gently but firmly took hold of the crook of her arm. The next thing she knew, he was steering her down the street. But before reaching their block, he followed the sidewalk on a cross street, then took them down the alley.

Down the alley.

The same way Brandan had brought her home on that fateful morning. Sneaking back after a night of sin.

She choked on a sob.

They entered Todd's yard through the back gate, and before long, Daisy sat at his kitchen table while he set a tea kettle on the stove.

Todd's intention in bringing Daisy into his house had been to give her time to compose herself before she went home. Whatever was wrong, he assumed a cup of tea and a sympathetic ear would make a difference. That's what his mother had taught him, and he thought it was worth a try now.

When the tea was ready, he set a cup on the table in front of Daisy.

She looked at it, smiled wanly, and asked, "Is it chamomile?" Then she covered her face with her hands and began to sob.

"Come on, Daisy. It can't be as bad as all that."

She released a strange-sounding laugh as she lowered her hands to look at him.

Todd reached across the table to push her cup and saucer even closer to her.

"I'm pregnant," she said, her voice flat.

The words seemed to suck the air out of the small kitchen.

"I think that's 'as bad as all that.' Don't you?"

Todd leaned against the back of his chair, not knowing what to say or do next. Never in a million years would he have expected *that* to be her problem. Lillian, maybe. But Daisy? Sweet, generous, thoughtful Daisy. No. She wasn't the sort of girl to fly in the face of propriety or the expected norms. She was . . . special.

"I don't know what to do," she whispered.

"Have you—" He broke off to clear his throat. "Have you told the . . . father?"

Her face paled. "I . . . I can't. He . . . he's overseas. He's in the service."

"Good lord," Todd said beneath his breath. Then, louder, "You need to write to him. You need to tell him."

Silence lay heavy over the room. Daisy's wounded, despairing expression made Todd want to go to her, hold her, promise her it would be all right. But how could he keep such a promise? The man who'd left her in this condition was in another country, fighting in the war. He stayed still, searching for something comforting to say. He wasn't sure what.

"Brandan's the father."

If her pregnancy had surprised him, this additional information was like a punch to his gut. It left him speechless.

"I don't know what to do." Her watery eyes beseeched him. "What am I supposed to do?"

Todd ran a hand over his face and released a breath.

Daisy pushed aside the cup and saucer, folded her arms on the table, and hid her face against them.

A hundred questions raced through Todd's head. Should he ask them? Was it any of his business? Would it help anything?

As if he'd spoken aloud, she lifted her head again and answered one of his questions. "We weren't lovers. It only . . . It only happened once. It was a . . . a mistake."

Todd wished he could get his hands on Brandan Gallagher. He'd like to throttle him within an inch of his life. Todd had begun to like Brandan, despite thinking he was sometimes cocky and thoughtless. And, to be honest, he'd envied Brandan his perfect health and good looks. But right at this moment, Todd despised him. Brandan already had Lillian Abbott's love. Why had he tampered with the younger sister? Why had he—

"It was my fault," Daisy said softly. "I . . . I've had a terrible crush on him for years, starting before he and Lillian became an item. I loved him and wished . . . wished for what I couldn't have. And somehow, one night, I just . . . lost my head."

That broke his silence at last. "It wasn't your fault, Daisy. He's a man. It was his responsibility to act like it."

She worried her lower lip as she looked at him, perhaps hopeful that what he said was true.

"You need to tell your parents."

"I can't. Not yet. I don't know if I ever can. I might . . . I might go away."

"Go away?" The thought of it squeezed his heart. He didn't want her to go away. "How far . . . How far along are you?"

"Six and a half weeks."

Her precision reminded him that she'd said it had only happened once. Again he thought of the satisfaction he would feel if he could smash his fist into Brandan's face.

"Lillian won't speak to me again if she finds out."

Todd leaned forward. "Do you mean you won't tell them who the father is?"

"Never." She shook her head. "I'll . . . I'll lie. I'll tell them it was somebody from the air base and that he's gone and that I don't know how to get in touch with him. I'll tell them I don't know his last name."

"You'd rather have them believe that about you than know the truth?"

She looked down, but not before he saw the shame written in her expression.

"Daisy?"

She lifted her gaze.

"You could marry me," he said.

Her eyes widened, and the expression she wore mirrored the surprise he felt. Had he really said those words aloud? He'd spoken before the thought had fully formed, but now he began to warm to the idea. It made sense. Todd and Daisy had known each other almost their entire lives. Todd loved the Abbott family as if they were his own. He would do just about anything for them. Marrying Daisy might protect her from gossip and scorn. It was possible no one would ever know she was pregnant out of wedlock. Besides, he could provide for her and her child. They wouldn't ever be in need. If she went away to have the baby, who would look out for her? Who would protect her?

Todd needed to protect her.

"You could marry me," he repeated.

"Todd, I don't—" She fell silent without finishing.

He understood what she'd almost said. "Listen, I know you don't love me. But you like me, and I like you. We know each other. You and your parents, you've all made me feel like a part of the family ever since my folks died." He thought especially of Carl and all the man had done for him. If he could save him some heartache, he would. "It isn't like you'd be marrying a stranger, Daisy. People might be surprised, but they wouldn't know the truth about . . . about you and him. They wouldn't talk, because you and I would be husband and wife. And I . . . I wouldn't expect us to live that way until you were ready." He felt embarrassed, saying those words to her, but he didn't look away.

Fresh tears ran down her cheeks. She brought a wadded handkerchief to her nose and wiped it. "I can't, Todd. It's kind of you to ask. Really." She took a clean edge of the handkerchief and dried her eyes. "I'd better go home. Mom will wonder what's keeping me." She pushed back the chair and stood.

Todd stood too. "Okay. But the offer stands."

He watched her leave, wondering if he'd lost his mind. But what else could he do to help Daisy? To help all the Abbotts?

But mostly Daisy.

Chapter 30

SUNDAY, OCTOBER 4, 1942

Todd Kinnear's offer of marriage stayed with Daisy in the days that followed. Every time she wondered what she was going to do, she remembered it. Every time she was sick in the toilet, she remembered it. Every time she looked at her stomach, still without any hint of a pooch, she remembered it.

And sitting in church the following Sunday, she remembered it too. Somehow, sitting in the sanctuary, her parents and sister right beside her in the pew, made the shame of what she'd done and the predicament she was in seem even worse. Somewhere, a few rows behind her, there was a man willing to marry her, willing to rescue her from the mess she'd made. He hadn't judged her. He hadn't told her what a foolish thing she'd done. He'd offered only kindness and protection.

She'd never thought of Todd in a romantic sense. He was her neighbor, a good guy. Decent enough to give her dad a job when he'd lost his old one. Todd wasn't bad looking either. He wasn't swoony, but he wasn't a dogface either. He was only a year or two older than Brandan, but it seemed like more than that. She supposed that was because, instead of college and the army, he'd run the family business from the time he finished high school. He was steady and reliable. Ordinary. Like her dad. Someone who didn't stand out in a crowd but who was dependable and caring.

But Todd had offered to give her his name. Without asking anything from her in return. Without asking *that* from her.

She couldn't do it. How could she do it? There had to be another way out of this mess. There had to be.

She closed her eyes. *Maybe I* should *write to Brandan. Maybe he could tell me what to do?*

But Brandan had already told her that *she* was a mistake, that he loved Lillian. And what could he do from a base in England? Nothing. He couldn't do anything. She had to figure this out on her own.

Lillian poked her in the ribs. "Hey," she whispered, "wake up."

Daisy glanced at her sister. "I wasn't asleep."

"You looked like it."

Daisy was tempted to stick out her tongue. But she couldn't do that. She wasn't a child any longer. She was going to have a child of her own. The fresh realization sobered her and chased the temptation away.

The congregation rose to sing the closing hymn. Afterward, as soon as she was out of the pew, Daisy slipped away from her family and made a beeline for the front doors. Her parents were never in a hurry to leave church, so she knew she might have a lengthy wait. She didn't care. The day was warm and sunny. Leaves had begun to change, marking the city with shades of red, orange, and gold, mixed among the remaining green.

She strode away from the church entrance, hoping to avoid any conversations. Her emotions couldn't be trusted. She'd managed not to cry so far today. But who knew how long that would last?

Stopping at the corner, she looked back to see if her parents and sister were behind her. They weren't. Undoubtedly, they were in the fellowship hall, and Dad was drinking a cup of coffee. She released a sigh, swinging her gaze in the opposite direction. Across the street and close to the alley, she spied Brandan's two younger brothers. Ribbons of smoke rose above their heads.

She headed toward them. "Are you two crazy?"

In unison the brothers looked at her while hiding their hands behind their backs.

"I could see those cigarettes from half a block away. Do you think your parents won't know about it if somebody else sees you?"

William, the middle brother, blew out a breath—and the smoke—he'd held. Then he coughed.

Yancy, the youngest Gallagher brother, said, "You're not going to tell, are you?" He frowned, waiting for her to confirm it.

"Not if you put them out and get back where you belong."

"You sound like our mom," William retorted.

He was right. She did sound like their mom. And her own mom. And Martha's mom. Is that what happened when a girl got pregnant? She turned into a mother even before the baby was born?

"Go on." She motioned with her head. "Get out of here."

They dropped the cigarettes and sprinted toward the parking lot, their laughter trailing behind.

Before she could squish the first butt with her shoe, she heard Lillian call her name. She finished her task before turning around. On the curb across the street, Lillian stood with Brandan's parents. Her heart started to race in her chest. Would they look at her and know?

Such a silly question. Even she knew the answer was no. They wouldn't have a clue. They still thought of her as an innocent girl. How wrong they were.

Drawing a steadying breath, she crossed the street a second time. As she got closer, she forced herself to smile in greeting.

"Daisy," Lillian said, "Mrs. Gallagher has invited me to their house for Sunday dinner. She's had another letter from Brandan. Would you like to come? You're invited."

Her pulse skipped erratically. "That's very nice, Mrs. Gallagher, but I can't accept. I . . . I promised Martha I would go to her house after church." A bald-faced lie, but hopefully she made it sound believable.

Lillian didn't seem to mind. "Have fun." She looped her arm through Elenore Gallagher's, and they turned to follow the sidewalk toward the parking lot. Andrew Gallagher touched his hat brim at Daisy before following after them.

Once they were out of sight, Daisy breathed freely again. How long could she get away with this? How long could she keep silent? How long could she tell one lie after another?

Chapter 31

PRESENT DAY–FEBRUARY

Daisy awakened with a start. She'd fallen asleep in the chair in her bedroom, her Bible open on her lap, her glasses perched on her nose. A dream lingered in her mind. So often, dreams evaporated the instant she came awake. Not this one. Perhaps because this one had been more memory than imagination.

O Father God, thank You for Your great mercy.

She closed the Bible and hugged it to her chest. Her husband had given it to her thirty years ago today. A Valentine's Day present. One of his final gifts in his last year of life.

The Bible's leather cover was worn and familiar beneath her touch. The edges of many pages curled from use and time. Throughout the much-beloved book, passages had been highlighted, and notes and dates and names had been written in the margins. Between some pages, slips of notepaper were stuck in the gutters. All of those things combined told much of her spiritual story of the last thirty years—and even longer than that. Sometimes she liked to flip through her Bible to remind herself of the lessons God had given her.

What would have happened in my life if I'd taken Your lessons to heart eighty years ago?

Eighty years. It seemed impossible that so much time had passed since the first year of the war. She'd been a child when Pearl Harbor was bombed. She hadn't thought so, of course. She'd thought herself all grown up, a woman ready to make her own choices. She'd thought herself in love, too, and had acted upon that emotion with complete disregard for God's loving instructions.

She closed her eyes and took several slow, deep breaths.

Her impetuous actions had caused harm to others and fractured more than one relationship. Even now, even many decades later, she felt deep regret for what she'd done. God had forgiven her, but the Enemy of her soul liked to remind her of her failures, of her sinful choices. What she'd done in the summer of 1942 was one sin the devil liked to taunt her about more than any others.

Brianna's pretty face popped into her mind, and she knew at once that it was a call to prayer. She didn't know why. Perhaps she saw something of herself, as well as Lillian, in the girl.

God, help her make righteous choices. Protect her from temptation.

Chapter 32

MONDAY, OCTOBER 5, 1942

Official word hadn't come down from the top brass, but there was a feeling around Station 102, Alconbury, that a big mission would happen soon, and this time the Americans would be involved.

Brandan found the idea of his first bombing mission of the war both exciting and nerve-racking. He'd known he and the rest of his group hadn't flown their B-24 Liberators from New Hampshire to England for the fun of it. Still, it had been fun, that flight across the Atlantic. *Whooie!* Way more amazing than the antisubmarine patrols they'd flown over the Gulf of Mexico earlier in the summer. But even with those patrols and the three U-Boats they'd destroyed, the war hadn't seemed real yet.

Now, it was real.

Dearest Lill,

I haven't heard from you since I left Boise. Not a single letter. They tell us all the time how slow the mail is. Letters take weeks and weeks to get to us, and plenty of times they get lost altogether. Maybe the mail's held up even more because of all the moving around we've done in the last five months, first back in the States, then in England. Or maybe you were waiting for me to write to say I'm sorry. I did write. I am sorry. I hope you got that letter. And I hope you'll write soon to say things are okay between us.

Everybody here thinks we'll be flying our first mission soon. Lots of speculation but no facts. Even if I knew for sure, I couldn't say. But the Army Air Corps didn't send us to England to sit on our cans. We'll go on our first mission, and it will be sooner rather than later.

Talking to the RAF pilots, I've got an even better understanding of how dangerous this can be for a pilot and his crew. I guess I tried to believe I'd be one of the lucky ones. But when we hear what this country's gone through over the past couple of years, it leaves a guy wondering if any of us will get out okay.

You might not like me saying this, but it makes me know I made the right decision. I wouldn't want you to be a war widow, Lill. And I wouldn't want you to get stuck with a husband who got burned or maimed either. Lots of that happening over here.

Brandan

As Todd waited in the kitchen of the Abbott home, along with several other guests—all of them female—he wished he'd declined Carl's invitation to participate in Daisy's surprise birthday party. It felt awkward and dishonest. He alone knew Daisy wouldn't want to celebrate right now, and he alone knew the reason why. But there was no getting out of it now.

Martha Neville whispered something to him.

"Sorry. I didn't hear you." He turned so his good ear faced her.

"I said, she'll be so surprised."

He nodded.

"She's been blue lately," her friend went on. "I don't know why. Daisy's usually the one cheering up everybody else."

Todd hadn't spoken to Daisy in the past six days. Not since she'd poured out her tale of woe in his kitchen. He'd seen her from the back at church on Sunday, but she'd left the instant the service was over. What had she decided to do? Obviously, her pregnancy remained a secret, or her parents wouldn't be hosting this party.

Lillian appeared in the doorway. "She's coming up the sidewalk now." She put her index finger in front of her lips. "Shhh." Then she stepped into the kitchen herself.

Whispers stopped at once. Todd held his breath.

From the living room, he heard Nancy Abbott say, "Oh, good. You're home. Can you help me with something before you go upstairs?"

"Sure," Daisy answered. "What do you need?"

The creak of a floorboard prepared them. A second later, led by Lillian, they all shouted, "Surprise!"

Todd stayed back while the rest of the party spilled from the kitchen into the dining room, but he could see Daisy's ashen face from where he stood. She looked like a deer in the headlights, frozen in place, waiting to be struck and killed. Her gaze shifted, meeting his, and he saw the panic in her eyes. He forced a smile and gave her a nod of encouragement as he stepped toward the doorway. It seemed to help. She smiled, too, and turned to speak, one by one, with her guests.

"Well, we pulled it off." Carl moved past Todd. "She was surprised."

"Yes, she was."

Carl struck a match and lit the candles on a cake. "Heaven knows when we'll have enough sugar for another cake this size." He lifted the platter and carried the cake out to the dining room table, singing "Happy Birthday" on his way.

"Make a wish," Lillian said above the din of conversations, "and blow out the candles."

Daisy glanced toward Todd, her smile faltering. Again, he gave her a nod. And again, he took a step forward. He saw her draw in a deep breath, saw her shoulders level and her jaw tighten with determination. Then she moved close to the table and cake, leaned forward, closed her eyes for a moment, then opened them and blew out the candles.

He wondered what she'd wished for. That God would make her troubles go away? That she would wake up and find it had all been a dream? Or a nightmare? That Brandan would miraculously come back from across the Atlantic and marry her?

His own jaw flexed as applause filled the small room.

Nancy moved close to her daughter. "I'll cut the cake for you."

"Just a small piece for me," Daisy answered.

Todd frowned. She wasn't just blue, he thought. She'd lost weight. And there were smudges under her eyes. How long had it been since she'd had a decent night's sleep? Weeks, no doubt. Had Nancy or Carl noticed the changes? Were they concerned about her?

"Here, Todd." Martha held out a dessert plate to him, pulling his attention from Daisy. A large slice of cake with chocolate frosting sat in the plate's center. "And here's a fork."

"Thanks."

He didn't have much of a sweet tooth, but even he had a hard time resisting Nancy Abbott's devil's food cake. And Carl was right. While the war lasted and rationing got tighter, this sort of dessert wouldn't come around often. Not even for a beloved daughter's birthday.

As he took his first bite, his gaze returned to Daisy. She continued to smile at her guests and family, as if enjoying her little party. But beneath the smile he saw the sadness within and wished he could make it go away.

Chapter 33

FRIDAY, OCTOBER 9, 1942

The mission: bomb Compagnie de Fives, a steelworks outside Lille, France.

Brandan's B-24 joined more than a hundred other bombers dispatched from the UK. It was the first US bombing raid to be flown over France. His mom had always wanted to go to Paris. She'd longed to see the Eiffel Tower in person. Now his plane would drop ten five-hundred-pound bombs on a city approximately two hundred and twenty kilometers to the north of it.

Besides Brandan, the pilot, there were nine crew members inside the *Boise Beast*: copilot, bombardier, nose gunner, navigator, radio operator, ball turret gunner, two waist gunners, and tail gunner. Each were in their appointed positions, all of them wearing their oxygen masks and freezing their tails off. It could get as cold as minus-fifty degrees Fahrenheit at the highest altitude missions. It was one of the few things Brandan hated about flying.

The planes flew in tight formation—B-24 Liberators and B-17 Flying Fortresses—and for a while, Brandan wondered if the bombing run would be accomplished without any resistance from the Germans. It was a foolish thought, and he knew it.

They came at them from all sides, the yellow-nosed fighters. The formation hadn't reached Lille yet when Brandan's plane was hit. In short succession, two engines were gone. A third was crippled, and his plane was soon falling behind the rest of the formation, making them even more vulnerable to the German fighter planes.

"Is anybody hit?" he shouted.

"I think we're all okay." The answer came from Benny, the navigator.

Brandan wondered if he could get the *Boise Beast* back across the English Channel before they were blown from the sky. He feared not. Not with only one good engine left. He had to make a decision before it was too late, before the plane got too low for the men to parachute to safety. Parachuting into the Channel was almost a death sentence. They needed to act now while they were still high enough that a jump was safe. They wouldn't be safe for long.

"Get 'em out!" he yelled at Wiley, his copilot. "Now! I'll keep us up as long as I can."

Chapter 34

PRESENT DAY–FEBRUARY

The last place Brianna wanted to be on that Friday morning was in her history class, despite the unexpected interest she'd taken in it. For that matter, she didn't want to be anywhere on that stupid community college campus. She was in a foul mood, and she didn't care who noticed it.

She hadn't heard from Greg all week. Not since his text that had let her know he would miss church. The same text that had said he would call her . . . which he hadn't done. He didn't seem the type to promise something and then not follow through.

"What sort of man is he? What is his character?"

She frowned, hating that GeeGee's questions persisted in her head. Hating that she couldn't seem to be rid of them. Hating that they made her wonder if she knew what she thought she knew. Was Greg the type to make a promise and then not follow through? What made her think he wasn't?

As if in answer, her phone pinged, and she checked the screen. Her heart fluttered at the sight of Greg's name. Finally.

Been out of town. Would like to see you. Lunch?

Sure. Where? Time?

Meet at our coffee shop. Will go to lunch from there. 12:30.

Our coffee shop.

She grinned as she sent him a thumbs-up, then set down her phone. She'd driven her mom's car to school that day, so she didn't have to worry about how to get to the coffee shop. A good thing since she didn't want to ask Hannah or Adam for a lift, nor did she want to ride the bus.

"You look like you're in a good mood." Adam slid into the chair to her right.

"I am."

"Good, because you've been a grump all week."

She wished she had a good comeback, but she didn't. Mostly because he was right. She had been a grump. But that was over. Wherever Greg had gone, whatever had kept him silent, he was back.

"Hey," Adam began, "would you like to—"

Professor Meyer stepped to the front of the class, essentially cutting off whatever Adam meant to ask. The instructor began to share information about an upcoming quiz and two important due dates. Then he dimmed the lights and started a video, one that should have interested Brianna since it was about life in America during World War II. But her thoughts had drifted back to Greg and the coffee shop—*their* coffee shop—and the lunch that would follow.

Less than two hours later, Brianna entered the coffee shop, feeling breathless. Greg was there, a beverage in hand.

"Am I late?" she asked as she approached his table.

"No. I was early. Do you want a coffee or shall we go get something to eat?"

"We can go. Do you want me to follow you in my car?"

He shook his head as he got to his feet. "Ride with me. I can bring you back when we're through."

"Okay." She hoped her silly grin didn't tell him how much she'd wanted that answer.

They left the coffee shop together and walked to Greg's newer-model truck. He opened the passenger door for her before he sprinted around to the driver's side and got in.

"I hope you don't mind this last-minute request. I like to be spontaneous rather than making plans. Having too much structure is boring."

She glanced over at him as she fastened her seatbelt. "Aren't most businesses structured?"

He laughed and started the truck without answering.

"Where were you?" she asked.

"Huh?"

"You said you were out of town. Where'd you go?"

"Oh. I had to go see my grandfather. He fell and needed some help."

"I hope he's okay."

"Yeah. He's a tough old bird."

Brianna realized he hadn't said where his grandfather lived, but it felt pushy to ask again. So instead, she stared out the window at the passing businesses. After a couple of miles, Greg pulled into a small strip mall and parked the truck in front of a restaurant.

"I heard this place is good," he said as he opened his door. "Hope you like Mexican."

"I do." She couldn't tell him that she would like whatever he liked. That sounded crazy, even to her.

When they both arrived at the front of the truck, Greg reached out and took her hand. It felt like the most natural thing in the world, and it started her stomach spinning and her heart racing until she was certain she wouldn't be able to eat a bite, whether or not she liked the food.

He smiled at her, almost as if he knew what she felt. "Hey, did I tell you how pretty you look?"

She shook her head.

"Well, you do."

For a moment she thought he might lean in and kiss her. But he didn't. Instead, he drew her to the restaurant entrance and pulled open the door.

Chapter 35

MONDAY, OCTOBER 19, 1942

hs 44 govt wux Washington, D.C. 743pm 10–19–42

Mr. Andrew H. Gallagher
1228 N. 22nd Street
Boise, Ida.

The Secretary of War desires me to express his deep regret that your son, Second Lieutenant Brandan H. Gallagher, has been reported missing in action since Nine October over France, if further details or other information are received you will be promptly notified.

C.W. Jones
The Adjutant General
857am

While holding the telegram and with Brandan's grim-faced father looking on from a few feet away, Lillian fell to the floor in a dead faint.

Daisy didn't faint when she heard the news, but she wished she could. Whatever fantasy she might have clung to for the past few weeks had been downed over France ten days earlier without her knowing it at the time.

Brandan was missing.

Brandan could be dead.

Brandan Gallagher, who'd stolen her heart before her fifteenth birthday, the boy she'd loved from afar for years.

Brandan—charming, dashing, handsome, confident Brandan—who'd fallen for Lillian, the wrong sister.

Brandan, the man Daisy had given herself to, all too quickly and against all reason.

Brandan, the father of her unborn baby.

Todd found her at the small park a couple of blocks from their homes. "I've been looking for you." He settled onto the bench beside her.

"You heard about Brandan?"

"I heard."

"I can't give the baby up for adoption. Not now. If Brandan's dead—" She broke off.

Todd nodded, and there was a wealth of tenderness in his eyes.

She drew a breath and tried again. "If he's dead"—she touched her belly—"This is all that's left of him."

"So you plan to tell them about the baby? About Brandan? Your parents. His parents. Lillian."

A chill shivered through her. "They'll hate me. They'll all hate me."

"They won't hate you, Daisy. Perhaps they'll be disappointed at first, but they won't hate you."

"My sister will."

Todd didn't respond. What could he say? Even he had to know how Lillian would react to the news.

"I can't keep the pregnancy a secret forever," she whispered to herself. "I'll have to lie about who the father is. That's all I can do. A GI who's gone now, and I don't know his name or address. Like I told you before. They won't think any worse of me than they would if they knew the truth."

A boy with a dog cut through the park. He waved at them. Todd waved back. Just as boy and dog disappeared around a corner, a couple of squirrels chased through the crunchy leaves on the ground, darting this way and that until, finally, they headed for different trees.

Todd cleared his throat. "What can I do to help?"

"Nothing. Nobody can help." She covered her face with her hands.

"You could rethink my offer."

Her breath caught as she lowered her hands again. She knew what he meant, of course. Still, she asked, "Your offer?"

"To marry me."

She twisted on the bench to face him. For the first time she truly considered it. She tried to imagine the future. Todd Kinnear would marry her. She would have a home. She would have his name. The baby would have his name.

A new thought came to her. "Even if I married you, the baby will come earlier than expected. People will know I was already pregnant. At least some of them."

"And everyone will think the baby is mine."

"But—" She broke off and swallowed hard. "You would do that for me?"

"Yes."

"People would look at you differently. My parents would look at you differently. I can't avoid that shame. You can." She shook her head. "I don't think I can tell them the baby's yours. Who would believe it? We've never even been on a date. My dad will ask so many questions if I tell him I want to marry you. I'm not that good of an actress. He'll demand to know why."

"Then we won't tell him beforehand. We can drive to Nevada. There's no waiting period there. We can go down and get married and tell them when we get back. We're both of age. We'll elope."

Daisy closed her eyes. *God, I've already ruined my life. Would it ruin Todd's if I do this? I don't love him. I've never thought of him as anything but a nice neighbor. Could I share his home? Really share it? Wear my robe in front of him. Take a bath in his tub. Could I pretend that we're more than friends?* Interrupting her desperate prayer, an accusatory voice in her head retorted, *You did worse than all that with Brandan.*

"Daisy?"

She looked at him.

"If you're wondering how I'll feel about the baby, I'll love him. Or her. I promise. I'll be a good dad."

She hadn't wondered, but now she did. "How can you be sure?"

"I'm sure," he answered softly.

Yes, he probably did know. He was that decent.

"And you could have your own bedroom. Like I said before, I wouldn't expect you to share my bed. We'd wait until . . . until you're ready."

What if I'm never ready?

"We could make this work, Daisy."

She tried to imagine the reaction from her family if she returned to her home with Todd as her husband. Shock. Disbelief. Suspicion. Yes, there would be suspicion. Suspicion that would be confirmed in a matter of weeks or months.

She was nine weeks pregnant now. How long before she couldn't hide her pregnancy? She didn't know and had no one she could ask.

Not true. There were people she *could* ask, if she wasn't the one expecting the baby or if she didn't care that they knew the whole sordid truth.

"We could go tomorrow morning," Todd said. "It'll take us about seven hours or a bit more. If we leave early, there'll still be time to get a license and find a minister to marry us before the end of the day." He turned his gaze toward the trees. "We'd have to wait to drive back the next day."

Daisy seemed to have two choices: face her unwed pregnancy alone, never telling anyone that Brandan was the father, or face her pregnancy as Todd's wife, with others thinking he'd been her lover before they married. But if she didn't marry him and her parents insisted she go away, that she have the baby and give it up for adoption, what then? Then Brandan's only child could be lost forever. No, she really only had one choice.

"All right, Todd. I'll marry you."

Chapter 36

TUESDAY, OCTOBER 20, 1942

Dear Mom and Dad,

I needed to go somewhere to take care of something. I didn't want to wake you this early in the morning, so I'm leaving this note instead. I'll explain when I get home tomorrow. Don't worry about me. I'm all right and with a friend.

Love,

Daisy

What an unusual day, Lillian thought as her mother drove the family car toward Gowen Field.

The city of Boise had given way to sagebrush and jack rabbits. Not a tree in sight this far out into the desert. The terrain left her with little to distract her thoughts.

The day had started out in a strange way because of Daisy. Her younger sister had left the house in the night or early in the morning hours while everybody slept, leaving behind a note that explained absolutely nothing about where she'd gone or why.

Then, only a short while after learning about Daisy's absence, Lillian had received the offer of a job as a civilian clerk at the base if she wanted it. She'd been so sure she wouldn't get the job, and now it was going to be hers. That made the day unusual in the best sort of way. At the base, she would work around a lot of airmen. Her life would be more exciting, less drab and boring. Surely her work at the base would take her mind off of Brandan. And she was desperate not to think about him. He'd refused to marry her when he could, and now he was missing in action, perhaps dead. Lillian was twenty-one years old and without someone to love her. When Brandan had been off to the university or down in Louisiana for his flight training, she'd known he loved her. And others had known he loved her too. Now all that had changed.

"Are you sure you'll be able to take the bus home?" her mom asked, breaking through Lillian's thoughts.

"I'm sure. That's what Mrs. Baker told me."

"She's your supervisor?"

"Yes."

"And she'll see that you catch the bus?"

"Yes, Mom."

"That's good. I won't have to worry about you." Her mom's voice sounded distant, and Lillian guessed that her thoughts had returned to Daisy's unknown whereabouts.

Lillian didn't particularly care where her sister had gone, but she did think Daisy was selfish and thoughtless, leaving the way she had. She knew how upset Lillian was about Brandan. She could have stayed home to provide emotional support instead of running off to heaven knew where. But no. She'd had somewhere to go and something to do. Something silly, no doubt. Silly and boring.

I'll Be Seeing You

Todd took the marriage license from the clerk and turned toward Daisy. Her face was pale, her expression tense. At the moment, she looked much younger than her nineteen years.

"Guess we'd better get over to the church," he said. "The minister is waiting for us."

She nodded.

As they left the courthouse, he wondered if he should tell Daisy she didn't have to do this. If she wanted, they could get back into the car and drive home to Idaho. Only, he didn't want to take her home. He didn't want her to change her mind. Would she be surprised to know he felt that way?

Neither of them had said much during their hours on the road between Boise and Winnemucca. The silence had given Todd plenty of time to consider what they were about to do. The longer he'd thought about it, the more certain he was that he'd done the right thing when he'd offered to marry her. It was better for her. Better for her and her baby. And maybe, just maybe, a good thing for him too.

The red-brick Methodist church sat on one corner of the block. The minister, a Reverend Sanders, had told Todd to enter through the side entrance next to the parking lot as the front doors would already be locked. The side door opened next to the church offices, and someone would be there to greet them.

The reverend was true to his word. A woman with gray hair and wearing a pale-blue dress smiled at them from behind a desk. "Are you the bride and groom?"

"Yes, ma'am," Todd answered.

Daisy merely nodded.

"I'm Mrs. Sanders." The woman stood. "Follow me. Reverend Sanders is waiting for you in the chapel."

The hallway she led them down was dimly lit, as was the small chapel. Late-afternoon sunlight filtered through a stained-glass window, throwing muted colors onto the pews and floor.

"Reverend Sanders," Mrs. Sanders called in a modulated voice.

Only then did Todd notice the two people who were seated on the front pew. They both stood and turned to watch as Todd and Daisy approached them, Mrs. Sanders following behind. The tall, angular man—undoubtedly the reverend given the black robe he wore—looked to be in his sixties with salt-and-pepper hair. The younger woman beside him bore enough of a resemblance for Todd to guess she was related. Probably his daughter.

"Ah, here you are." The reverend held out a hand toward Todd. "My wife and daughter are here as your witnesses."

Todd nodded to each in turn. "Thank you." He handed the license to the reverend.

Mrs. Sanders asked, "Would you like me to play the 'Wedding March' or a hymn on the organ?"

Todd looked from the woman to Daisy, who gave a brief shake of her head. "No. I guess not."

"Well, then," Reverend Sanders said, "let's begin." He told them where to stand, then he took his place and opened his Bible. "Dearly beloved . . ."

Todd's bride didn't wear white. She wore a light-brown dress, one he'd seen her wear a number of times to church. It surprised him that he recognized it. He didn't usually make note of what girls wore. Not in church or elsewhere. Her brown hat had a veil, and in the muted lighting of the chapel, the veil made it difficult to tell if there were tears in her eyes. He thought maybe there were.

The minister arrived at the portion in the ceremony when the bride and groom exchanged their vows. Strange that he hardly needed Reverend Sanders to give him his lines.

"I, Todd Robert Kinnear, take thee, Daisy Henrietta Abbott, to be my wedded wife, to have and to hold from this day forward, for better, for worse, for richer, for poorer, in sickness and in health, to love and to cherish, till death do us part, according to God's holy ordinance; and thereto I pledge thee my faith."

He hadn't known her middle name until they obtained their marriage license. She probably hadn't known his either. There were many, many things they didn't know about each other, but he meant the words he'd spoken all the same. He meant to honor his vow before God. He hoped she understood that.

Tears appeared on her cheeks below the veil, confirming his earlier suspicion.

He took the ring from his pocket and slid it slowly onto her finger, echoing the reverend's prompt. "I give you this ring as a sign of my vow, and with all that I am, and all that I have; I honor you in the name of the Father, and of the Son, and of the Holy Spirit. Amen."

Daisy recited her vows, Reverend Sanders said a few more words, then, "You may kiss your bride."

Todd's breath caught in his chest. Did she want him to kiss her? She didn't love him. She appreciated him. They were friends. But nothing more.

As if reading his thoughts, she gave him the slightest of nods and tilted her head. After a moment's hesitation, he brushed her lips with his. Some men, at this point in the ceremony, laid claim to their wives. He couldn't do that. All he could do was promise he would take care of her and honor her wishes.

Daisy Kinnear

Mrs. Todd Kinnear

Daisy Abbott Kinnear

Daisy Henrietta Kinnear

As Todd unlocked the door to the hotel room—*their* hotel room—the various versions of her new name played in Daisy's head, none of them sounding real to her. None of them sounding right. But it was done. She'd married Todd, the boy next door. The man next door. She'd married Todd Kinnear while carrying Brandan Gallagher's baby.

Will he grow to hate me for what I've done? Her stomach clenched. *God, do You hate me for what I've done?*

The room was plain but looked clean. It had a double bed as well as a dresser, a small round table, and two chairs.

While Daisy stood just inside the doorway, Todd set their bags on the floor and went to the closet. Looking inside, he said, "There's extra blankets and pillows. I'll sleep on the floor."

"I can't let—" she started, then broke off. She could and she would let him sleep there.

"Why don't you use the bathroom. I'll . . . take a short walk. I could use a stretch of my legs." He was a bad liar but a kind one. "Do you need me to get anything for you? There's a drugstore at the end of the block."

"No. I have everything I need. Thank you, Todd."

"Some crackers, maybe. You didn't hardly touch your dinner."

"I'm fine. Thanks."

"Okay. Back in a while."

She washed hurriedly and donned her pajamas, then got into the bed, pulling the covers up to her chin. After a short while staring at the ceiling, she rolled onto her side, her back to the door, and closed her eyes. She wanted to fall asleep but knew she wouldn't. Not while she waited to hear the sound of the key in the lock. It was a long while before that happened. So long she began to wonder if something had happened to Todd.

But at last he returned. When the door opened and he entered the room, she held her breath. Would he speak to her, check to see if she was awake?

He didn't. She listened as he moved around the room, going to the closet first. Her eyes still closed, feigning sleep, she could only assume he made his bed on the floor with the extra blankets and pillows. Finally, he went into the bathroom. After a short while, she heard the flush of the toilet and water running in the sink.

How could something so ordinary sound intimate? As if she were invading his privacy.

She remembered the night that had brought her to this moment. She thought of Brandan, so handsome in his uniform, even when tipsy. She remembered his smile and the twinkle in his eyes and the sound of his voice. She recalled the heavens above his convertible as she drove his car into the foothills, the stars splashed across the inky expanse. She could almost smell the sagebrush and feel the hushed night air all around her. Tears fell from her eyes, soaking the pillow, as she remembered the way Brandan had reached for her, the way he'd drawn her across his lap and kissed her. Kissed her as she'd dreamed he would kiss her for such a long, long time. She remembered the way he'd touched her, and the way she'd acquiesced with so little effort on his part.

I'm sorry for what happened, he'd written weeks later. *But it's Lillian I love.*

Shame washed over her once again. White-hot shame. Scalding hot.

She'd ruined her life for a man who didn't care about her, for a man who'd scarcely known she was alive. And today she'd ruined Todd's life too. She'd tied him to a wife he never would have married if she hadn't been in trouble. She'd tied him to a child that wasn't his.

O God, I'm sorry. I'm sorry. Please don't let me make him sorry too. Help me be a good wife, despite how things are.

Todd came out of the bathroom. She listened as he settled onto the hard floor. She heard him release a soft sigh. After a few moments, he whispered, "Good night, Daisy."

Her throat tight with emotion, she couldn't answer, so she let him think she slept.

Real sleep evaded her for hours.

Chapter 37

PRESENT DAY–FEBRUARY

Outside Brianna's house, another snowstorm was blanketing the ground in white, while inside, a lively discussion took place around the Sunday dinner table in the Hastings house. Dirty dishes had been cleared away, and now the family and guests lingered at the table over their coffee and other beverages. Seated with Brianna were her mom and dad, her great-aunt Elizabeth and GeeGee, plus Hannah Smith and Adam Wentworth. She'd also invited Greg, but—much to her disappointment—he'd had a family obligation and couldn't come.

It was Adam who had started this newest topic for discussion when he'd asked if telling a lie was always wrong—a question that had come up in his philosophy class. But Adam wanted the answers to come from a Christian worldview rather than a secular one.

"Rahab lied to protect the Hebrew spies," Hannah said, leaning forward so she could look around the table. "And then she's included in Hebrews in that hall-of-fame list. Wasn't one of her acts of faithfulness that she lied to save their lives?"

Brianna's mom flipped through her Bible. "Perhaps. But Psalms and Proverbs both mention a lying tongue as something to be avoided.

And Colossians 3:9 says, 'Do not lie to one another, since you laid aside the old self with its evil practices.'"

"'Do not lie to one another,'" Adam echoed. "So does that mean don't lie to another believer or to anybody at all at any time? What if you tell a lie for a good reason, like Rahab did? To save a life."

"Or like the midwives did," Hannah added. "They lied to save the lives of the baby boys that Pharaoh ordered them to murder."

Brianna had been satisfied to just listen, but then she thought of what she'd learned in her history studies in recent weeks. "What about the gentiles in Germany and the rest of Europe during World War Two? They lied to save Jews who were being killed in concentration camps. Surely those lies were righteous." She looked toward her great-grandmother. "What do you think, GeeGee?"

GeeGee's expression was enigmatic. Brianna had learned that such a look meant her great-grandmother was giving the matter thought. An answer would eventually come. As the silence lengthened, everyone else at the table also looked in the older woman's direction.

"One thing I have learned in my life," GeeGee began at last, "is that many questions don't have easy answers, even for believers with the Word of God to guide them. Few decisions that matter are made without deep thought, without wrestling for an answer, without prayer. Do I believe lying is wrong? Yes. God's Word tells me I shouldn't lie. Yet I have told lies. I have lived a lie in the past. I have asked forgiveness for those lies. And there are consequences when we don't walk uprightly before the Lord. But is lying *always* wrong?" Her eyes took on a faraway look. "I remember the photographs of the concentration camps after they were liberated. I remember the horror and disbelief at what had happened there as the truth came out. If I could tell a lie that would have saved one of those people, I would do it in an instant. Or at least I want to believe I would. There were great dangers for those who did so. There are many examples during that war of people who laid down their lives for another. Choosing to lie in order to save a life is, I believe, preventing a worse atrocity. People are made in the image of God. We are to respect human life. Not lying to the Nazis would have been to submit to an ungodly and immoral government."

Another silence followed before Adam asked, "What about the ninth commandment? Doesn't it say that we shall not lie? Doesn't that make all lying wrong?"

Brianna's dad said, "I believe a truer translation for that commandment is not to bear false witness against your neighbor. So I suppose that is a very specific kind of lie that is prohibited."

Several people spoke at once, and Brianna's attention drifted back to GeeGee's answer. She'd said she'd told lies and had lived a lie. What had she meant by that? Brianna couldn't imagine GeeGee telling a lie, let alone living one. She would have to ask her about it the next time they were alone together.

The conversation began to die down, and Adam grinned as he stared around the table. "I wonder what my professor would think if he could have listened in."

"May I add something?" GeeGee asked softly.

Again, all eyes turned toward her.

"Some time after the war, I read that more Jews were rescued by ordinary individuals who made split-second decisions than from organized efforts. I used to ponder that, to wonder if I would have had the courage to make one of those split-second decisions. I finally came to the conclusion that no one can really know what we would do in dire situations like the ones that happened in the war. We hope that our character is such that we will do the right thing, but it is in the moment when those situations arise that God gives us the grace, the courage, and even the wisdom to know what we must do."

"Which means we must know His voice," Great-Aunt Elizabeth said, speaking for the first time since Adam had posed his question.

"We must both know His Word and be attuned to His Spirit. Only then can we know what He's calling us to do."

Brianna frowned as she mulled over what both her great-grandmother and great-aunt had said. Did she know God's Word and the voice of His Spirit the way she should? She hoped so.

Chapter 38

WEDNESDAY, OCTOBER 21, 1942

The bus that took civilian employees back into town from Gowen Field was noisy and smelly, but at the end of Lillian's first full day of work on the base, she wasn't about to complain. The bus would drop her within a few blocks of home. That was all she cared about at the moment. Her brain churned with the rules and regulations of the base, the dos and the don'ts she had to follow, both at work and in her private life. Right now, she wanted nothing so much as a hot bath and a good night's sleep.

Half an hour later, she opened the front door of the house and started to call, "Mom—" But the rest of her words stopped in her throat when she saw her parents, Daisy, and Todd Kinnear seated in the living room, all of them wearing somber expressions. Her gaze shot back to her sister on the sofa beside Todd. "Where on earth did you go for two days?"

"Sit down, Lillian," her dad said.

She wanted to argue, but something in his tone made her swallow a retort. She crossed the room to take the only vacant chair.

Her mom said, "Daisy and Todd were telling us their news."

"'Their news'?" Again, her gaze went to her sister.

Todd reached for Daisy's hand. "We're married."

Lillian drew back. Was this some sort of practical joke?

"We drove to Winnemucca yesterday and got married."

Lillian gave her head a slow shake, denying the possibility, but when she stopped and looked at them, she caught the sparkle of a ring on Daisy's left hand. Even so, even with a ring on Daisy's finger, the idea was too preposterous to be believed. Daisy *married*? Daisy married to Todd? Why would he want to marry her? And why on earth would she marry him, even if he asked her? Daisy might not be a knockout, she might not have boys hanging around all the time, but she didn't have to settle for somebody like Todd Kinnear. Oh, sure. He was nice and all. But he was as dull as ditchwater.

Todd looked at Lillian's dad. "Sir, I know you're disappointed in me for doing it this way. But we"—he looked at Daisy—"talked about it and decided this was for the best, what with the war and all. No fuss over a wedding or a reception." His gaze returned to her dad. "This way, nobody will spend money they can't afford. We both wanted something simple. But we were married by a minister, not by a justice of the peace. We wanted to do it right."

Good grief! It was true. Daisy was a married woman. Lillian hadn't even managed to get engaged before her younger sister got married. And now with Brandan missing in action and probably dead, who knew when she would get to buy a fancy dress and walk down the aisle. It was wrong. It was all completely wrong.

Her mom rose from her chair and crossed the room. Leaning down, she kissed Daisy on the cheek, then repeated the action with Todd. "I wish you both great happiness."

"Thank you, Mrs. Abbott."

"Nancy." She smiled at Todd. "Or Mother Abbott, if you choose."

It was his turn to smile. "I would like that."

What was wrong with her parents? Why weren't they reading the riot act to both Daisy and Todd? They'd eloped. They'd been selfish and thoughtless.

As if in response to Lillian's thoughts, her dad followed the same path across the room, kissed Daisy's cheek, and offered his hand to Todd. "You're both adults. I trust you've done the right thing."

"I'll take care of her, sir. She'll never be in want."

"I know that, son. I know that."

"Oh, for pity's sake!" Lillian hopped up from the chair. "This is the most screwball thing I've ever heard." With a toss of her head, she left the living room and ran up the stairs to her bedroom, making sure she slammed the door behind her.

She looked out the window over her desk. Light was fading, and the sky looked gray. Gray like her life. Her gray, dull life. Even her new job couldn't brighten things up. She'd waited and waited and waited for Brandan. She'd loved him, but he'd refused to marry her when she wanted. Now he was gone.

And it was Daisy who got married. Daisy who would have a home of her own. Daisy who would get congratulations from friends and neighbors.

"Lillian, may I come in?" The door creaked open. "Please."

She faced her sister and crossed her arms over her chest. "How could you pull such a stupid trick?"

Daisy stepped into the room. "It wasn't stupid."

"You eloped with Todd Kinnear. Sounds stupid to me."

"He's a good man."

Lillian narrowed her gaze. "You two never even went out."

"We've been friends a long time."

"'Friends'?" She snorted in disbelief. "How could you not tell me what you planned to do?"

Her sister took a step back. Tears glittered in her eyes. "I couldn't tell you because I knew how you'd react. I knew you were feeling bad about Brandan. And I . . . I wanted to marry Todd."

"Don't act like you kept it a secret because I was feeling bad. You're just selfish. That's all. Selfish and thoughtless." She flicked her hand toward the door. "So go. Go be with your new husband."

Daisy stood still a long while before turning away. "I love you, sis," she said as she disappeared into the hallway.

With a huff, Lillian faced the window again, surprised by the tears that welled in her eyes and trickled down her cheeks.

Lying in a cold, windowless cellar, his body ravaged by pain and fever, made it impossible for Brandan to keep track of the passage of time. When he opened his eyes, he didn't know if it was day or night. In his more lucid moments, he tried to piece together what had happened, but there were holes in his memory. He remembered commanding the men to bail out of the stricken B-24. He remembered the plane was already too low before he could have followed them, so he'd brought the bomber down in a field. He remembered the first hard impact and not much after that. Bits and snatches. Voices saying things he couldn't understand. Arms dragging him across uneven ground. The pain.

He remembered the pain. Easy enough to do since it was with him still.

He knew something else. The Nazis didn't have him. He was with the French. For now, strangers were keeping him safe, hiding him beneath a house in a space that barely had enough room for him to sit up. The girl who brought him soup and dry, tasteless bread and who tended to his broken leg and other wounds didn't speak English. He'd never learned to say anything in French beyond *oui* and *merci*. So he couldn't ask her any questions. All he could do was lie there and hope they were good at keeping secrets and hadn't left any clues behind at the downed plane. His life and theirs depended on it.

Chapter 39

PRESENT DAY–FEBRUARY

It had been more than thirty years since Daisy last read the letter she'd received from Brandan Gallagher, the one mailed in September of 1942. She hadn't kept it with the other bundles of letters she'd saved through the years. This one had been tucked away in a keepsake box that held other small remembrances of her past.

> Daisy,
>
> I'm sending this letter to Jack and asking him to get it to you. I don't want to take a chance on anybody else seeing it.

She didn't have to keep reading to remember the words he'd written to her so long ago. She even remembered the pain that had come with them, although time and God had taken away the sting. It was the discussion around the dinner table on Sunday that had caused her to look for the letter. As if it were yesterday, she remembered being closed in the upstairs bathroom, two truths staring her in the face. One, Brandan hadn't loved her and never would love her. And two, she was going to have his baby.

That was the moment when the first life-changing lie had been born.

"I have told lies. I have lived a lie . . ." That's what she'd said to everyone on Sunday.

Was it ever okay to tell a lie? Several examples had been given around the dinner table, both from the Bible and from history. She did believe that lying to save another life was the right thing to do. That was an unselfish act. But most lies were so much more selfish than that. Most lies were told to hide from the truth, to protect oneself, not to protect others. Most were told to try to avoid personal consequences. Lies were told to others and whispered to one's own heart. Lies were made up of what was said and what went unsaid. Overt and covert.

"O Father, whatever would I have done without Your mercy and grace?" She reached for her Bible, opened it to the first chapter of Galatians, and read aloud the note she'd written at the top of the page, dated 1992. "Mercy is *not* getting what we deserve (Hell). Grace is getting what we don't deserve (Heaven)."

Rather than put the letter from Brandan back into the box, she stuck it in the Bible. For surely, if there was ever a good example of God's mercy and grace, it was represented by this letter written nearly eighty years before. She would do well to remember and thank Him for it, over and over again.

Closing the Bible on her lap, she leaned her head against the back of the chair and closed her eyes, more memories rising up.

Her lie had been exposed, of course, in time. Not to everyone, but to a few. To people she'd loved. They'd all discovered the truth eventually.

"'Be sure that your sin will find you out,'" she quoted softly, knowing the words of Scripture to be true.

Chapter 40

THURSDAY, OCTOBER 22, 1942

Daisy awakened slowly, surprised to see how much sunlight spilled into the room from beneath the curtains. She rolled onto her side to look at the clock on the bedside stand. Eight thirty.

She sat up quickly. Too quickly. The room spun, and she had to lie down again to wait until her stomach settled. When it did, she got out of bed, reached for her robe, and hurried out to the kitchen. Todd wasn't there. She'd known he wouldn't be. Not this late in the morning. After missing the past two days at the factory while he drove to and from Winnemucca, he'd gone into work this morning on time. And he'd gone without her fixing him breakfast. He should be able to count on his new wife to do that much for him, but she'd failed. Miserably.

Despondent, she turned and walked to the bathroom so she could get ready for the day. Not that she had a lot awaiting her. She didn't have her regular job to go to. She'd called Mr. Armstrong on Monday night and resigned. When he'd learned the reason why, he'd told her he wouldn't require a two-week notice. "Stay home with your husband where you belong," he'd said, ending with a hearty congratulations to them both.

Half an hour later, with her hair tied up in a scarf, Daisy began to clean Todd's house. Like her mother would have done, she set the kitchen chairs onto the table, legs up. Then she swept and mopped the floor. The living room, hall, and bedrooms were next. All went well until she entered Todd's bedroom. There, she stopped and wondered if he would want her in there. Would he want her moving around his things, dust mopping the floor, changing the sheets?

I'm his wife. Of course he wants it. She sank onto the side of his already made bed. *What else am I good for?*

Last night, after leaving her house—no, her parents' house—Todd had brought her into his home. She'd been inside the Kinnear house countless times over the years. For Daisy, it had been like having two homes on the same block. But she hadn't come inside often after Opal Kinnear's passing. Perhaps two or three times since the funeral in 1938. Now, she felt like an intruder. Not even a guest. An interloper.

What would Todd's mother think of what we've done? She let her gaze roam over the room. *Wouldn't she want him to marry for love?*

The telephone rang, and her heart quickened at the sound. The feeling that she didn't belong intensified. Should she answer it? She wasn't sure if that was his ring on the party line. The call could be for someone else.

The phone rang and rang, but she didn't budge. Finally it stopped, and she breathed a sigh of relief. Then it started ringing again. This time she rose and went to the living room.

With the handset to her ear, she said a tentative, "Hello?"

"Daisy." Todd's voice came through the wire. "I was getting worried. Are you all right?"

"Yes. I'm fine. I . . . I wasn't sure if I should answer."

"You can always answer. I've got a private line. It only rings when the call's for us."

She nodded as if he could see her.

"You were sound asleep when I left. I didn't want to disturb you. How are you?"

"I'm fine. I was . . . I was just . . . tired after all the driving."

"I left some money in the drawer next to the back door. In case you want to get anything from the market."

Dinner. Of course. She should think about dinner. "Okay."

"Call me here at the factory if you need anything. The number's there by the phone. I wrote it down this morning."

She found the slip of paper with her eyes. "I see it."

"All right, then. I'll let you go. I'll be home around six."

She said goodbye and placed the handset in its cradle.

Pull yourself together. You're not a child. You know how to clean and cook and shop.

Drawing a deep breath, she went to the refrigerator to see what was there. Not much to choose from. The cupboards didn't offer many choices either. She would need to go to the store.

Daisy had helped her mom in the kitchen since she was a little girl, but she'd never been in charge of planning a meal, and her shopping for groceries had been mostly as an errand girl. Her mom would need flour and send Daisy to the store for it. That sort of thing.

Everyone said that more serious rationing was coming soon, but so far, sugar was the only restricted edible commodity. Since she didn't plan to make dessert, she wouldn't need her ration book. But knowing what to prepare did require some thought. After all, she had no idea what Todd liked to eat.

Except for one thing. He liked hamburgers. She remembered from the last barbecue they'd had in the Abbott backyard. She could make meat and potato patties tonight. And they could have pears. There were a couple of jars of them in the cupboard. He must like those, too, since he was the only person who lived there.

The only person up until yesterday.

Next summer, she could plant a victory garden and grow their own tomatoes and carrots and peas and beans. The yard was big enough for a few rows of corn too. Of course, she would have had the baby by then. Maybe she wouldn't have enough time to tend a garden.

She grew still, and her hands overlapped on her belly. Still flat, but she thought there was a firmness she hadn't noticed before. And perhaps not completely flat. It did seem a little round.

Her heart skittered. Not with fear. Not with shame. But at a fresh realization that a tiny human being grew inside of her.

Interactions with Carl were awkward throughout Todd's first day back at work. Other employees congratulated him on his marriage. Men slapped him on the back, and women wished him well. But Carl avoided him when possible, and when they were together, he remained silent and withdrawn.

Todd couldn't say he blamed his new father-in-law for reacting that way. Look at all that had happened. First, Todd had become Carl's boss. Weeks later, he'd eloped with his daughter. Maybe if Carl was the boss, it wouldn't feel quite as strange. Maybe if Todd hadn't taken questions and concerns to Carl so often in the past, his father-in-law wouldn't think Todd had betrayed a trust by running off with Daisy. And it had been a betrayal of trust, whether Todd wanted to admit it or not.

An uncomfortable silence stayed with them on their walk home that evening. Todd tried to come up with something to say but discarded every idea. Finally, at his front walk, he stopped. "See you in the morning."

"In the morning, son." Carl moved on toward his house.

Being called "son" helped a little. Perhaps what had been fractured could be mended.

Todd noticed two things when he opened the front door: the absence of dust on the floor and other surfaces in the living room and the smell of fried beef coming from the kitchen. His stomach growled in response to the latter.

"I'm home!" he called, the same way he used to hear his dad call to his mom.

Daisy appeared in the kitchen doorway. "Hi."

"You made dinner. Smells good." He turned toward the coat closet and removed his jacket.

"It's ready when you are."

He faced her again. She wore an apron over a pale-yellow dress. Her brown hair was tied back with a matching yellow scarf. She looked younger than her years, which made him feel older than his own. She looked tired as well. Much too tired. And what he wanted was for her to look happy.

"Looks like you . . . like you've been settling in."

"I hope it's all right." She glanced around the living room as if worried he would find something out of place.

He tried to reassure her. "Everything looks great. The house hasn't been this free of dust in years." It sounded more like he was complimenting a maid instead of his bride of two days.

She dipped her head and returned to the kitchen.

Todd followed after her, arriving in time to see her take a platter of meat patties from the oven. She carried the warm platter to the table and set it in the center, between a bowl of green beans and another of pears. Off to the side sat a plate with sliced bread on it, a saucer of butter nearby.

She turned and looked at him, uncertainty still in her eyes.

"I'll wash up," he said, "and be right back."

She's nervous. I'm nervous. Lord, help me make things better between us.

He washed his hands in the bathroom sink, and when he was done, he splashed his face with cool water, hoping it would help him think more clearly. After drying off, he ran a comb through his hair. It didn't do much to improve his looks, but it was better than nothing.

He returned to the kitchen. Daisy was seated at the table, waiting for him. He took the chair opposite her. Their gazes met and held a short while. Then he bowed his head and said the blessing he'd learned as a young boy. Her soft "Amen" echoed his, and then they both looked up.

"This looks good, Daisy."

"I hope so. It's not much."

"I don't require much."

"I'm sorry I didn't pack a lunch for you."

"I'm used to doing it, and you needed your rest."

The conversation remained as stilted as before. It felt worse to Todd than pure silence would have been. He lifted the platter and slid a couple of patties onto his plate, then offered it for Daisy to do the same.

He was wrong about silence, he decided awhile later. Even stilted talking had to be better than more silence. There'd been too much of that, starting with the long drive down to Winnemucca.

He slid his now-empty plate a couple of inches away from him. "Daisy . . ."

She lifted her eyes.

"We've always been able to talk to each other. We've been friends. I don't want us to become strangers now."

"I'm sorry. I didn't—"

"Don't apologize. I'm not looking to make you feel bad." He drew a deep breath and let it out. "No matter why and how we got married, you're my wife. This is *our* home. You aren't a guest here. If there's something you want to change, change it. If there's something we need to buy to make you more comfortable, we'll buy it."

She didn't respond except to blink back tears.

He hadn't wanted to make her cry any more than he'd wanted her apology. *I'm making a muck of this.*

Daisy intruded on his thoughts, saying softly, "A friend told me once that her sister cried at the drop of a hat throughout her pregnancy. It's not your fault when I get like this."

Maybe not this time. Or maybe she was just being sweet to him.

He took in another breath and released it. "We'll figure this out. I know we will."

She nodded, a couple of those tears breaking free despite her best efforts.

"Why don't I do the dishes, and then we can listen to the radio."

"Don't be silly," she protested. "You worked all day."

"From the look of things, so did you."

He stood, stacked both his plate and hers on top of the empty meat platter, then carried them to the sink. By the time he turned around, she was repeating his actions with the serving bowls. Before she could order him from the kitchen—the same way he'd seen her mother do to her father—Todd faced the sink again, put the stopper in the drain, and began to fill the basin with hot water and soap suds.

We're a team, he wanted to say to her. Then he thought of something better. His dad had liked to quote Charles Spurgeon: *"Begin as you mean to go on, and go on as you began, and let the Lord be all in all to you."*

He turned off the water and glanced over at Daisy. "Let's begin as we mean to go on."

She eyed him as if not understanding.

"We're in this together, Daisy. As my wife, you're my helpmeet, but I'm pretty sure that a husband being willing to die for his wife means I'm your helpmeet too. Don't you agree?"

Now she frowned. "You don't think like most men, do you?"

He chuckled as he put his hands into the dishwater and began washing a plate.

Chapter 41

PRESENT DAY–MARCH

Brianna laughed nervously as Greg unlocked the back door of the house. "Are you sure we should be here when your parents aren't home?"

"I'm sure. My folks let me drop by whenever I want. That's why they gave me the key." He pushed open the door and immediately entered a code into the security system. It beeped its acceptance.

"But you don't live with them."

It was Greg's turn to laugh. "No. I share a house near the university with a bunch of other guys. BSU students, like me. The last thing I want to do is live with my parents at my age."

His comment made her feel like a child. She was only a year younger than Greg, and she still lived at home. She still depended upon her parents for pretty much everything, including transportation. She might as well be twelve.

"Want something to drink?" Greg asked.

"Sure."

She moved through the kitchen into the dining room where the window overlooked a large deck and, beyond it, a fenced yard that must be stunning in the spring and summer when the grass turned green, the flowers were in bloom, and the waterscape gurgled. She turned and looked into the formal living area. Nothing out of place. Everything looked elegant and, for that matter, never used. Like a showroom in an upscale furniture store.

"Here you go." Greg stepped to her side and held out a glass with ice and, she assumed from the fizzing, cola.

"Thanks." She took it from him, their hands touching.

That was the moment when she noticed the stillness that surrounded them. The silence made her feel oddly vulnerable. It wasn't as if she'd never been alone with a guy before. But this seemed . . . different.

She moved around the room, pretending to look at a couple of prints hanging on the wall. "What do your parents do?" she asked, more to create some sound than from true curiosity.

"Mom's in real estate. Dad's a financial planner."

She turned to look at him. "Where do they go to church?"

His eyebrows raised. "Mom and Dad?" He laughed again. "I doubt they've ever darkened a church door except for maybe to attend a funeral."

"Then how did you come to know Christ?"

He shrugged. "A friend." He motioned with his head. "Come on. Let me show you the family room. They've got a massive TV with surround sound. We can watch a movie. Or Dad's got a PlayStation 5. You could take me on in *Spider-Man*." He grinned. "But I warn you, I've never been beat."

"I'm afraid I wouldn't know what I'm doing. Haven't ever played it." She hadn't ever played much of anything when it came to video games.

"A movie it is." He reached for her hand. Brianna stepped forward to let him take it, nerves tumbling in her stomach once again.

The family room in the basement was enormous, and the

large-screen TV was unlike anything she'd seen before. Three rows of leather recliners had been placed in front of it on a sloping floor. A movie-style popcorn popper stood against one wall. The high windows all had drawn blinds, casting the room in shadows even with several lamps turned on.

"Wow." Brianna breathed out the word in a near whisper.

"Yeah, it's something, isn't it? Dad's hardly ever around, but he's always wanted a home theater. I use it way more than he does, and I don't even live here."

"There must be room for you if you wanted to live with them."

"I guess. But I don't want to. I like my freedom."

He drew her closer. His eyes searched hers for a moment. Then he leaned in and kissed her. His lips felt light upon hers, almost tentative. But it caused an explosion of sensations on her insides. One of his hands touched her back between her shoulder blades and drew her closer to him. As the kiss deepened, the hand slid slowly down to the small of her back. It seemed it might go lower still.

She sucked in a small breath as she stepped back from him, breaking both the kiss and his embrace. "Maybe we should watch that movie," she managed to say after a moment.

Did the shadows play tricks, or did he look irritated? Almost angry.

But then he smiled that smile of his. "Sure. A movie's good." He motioned toward the recliners. "Pick a chair. I prefer the back row, but they're all good."

Tingling sensations continued to move through her as she walked to the rows of recliners. Sensations that seemed both wonderful and frightening.

Maybe I should leave. Maybe it isn't smart to be here when no one else is in the house.

She could imagine her mom's response to that thought. She would say there was no maybe about it. But wasn't that just an old-fashioned way of thinking? They weren't doing anything wrong. They were both adults. They were both Christians. What harm was there in watching a movie together? There wasn't any harm. She was being silly. That was all.

Chapter 42

MONDAY, NOVEMBER 2, 1942

Daisy chose not to see the Abbott family physician, the man who'd cared for all members of her family, including her grandparents, since before Daisy was born. What if he inadvertently let something slip to her mom or dad, should they happen to need his care too? So she made an appointment with Todd's family doctor and went to see him alone.

When Daisy was dressed again after the examination, she joined Dr. Hamilton in his office. He had a somewhat brusque manner, his questions and comments brief and to the point. But he wasn't an unpleasant sort. If not for her embarrassment over the intimate exam, she thought she might like him.

"You are about thirteen weeks along, Mrs. Kinnear," he said, looking at some papers on his desk. "Based upon the date of your last menstruation."

She didn't need him to tell her that particular bit of information. She knew exactly how far along she was, and he was over by about twelve days. She was eleven weeks and two days pregnant, to be precise.

"I estimate your due date to be the seventh of May." He glanced up. "Why have you waited so long to see me?"

"I felt fine. It didn't seem urgent." Heat rose in her cheeks, and she was thankful the doctor had looked down again.

"No morning sickness?"

"Yes. Some. But it's been better in the last week or so."

"Good. Good." He nodded and made a note. "You are slightly underweight for an expectant mother. Do you have a good appetite?"

"Usually, yes."

"Be sure you eat three meals a day. You're young and healthy. There's no reason to expect any problems. You may continue with your daily routine for now. I suggest you avoid large, crowded events and limit the amount of time you spend listening to the radio, especially with the volume too loud. My nurse will give you a brochure to help guide you through the remainder of your pregnancy."

"Thank you, Doctor."

He stood. "And give my best to your husband. I didn't know Todd had found himself a wife. I'm pleased for you both."

"Thank you," she repeated softly, also rising.

He instructed her on making her next appointment, then walked her to the door of his office and saw her out.

A short while later, after making her follow-up appointment, she stepped outside the building. Blustery weather caused her to pull up the collar of her coat as she started to walk toward home, leaning into the wind.

She wished she had someone to talk to about her pregnancy. Her mom would be able to offer so much wisdom, but she couldn't tell her yet. Later, most everyone would guess the baby hadn't arrived early. Which was also the reason she couldn't tell Martha. In fact, she wasn't sure her best friend had forgiven her yet for eloping.

As for Lillian . . . Daisy frowned. Her sister had been so unpleasant the night she'd learned of Daisy's marriage. What would she be like when she discovered her younger sister was expecting a baby? And if she ever learned that Todd wasn't the father—

She wasn't sure if it was that thought or a blast of cold air that caused her to shudder.

Todd stood at the window overlooking the factory floor, but his thoughts were on Daisy. Her first appointment with Dr. Hamilton had been this afternoon. Most likely, she was on her way home by now.

Had the appointment gone well? Was the doctor concerned about anything?

Maybe he should have insisted on going with her. It was her first time to meet Dr. Hamilton. But she'd insisted she was all right, that she preferred to see him alone.

"Mr. Kinnear," a female voice intruded on his thoughts.

For a split second, he expected to turn and see Daisy. But of course that wasn't who'd spoken. It was one of his floor managers. He didn't have to search his memory for her name. Gladys Myers stood out from the other women who worked for Kinnear Canning. She was taller than most women. A lot taller. And with her platinum-blond hair and startling blue eyes, she looked like someone who belonged on the silver screen opposite John Wayne, not making compasses in a former canning factory.

"Yes, Mrs. Myers."

"It's . . . it's Mr. Jamison. He's causing a commotion in the lunchroom."

"A commotion?"

"I believe he's had word about his son."

"Harry." A sick knot formed in Todd's gut. "I'll go now." He hurried away with long strides, taking the stairs three at a time, and hit the ground floor almost at a run, drawing the attention of some of the workers before he disappeared from view.

Whatever commotion there'd been, it was over by the time Todd reached the lunchroom. The only evidence of anything untoward was an overturned waste can and two chairs lying on their backs. Any witnesses had disappeared before the boss arrived, and Roy Jamison was alone in the room. A glass three quarters full of amber liquid sat on the table before him.

In the ten months since Harry Jamison had left for boot camp, Roy hadn't shown any signs of drinking during work hours. It had seemed to Todd that the man's demons had been defeated. Not so today.

Roy looked up as Todd approached the table. "He's dead." His voice was flat. His eyes were blurry. The unmistakable smell of whiskey lingered in the air.

Todd sat opposite him. "I didn't know he was in combat yet."

"DNB."

"What?"

"His casualty code. DNB. Died Non-Battle." He lifted the glass and took a long swallow. When he set it down again, whiskey sloshed over the sides to pool on the table. "A transport plane crashed. No survivors."

"I'm sorry, Roy. Truly sorry for your loss." Todd drew a deep breath, steeling himself for what he knew he had to say. "But I can't have you drinking at work. Not even under these circumstances." His words sounded cold and calloused in his ears, but he pressed on. "We have a government contract. Our work matters to the war effort. All of our work. Yours too."

Roy stared at him blankly.

"I put up with your drinking in your office a year ago. I can't put up with it now." He pushed back the chair and stood. "You need to go home. Take a couple of weeks off. Sober up. Be there for your wife. Mourn your son. But when you come back, you can't bring any liquor with you. Understood? There won't be any drinking on company property in the future. None. If this happens again, you'll be fired on the spot."

Todd wouldn't have been surprised if the older man called him a string of foul names. He figured he deserved them. Last December, he'd put Roy Jamison into his car and driven him home. He wanted to show the same compassion now. Especially because Harry was dead. But he couldn't. His gut told him he had to be firm this time around, even in the face of such tragedy.

"Is your car here?" He knew what the answer would be. Roy hadn't given up driving his car to work and wouldn't until gas rationing made it impossible for him to continue.

The older man nodded.

"I'll get someone to take you home." He turned on his heel and walked out of the lunchroom.

Carl Abbott waited not far from the doorway. "I'll take him home."

"Was I too hard on him?" Todd asked in a low voice, forgetting the awkwardness that lingered between them, desperate to have Carl confirm he'd done the right thing.

"No. You needed to say what you said. He needed to hear it."

"He just lost his son."

"Yes, he lost his son, and we must offer him Christian compassion and understanding. But we must also give him truth. Compassion doesn't mean lying to someone to save their feelings."

Todd winced on the inside, reminded of the lie he and Daisy planned to tell the world about her baby. Was it wrong to lie to protect someone? To protect Daisy? To protect an innocent child? Was it wrong to lie to a man he respected so much, even for a good reason?

Something crashed in the lunchroom, pulling Todd's thoughts to the matter at hand.

"I'll take him to his house now." Carl stepped around Todd. "And I'll give the car keys to his wife. Hopefully, she'll have the good sense to hide them from him."

Todd checked his watch. "Don't bother to come back to work. It's almost quitting time. Just go home afterward."

His father-in-law looked back at him and nodded before disappearing through the doorway.

Todd turned toward his office. He would get his coat and head home a little early himself. He was eager to know what the doctor had to say to Daisy.

The brochure Daisy brought home from the doctor's office suggested the best activity for an expectant mother was the preparation of the nursery and layette. How many hours a day could a woman do that? And she couldn't very well start knitting baby booties yet. At least not where anyone might see her. She wasn't supposed to know she was pregnant.

She paused in front of the dressing-table mirror in her room, turned sideways, and pressed her hand against her belly. It didn't look like there was a baby growing inside of her. Would it happen suddenly? Would she wake up one morning and find her stomach as large as a pumpkin or a watermelon?

A couple of girls she knew from high school had married and had babies already, but neither of them were close friends. She hadn't seen them when they were expecting. If only there was someone she could—

"Daisy, I'm home."

Her pulse skittered at the sound of Todd's voice. Was she running late or was he early? She hurried out of the bedroom in time to see him hang his coat in the closet.

He faced her with a smile. "I'm early," he said as if to answer her silent question.

"I haven't started dinner."

"That's all right. I'd rather hear about your appointment with Dr. Hamilton."

She felt warmth rise in her cheeks. It remained difficult, embarrassing even, for her to talk about her pregnancy with him. Looking down at her hands, folded before her, she answered, "The doctor said I'm healthy, but he thinks I'm too thin. He wants me to be sure to eat three meals a day."

"You are too thin."

Her gaze darted up. Did he think her unattractive? In comparison to her sister, she was certain everybody thought so. In her memory, she heard Brandan whisper Lillian's name, even as Daisy lay beside him.

"I noticed when you lost weight," he continued. "You didn't have any extra to lose. That's why it was obvious. I know now it's because you were worried and . . . and sick in the mornings."

The heat in her cheeks worsened.

"I . . . I'll fix dinner." She started for the kitchen. "Soup and grilled cheese sandwiches. I hope that's all right."

He followed her. "Daisy. Wait."

She faced him again.

"I thought we were doing better. I thought you'd stopped feeling . . . I don't know . . . Awkward around me."

He was right. Things hadn't been as strained between them as in the beginning. She often remembered what he'd said after the first dinner she'd prepared in his home. In *their* home. That they needed to begin as they meant to go on. She appreciated him so much for trying to make this unexpected marriage work between them. Still, talking to him about her pregnancy felt wrong. It must remind him of the sin she'd committed, and the consequences of that sin she had to live with. And now he had to live with as well. Two centuries ago, she would have been labeled with a scarlet letter. In the days of the Bible, she would have been stoned to death.

"Daisy?"

She blinked away her darker thoughts. "I'm sorry."

She saw him take and release a breath, knew that he wanted to tell her again to stop apologizing. But how could she? She had a great deal to be sorry for.

Chapter 43

PRESENT DAY–MARCH

Hannah dropped her bag onto the table opposite Brianna. "What is up with you?"

"Nothing."

"Don't give me that. You skipped classes yesterday." She pulled out a chair and sat on it.

Brianna closed her laptop. "I had something to do." She crossed her arms defensively. "It's not like I robbed a store or something. I just missed a couple of classes."

"Adam was looking for you. Said he ran across something you might want for your history class."

She remembered getting a text from Adam while she and Greg were watching the movie. She hadn't answered and then had forgotten about it. Until Hannah's reminder. "I know. He sent me a message. He'll tell me whatever he's got in class." She checked the time on her phone. "I probably ought to go."

"Brianna, be careful."

"What do you mean?"

"Nothing. Just be careful."

Brianna sighed as she put her laptop away.

"Adam's a good guy," Hannah added.

"I know that."

"Don't be careless with him."

"Hannah, you're not making sense."

Her friend gave her one of those who-are-you-trying-to-fool looks. "Adam likes you."

"We've talked about this before. I like him too."

This time Hannah's look was more scolding.

Brianna reacted with a spark of anger. "I've gotta go." She grabbed her case and left the small study area. What had gotten into Hannah anyway? She was supposed to be Brianna's friend, not a second mother. Brianna didn't need to be told what to do. She certainly didn't need to be told that Adam was a good guy and that he liked her.

Her footsteps slowed. She and Hannah and Adam had been friends for years. Good friends, the three of them. They'd gone to school together for most of their lives. All three were believers in Jesus, although Adam didn't go to the same church as Hannah and Brianna. Adam was the brainy one of the group. Hannah was the most spiritual. Brianna? Well, she wasn't sure that she was "the most" in any category, but she did know how to be a good friend. She wouldn't do anything to hurt either Hannah or Adam.

"Adam likes you."

She came to a standstill, forcing other students to go around her on their way to their classes. Was Hannah right? Was Brianna being careless with Adam's feelings? Just because she didn't want their friendship to change didn't mean she was doing anything wrong. Did it?

She gave her head a shake and hurried on her way. In the classroom, she took her usual seat in the back corner of the room and watched the doorway for Adam. But he never came. Unlike Brianna, he wasn't the sort of student to skip a class. Not if it could be helped.

Doubt niggled at her as she took out her phone and replied to the previous day's message.

Sorry didn't get back to you. Will explain later. Are you on campus? Don't see you in class.

She pressed Send and waited. And waited. But no reply came. That wasn't like Adam to ignore her text. Come to think of it, it shouldn't be like her either. But she'd had her reasons yesterday. It would have been rude to answer a text in the middle of a movie. It might have upset Greg.

But Brianna didn't want to hurt Adam's feelings either. She would make sure things were okay between them just as soon as this class was over.

As it turned out, Brianna didn't have to look for Adam when the class was over. He was waiting near the door as students spilled out of the classroom.

"Hey." He held up his phone with the message app open. "I got your message."

"Not like you to miss class."

"I didn't. I slipped in late and just sat in the first open chair."

It hurt a little that he hadn't come to sit beside her. "Oh."

"Want to talk a bit?"

"Okay." She fell into step beside him.

It didn't take them too long to find an unoccupied corner with a couple of empty chairs around a small table. Brianna dropped her bag on the floor and sat down.

"Want something to drink?" Adam asked.

"Sure."

"I'll get them." He went to a nearby vending machine and returned with two cold bottles.

Brianna twisted off the lid of her orange soda. "Sorry I didn't answer your text yesterday. I was . . . in the middle of something."

"With Greg?"

Part of her wanted to lie about it for some reason. She didn't know why. "Yes. We were watching a movie."

He nodded before taking a swig of his Coke.

"I feel bad that I didn't get back to you. Really. I just . . . I just forgot."

There was something tender about the way he looked at her now. "Be careful, Brianna."

What was it with her friends? First Hannah, now Adam, both of them telling her to be careful.

Adam reached across the table and covered her left hand with one of his. "I don't want you to get hurt. I care about you."

"I know you do." Her throat felt tight all of a sudden.

His eyes narrowed slightly. "I'm not sure about that guy."

Defensiveness rose in her chest.

"I don't want you to get hurt," Adam repeated.

She remembered the vulnerable feeling that had gripped her yesterday when she was alone with Greg. She remembered that almost angry look he'd given her when she'd ended the kiss. But surely she'd had nothing to be nervous about, and neither did Adam.

"I won't get hurt," she answered at last. "You don't have to worry about me."

He looked as if he'd like to say more, but instead, he squeezed her hand.

Her heart gave a strange little flutter in her chest. But she ignored it. After all, it was nothing like the crazy way Greg made her feel.

Chapter 44

SATURDAY, NOVEMBER 7, 1942

Lillian didn't mind missing breakfast if it meant another hour or two of shut-eye. Especially after an evening out with some new friends from the air base. They'd gone dancing at the Starlite, and it had been so much fun.

Smiling, she rolled onto her side, away from the daylight spilling through the curtains. It felt like years since she'd had that kind of fun. She could hardly remember the last time Brandan had taken her dancing. No, she did remember. It had been after his graduation. May of 1941.

Brandan.

She felt a twinge of guilt. She hadn't been to the Gallagher home in a while. His parents must still be worried sick about him. Not that she wasn't worried too. She was. But what could she do? Nothing. Absolutely nothing. Better not to think about him. Better to move on and live her own life. She didn't want to be sad, and thinking about Brandan and seeing his parents made her sad. She'd had too much fun last night to ruin her morning with sorrowful memories.

Outside, Jupiter started barking up a storm. Lillian was about to pull the pillow over her head when, despite the closed window, she heard Daisy's voice call the dog's name. Jupiter fell silent.

Lillian hadn't spoken to her sister in over two weeks. Not even at church the past two Sundays. It had sickened her, the way people congratulated the couple. No one had scolded them for eloping. Of course, elopements and quick marriages happened a lot these days.

For everybody but me.

Brandan.

She'd promised to wait for him while he was off fighting Hitler and the Nazis, but if Brandan was dead, there was no reason to wait. There was no hope left that she would become Mrs. Brandan Gallagher. No more drives in his convertible. No more kisses in his arms. No more listening as he whispered he loved her. Was she supposed to stop living when there was little hope, if any, that he'd survived?

"*Missing in action*" was what the telegram had said. He could be alive. He might be a prisoner of war. But if he was a prisoner, wouldn't the Gallaghers have heard something by now? Almost a month had passed since his plane went down over France. That was surely enough time for the Germans to tell the Americans they'd captured one of their pilots. Or maybe not. She didn't know how such things worked.

All hope of returning to sleep lost, she sat up on the side of her bed, wishing that she'd arranged to meet her friends at the Starlite again tonight.

Jupiter sat near the kitchen table, eyes watchful and ears on alert, while Daisy wiped the counters with a cloth.

"Hey," Todd said from behind her. "What's he doing here?"

She turned quickly. "He was barking a lot, so I brought him in with me. You don't mind, do you?" The Kinnears had never owned a dog. Maybe Todd didn't want one in his house.

"No, I don't mind." He bent down and scratched Jupiter behind one ear. "You're always welcome. Aren't you, boy?"

As he straightened, Todd met her gaze, and his tender smile caused something warm to blossom in her heart.

"If you're feeling up to it," he continued, "I thought we might look at some things we'll need for the baby when it comes. A crib. A carriage. That sort of stuff."

Her pulse quickened. Buying baby furniture made the future seem ever more real. "There's no hurry. We've got six months before the baby's due."

"Who knows what will be rationed next? By spring, parts for a baby carriage or crib might be hard to find. We don't need to buy today, but it doesn't hurt to look."

"What if someone sees us?"

He looked confused.

"We've been married less than three weeks," she explained, feeling that all-too-familiar flush rising in her cheeks.

"Oh." He shrugged. "Well, if we see someone we know, I'll tell them we're dreaming for the future. You know. Anticipating a blessed event."

Something about his expression told her he meant what he said. He did anticipate the arrival of the baby. Would Brandan have felt the same if circumstances had been different? Cold reality washed over her at the thought. She knew the answer. He wouldn't have been happy about it, and he would have despised her for trapping him.

A knock at the back door caused Daisy to jump in surprise. Todd pulled the door open to reveal Lillian standing on the back porch.

She glanced at Jupiter, then fixed Todd with a hard look. "Are you stealing our dog as well as my sister?"

"Lillian, please," Daisy whispered.

Apparently not offended, Todd grinned as he opened the door wider. "Come in out of the cold."

Lillian stepped inside, finally glancing in Daisy's direction. "I guess he always was more your dog than mine."

Daisy felt a spark of hope that she'd been forgiven. "Would you like a cup of coffee? There's still some in the pot."

"Sure. I'll enjoy it while I can." Lillian moved to a chair at the table.

Todd looked at Daisy. "I've got some work to do in the garage." He stepped closer and gave her a peck on the cheek. She knew the kiss had been for Lillian's benefit, but there was a small part of her that wished he'd wanted to kiss her for a different reason.

Daisy took a cup from the shelf and filled it with coffee. Then she got cream from the refrigerator. By the time she sat opposite her sister, Lillian was stirring a large spoonful of precious sugar into her cup. But perhaps it didn't matter. Todd didn't have much of a sweet tooth.

"So," Lillian said after a sip, "how does married life suit you?"

Here came that blasted blush again. Trying to make it go away kept her from answering.

Lillian laughed. "Oh my goodness. You're embarrassed. Do you think I don't know what goes on in a marriage?"

"No. It's just . . . No, I—" She took a quick breath. "You've forgiven me? For eloping?"

"I suppose." Lillian held her coffee cup close to her mouth, her elbows on the table. "I guess I must. I miss having you around."

"I've missed you too."

"Really? I thought you'd be too wrapped up in your new husband to think about me."

Daisy managed not to blush this time, but she was even more determined to change the subject. "Do you like working at the base?"

"I love it. There's so much energy around Gowen Field. It pulses with it. My work isn't exciting, but there are so many new people to meet, it makes the days go by fast. There are airmen from all over the country. You should hear the mix of accents." She set down her cup. "If you hadn't gotten married, they might have hired you too."

"They don't hire married women?" Daisy knew that wasn't true, but she asked anyway.

"Well, yes. There are married women working there. Of course there are. But you weren't home to get a phone call, were you? You were off marrying the next-door neighbor. Remember?"

Daisy swallowed a reply. What did it matter? Even if she'd gotten a job at the base, she would have had to quit once her pregnancy started to show. Pregnant women couldn't keep working there. Or most other places either.

Lillian didn't seem to notice Daisy's silence. "I've made some terrific new friends. June Olson and Rose Forest. They're both single girls, like me."

Single? What about Brandan?

"We went to the Starlite last night with some of the airmen from the base."

"'The Starlite,'" Daisy whispered as her breath caught and her stomach knotted.

"The place was hopping. I don't think I danced with the same guy twice the whole night."

What about Brandan? she wondered again. But it was obvious Lillian hadn't given him a moment's thought. Lillian hadn't thought about Brandan or his worried parents. Only about herself.

Her sister rattled on for a long while about her night out before saying she needed to go home.

The back door opened a few minutes after Lillian's departure, and Todd entered. "Things better between you two?"

Daisy nodded.

"I see she didn't take Jupiter home with her."

Daisy looked down at the dog, lying with his head on folded paws. "No. I think she forgot he was the reason she came over." She leaned forward and gave Jupiter a few pats on the head. "Maybe he's got a new home." *Like me.*

"Are you ready to go look at baby things?"

"Yes. But could we go by the Gallagher home first? I'd like to see how the family is doing, and they haven't been to church since they got that telegram."

If Todd minded the request, he didn't show it. "Sure. That's a good idea."

"I baked bread yesterday. I'll take them a loaf."

Worry and grief had etched deep lines in Andrew Gallagher's forehead and painted dark circles beneath his wife's eyes. They both seemed to have aged a decade since the summer picnic in the Abbott family's backyard. That had been only three months ago, but it felt like a lifetime to Todd.

"This is so kind of you." Elenore carried the loaf of bread to the kitchen, and when she returned, she insisted her guests sit and stay awhile.

Todd let Daisy lead the conversation. While he listened, he studied the framed photographs that covered a low bookcase to his left. Mostly they were photos of the three Gallagher boys at different ages. In the center was one of Brandan in his dress uniform. Perhaps it had been taken during his leave in August. He was a tall, good-looking guy with black hair and a square jaw.

No wonder Daisy fell for him.

"Todd?" Daisy's voice drew his attention from the photos. "Mr. Gallagher wondered how production is going at the factory."

He looked at the man. "Good. The transition was smoother and faster than I anticipated. Carl's help was indispensable. I'm fortunate he came on board when he did."

"I've encouraged William to apply for work at your factory when he graduates in the spring." Andrew gave him a hopeful look.

"Sure." Todd's gaze slipped to the photographs, falling on one of the three brothers together, then returned to the boys' father. "Yes, he should apply. We're always in need of good help."

Andrew exchanged a look with his wife. "We're afraid he'll enlist the minute he turns eighteen in February. He wants revenge for . . . for Brandan."

Empathy tightened Todd's chest, followed by shame. He shouldn't resent a man who may have given his life for his country. No matter how jealous he was.

Jealous?

He glanced at Daisy, then back at Andrew Gallagher. "Maybe we could put him to work part time now. Who knows? The war could be over by the time graduation rolls around."

No one in the room believed that was likely, but they all *wanted* to believe it. The whole country wanted to believe it.

Todd continued, "Have him come by the factory after school this coming week. Tell him to ask for me."

Relief crossed the older man's face. "I'll do that. Thanks. Can't tell you how much I appreciate it."

"It's the least I can do."

A realization hit him with force: he was seated opposite the grandparents of Daisy's baby. Grandparents who, if all went according to plan, would never know the child was related to them. It was a complication he hadn't considered, and he felt the weight of the lie grow heavier on his shoulders.

Elenore's eyes widened. "Good heavens. We didn't even congratulate you two on your marriage. Where on earth are our manners? We're so happy for you both."

Todd reached for Daisy's hand. "Thank you."

"It certainly took the ladies at church by surprise. My women's circle was all abuzz."

"It took us by surprise too." Todd hoped the older couple wouldn't ever know how true those words were.

Daisy squeezed his fingers, and he saw a silent request in her eyes. He stood, drawing her up with him. "We don't want to be rude, but Daisy and I have errands we need to take care of today."

Elenore's smile was tinged with sadness as she and her husband rose as well. "Of course. We understand. Young people always have a great deal on their plates. Don't they, Andrew?"

"Yes. They do."

The woman reached for Daisy's free hand. "Please tell Lillian that we're thinking of her. Give her our love. Tell her we long to see her when she's able."

"I will," Daisy answered softly. "And I . . . we're all praying for Brandan to be found."

"Thank you." Andrew put an arm around his wife's shoulders. "That means the world to us."

Guilt snaked through Todd. He hadn't prayed for Brandan to be found. Not even once since hearing the news of his plane going down in enemy territory. And that shamed him. No matter what he thought of Brandan personally, he was called by God to pray for him.

Daisy released Todd's hand and gave Elenore a quick hug. When they parted, both women had tears in their eyes.

Outside a cold wind pushed against them as they walked toward downtown.

"You okay?" Todd asked after a couple of blocks in silence.

"Yes. But I feel bad for them. Is it worse not knowing what's happened to Brandan?"

In the window to his left hung a service flag with three blue stars on it. Next door, the service flag had one blue star and one gold. Blue for a son in the military. Gold for a son killed in service. Would the blue star in the Gallagher window eventually be changed to gold?

"I don't know," he answered Daisy at last.

She looked up at him. "Are they holding onto hope when there isn't any?"

Another question he couldn't answer. But it made him wonder: Was Daisy holding onto hope for Brandan's return? And what would happen if he did?

Chapter 45

PRESENT DAY–MARCH

Daisy looked out the family-room window. Although still officially winter, there were signs of spring in the new buds on the trees and in the yellow and purple crocuses blooming in the garden. She loved spring—a season that brought hope and a sense of life renewing itself.

"That year—nineteen forty-two—was a hard year," she said at last, answering the question Brianna had asked moments before. "News of the war always seemed to be bad. So many defeats in the Pacific. As for the war across the Atlantic, nothing seemed to happen there. Our air force had joined the British in bombing the enemy in occupied Europe, but it didn't seem as if anything would change on the ground. Finally, in November, the US forces invaded North Africa."

"What about Aunt Lillian's boyfriend? You said he was shot down over France in forty-two."

Daisy blinked as she turned to look at her great-granddaughter. "Did we talk about that already? I'd forgotten."

Brianna offered a smile but no comment.

"Yes, that bombing run you asked about happened in October of nineteen forty-two. The ninth of October. The first time our boys joined with the British in the air. But it would be a very long time after that before American soldiers set foot in France. A very long time before so many oppressed people were liberated." She shook her head, remembering. "And if it seemed long to those of us on the home front, imagine how long it felt to the people living under that evil regime."

"At least something like that can't happen today."

Daisy stared at the girl. Could anyone be that naive? Yes, she supposed they could. Especially the young. Daisy herself wouldn't have believed such horrors possible when she was the same age. At that age a girl believed herself invincible. Or, if not invincible, at least that nothing truly bad would happen to her.

"Brianna, there's a saying that goes something like this: those who don't learn history are doomed to repeat it. Do you believe the genocide that happened during the Second World War was the first or last time such a thing has happened throughout history? It isn't and it wasn't. Until the Lord comes, sinful people will choose sinful paths, and that includes killing the innocents."

"Why doesn't God stop it? He could. Why doesn't He?"

Daisy reached forward to touch the back of Brianna's hand. "Perhaps, as Jesus said, His time has not yet come. We live in the tension between the first coming of the Messiah and what will be His second coming. The kingdom is here now, and yet it isn't fully here. We catch only glimpses of what shall be. When Christ returns, every knee will bow to Him. The kingdom will be here in full. But today, the devil continues to roam the earth, seeking to devour and destroy whoever he can."

"GeeGee, I'm a Christian. I trust Jesus for my salvation. But sometimes I don't understand everything."

"If we understood everything, we would be like God." Daisy shook her head once more. "We will never understand everything. We will never be like God, although that's one of the lies of Satan, whispering to us that we can be. It began with Eve and has never stopped. It's why faith is so important. We must have faith, especially when we don't understand."

Brianna nodded, her expression thoughtful. "Was it easier to be a Christian back then? During the war."

"'Easier'?"

"More people went to church. More people believed the same thing. Right?"

"Well, yes. I suppose that's true. The majority of Americans attended church on Sundays when I was a girl. The majority were church members. I would venture to say that even those who never went to church had some basic understanding of what it meant to be a Christian. Most would have known that America itself and our system of laws were founded on Judeo-Christian beliefs. So in that sense, I suppose it was easier." She looked at Brianna. "Why do you ask, dear?"

Her great-granddaughter shrugged. "I don't know." She turned to look out the window.

Daisy waited patiently for the girl to continue.

"My two closest friends, Adam and Hannah—they were at dinner with me three Sundays ago."

"Yes, I remember."

"They're both believers. Hannah loves to talk about the sermons we've heard and what she's been reading in the Bible or in books. But other kids I know, they're, like, hostile to what we believe. So I never mention my faith when I'm with them. I just keep quiet, even when I know they're wrong about something. Even when they say stuff that isn't true about Christians. Is that awful of me?"

"Perhaps *human* is a better word." She resisted the smile that tried to come, not wanting Brianna to think the subject wasn't important. It was. "I've had to struggle with knowing how to explain or show my faith. Certainly it's clear that believers can't deny Christ and still be

His. But sometimes we must preach the gospel without using words. I don't know who said that, but it's true. We must live the gospel. We must let others see how Jesus changed us and how He's still changing us."

"Still changing you? GeeGee, you're ninety-eight."

Daisy laughed softly. "And desperately in need of His grace, every moment of every day."

Chapter 46

TUESDAY, DECEMBER 1, 1942

The Frenchman's English wasn't good. Brandan got lost, trying to figure out what he said. But he understood enough to know the people who'd sheltered him all this while planned to move him soon. Probably tonight. He hoped running wouldn't be required because he wasn't sure he could walk any faster than a snail's pace.

He would have liked to see the sun after nearly two months in a cellar. Unfortunately, when he emerged into the outdoors, he discovered it was night—a cold and cloudy one. No moonlight reflected off the snow-covered ground. Safer, of course, but disheartening.

The boots he wore were a bit large for him, but he understood the dangers if he was seen in his military-issued boots. The gestapo watched for mistakes like that. American boots would be a dead giveaway.

"Come," a man whispered to him.

He followed as fast as his bad leg allowed.

As they moved through the trees, he thought of Todd Kinnear's slight limp, the one that had played a part in his 4-F classification. Wouldn't the two of them be a pair if they were walking together now?

"Hurry!"

The urgency in the single word chased away all thoughts except to keep going as fast as he possibly could.

Chapter 47

MONDAY, DECEMBER 21, 1942

Daisy was about to take a meatloaf from the oven when a fluttering sensation caused her to stop still. Her hands went to her belly where she felt the rounding beneath her skirt. The bump wasn't large, and it was easily hidden beneath the dresses and skirts she wore. But it was noticeable to her. Todd had noticed it too. Not that he'd said so. It was more in the way she caught him looking at her sometimes.

It's time to tell my family.

The thought caused a different type of flutter in her stomach. She closed her eyes and forced herself to inhale slowly and exhale the same way. She did it again and again until she felt the tension leave her. Then she opened her eyes. At the same moment, the front door opened. Jupiter rose from the bed of blankets Daisy had made for him near the back door and trotted into the living room.

"I'm home!" Todd called, the way he always did.

A smile tugged at the corners of her mouth. There was something comforting about the sound of his voice at the end of the workday.

"I'm in here. Dinner's about ready." She turned to the oven, hoping those extra few minutes lost in thought hadn't burned the main course.

"Smells good. I'll wash up and be right there."

The top of the meatloaf was a little dark but not burnt. She set the pan on the cooling rack before removing the baked potatoes from the oven. By the time Todd entered the kitchen, Jupiter on his heels, their dinner was on the table.

"Anything I can do to help?"

"No. Just take your seat."

Over the past two months, more of the awkwardness had eased between them. Especially, it seemed, at dinner time. Todd never failed to offer to help. He never failed to compliment her cooking. And he seemed able to tell when she wanted to talk and when she preferred silence. Did he know how much she appreciated his many small kindnesses to her? She hoped so.

Tonight she steered the conversation to work at the factory. Eventually, she asked about Roy Jamison.

"He seems to be doing better. No drinking at work, as far as I can tell. No sign that he's spent his lunch hour in a bar. He's grieving, but he's dealing with it better."

"Does he have a pastor who can provide comfort and counsel?"

"Not that he's mentioned. He's never talked about church."

"You could ask him and his wife to join us for the Christmas Eve service."

Todd reached across the table to touch the back of her hand. "You wouldn't mind?"

"Of course I wouldn't mind."

"Then I'll pass along the invitation to Roy tomorrow. And just to be sure she knows about it, I'll call Mrs. Jamison."

Daisy placed her fork on her empty plate. "There's something else we need to do."

Todd's eyebrows rose in question.

"It's time." She placed her right hand on her stomach. "It's time to tell my family that I'm expecting."

He didn't smile, but the look he gave her was filled with tenderness and compassion.

"I think . . . I think we should do it Christmas Day, when we're at their house for dinner."

Todd nodded. "Whatever you think is best."

She lowered her gaze. "It won't be long before they'll know I'm more than two months pregnant. Perhaps I can disguise it another couple of months."

He was silent.

"Are you prepared?" She looked up again. "For them to know I was pregnant when we eloped?"

"I've been preparing for it since the day I asked you to marry me."

Sadness pricked her heart. He hadn't asked her to marry him. Not the usual way, at any rate. In actuality, he'd offered an escape route. He hadn't proposed so much as he'd rescued.

"It'll be all right, Daisy. We'll weather whatever comes."

Sometimes, when she was cleaning house or planning a meal or mending clothes, it was easy to pretend that she'd married Todd because that was what she'd wanted. Sometimes she could almost believe she was happy to be his wife and eager to have his baby.

Only she wasn't truly his wife, as others believed, and the baby she carried wasn't his. That truth always brought her imaginary life crumbling down around her ankles.

She swallowed threatening tears and gave her head a little toss. "Yes. We'll weather whatever comes."

Chapter 48

PRESENT DAY—MARCH

About ten minutes remained in Brianna's English class when her phone vibrated. A quick glance made her smile. Greg! She moved the phone to her lap to read the text.

> In parking lot. Will take you home.

She answered with a thumbs up before closing her laptop and preparing to make a quick exit the instant the professor stopped talking.

One thing she'd learned about Greg in the six weeks she'd known him: he wasn't fond of either texting or chatting on the phone. Sometimes he went days without contacting her or responding to one of her texts. His lengthy silences sent her into the pit of despair. But all it took was one text from him, and her feelings soared to the heights again. It was exhausting. Wonderful and terrible at the same time.

Was it like this for everyone? When a girl met that certain special someone, did she always feel these crazy highs and lows? If only she had someone to talk to about it. She couldn't ask Hannah. Her best friend seemed to have a growing distrust for Greg Truman. As for Adam, she couldn't bring it up with him. For one thing, he was a guy. Plus, now that she believed he wanted more than friendship, she would feel awkward talking about Greg. She supposed she could mention him to GeeGee again, but even that felt wrong. Her great-grandmother would want to know more about his character. What more did Brianna have to say about that? She only knew him slightly better than the last time her great-grandmother asked.

She glanced at the time on her phone. Still five minutes before the hour. Would the professor ever stop talking?

As if in answer, her instructor said, "That's it for today. Don't forget your paper is due to be uploaded no later than Sunday night."

Brianna scooped up her bag and headed for the door. A moment later she was plunged into the stream of students in the hallways. She flowed along with them until she reached the main exit. As soon as she stepped outside, a strong March wind pushed her sideways, and she paused to catch her balance while looking for Greg's familiar truck. She finally found it off to her left. Greg had taken the last handicapped space on that side of the building. She could almost hear what Hannah would say: *"How thoughtless."* But he was only there for a few minutes. Just until she found him. It wasn't a crime. Someone who needed that parking space could have it in no time at all.

She hurried toward him, smiling when she knew he'd caught sight of her. As she got closer, Greg motioned for her to go to the passenger door, and she did so.

"I didn't expect to see you," she said as she got in. The truth was she never knew what to expect when it came to Greg, but she wouldn't say that to him. It might sound like a complaint.

"Thought I'd surprise you."

"You did."

He turned the key to start the engine. "I've got another surprise." He glanced at her, then focused on backing the truck out of the space.

"What?"

"It's about spring break. What are your plans?" He checked both ways, then pulled out of the lot, heading for the main thoroughfare.

"I don't have any plans. I'll just hang with friends, I guess, or do nothing at all."

"Sounds boring."

"Does it?"

"Do you ski?"

"Yes. I'm not great, but it's fun when I get to go."

"Then let's go skiing. You and me."

"I'd like that. Bogus usually has good snow conditions this time of year. Even into April."

"I was thinking more of a spring-break vacation. I've heard Brundage Mountain is great, and I was able to get a time-share in McCall."

"For the two of us?" The question came out in a near whisper.

"Yeah." He grinned as he glanced over at her. "There's two bedrooms, plus the living area and kitchen. All very respectable."

Her parents would never approve of such an arrangement, even with separate bedrooms, but telling Greg would make her sound like a child. She wasn't a child. She could make her own decisions. They'd been alone in his parents' home for that movie and nothing untoward had happened. He'd acted the gentleman the whole time. They'd kissed, but nothing else. Not really. What could it hurt to spend a few days of spring break with him?

"The place has a heated pool and a hot tub. So when we're not skiing, we can kick back and relax. What do you think, Brianna?"

"For the whole week?" Her voice sounded small in her own ears.

He laughed. "No. I couldn't afford a whole week. I've got the place for three nights. We can drive up on Monday, ski on Tuesday and Wednesday, then drive home on Thursday. If we want, we could even get in a few runs on our last day before driving back to Boise.

I've got the time-share already. You'd have to pay for your own ski pass, and we can share the cost of groceries. Sound good?"

"Sounds like fun, but I'm not sure I can."

Greg pulled into her subdivision. "Don't you want to spend the time with me?" The look he cast in her direction was filled with disappointment.

"You know I do," she answered quickly. And she did. She wanted to go more than she could say.

"Then let's do it."

"Okay." The word made her feel breathless. "Okay, I'll go."

Chapter 49

FRIDAY, DECEMBER 25, 1942

Todd awoke on Christmas morning with a knot in his belly. Tension had been building all week, ever since Daisy told him it was time her family knew she was pregnant. It wasn't telling her family about the baby that worried him. Today would be okay. There would be congratulations and celebration. But this would begin the countdown to the moment when they realized Daisy had lied to them. That Todd had lied to them. That's what bothered him. That's what had his gut in knots. He preferred to be an honest man, but he'd chosen to live a lie because of this unborn child, because he wanted to shelter and protect Daisy and her baby.

He got out of bed and put on his robe and slippers. Then he headed for the kitchen, pausing long enough to plug in the lights on the Christmas tree. He hadn't bothered with a tree in the years after his mom died when he'd lived in this house alone. He'd hung a wreath on his door and set out his mom's favorite Christmas candles, but he'd done without a tree. This tree had been Daisy's idea, and he was glad she'd suggested it. It brightened the living room and lifted his spirits.

Humming a Christmas tune, he entered the kitchen. Before

long, coffee was percolating on the stove. Because of rationing, Todd didn't drink coffee every day, but on Christmas morning he could treat himself.

"Merry Christmas."

He turned toward the sound of Daisy's voice. She stood in the kitchen doorway, wearing a robe and slippers like him, her hair delightfully disheveled. "Merry Christmas," he replied.

"You're up early." She pushed hair off her forehead.

"Guess it's the kid in me. Wanted to see if Santa came."

She smiled. "Did he?"

"Forgot to check after I plugged in the lights. Wanted coffee more than anything else."

"Well, I think Santa did come in the night. I saw a package under the tree with your name on it."

And he'd thought he would be the one to surprise her. But she hadn't seemed to notice the small box he'd stuck between the branches of the tree. So his surprise might still work.

He remembered another Christmas morning, back before his dad died. Daisy had been eight years old that year, as he recalled, and Santa had brought her a brand-new bike. A bright-red bike with a basket and a bell. Despite a dusting of snow on the ground and frigid temperatures, she'd been out on the sidewalk as the sun came up, riding around the block, the bell ringing. Todd had gone out to the front yard to watch her sail by. He remembered how her joy seemed to radiate all around her, making him feel joyful too.

She still makes me feel that way.

He wanted to pull her into his embrace and kiss her. Really kiss her. No light brushing of his lips on hers, a show for the sake of others, like he'd done at their wedding. He wanted to kiss her all for himself. He wanted to taste her, to drink her in.

"Oh." A look of surprise crossed her face, followed by a smile as her hands went to her stomach.

Despite her smile, he felt alarmed. "Are you all right?"

"Yes. I just . . . I felt the baby move. It . . . It happened the other day, too, but I wasn't as sure that's what it was. I'm sure now."

"Is it like a kick?" He stared at her abdomen, her hands folded over her belly.

"No. It's more like a . . . like a flutter. Like butterfly wings maybe."

"'For thou didst form my inward parts,'" Todd whispered. The verse had been repeating in his mind and heart for weeks, and now he spoke them aloud. "'Thou didst cover me in my mother's womb. I will give thanks unto thee; for I am fearfully and wonderfully made.'"

Tears glittered in Daisy's eyes, and he couldn't resist the need to hold her any longer. He stepped forward and drew her close to him, resting his cheek on the top of her head.

"Think of that, Daisy. God is forming this baby's inward parts right now, inside of you. This child is fearfully and wonderfully made, and God loves him. Or her. God loves your baby even more than we do."

One of her tears tickled his skin as it slid down from his collarbone to a place beneath his robe and pajama top. While he couldn't kiss her the way he wanted, he could—and did—kiss the top of her head. He heard her draw a shaky breath before she withdrew from his embrace. Reluctantly, he let her go.

"Your coffee's ready," she said softly.

"You're right." He cleared his throat as he turned away. "I'd better take it off the burner before it boils over."

"Jupiter and I will wait for you by the tree."

Alone in the kitchen, Todd leaned his hands against the counter, his head bowed, wondering at all the emotions that swirled inside of him. He'd always liked Daisy, and last summer, he'd admitted to himself that he'd felt a growing attraction to her. But for some reason he hadn't expected to . . . to desire her. Not yet. Not now. Not when she carried another man's child.

But he did desire her. He desired her and . . . and—

I'm falling in love with her.

No. Not falling. Had fallen.

Todd Kinnear loved his wife.

A little before noon, Todd and Daisy left their home through the back door, Jupiter leading the way. Todd wore the new gloves Daisy had given him, and she wore the lovely cross necklace he'd given her. On the surface they looked like any other young, happily married couple who'd enjoyed their first Christmas morning together. But Daisy knew it was a charade, one that she would have to live out for the rest of her life. And soon she would play her part in the next scene in this small drama of theirs.

"Merry Christmas!" her mom exclaimed as they entered through the back door.

As soon as they shed their coats, Daisy was wrapped in her mom's embrace. Todd received the same treatment a moment later.

In the doorway to the kitchen, her dad held up a crystal cup. "How about some eggnog, you two?"

Todd answered, "Yes, please." Then he looked at Daisy, and she nodded. "Make that two, Carl."

The two men moved out of view.

"Where's Lillian?" Daisy asked.

"Upstairs. She had letters to write."

Daisy wondered who the recipients might be. With Brandan missing in action, who did her sister have to write?

Her mom said, "We invited the Gallaghers to join us for Christmas dinner, but they said they preferred a quiet day." She drew a breath and released it on a sigh. "My heart breaks every time I see them."

"Mine too."

"I've encouraged Lillian to spend more time with Brandan's parents and brothers, but she's so busy with her job at the base and with her . . . new friends." Concern drew her mom's eyebrows together. "I thought it would be good for her to return to work, but now I'm not so sure."

"I've hardly seen her for weeks, except at church." *And she doesn't speak to me when we're together.*

From all appearances, Lillian was no longer upset about Daisy's marriage to Todd. In fact, she seemed to have forgotten her entire family right along with forgetting Brandan, all of them replaced by the girls who worked with her at the base. And some of the airmen too.

She glanced up, as if she could look into her sister's bedroom from the kitchen. Was Lillian writing to other airmen, to men she'd met on the base? Could she have forgotten her feelings for Brandan already?

Daisy tried to shake off that alarming suspicion. "Can I help with anything, Mom?"

"No, darling. Dinner is almost ready. Go get that cup of eggnog from your dad and relax with your husband."

"If you're sure."

"I'm positive." Her mom gave a little shooing motion with her hands.

The dining room table appeared festive with its red candles, evergreen branches, and gold napkin rings. A set of Mr. and Mrs. Santa Claus salt-and-pepper shakers sat in the middle of the table. The best china—which only came out on Thanksgiving, Christmas, and Easter—completed each place setting.

"Everything looks pretty, Mom."

"Thank you, dear."

Daisy moved through the dining room and into the living room. Her dad stood near the tree with a cup of eggnog in his hand. He held it out to her.

"Here you go." He smiled as she took the cup from his hand.

"Thanks." She took a sip. "It's good, Dad."

"Christmas dinner wouldn't feel right without a cup of eggnog," he replied.

Daisy looked at Todd, who stood near the sofa, cup in hand. She felt a strange tug-of-war inside her. The familiarity of her girlhood home wanted her to stay near her dad and the Christmas tree where all the well-known ornaments hung from the branches. But the look on her husband's face made her want to stand beside him, to show themselves united on this day when Christians around the world celebrated the birth of a child. As if to help make up her mind, that fluttering sensation returned to her belly, and she moved across the room to Todd.

Her mother came into the living room. Taking hold of the banister, she called up the stairs, "Lillian, come down! Daisy and Todd are here, and dinner is ready to go on the table."

"I'll be down in a minute."

Daisy drank the rest of her eggnog. "I should help Mom. Thanks, Dad." She held out the cup toward Todd. He took it, and she returned to the kitchen.

Mother and daughter fell into a comfortable routine, carrying food to the dining room table. They had served many Christmas dinners in this same way, and Daisy knew where the platter of ham should go—on her father's right—and where each serving bowl should be set around the cheery table. Before they were finished, Todd came to light the tapered candles, and Daisy realized that he had done the same at more than one Christmas gathering.

As if knowing the work was done, Lillian appeared in the archway to the dining room. "Sorry I took so long." She smiled at the room in general as she went to her usual place. "Merry Christmas, everybody."

While Daisy's dad held out the chair for her mom, Todd did the same for Daisy, then went around the table to repeat the action for

Lillian. As soon as the men were settled, her dad held out his hands to his daughters. The chain continued from Daisy to Todd to her mother. Her dad led them in a traditional blessing, and before long, they were enjoying their Christmas feast.

At the end of the meal, before Daisy's mom could rise and begin clearing the table, Todd reached for Daisy's hand.

"Daisy and I have an announcement," he said, drawing everyone's attention.

Daisy felt the food in her stomach turn, and her mouth went dry.

Todd looked at her, and she nodded.

"We're going to have a baby," he said.

Her mom squealed with joy. Her dad leaned back in his chair, wearing a stunned expression. And Lillian? Daisy wasn't sure what she saw in her sister's expression. Was it resentment? Disinterest? Lillian stared down at her plate and moved the last bits of food with her fork, as if drawing a picture with it.

"Oh my goodness." Her mom got up and came to give Daisy a hug. "We hoped we'd have a grandchild one day. We didn't expect it to be so soon."

That all-too-familiar feeling of guilt sluiced through Daisy. The first Abbott grandchild would arrive sooner than her mom thought. About nine and a half weeks early. And then the looks on her parents' faces would be something very different from what they were now.

Chapter 50

PRESENT DAY–MARCH

The restaurant buzzed with voices as Daisy rolled her walker toward the table where the hostess awaited her. Brianna and her mother, Jennifer, followed right behind Daisy, no doubt made impatient by her slow speed. But there was nothing to be done about that.

At the table, she dropped onto the nearest chair with a smile. "Isn't this lovely?" She glanced around. "I don't believe I've been here before."

"Dad brought me here for my eighteenth birthday," Jennifer said as she settled onto the chair opposite Daisy. "So it's always been a favorite of mine."

Daisy did a quick mental calculation. Or as quick as was possible at her age. Jennifer had been born when her father, Bobby, was thirty. That she knew without doubt. Which meant Jennifer had turned eighteen . . . *oh, my goodness* . . . nearly thirty years ago.

Brianna broke into her thoughts. "Mom and Dad brought me here after my graduation from high school."

"Well, it seems I'm the only one who didn't even know about it." Daisy looked at her granddaughter. "Is this a special occasion?"

Jennifer smiled. "Not really. We wanted to thank you for all the time you've given to Brianna for her history assignment."

Their server arrived with ice water.

"Thank you, dear," Daisy said.

The girl—probably no older than Brianna—smiled at her. "Do you need a moment to look at the menu?" Her gaze moved to the other two at the table.

"I know what I want," Jennifer answered, "but my grandmother will need to look at the menu."

"Okay. I'll be back in a few." The server moved off to another table.

Daisy opened her menu but looked at her granddaughter. "What are you having, Jennifer?" After she answered, Daisy repeated the question to her great-granddaughter. She considered their choices, but in the end, she decided on a French-dip sandwich.

After the server returned and they'd placed their orders, Daisy said to Jennifer, "I used to make French dips often when your grandfather was alive. They were one of his favorites."

"As I recall, you loved to cook for Grandpa."

"Yes." She smiled, times in her kitchen rushing through her memory. "I did. But he was an easy man to please. I was fortunate in that regard."

"Were you a good cook, GeeGee?" Brianna asked.

Daisy nodded. "I think so. I was often told so, anyway. I began helping my mother in the kitchen when I was a young girl, and she taught me well." She laughed softly. "It was certainly a challenge to be a good cook during the war."

"Because of the rationing?"

She nodded again. "And shortages. Even some things that weren't rationed were in short supply. I never knew for certain what I'd find on the store shelves when I went shopping. And it wasn't just food items. Cigarettes, for example, were difficult to come by. Smoking was a popular thing to do in the forties, but 60 percent of the cigarettes made in America went to our GIs, which meant civilians often went without. Better for their health, as it turned out."

"Did you smoke, GeeGee?"

"Good gracious, no." She wrinkled her nose. "Filthy habit. But I had friends and some family who did. Heavens, there were doctors who *suggested* smoking for various ailments. To calm oneself and other such things. They didn't understand the damage it did to a person's health." She pointed a finger at Brianna, smiling to soften the gesture. "Don't be foolish with your health, my dear."

"You don't have to worry about that," the girl answered. "I think it's a filthy habit too."

Daisy saw a great deal of Brianna's grandfather in the girl's expression. Bobby had been a headstrong boy, so determined to get his own way. While he—and his sister, Elizabeth—had been the joy of Daisy's life, Bobby had tested her patience to the absolute limits, especially during his teen years. Did Brianna do the same thing to Jennifer?

A silly thought, she supposed. All children tested their parents at one point or another.

She reached across the corner of the table to pat Brianna's hand. "Wise girl. Keep your head about you, and you'll do well."

Chapter 51

THURSDAY, DECEMBER 31, 1942

The Starlite was packed on New Year's Eve, and Lillian hadn't been without a dance partner all evening. But as the hour neared midnight, she felt an urge to escape the crowded dance floor and the airman who had led her in a rousing jitterbug. She didn't know him at all beyond as a dance partner. Still, she had a niggling sensation that he would want to kiss her when the clock struck twelve, and she wasn't interested. There was an unhappy tightness in her chest at the mere thought of it.

She hadn't been kissed by any other guy since her first date with Brandan. More than five years, and her lips had only touched his in that time. There was a part of her that wanted to explore what it would be like. Another part of her was afraid nobody else could make her feel the way Brandan had.

"Excuse me," she said to the airman, then immediately worked her way through the crowd to the table where her friend Patty sat, guarding the coats and purses. "Have you danced at all?"

Patty shook her head.

"Are you ready to leave?"

A look of relief washed over Patty's face as she nodded again. "Yes."

This was the first time Lillian had invited her good friend to come along with her, Rose, and June. But asking her appeared to have been a mistake. Patty wasn't having a good time.

"All right." Lillian reached for her coat. "We can go."

"I don't want to spoil your fun."

"You won't. I'm danced out." She grabbed one of the party hats in the center of the table. "But let's not miss out on these." She put it on her head. With elastic in short supply, this one had to be tied on with string. She didn't care. It wasn't a fashion statement.

The girls made their way through the throng of people. The smells of warm bodies and various perfumes mingled in the air. It wasn't a pleasant odor. Lillian welcomed the frigid night that greeted them as they stepped outside. She was about to loop her arm through Patty's when a voice stopped her.

"Lillian Abbott! Is that you?"

She turned to see Susan Malloy, an old friend from high school.

"Gracious. I haven't seen you two in ages." Susan glanced at Patty, including her in the comment.

"I thought you moved to California," Lillian replied.

"I did. To Los Angeles. It's heavenly there. I only tolerate this cold weather to visit my parents for Christmas and New Year's." She pulled her gorgeous fur coat closer around her. Lillian suspected the action wasn't as much for needed warmth as to draw attention to it. Susan had never shied away from flaunting her family's affluence, not even during the worst years of the Depression.

Susan reached out and put a hand on Lillian's arm, her expression softening. "I heard about Brandan. I'm sorry. But were you two still an item when he left? Someone told me he was here"—she glanced up at the Starlite sign—"just before he shipped out, and he came without you." She leaned closer, lowering her voice. "He was drinking and left with a girl, weaving all over the place. I'll bet it was Betty Lou. She always had her eye on him. Such a tramp."

A hundred different thoughts and emotions seemed to explode inside Lillian as Susan spoke.

Patty—dear, sweet Patty—spoke up. "It's almost midnight, Susan. You'd better get inside if you don't want to miss the countdown."

"What about you?"

"We're headed home," Patty replied. "And it's much too cold to stand here chatting. it was good to see you, Susan. Happy New Year, and have a safe trip back to California." She drew Lillian away as she spoke. As soon as they were out of hearing, darkness closing around them, she added, "Lillian, don't you pay any attention to her. Susan doesn't know what she's talking about. Brandan wouldn't ever come to the Starlite without you, and you know it."

Lillian loved her friend for saying what she did. But Patty didn't know how awful Brandan's last week at home had been, how Lillian had refused to go anywhere with him, how she hadn't even taken his call on the Friday before he left. Was it possible he'd come here without her? Was it possible he'd chosen to leave with Betty Lou Southern? And if so, what had happened next?

> I messed up. I hurt you, and I never meant to do that. I love you, Lill.

The words from his one and only letter from England seemed to burn in her chest. She'd thought he meant only that he'd messed up by not proposing, by not seeing that she was right, that he'd hurt her by leaving without putting a ring on her finger.

But what if that wasn't what he'd meant? And did it make any difference now that he was missing in action?

Chapter 52

WEDNESDAY, MARCH 10, 1943

"Honey!" Daisy's mom called. "Are you napping?"

Smiling, Daisy left the baby's room. "No, I'm not napping."

Her mom waited in the kitchen. "Good, because I had to come over right away. I couldn't wait a minute. Look at what the ladies in my church circle sent to you." From a canvas bag she poured out baby clothes and diapers onto the table. "Mrs. Humble knitted this yellow sweater. Isn't it adorable? And Grace Henry's daughter passed along lots of her baby things. She says she's done having kids, that four are enough." After a light laugh, she kept going, picking up various items and telling who'd given each one until all were accounted for.

"Mom, this is wonderful. Your friends are so kind."

"They all hope you'll become part of the circle after the baby's born."

"I'll see, Mom. I . . . I imagine I might be a bit busy at first."

"Of course you will." Her mom sat on one of the chairs. "But that won't last forever. You'll want to spend time with other wives and mothers. We only meet once a month, and the fellowship is good for every one of us."

"Someday." Daisy reached for the delicate yellow sweater. It was so tiny. Would she really be responsible for the little human being who would wear it? What if she wasn't able? What if she was a horrible mother?

"Mrs. Humble says she wants to host a tea in your honor before the baby comes. Possibly late June. Her flower gardens are exquisite in June."

Daisy closed her eyes. June would be too late. She would have the baby in her arms by then. But she couldn't tell Mom that.

"Are you sleeping all right, dear? You look tired."

"I'm sleeping fine." She put down the sweater. "Why don't I make us a cup of tea?"

"Sounds lovely, but let me make it. You sit there and rest for a moment."

Daisy obliged. Her mom was right. She *was* tired. The baby had been more and more active recently, and his busiest hours for kicking and changing position were in the wee hours of the morning. But Daisy couldn't complain to anyone except Todd and the doctor because she wasn't supposed to be seven months along. And she hadn't bothered to tell either of them anyway. They were men. They couldn't possibly understand. Oh, how she longed for a female confidante.

With the kettle heating on the stove, her mom returned to the table. In unison they began to fold and stack the clothes. Not long after they were finished, the kettle whistled.

"You fix the tea." Daisy stood. "I'll put these things away."

"I could do that for you before I go."

"No thanks, Mom. I've got it."

The truth was she didn't want anyone else going into the baby's room. Because, of course, it was her bedroom too. Not that it was obvious she slept there. It looked like nothing more than a spare bed ready for a guest. The baby's crib, dresser, and changing table sat against the opposite wall, leaving not much room to turn around. This was definitely a room for a baby, but Daisy still worried someone would see something out of place and guess the truth.

She gathered the folded clothes to her chest.

Living a lie was exhausting. Did it improve her life to put off the truth for another time? She didn't know. Perhaps it only proved she was a coward.

In the baby's room she opened the dresser and began putting all of the gifted items into drawers. The kindness of the women from church suddenly overwhelmed her. Tears sprang to her eyes and slipped down her cheeks. She didn't deserve their generosity or goodwill.

I'm a pretender.

"Tea's ready!" her mom called.

Daisy wiped away the tears, pasted on a smile, and returned to the kitchen.

Her mom sat at the table, a cup held between her hands. "This is nice. Spending some time in the afternoon with my daughter. Our house is so quiet during the week, with your father and sister both at work and you gone from home. There isn't enough for me to do anymore." She cast a glance in the direction of Jupiter, who slept in his bed in the corner. "Even the dog deserted me."

"Nobody deserted you, Mom."

"It feels that way. You'll see. In another eighteen or nineteen years, your son or daughter will go off to college or work or get married, and you'll be all alone in the house. I told your father that I should get a job. Women are needed everywhere. Perhaps I could go to work out at the base with your sister."

Daisy looked into her teacup. Lillian wouldn't like it if their mom joined her at Gowen Field. She would feel spied upon.

"But I've never done any kind of clerical work," Mom continued, "so I doubt the army would want me there. Perhaps Mr. Armstrong still needs help at the drugstore. Do you think I could do that sort of work?"

"Mom, you could do anything you put your mind to. The women who're building airplanes and battleships today never did it before our country needed them. The women who work for Todd never made compasses before, either, but they're doing it now. Anybody would be lucky to have you work for them."

"Thank you, dear. I needed a pep talk."

Odd, wasn't it? Daisy had never considered that her mom might want to do something besides raise her daughters, clean the house, and prepare her family's supper every night. If not for the Depression, Daisy might have gone to college after finishing high school. If not for getting pregnant, she might be riding the bus with Lillian out to the air base each morning. So why hadn't she considered that her mom might want something more to do?

Will that be me someday? Will I want something I never had?

Like love.

In February President Roosevelt had ordered that all war plants maintain a minimum of a forty-eight-hour work week. The order hadn't impacted Kinnear Canning since their workers already worked six days a week, eight hours a day.

If his employees were exhausted by the schedule, Todd couldn't tell when he looked into the lunchroom a little after noon. The women were engaged in lively—and somewhat loud—conversations while they ate the sandwiches they'd brought from home. The few men still working for Todd, the ones who hadn't left factory work for service in the military, had gone elsewhere to eat. Probably outdoors to enjoy the pleasant weather—sunshine, no wind, and sixty degrees. A welcome change from winter.

He moved along the corridor but slowed his steps when he saw Carl waiting for him with a boy of about eleven or twelve. The kid had been crying. He'd dried his cheeks, but his eyes were still red. That was apparent even before Todd reached them.

His gaze met Carl's.

"This is Peter Mason. He's Teresa Lewis's brother." Carl placed his hand on the boy's shoulder, a protective gesture. "He's come to take her home."

Todd didn't need further explanation. Someone close to Teresa Lewis had died. He pictured the young woman, the place where she worked on the factory floor. She was a year older than Daisy and lived at home with her parents because her husband was serving in the Pacific. Her older brother was with the army in North Africa the last Todd heard.

Following his own father's example, Todd had made it a point to get to know his employees, from the janitor to the manager and every position in between. The practice had served him well. The people who worked for him were loyal and dedicated. But it wasn't as easy with the country at war, for it meant Todd shared their pains as well as their joys.

He looked down at the boy. "I believe I saw your sister in the lunchroom. Let me take you to her." He gave a nod to Carl, then turned, placing his hand on Peter's shoulder the way Carl had moments before.

He shortened his stride, not hurrying the kid on an unpleasant errand. When they reached the doorway to the lunchroom, he stopped and Peter stopped beside him. Conversations hadn't slowed when he'd looked into the room a short while ago, but they did now. It took mere seconds for the room to grow quiet, all eyes turning in Todd's and Peter's direction. They knew, just as he'd known when he saw the boy, that bad news awaited someone.

After a short hesitation, Teresa rose and moved away from the table, her eyes locked on her brother. "Peter?"

"You need to come home, Terri. We got a telegram." The kid crushed his sister in a hug and started to cry again.

All color drained from her cheeks. "Who . . . Who is it?"

"It's Donny." The answer was muffled as Peter's face pressed against his sister's chest. "He . . . he's dead."

Donny. The brother in Africa.

Teresa looked up at Todd. Her eyes glittered, but she blinked back tears. Her tongue moistened quivering lips. He sensed her fighting for control, a determination not to let her little brother see her crumble too.

"Go home," he told her. "Your shift is covered. Let us know how you're doing when you can."

She nodded, mouthing *Thank you*. Then she guided her brother past Todd and down the corridor.

Todd looked at the rest of the silent women in the room. He could almost hear their thoughts as they silently prayed for their men, for their loved ones who were fighting somewhere on the other side of the world.

For the first time, a feeling of relief washed over Todd, thankful he wasn't in the military. Not now. Not ever. The reason wasn't because he didn't want to fight. He still wished he could. But he was thankful Daisy would never need to imagine the worst happening to him. She wouldn't have to fear the arrival of a message from the adjutant general the way the other women in this room were fearing it now.

Then again, she'd already experienced that pain because of Brandan Gallagher. Would she suffer the same way if Todd was the one who went missing?

Chapter 53

PRESENT DAY–MARCH

At church the next Sunday—the first Sunday of spring break—Brianna sat with her usual group of friends. Once again, Greg had missed the service. But it wasn't his absence that distracted Brianna from listening to the pastor's sermon. It was the guilt she felt for the lie she'd told her parents. She'd made up a school friend who had invited Daisy to join her and her parents in McCall. She'd needed a reason to be gone for a few days. She'd needed a reason to take her skis, boots, poles, and winter clothes with her. The lie held just enough truth that she hoped it wouldn't trip her up.

It's their fault that I have to lie to them. I'm twenty years old. I shouldn't have to get their permission. I shouldn't have to make up excuses.

True enough. But she did live with her parents, so she did have to abide by their rules. And she knew what both her mom and dad would think of her going off for a few days alone with a boyfriend.

She frowned. Was Greg her boyfriend? Sometimes she thought so. Sometimes she wasn't so sure. But if he wasn't, why would he ask her to go away with him? Why would he want to take her to McCall?

Wasn't there romance involved in spending several days together while on spring break? When they returned to Boise, he would definitely be her boyfriend. Wasn't that a good thing?

The trickiest part of her plans had been how to leave the house without Greg coming to get her. But as chance would have it, her mother was taking a friend to a doctor's appointment in the early afternoon. It had given Brianna the perfect window of time for Greg to pick her up. The two-hour drive, plus a stop for groceries, would get them to the condo right about check-in time. Perfect.

And then we'll have the evening together.

Her stomach tumbled at the thought. A whole evening, just the two of them. And not only one evening. Three. Three nights in a condo alone.

Am I crazy to go with him?

Hannah would tell her yes. Yes, it was crazy. Hannah would remind her of things like purity. But it wasn't as if anyone would even know Brianna had gone away with Greg, and she didn't plan to sleep with him. She knew what was okay and what wasn't. She'd grown up in church. She was a Christian. So was Greg. Together they would make the right choices.

A new slide went up on the screen, and it drew Brianna's gaze as Pastor Moore read the words aloud.

> But if any of you lacks wisdom, let him ask of God, who gives to all generously and without reproach, and it will be given to him. But he must ask in faith without any doubting, for the one who doubts is like the surf of the sea, driven and tossed by the wind.

She didn't listen to what the pastor said next. Instead, she stared at the words on the screen as a softer voice seemed to speak into her heart, asking her if she lacked wisdom. There was more the small voice wanted to say to her, but she closed her eyes, at the same time closing her ears. She had made her decision. The plans were in motion. All would be well.

Chapter 54

FRIDAY, MARCH 12, 1943

Brandan turned his face toward the sun, enjoying the warmth on his skin. It seemed he hadn't known true warmth in months.

Five months.

Five months in France through a harsh, bitter winter.

Focusing once more, he followed the Frenchman along a narrow street to a new location, his bad leg throbbing with each step he took. He'd lost track of the number of places he'd stayed in while avoiding the Nazis—a night here, a week there—and he was well aware of the risk each person involved had taken in order to keep him safe. And what was he to them? Nothing. Nobody. Just an American pilot from Boise, Idaho, a place they'd never heard of. He wasn't important in the big scheme of things. They would all be safer if they let him be caught and made a prisoner of war. Instead, they continued to put their own lives in danger to try to save his.

Five months of it. Five months of hiding, of fear, of cold, of hunger, of pain.

How much longer could he stay out of sight? How much longer could he evade the enemy? According to the French, the Allies were no closer to invading Europe than when he'd crashed his plane. Could he manage to hide for another five months? A year? Longer?

His guide stopped before a door, looked up and down the street, then rapped twice, then again. The door opened, and the Frenchman led him into a dimly lit interior. The air smelled of cooked cabbage, and his stomach growled, despite his dislike of the vegetable. Anything in his stomach would be welcome. Daily rations for the people in this country were hardly enough to keep a bird alive. Yet they shared their food with him. Their generosity humbled him, and he swore that if he managed to get out of France alive, he would do his best to be generous to others. So help him, he would.

"Welcome," a young woman said in a thick accent.

She reminded Brandan of Lillian. Maybe it was the color of her hair or the fullness of her lips. Or maybe she looked nothing at all like Lillian. It was hard to remember for sure. He had no photo of the woman he loved. Before a mission, pilots and crew had to leave all of their personal effects with the purser. They weren't allowed to keep personal items with them in case of capture. He'd made it out of the downed plane with his aid box—he didn't remember how—and some of the things from that box were still with him, although well hidden, including the remaining francs he'd discovered in a red purse in the survival kit. But there wasn't anything tangible from home—no photos, no letters—and at times the lack of such items made him wonder if anything he remembered was true.

"This way." The woman motioned for him to follow, then led the way up a narrow staircase.

He was thankful they were headed up instead of down. Dank, dark cellars were the worst.

Chapter 55

SUNDAY, APRIL 18, 1943

Would Daisy ever again draw an easy breath or sleep through the night without having to go to the bathroom multiple times? Sometimes she feared not. Thankfully, for the purpose of her masquerade, she appeared smaller than many women in their final month of pregnancy. Dr. Hamilton said that wasn't cause for concern. She was young and healthy and so was the infant she carried.

If the baby came precisely on schedule—which everyone had said almost never happened—Daisy had less than three weeks before she would give birth. Some mothers at church had mentioned the first baby often took longer and not to be surprised if she went two weeks, even three weeks, over. Daisy hoped that would be true for her. But even another two or three weeks wouldn't be enough to continue the lie. Eventually, the truth would be revealed. The whispers would start, and people would look at her—and at her parents—in a different way. Daisy knew whatever was said, she deserved it. But she hated that her parents would have to shoulder her shame as well.

All this was going through her mind again as Daisy washed the last of the Sunday dinner dishes.

"Let's take a walk," Todd suggested as he dried a plate.

She considered begging off. A nap sounded ever so much more enjoyable. But maybe a walk first would make the nap even better. "Okay."

Her husband put away the last few items and closed the cupboard. "Do you want your sweater?" He moved as if to fetch it for her.

"No. It's lovely out. I don't need it."

He stopped and looked at her. "Are you sure?"

She nodded. "I'm sure."

As if understanding the conversation, Jupiter came to stand by Daisy.

"I'll get the leash," Todd said.

Daisy leaned over enough to stroke the dog's head. "He does so much for us," she whispered.

Jupiter wagged his tail.

"He made a poor bargain when he married me."

Todd stepped into the kitchen. "Did you say something?"

"Just talking to Jupiter."

Todd smiled, a tender look in his eyes, and her heart ached in response. For all of her stupid mistakes, for all of her sinful choices, God had blessed her with a caring husband. She didn't deserve his many kindnesses. They hadn't married for love. Only for necessity. Only because he wanted to help a childhood friend in desperate need. And yet, there were moments when she thought—

"Ready?" he asked.

"Yes." She swallowed. "Yes, I'm ready."

Outside, spring was in full display. Lawns had turned green. Flowers brightened beds along sidewalks and surrounding porches. Leaves in varying shades of green had unfurled in many trees while other late bloomers languished in their winter nakedness. The air was fresh with a touch of warmth, a promise of summer to come.

They'd walked for a couple of blocks when they saw several children playing. Two girls drew a hopscotch outline on the sidewalk with chalk while three boys constructed a building with interlocking blocks.

With his hand beneath her elbow, Todd guided Daisy onto the grass between sidewalk and street. "What's that going to be?" he asked the boys.

"A skyscraper." The kid—with curly red hair and freckles—held up one of three boxes. "Like that one." He pointed to a picture on the lid.

"Impressive." Todd leaned down and lowered his voice. "But don't you think it'll be hard to move out of people's way when you're finished?"

"Nah. We'll take it apart. We'll wanna build something else later."

As Todd straightened, he smiled at Daisy. "He's got a point. After you've built something, it's time to move on to the next thing."

Once past the children, they returned to the sidewalk.

"You like kids," Daisy said.

"Sure. What's not to like?"

She narrowed her eyes and tilted her head to look up at him. "I'm starting to believe you're a big kid yourself."

He laughed.

Something warm curled inside Daisy, for she knew Todd would be a good father to her baby.

But then she thought of Brandan. Even should he return from the war—which seemed unlikely after all this time—he must never know the truth. Everyone must believe Todd was the baby's father. To protect her child from being teased or rejected or called bad names, everyone must believe it.

For a moment, she seemed to hear Brandan whisper her name as he had on that fateful night that changed her life forever. She remembered the scents and sounds, could almost feel the summer breeze upon her skin, and she wanted to weep.

"Daisy?" Todd stopped and took hold of her upper arms with his hands, forcing her to face him. "Are you in pain? Is something wrong? Is it the baby?"

She shook her head, nodded, shook her head again.

One of his arms went around her back as he stepped to her side. "We'd better get you home."

"No. I'm fine. It's nothing."

"Are you sure?"

"I'm positive. Let's keep walking. It's too lovely outside. Besides, the exercise must be good for me. I breathe easier when I'm moving."

"Okay," he said, but his eyes showed his uncertainty.

How she wished she could take away Todd's concern. But what was there to say to him? She had no words of comfort to offer. She couldn't explain her feelings when she didn't understand them fully herself. She'd loved Brandan Gallagher from afar for years. She'd wanted him to love her. She'd given herself to him, despite knowing he belonged to her sister. Now she carried his baby while his fate remained a mystery.

What was she supposed to feel for Brandan now? Especially since she was married to another man. A good man. A decent and caring man who deserved more than she was ready to give him.

She turned away. "Maybe you're right. Let's go home."

Chapter 56

PRESENT DAY—MARCH

Brianna stared at the pile of clothing on the bench at the foot of her bed. It seemed a ridiculous amount for four days and three nights, but she needed to plan for almost anything. Other than skiing and swimming, what activities might there be? Greg hadn't been very clear in that regard. Would they dine in a nice restaurant? Would they go dancing somewhere? Would they attend a play or a movie? Did he like art shows? She hadn't a clue.

"We'll just do whatever," he'd said when asked.

She would need a dress in case they went dancing. She would want something to relax in. Several somethings, as she didn't want him to see her in the same outfit every day. She would need to be able to layer. Spring in the mountains could be freezing or sunny and warm. It might even be both while they were there.

In addition to the matter of clothes, there was makeup and hair products. And a book was always a good idea.

Her phone rang, and GeeGee's smiling face popped onto the screen. She considered ignoring it, then decided she couldn't. "Hi, GeeGee."

"Hello, dear. I was wondering if you might like to come over tomorrow. I found a couple of old scrapbooks that I thought might interest you for your history project."

"I'd love to see them, GeeGee, but I'm going to be out of town for a few days. It's spring break, and I'm getting away for some skiing with . . . friends."

Her great-grandmother was silent for a few moments before saying, "I hope you'll have fun. It's so warm here in the valley, it's difficult to imagine anywhere with snow."

"There's still plenty in the mountains." The guilty feelings from earlier that morning came back in a rush. Why did GeeGee have to call her now? She'd just begun to feel some excitement about the trip, and now she was second-guessing herself.

"Is Greg one of the friends?"

Brianna sank onto the side of her bed. Whether she said yes or no, she would be lying. Greg was going, and there weren't going to be multiple friends. Maybe it would be better to say no since she hadn't mentioned Greg to her mom. On the other hand, it felt even more wrong to tell her great-grandmother that she wouldn't be with him. "Yes," she answered at last.

"Do me a favor, Brianna."

"What's that?"

"Be very careful with your heart."

Defensiveness rose up. "What do you mean?"

"Only that, dear girl. Be careful."

She released a breath through her nose before saying, "I will."

Chapter 57

SATURDAY, MAY 22, 1943

Todd and Carl were quiet on their walk home from the factory on the fourth Saturday in May. It was the end of a long work week, and in addition to some supply foul-ups that put stress on fulfilling their government orders, two more women had received telegrams telling them that loved ones had been killed in action. Two more gold stars to hang in windows. Two more families in mourning.

"Try not to let it weigh on you," Carl said, breaking the silence.

Todd glanced at him, not surprised that his father-in-law had read his thoughts. "Annie Smith has three kids. The oldest one is five."

"I know. It's hard news. At least she's got her mother and mother-in-law to help with the little ones."

Todd thought of the Gallaghers, a family still waiting for answers. Still hoping despite no word of their son. Was it better to know or not to know? It was a question he'd wondered for many months.

Carl put a hand on Todd's shoulder. "It makes everyone anxious when one of those telegrams comes. The mood on the floor changes every time it happens."

"I guess we can be thankful that there's been good news on the war front for a change."

Todd didn't have to explain what he meant. Americans had recently learned of the end of the North African campaign and the capture of General von Arnim and other Axis officers in the Cape Bon Peninsula. And Winston Churchill's address to Congress, saying that Japan's war machine would not survive after the Allies defeated Hitler's armies, had shored up more than one flagging spirit in the nation.

The two men stopped at the walkway to Todd's home.

Carl said, "Try to rest tomorrow. Don't let thoughts of the factory spoil Sunday for you."

Todd nodded.

"Give Daisy my love. We'll see you at church in the morning."

"In the morning." Todd turned and headed for the front door. The moment he opened it, he called, "I'm home!" His usual greeting was met with silence. "Daisy?"

More silence, and then he thought he heard a sound coming from the baby's bedroom. The door was shut. Todd rapped on it softly, thinking Daisy might be napping.

He was about to turn toward his own room when he heard something again. Something like a gasp.

"Daisy?" He took a breath and opened the door.

She stood beside the crib, gripping the headboard and leaning forward, staring at the floor.

"Daisy."

She looked up at last. "I think . . . I think it's time."

"'Time'?"

"To go to the hospital."

Two weeks. They'd made it a little over two weeks past the due date Dr. Hamilton had set. They'd hoped for more, but now the time had come. The baby was on its way. Todd's mind went momentarily numb. Another groan from Daisy brought him to his senses. "I'll get the car."

"Just take me with you." She had one hand on her lower back. With the other, she pointed. "We need to take that with me."

He saw the small suitcase beside the door and grabbed it. Then he went to Daisy and took hold of her arm. "You set the pace."

She took only a couple of steps before she stopped and bent forward again.

"Should I get your mom?"

"No!" She looked up at him in alarm. "No, I don't want her to know yet."

"Daisy, I think—"

"After the baby comes."

He disagreed with her decision—now, of all times, she should have her mother with her—but he kept his opinion to himself. He wanted to get her into the car and to the hospital.

"When did the pain start?" he asked as they got closer to the detached garage.

"This morning. After you left for work."

"Why didn't you call me?"

"I don't know. It didn't . . . It didn't seem that bad."

He released an exasperated breath as Jupiter moved in front of them, wagging his tail in excitement. "Get back. Stay." After the dog obeyed, Todd opened the door to the garage and helped Daisy through the opening. Before long, they were both in the car and on their way.

There was almost no traffic between their house and the hospital, and Todd was able to get there in under fifteen minutes. But those fifteen minutes felt like a thousand, especially every time Daisy released a moan or drew in a sharp breath. And he didn't draw a deep breath of his own until Daisy was seated in a wheelchair and on her way to the delivery room.

He managed to find the fathers' waiting room. Once there, he commenced pacing.

"Mr. Kinnear?"

He whirled toward the voice, his heart rat-a-tatting in his chest.

"Your wife is fine. She's dilating, and the doctor is on his way to the hospital. But you still may have several hours to wait, so don't be anxious if you don't hear anything for a while."

"Thanks."

"You might want to go to the cafeteria for some supper."

"That's all right. I'll wait here."

The nurse smiled at him—as she'd undoubtedly smiled at dozens of expectant fathers before him—then disappeared down the hallway on her silent white shoes.

Todd tried to settle on a chair, but it didn't last long. And the longer he paced, the more convinced he was that Daisy was wrong not to let her parents know she was in labor. Finally, he went in search of the pay phone.

Robert Carl Kinnear—named for Todd's and Daisy's fathers, respectively—entered the world at precisely 11:30 p.m., a healthy seven pounds two ounces. Sometime after midnight, once Daisy was settled into a hospital bed in the maternity ward, Todd was allowed to see her.

"Only a few minutes," the nurse told him in a hushed voice. "Your wife needs her sleep."

"Yes, ma'am. I understand." He moved across the room. When he reached the bed, he took hold of Daisy's hand. "How are you? It seemed to take forever."

"I'm fine. Only tired." She gave him a brief smile. "Have you seen him?"

He nodded. "I've seen him. He's . . . perfect."

"Perfect," she whispered.

Todd glanced around the large room. "No other mothers, I see."

"Not yet. It's like a private room for now. But the nurse said there are other women in labor, so I don't expect to be alone for long." Her eyelids fluttered closed.

"I'd better let you sleep."

"Mmm."

Todd brushed her forehead with his lips. "I'll be back in the morning for visiting hours. Your mom and dad said they'll come to see you after church."

"'Mom and Dad,'" she echoed, the words mumbled as she drifted toward sleep.

"Sleep well, my love."

Chapter 58

SUNDAY, MAY 23, 1943

Todd saw the understanding dawn as his in-laws looked through the plate-glass window at the infants in the nursery. Carl and Nancy could tell that little Bobby Kinnear hadn't arrived six weeks early, and when they looked at Todd, he recognized their surprise and disappointment.

They didn't speak of it aloud, of course. People rarely did, except for those who loved to gossip. It was a private matter. A private shame. But Todd felt himself become smaller in their eyes, and it hurt. Even more than he'd anticipated. It was like losing a father for the second time. For that's what Carl had been to him these past years. A father. And, unspoken, something had died between them. When Carl looked at Todd, he thought he was looking at the despoiler of his youngest daughter, and there was nothing Todd could say or do to change that. Not if he meant to protect Daisy's secret as he'd promised he would.

He cleared his throat. "Daisy's waiting to see you."

By now there were three more mothers in the ward with his wife, and each of them had at least one visitor at her bedside. When Todd led the way into the ward, Daisy was sitting up in bed, several pillows at her back. She wore a pale-pink bed jacket that her mom had made for her, and her hair was caught back with a scarf of the same color. She looked fragile and frightened, and he longed to protect her from the censure—silent or otherwise—that was to come.

As it turned out, Carl and Nancy had gathered themselves by the time they approached their daughter's bed.

"Darling." Her mom leaned in to kiss Daisy's cheek. "We're so happy all went well for you."

"You look good," her dad added. Then he, too, kissed her cheek.

Daisy glanced at Todd, then back to her parents. "Have you seen the baby?"

"Yes." Nancy nodded. "He's beautiful. You both look well."

"Did Todd tell you his name?"

"Bobby, wasn't it?"

Todd moved to the opposite side of the bed from his in-laws and took hold of Daisy's hand. "Bobby for short. His full name is Robert Carl. Robert Carl Kinnear."

"Isn't that nice, Carl?" Nancy hugged her husband's arm to her side. "They're honoring the baby's grandfathers."

Did Todd imagine it, or did a look of pain cross Daisy's face? Did she think about Andrew Gallagher and feel guilty that his name hadn't been used as one of the grandfathers? But how would they have explained that choice? They couldn't. Their way was set.

Nancy took hold of her daughter's free hand. "You're blessed. Your son is healthy and strong. We thank God for that. And you are well too." There was a stiffness in her words that she wasn't able to hide.

Tears glittered in Daisy's eyes. "Thanks, Mom."

"Lillian sends her love. She was busy with friends after church or she would have come with us to see you and the baby."

"I understand."

"We should let you rest." Nancy released Daisy's hand and

stepped back from the bed. "Is there anything you need me to do to get ready for the baby to come home?"

"No. I think we have everything ready." Daisy glanced up at Todd.

He nodded as he squeezed her hand. "We're ready."

Carl leaned down and kissed the top of Daisy's head. "Congratulations to you both." He stepped away from the bed, as his wife had done moments before, and avoided looking at Todd before he and Nancy turned to leave the ward.

"They know," Daisy whispered after they were gone.

"They know."

"Oh, Todd. I'm sorry."

He squeezed her hand again. "Bobby is healthy, like your mom said. He's perfect. Got his ten fingers and ten toes and a good set of lungs. We've got lots of be thankful for, Daisy. We're a family. The three of us." *And I love you both*, he added silently.

She turned and pressed her face into his chest. He heard her catch a sob while her tears dampened his shirt.

"We'll get through this." He stroked her hair, silently praying that his words were true.

"Excuse me, everyone, but visiting hours are over."

Todd looked toward the nurse in the entrance. The last thing he wanted to do was let go of Daisy now. As if sensing that, the nurse walked toward him.

"Don't worry," she said. "New mothers are often emotional, Mr. Kinnear. We'll take good care of your wife. And it's almost time to feed the baby. On your way now. Scoot."

Daisy drew her head back and looked up at him. A sad smile tugged at the corners of her mouth. "I'm all right. You can go. I'll be fine."

"You sure?"

"Yes."

"As I said," the nurse intruded, "it's very normal for Mother to be a bit teary. Don't you worry yourself. She'll be right as rain before you know it." She motioned him away with both hands.

His instincts demanded he stay, but Todd, along with other fathers and family members, were driven from the room by the ever-so-efficient nurse.

Chapter 59

PRESENT DAY–MARCH

"Have I done wrong, Father? To continue to keep silent about some things from my own past?"

Daisy lifted the leg rest on the recliner and closed her eyes.

"I told so many lies back then. *We* told so many lies. I believed for a long time that I had made my bed and had to lie in it. But then You remade the bed, didn't You? You took me from a place of misery into a place of happiness, step by step. I didn't deserve any of it. But look at the life I've had. Blessing upon blessing. Yes, hardship too. But blessings still. So much grace, Lord. So much grace."

Memories flitted through her mind. Memories of each time she'd told the truth about Bobby's conception to the people in her life who'd needed to know. Oh, it had been hard. Admitting one's failures was never easy. Sin had consequences, even confessed sin that God forgave. But there was blessing to be found in truth-telling as well. God had been faithful, letting her know when it was time to speak, guiding her as she faced her own emotions and the emotions of others. He had refined her and sustained her, and she was grateful.

Brianna's face replaced the memories of people now dead.

O Father. It's a different age. It seems like a different world sometimes.

But the dangers are much the same. Our adversary, the devil, prowls around like a roaring lion, seeking someone to devour. Jesus, don't let that someone be Brianna. Guard her heart and mind. Don't let her be deceived by the lies of the Enemy. Not by clever words from a young man or from her own wishes and desires. Don't let her justify bad actions rather than submit to Your authority. Make her strong, Lord. Make her strong in You. Stronger than I was. Increase her faith and grant her wisdom beyond her years.

Chapter 60

FRIDAY, MAY 28, 1943

Daisy was settled into the wheelchair, a well-swaddled Bobby in her arms, when Todd arrived in the ward late on Friday morning.

He grinned when he saw the pair of them. "Ready to go home?"

"Yes." She could hardly express how ready she was. She was tired of someone else deciding when she could hold and feed her baby. She was tired of being on the hospital's schedule, waking up when they wanted, trying to sleep when they said she must, eating when they brought trays of food, whether or not she was hungry. She was tired of restricted visiting hours, even if it was only Todd who came to see her after that first day. She was tired of sharing a room with three strangers, as nice as those ladies all were.

Todd gave her a slight bow. "Your chariot is parked outside. And your mom went to the market to make sure we had food to see us through until you're up and around."

She wanted to ask him if her parents had forgiven her for the deception, but she pressed her lips together, unwilling to ask such a thing in front of the nurse who stood nearby. But even once they were in the car and driving toward home, she didn't ask. What could he tell her? She understood that no one close to her would talk about the date of Bobby's conception. Her family and true friends would go on pretending that he'd arrived six weeks early instead of just over two weeks late. She suspected that even Todd wouldn't mention it unless she brought it up first.

The baby slept soundly throughout the ride home and didn't stir during the transfer from Daisy's arms into the cradle—the cradle that had been Todd's but looked brand new.

"Mom never could bring herself to give it away," he had told Daisy the day he brought it in from the garage, newly sanded and varnished, "even after she knew there wouldn't be any more babies for her and Dad."

Now, looking down at Bobby, he said, "Mom would be happy to see us using it. She always was sentimental about this cradle. Don't know why."

"I know why."

"You do? What?"

"It isn't something you can put into words. It can only be felt." She placed a hand over her heart. "It has to be felt here."

"And you've learned this from all your time as a mother?"

She laughed. "Exactly."

He looked at her for a long while without saying a word. So long she began to feel uncomfortable beneath the gaze. No, not uncomfortable. Just . . . strange. It was as if he could look beyond her appearance and right into the heart she'd indicated moments before.

She drew a quick breath. "I think I'll take a nap while the baby's sleeping."

"Sure. Good idea." Todd moved toward the bedroom doorway. "I'll keep the food hot for when you're hungry."

As soon as the door closed behind him, Daisy sank onto the bed. She placed her hand on the siderail of the cradle, causing it to swing a little.

I'm sorry, God. I'm sorry for all of the lies. Thank You that Bobby arrived safely. Help me to keep him safe. Help me to raise him to be a follower of Your Son. Keep me from intentional sin. Let me be the right kind of mother for him.

She drew in a deep breath and released it.

And Father God, thank You for giving me a kind man to help raise Bobby. Don't let me hurt Todd. Don't let me ever forget what he has done for us.

She laid back on the bed and closed her eyes.

Thank You because I know he . . .

Chapter 61

SUNDAY, MAY 30, 1943

Lillian didn't spend a lot of time with her parents these days. Between work and going out with friends, sitting down to dinner with Mom and Dad a few times per week was the most she managed. But even being away as much as she was, she still felt the strange mood that lingered in the air when she was home. What was the matter with them? Those odd looks they exchanged. The strained silences. The stiff expressions. It was enough to drive a girl crazy.

Visiting her sister on that Sunday had more to do with escaping her parents' strange humors after dinner than it did with seeing her nephew for the first time. She supposed she should feel guilty for not being more excited about the baby's birth, especially since he'd arrived weeks early, but she simply wasn't able to manufacture any real elation. She liked babies well enough. In fact, she'd often imagined she would have a baby of her own by this time. But Brandan hadn't married her before deploying, and she was no longer eager for marriage or motherhood. She was having too much fun as a single woman.

She knocked on the Kinnear back door, then opened it. "It's me. Are you up for a visitor?"

Todd stepped into view in the archway between the kitchen and living room. He held a tiny bundle in his arms and swayed gently as he grinned at her. "Of course. Come in."

For some reason, she hadn't expected to see Todd holding the baby. Wasn't that the mother's job? Yet there he was—and looking very pleased with himself at that.

"We wondered when Aunt Lillian would come for a visit." Todd's grin widened.

As Lillian moved through the kitchen, Daisy came into view. She sat on the sofa, still in her robe and slippers.

"Do you want to hold him?" Todd asked.

"Oh, I don't think—"

"Here." He motioned with his head. "Sit next to Daisy, and I'll put Bobby in your arms."

"Oh, all right." She sank onto the sofa. The next thing she knew, she held the baby, his little head resting in the crook of her left arm.

A tingle of surprise went through Lillian as she looked down. Bobby was a lovely infant. Unlike some newborns, his features weren't smooshed, his complexion was flawless, and he had a full head of dark hair. She couldn't see any resemblance to either Daisy or Todd in his face.

Her sister leaned close. "He's beautiful, isn't he?"

"Yes. He is."

Todd said, "He has Daisy's nose."

Lillian didn't see it, but she nodded as if she agreed.

Bobby wriggled. His little mouth pursed, and he made a kind of kissing sound, quieted, then squeaked.

"He's getting hungry again." Daisy made it sound as if this were some huge achievement on the infant's part. "I'd better change his diaper before I feed him."

"I can change him," Todd said. "You stay with your sister." He took the baby from Lillian's arms and disappeared into the baby's room.

Lillian looked at Daisy. "He changes diapers?"

"Yes. He's hardly let me lift a finger since he brought us home from the hospital. He's very caring."

"Did Dad ever change *our* diapers when we were babies?"

"I doubt it." Daisy laughed softly. "But maybe he wasn't as smitten with us as Todd is with Bobby."

Lillian bristled. "Dad loves us."

"I didn't say 'love.' I said 'smitten.' Todd's just about over the moon. I didn't expect it, but he is."

Lillian got up from the sofa and went to the front window. It was silly to be angry with Daisy, but she was. She didn't understand why. Because Todd changed the baby's diapers? Because Daisy said he was smitten with his son? Because her sister was living the life Lillian had imagined she would have?

A knot formed in her belly.

She tried to picture Brandan happily carrying a baby off to change its diaper, but she couldn't do it. Not even with her active imagination. Brandan would say diaper changing was woman's work. But then Brandan was more of a take-charge kind of guy. A physical kind of guy. A man who liked to hunt and fish and fly airplanes. Lillian had loved that about him . . . until he hadn't bent to her will. Then he'd frustrated her, angered her, hurt her. And finally he'd left her.

Shaking off her dour thoughts of Brandan, she turned from the window.

Todd reappeared from the baby's room and transferred Bobby—who was fussier now than before—into Daisy's waiting arms. Then Todd used both hands to help his wife rise from the sofa.

"I'm going to go feed the baby," Daisy said to Lillian. "We can visit more when he's finished, if you like."

"Another time." Lillian took a few steps toward the kitchen. "I'm going with friends to a matinee. *How Green Was My Valley* is back at the Pinney Theater. I need to get home and fix my hair and makeup."

Daisy looked as if she might protest Lillian's departure, but Bobby interrupted with a more insistent cry. With a nod, Daisy hurried toward the privacy of the bedroom to nurse her son.

Lillian said goodbye to Todd and left almost as quickly.

Chapter 62

PRESENT DAY–MARCH

Unlike her great-grandmother's call the previous day, Brianna ignored the one from Adam when her phone rang on Monday morning. She didn't want to talk to him while she packed for her getaway with Greg. It felt . . . wrong. She didn't want to tell him the truth, nor did she want to lie to him. It was better not to talk to him at all. The same would be true for Hannah. But luckily, Hannah hadn't asked what Brianna's plans were for spring break. A good thing, because her friend had an uncanny ability to tell what Brianna was thinking. Especially if she was trying to come up with a reply that wasn't completely honest.

After a short while, her phone pinged to let her know there was a voice mail awaiting her. She tapped the screen to retrieve it.

"Hey, Brianna. It's Adam. Would you like to go see a movie Wednesday night? Maybe we could grab dinner first, if you want. Give me a call. Later."

A movie. Dinner. Did that sound like a date? Like Adam wasn't willing to leave things as they were? Like Adam wanted to change their relationship, despite knowing she was seeing Greg?

"I'm not sure about that guy."

Was it possible Adam was more than a concerned friend? Could he be jealous? If so, it wasn't her fault. She hadn't encouraged him. He and Hannah were Brianna's best friends. Couldn't that be enough?

Have I been unfair to Adam? a small voice asked.

Before her conscience could continue, she shoved the last of her clothes into the suitcase and zipped it closed. Her skis, poles, and boots sat against the wall near the door. While it would be nice to move everything downstairs, she decided to wait. No need to remind her mom that she would be gone for a few days. No need to invite questions about this ski trip. No reason to risk even more lies.

This time it was GeeGee's voice she heard in her head: *"Be very careful with your heart."*

Brianna cringed at the warning. But the words kept repeating in her memory. She reached for her earbuds, stuck them in place, and turned on the music on her phone. If she couldn't block the warning with sheer determination, she would blast it out with an upbeat tune.

Chapter 63

SATURDAY, OCTOBER 9, 1943

For Daisy, days melded into weeks, and weeks into months. Time seemed to heal the distance between her and her parents, although her dad remained somewhat cool toward Todd. If friends and neighbors noticed what a big baby Bobby was despite arriving six weeks early, no one let on to Daisy herself. Perhaps it helped that she'd stayed home for the first two months following the birth, and only a few people saw Bobby during those eight weeks. Perhaps no one, other than her parents, had guessed the truth. Or at least the partial truth.

Motherhood, Daisy had decided, was better than she'd hoped it would be. She'd treasured the baby's first real smile, that day when she knew he saw her clearly, the time he rolled over by himself. And today, when Bobby—not quite five months old—sat upright and stayed upright without any help from his mom at all.

"Oh, you big boy! You'd better be able to do that tonight when your daddy gets home. Because he'll want to get out the Brownie and take pictures."

As if summoned by her words, the front door opened, and Todd called, "I'm home!"

It surprised her how she'd learned to listen for those words at the end of every workday. "You're early."

"I know."

"I haven't started dinner."

"No problem." Todd stopped and stared at Bobby. "Look who's sitting up by himself."

Daisy grinned. "I knew you'd be excited to see that." She got up from the floor, intending to pick up the baby.

Todd beat her to it. He whisked Bobby into his arms and held him above his head for a moment, then drew him down close to his face so that their noses touched. Bobby giggled. The sweetest sound in the world.

They didn't look at all alike, Todd and Bobby, but no one would ever guess that they weren't related by blood. Not with the way Todd behaved around the baby. It both warmed Daisy's heart and alarmed her—because sometimes she wished Todd *was* Bobby's father. And today of all days, wishing that felt wrong. Because today was the anniversary of Brandan's crash in France. He'd been missing for a full year now. To wish that Bobby wasn't Brandan's child seemed the same as wishing Brandan dead instead of missing.

"If you'll watch him, I'll start dinner."

"Of course."

She headed for the kitchen. "Why are you home early? Did something happen?"

"No. I just thought . . . I figured you might want some company today. Somebody besides this little guy."

She turned from the refrigerator to look at him. "Why today?"

"I noticed the date."

"The date?"

His expression was serious and tender at the same time, telling her everything she needed to know.

She hadn't expected Todd, of all people, to remember the date

Brandan had gone missing, but he had. Others would have remembered too. His parents definitely would. Lillian might. But that Todd remembered and cared enough to come home so she wouldn't face the memory alone moved her in an unexpected way.

I don't deserve you, Todd Kinnear.

Todd wondered if his heart might break in two as he looked at Daisy. He loved her, and he desired her. He wanted their marriage to be real and whole. And right at this moment, he hated the man who'd sired the baby in his arms, because he knew Daisy still thought about him. He resented that Bobby wasn't really and truly his son, as everyone believed. As he was able to believe most of the time.

"I'm going to get the camera." He tried to make his voice sound normal. "I want to get some photos of this little man sitting on his own."

He turned away before Daisy could read more in his eyes than he wanted her to know.

I made this bargain. I've gotta live with it. He went to his bedroom—his solitary bedroom. *For as long as it takes, I've gotta live with it.*

He'd promised Daisy he would never ask more of her than she could give. But when he'd made that promise, he hadn't realized he was halfway in love with her already. He hadn't realized that, by pretending they had a marriage based on love in order to fool others, he would be fooled by it too.

I should've known.

He grabbed the Brownie box camera off of his dresser and took it out to the living room, where he set Bobby on the floor. Unlike even a week ago, the baby didn't wobble uncertainly. In fact, he squealed his delight as he clapped his hands together. The action brought a smile to Todd's face, too, lifting his mood at last.

Bobby was the reason he'd offered to marry Daisy. No matter what else happened or didn't happen in this pseudo-marriage of theirs, this little boy made everything else okay. Legally, Robert Carl Kinnear was Todd's son, and Todd would move heaven and earth to give this boy the best life possible. No one and nothing would get in the way of that.

Chapter 64

SUNDAY, OCTOBER 10, 1943

With the strains of the closing hymn lingering in the air, Daisy left the pew and hurried to the nursery to get Bobby. By the time she returned to the narthex, her son riding on her hip, Todd and her parents were visiting with Elenore and Andrew Gallagher. Neither Lillian nor the two youngest Gallagher brothers were in sight. Daisy quietly stepped to Todd's side.

"William will turn eighteen next week," Elenore said, and the tension written on her face said what she hadn't. Another son would be old enough to enlist or be drafted.

Daisy's mom reached out to squeeze Elenore's hand, a silent gesture of encouragement.

After nearly two years of war and the rationing of everything from tires to shoes to canned goods to meat, fat, and cheese, everyone felt the need of encouragement at times. But Daisy thought the mothers of boys about to turn eighteen must surely need it the most.

Still, this year the tide of the war had shifted in favor of the Allies. In August, Kiska in the Aleutians had been retaken by American and Canadian units. In September, Italy had been invaded by Allied forces and in less than a week had surrendered unconditionally. As Daisy looked at Brandan's mother, she wondered how long it would be until the Allies made it into France. And when they did, would they find Brandan as well?

Bobby chattered a bit, which drew Elenore's gaze to him. A smile broke through her concerned expression, and she reached out to touch Bobby's chubby cheek with her fingertips.

"He's so adorable, Daisy. I remember when my boys were that age. Exhausting, but wonderful at the same time." Elenore paused, her head tipping slightly to one side. Then tears flooded her eyes. "I'm sorry." She took a handkerchief from her pocket and dried her tears. "Looking at Bobby made me think of Brandan when he was a baby on my hip."

Todd's arm slipped around Daisy's back, as if he'd guessed her sudden desire to bolt. Did others look at Bobby and think of Brandan? Or would Elenore have said the same thing to any woman holding a baby boy? Any baby boy.

His arm still around Daisy, Todd said, "I think I'd better get my little family home. Bobby's cheerful now, but he gets cranky when he doesn't go down for a nap at the usual time."

What he said was both the truth and an excuse. Daisy didn't care which way he'd meant it. She was thankful for any reason to leave before her anxiety began to show to others.

"And I get cranky," Todd added with a grin, "when I don't get my Sunday dinner on time."

Everyone laughed, as expected.

As soon as they were beyond the church doors, Daisy said, "Thank you."

Without further comment, Todd held out his arms and took Bobby onto his own hip as they walked toward home. The weather was mild, Indian summer still having its way in the valley. Daisy wouldn't mind if it stayed like this into December, but she knew it wouldn't.

It would change suddenly, warm one day and cold and blowing the next.

After a lengthy spell, Todd broke the silence. "You don't need to worry. She didn't see Brandan in Bobby. Her son's on her mind. That's all."

He didn't say, *Like he's on yours too*, but she seemed to hear it anyway. Yesterday, she'd thought him thoughtful, coming home early to offer his support. Now, she heard something else in his voice. An edge. A sharpness. And she wasn't sure how to respond. What did it mean? Was he angry with her? Was he worried even when he told her not to be?

Once at home, Todd carried Bobby to his bedroom, changed his diaper, and got him settled for a nap. Daisy watched it all from the bedroom doorway, touched by the way he spoke soft nonsense to Bobby, soothing him, allowing drowsiness to overtake him. It didn't seem long at all before the baby was asleep.

Todd looked toward Daisy then, and she had the sudden feeling he wished she would leave. But how could she? She needed to change out of her Sunday clothes, and this was her room as well as Bobby's. As if he realized it, he gave her a nod and walked toward her. She stepped out of his way to let him pass.

Sadness washed over her. It felt as if she'd lost something precious, although she couldn't say what that something was.

Chapter 65

PRESENT DAY–MARCH

Won't she ever leave? Brianna stared at the clock. Greg was due to arrive in less than ten minutes, and Mom was still in the house. Anxiety twisted her gut as she waited . . . and waited.

"Honey, I'm leaving now."

Brianna left her room and walked to the top of the stairs. "Okay. I'll see you Thursday."

"Don't I get a hug and a kiss goodbye?"

"Mom, I'm only going on a ski trip. It isn't like it's a big deal."

"Please."

Expelling a breath, she hurried down the stairs and gave the requested hug and kiss.

"Be careful," her mom said as she drew back.

"I will. No broken bones or anything."

Mom smiled, then turned and left through the door in the kitchen. Moments later, the garage door opened and the car backed down the driveway and into the street.

Brianna drew in a quick breath of relief before rushing back up the stairs to get her things. She'd just set her suitcase beside the rest of the equipment when Greg's truck pulled into the driveway. Not willing to waste a second, Brianna opened the door and headed outside with her skis and boots.

"Hey there." Greg stepped down from the cab.

"Hey."

"Am I late?"

"No. Right on time."

"Good." He went to the back and lowered the tailgate, then took the skis and boots from her. "Got much more?"

"Not a lot. I can get it." She went back inside.

Within minutes, the truck was loaded and the front door to the house was closed and locked. After they were both in the cab, Greg leaned over and gave her a quick kiss. "This is gonna be fun," he said as he pulled back.

The flutter of nerves she'd felt most of the morning exploded in her stomach. She felt breathless and lightheaded and . . . and a little afraid. Her hand alighted on the handle, and for an instant she considered opening the door and jumping from the truck before they could leave.

Don't be silly. There's nothing to be afraid of. We're not doing anything wrong. This is going to be fun, just like he said.

Greg started the engine, put the truck in gear, and backed out of the drive.

Chapter 66

MONDAY, OCTOBER 11, 1943

The old man's name was Pierre Benoit. Over five months ago he'd brought Brandan south into what had once been the free zone. The plan had been for Brandan to be guided over the mountains into Spain, but the gestapo had captured and tortured some members of the Resistance, and Brandan's departure had been postponed several different times.

Instead of an escape, he'd been taken to a farm where he labored in the open, the story being that he was a cousin of the farmer and both deaf and mute. Pierre labored beside him, supposedly another, more distant cousin. Brandan had been rigorously trained by the old man not to react to sounds of any kind. The drills and tests had seemed never-ending, but the exercises had served him well the times Pierre and he had been stopped, their papers demanded by the Germans.

Brandan and Pierre slept in a shed near the barn. While they had a small stove, the fire did little to remove the chill from the air this time of year. Brandan often wondered if he would ever be warm again. Could he survive another winter in occupied France? He wasn't sure he could. Despair often pressed on his heart, as it did tonight.

"The Allies," Pierre said into the darkness, perhaps sensing Brandan's mood. "They are in Italy. It will not be long."

"Not be long." Brandan let the words repeat in his mind, although he took little encouragement from them. He'd been in France for thirteen months. His body still ached from the injuries he'd sustained in the crash. And although he'd evaded capture by the Nazis multiple times, thanks to the courage of men and women who fought any way they could, he knew he could lose his freedom—and possibly his life—at any moment. *"Not long."* Did that mean a few months? Another year?

His stomach growled. He was hungry. He was always hungry. And everyone around him, even on a farm, was hungry too. Everyone except for the Germans who patrolled the land and controlled the cities and towns. They took the food and left others to starve, from the very young to the very old.

Pierre rolled onto his side on the bed of straw, his face illuminated by the light from the stove. "God is with us, my friend."

In their months together, Brandan had learned that the Frenchman's faith was unshakeable. Prayer wasn't a religious practice to him. It was a conversation with God. A constant conversation. There had been many times when Brandan envied Pierre his certainty in what he believed and Who he believed in. And lately, he'd begun asking questions. Pierre was never quick to respond. He pondered Brandan's questions first and often challenged him with his answers.

Was it the constant possibility of death or the long separation from the people he loved that caused Brandan to wonder more and more about the type of man he was? And to consider the kind of man he wanted to become. He thought about Lillian and Daisy often. He'd asked God to forgive him for what he'd done the weekend before he left Boise. But had he truly repented of his actions?

"Pierre?"

"Oui?"

"What is true repentance? Not just being sorry for something I did. How do I repent in a way that makes me a better man than I was before?"

"Oh, my friend. Are there hours enough in a night for such a question?"

"I've hurt people back home."

Pierre sat up, braced by one arm. "To repent means to turn away." He mirrored the action with the fingers of his free hand. "To turn and to walk in the opposite direction. See?"

"How do I do that in France?"

"God will show you." The old man lay down again, his expression serene. "Ask Him, and He will show you. Perhaps now is the time for God to increase your faith so that when you go home, you will be ready."

Weariness overcame Brandan, and his eyes drifted closed. "I hope you're right, Pierre. I hope you're right."

Chapter 67

WEDNESDAY, OCTOBER 20, 1943

A week before their first anniversary, Todd lay awake in the middle of the night, staring up into the darkness of his room, his thoughts in turmoil. Then, out of the silence, he sensed God speaking to him: *"Husbands, love your wives, even as Christ also loved the church, and gave himself up for it."* In the same instant the verse echoed in his mind, Todd felt the resentment and jealousy that had been building in his heart loosen their hold.

He released a deep sigh, and as he drew in another breath, clarity came with it. He hadn't been giving Daisy time to grow to care for him, as he'd told himself. He wasn't being sensitive to her needs when he didn't share his feelings with her. He'd been a coward. His actions—or lack thereof—had been meant to maintain the status quo, to keep from rocking an already unstable boat. Only he didn't want the status quo. He wanted his wife to love him as he loved her. And how could that happen if he didn't show her what he felt? Really show her. He needed to woo her. He needed to sweep her off her feet, if possible. He couldn't stand back and let life pass them by. They were married. They needed to live like it. Really live like it. Not just pretend.

The next day, he put a plan in motion, beginning with an arrangement for Carl and Nancy to watch Bobby on the night of Daisy and Todd's anniversary. Once that was done, he made a dinner reservation at a fine restaurant in town. Common sense told him he couldn't spring the evening on her. She would want to dress appropriately for a night on the town. So he told her they would be going out to eat on Wednesday night.

While dinner out couldn't be a surprise, he could surprise her with a gift. All he had to do was find the perfect one. He found it in a jewelry store in downtown Boise. A slender gold bracelet with a cross charm set with a small diamond at its center. The moment he saw the bracelet, he knew it was perfect for Daisy. Normally, she didn't wear jewelry other than the simple wedding band he'd put on her finger in Nevada and, on Sundays, the necklace he'd given her for Christmas. But he hoped she would want to wear this bracelet too.

When he arrived home from work on the appointed evening, Nancy had already taken Bobby home with her. Daisy waited alone in the living room, wearing a butter-yellow dress. She looked nervous, not unlike the day he'd married her.

"I'll wash up and change my clothes," he said. "We'll take the car tonight."

Daisy nodded.

As he headed for his room, he scolded himself. Unlike Brandan Gallagher, Todd had never been at ease with girls. He'd never known how to flatter or impress. But shouldn't it be easier with his own wife? Why hadn't he told her how pretty she looked? He could have said the color of her dress made her seem to glow. Anything would have been better than nothing.

You're not off to much of a start for the night.

He thought of Brandan again. Why did sweeping a girl off her feet come so easily to a guy like him? It had to be more than his movie-star good looks. What—

Todd shook his head to drive out the questions. It served no good purpose to compare himself to Brandan or any other man. Winning his wife's heart was up to him. He and Daisy were good friends. They'd found a way to live in unity for an entire year, sharing a home, parenting a baby, learning each other's little habits, establishing routines. To their friends and family, they appeared to have a good marriage. It wasn't *all* pretend. It couldn't be. There was more between them, even if Daisy didn't realize it yet. He was sure of it.

He held onto those thoughts as he finished dressing, as he escorted Daisy to the car and helped her into the front seat, and as he drove downtown. He reminded himself of what he wanted most as he held her arm and walked her from the parking lot into the restaurant.

There was more that was true between them than was false, and tonight, he meant to make her see it too.

Daisy wasn't sure why she felt uneasy. It wasn't as if she'd never eaten in a nice restaurant before. It certainly wasn't because she was never alone with Todd as a couple. Perhaps it was the way he'd looked at her tonight. There was something different in his gaze, although she wasn't sure what it was or what it meant.

After the hostess left them at their table, Todd leaned forward. "Get whatever you want. Don't even pay attention to the prices. This is our special night."

She smiled, then glanced down at the menu. As instructed, she wouldn't look at the prices. It was much more fun to simply look at her choices. All too often, what she wanted to buy at the store wasn't available, even if it wasn't rationed.

Mostaccioli with Chicken . . . Chicken a la Cacciatora . . . Breaded Veal Cutlet . . .

Her mouth began to water as her eyes scanned the menu.

Broiled Lobster Tail . . . Broiled Red Snapper . . . Filet Mignon . . .

She knew what she wanted, but then she read the notice printed at the bottom of the menu.

> Due to rationing and shortage of foods, these menus are subject to change without notice. All prices are our ceiling prices or below. By O.P.A. regulation, our ceilings are based on our highest prices from April 4 to 10, 1943. Our menus for that week are available for your inspection.

"Have you decided?" Todd inquired.

"Yes." She looked up. "The filet mignon with a baked potato and a salad."

He nodded. "Sounds good. I'll do the same."

"If they have it." She glanced toward the kitchen.

"They'll have it."

"How do you know?"

He grinned. "I have a feeling. It's our anniversary, after all."

One year. I've lived with this man for a whole year. Bobby will be five months old in two days, and soon he will call Todd "Daddy" or "Dada." But what about me? What do I want to call him?

Todd reached into the pocket of his jacket and removed a small box. He set it on the table and slid it toward her. "Happy anniversary."

"Todd, you shouldn't have—"

"Yes, I should have. Because you're my wife, Daisy, and I—"

He broke off when the waitress arrived with glasses of water.

"Good evening," she greeted them as she readied her order pad.

Daisy saw a flicker of frustration cross Todd's face at the interruption, although he hid it quickly. He smiled at the young woman and thanked her for the water. Then he said, "We both want the filet mignon with a baked potato and a salad."

"Would you like a glass of wine with your dinner?"

Todd looked at Daisy with a question in his eyes.

Her parents were teetotalers, so there had never been wine or spirits of any kind in the Abbott home. She was tempted to say yes. After all, would it be so awful to have her first taste of wine? But then she remembered Brandan on the night they'd gone into the foothills. He'd been drunk, and he hadn't thought straight because of it. If he hadn't been drinking, he never would have left the Starlite with Daisy. He never would have made love to her, and she wouldn't have gotten pregnant. Nor would she be married to Todd Kinnear.

"No." Her gaze fell to the box near her plate. "No wine for me."

"What's wrong?" Todd asked the moment the waitress left the table.

She shook her head. "Nothing."

"You look . . . sad."

She met his gaze again. "I'm not sad."

As she spoke the words, she realized how true they were. She wasn't sad. Her world could have completely fallen apart because of her sinful choice, because she'd lusted after a man who didn't belong to her. A man who didn't love her but took her anyway. A man she'd idealized in her mind. But God, in His mercy and grace, had provided her with another man, a good man, a good husband, a good provider. And now a good father to her son.

No, she wasn't sad. She was thankful. It was time to put her past behind her. Truly behind her. Could she do that?

"Wherefore if any man is in Christ, he is a new creature: the old things are passed away; behold, they are become new."

As the words from Scripture passed through her mind, warmth blossomed in her chest. She was new. Christ had made her new. When she'd confessed her sin, He'd forgiven her.

"There is therefore now no condemnation to them that are in Christ Jesus."

"'No condemnation,'" she whispered, the realization of what it meant sending little shockwaves throughout her body.

"What?"

She smiled at Todd through unexpected tears. It wasn't only that God didn't condemn her. Todd didn't condemn her either. He never had.

"Happy anniversary," she answered, her voice catching on the words.

Wisely, he asked for no further explanation. Instead, he reached out and pushed the box a little closer to her. "Open it."

She blinked back the tears, waiting until her vision was no longer blurred before she untied the narrow ribbon and lifted the lid. Laying on a bed of cotton was a gold bracelet with a small charm in its center. She slid the fingers of her right hand beneath the delicate chain and lifted it from the box.

"Do you like it?"

She looked from the bracelet to him. "Todd, I love it." Her pulse quickened in her chest as she looked at him, almost as if seeing him for the first time.

Bobby was in a deep sleep when Todd lifted him from the sofa in the Abbott living room.

"He's such a good boy," Nancy said as she stroked Bobby's pudgy cheek. Then she lifted her gaze to Todd. "Did you and Daisy have a nice evening?"

"Very nice."

"Good. I'm glad." She touched Todd's cheek, exactly as she'd done to her grandson moments before. "Give her my love."

"I will."

His mother-in-law tucked a warm blanket around Bobby, then

Todd carried him out into the crisp night air, following the path from one backyard to the other. Daisy waited for them in the living room, and when Todd headed straight for the bedroom, she followed.

"Does he need changed?" she asked.

"No. Your mom said she changed him an hour ago." Todd lay Bobby in his crib and placed the blanket over him. "He's knocked out."

The lamp in the corner was on, and it cast a soft yellow light over the crib and baby. Todd leaned down and kissed his son's cheek. By the time he straightened, Daisy stood beside him.

She repeated his actions. Then she looked up at Todd. "Maybe he'll sleep through the night."

"I hope so." Without thinking, he reached out and swept a loose strand of hair from Daisy's cheek, tucking it behind her ear.

Her eyes widened.

His pulse quickened.

All evening long, he'd thought about kissing Daisy. Really kissing her. In truth, he'd longed for such a moment between them for many months. Loving her from afar had stretched him almost beyond endurance. But tonight, from the instant she'd smiled at him through her tears and wished him a happy anniversary, he'd known something had changed between them. Something good. Perhaps something lasting.

"Daisy," he whispered.

"Yes?"

He leaned toward her.

She tipped her head back.

His lips met with hers. But unlike those infrequent kisses in the past, when he'd brushed his lips across hers and withdrawn, this time he drew closer, his mouth lingering, tasting, savoring. He wasn't sure how long it was before he felt her hands wrap around the back of his neck, almost as if she wished to pull him closer still.

They were both breathing fast when at last they broke the kiss. Todd stared down into the face he dreamed of at night and thought about so often throughout the day. She looked back at him, a flicker of uncertainty in her eyes. But not fear. Not rejection. Just uncertainty.

"Daisy, I . . . I love you."

The uncertainty left her gaze. "I know."

He'd hoped she might respond with words of love of her own. Foolish, perhaps, but he'd wished it. Yet he wasn't surprised. She was too honest to say something she didn't feel or believe. Maybe it was time he left her alone. Maybe he was moving too fast. He'd determined he would woo her, win her. One dinner out was not enough.

But before he could bid her good night, she took his hand and brought it to her lips, then pressed it against her breastbone. He felt the racing of her heart.

"Daisy . . ."

A soft smile curved the corners of her mouth. Then, keeping hold of his hand, she led him out of the baby's room—her room—and into his.

Chapter 68

PRESENT DAY–MARCH

Brianna and Greg talked only a little during the two-hour drive to McCall. Mostly they listened to music. Greg's preference ran more toward classic rock. Brianna loved contemporary Christian music and often shared her playlists with Hannah and vice versa.

Thinking of her best friend, she felt the butterflies take control of her stomach again. Hannah would be disappointed in her if she knew where she was going and with whom. Well, Hannah didn't know, and she didn't need to know. Not ever. No matter what.

"Something wrong?" Greg asked.

She glanced his way, forcing a smile. "No."

"You looked gloomy."

"Sorry. Just lost in thought, I guess."

"Good. No gloomy people on this trip. No homework. No chores. Nothing but skiing, good food, relaxing in a hot tub." He paused, then said, "You did remember your swimming suit, didn't you?"

"Yes. I remembered to bring it."

"Good. I'd hate to have to go in that hot tub by myself."

"There must be swimsuits for sale some place in McCall."

"Sure. But who wants to waste time shopping? Not me."

His reply bothered her, although she couldn't say why.

The two-lane highway carried them over a rise, and they caught their first glimpse of the outskirts of McCall. A short while later, Greg pulled into a grocery-store parking lot.

"Let's make sure we get everything we want now," he said as they walked toward the entrance.

"I made a list."

He shot her a smile. "Good on you. I was hoping you would."

Brianna didn't pretend to be much of a cook, but she'd helped enough while growing up to know her way around the kitchen. She also knew she didn't want to live on snack foods for three days. Instinct told her that's what would happen if she left matters up to Greg. She pulled up the list on her phone. Eggs, butter, bacon, bread, peanut butter, cereal. All of the makings for tacos. Hot-chocolate mix. Milk and sodas. Burgers, hot dogs, and buns. Ketchup and mustard and pickles.

Greg grabbed a shopping cart and pushed it toward the first aisle. Sure enough, it was the snack-foods aisle. Brianna added up the cost as he put bags of chips into the cart. They'd barely begun shopping, and she already wondered if she would have enough money to cover her share as agreed. By the time they left the store, Brianna's wallet was close to empty, and it seemed to her they had enough food to feed themselves for two weeks rather than a mere four days.

She could almost hear one of her dad's lectures about the real world and the importance of wisdom and common sense. Not to mention how to manage her money. Her dad was especially fond of that one. With determination, she refused to let those words of advice break through. Not now. Not when she was already in McCall with Greg. She was going to have fun and would worry about her savings later.

It took close to twenty minutes to drive to the condos on the east side of the lake. Snow was still packed high on the edges of the parking lot, but the roofs of the condos were clear and dry. Although the lake sometimes froze in winter, there was no sign of ice now. Spring was on its way to this resort community. Before long, there would be golfers on the greens instead of skiers on the slopes.

It took Greg and Brianna several trips to get everything into their second-floor unit. Greg took the lakeside bedroom, leaving the smaller one that overlooked the parking lot for Brianna. Not that she minded. She assumed they would spend most of the time in the living area, which also overlooked the lake.

When they were settled in, Greg flipped the switch on the gas fireplace, then took Brianna by the hand and drew her to the sofa. "Let's relax a bit before we worry about dinner."

"Okay." The word came out as a whisper as nerves ignited in her belly.

Chapter 69

TUESDAY, DECEMBER 21, 1943

Even as the jeep barreled toward an opening at the base of the Rock of Gibraltar, Brandan couldn't believe he was there, that he was free. After his many months in hiding and the torturous and deadly trek over the mountains from France, followed by his hastily arranged departure from Spain, it didn't feel real to be sitting in a vehicle with another American soldier at the wheel. Crazy as it was, he half wished he was back with Pierre Benoit.

Once inside the mountain, his driver told him that thirty thousand soldiers—American and British—lived within the complex. A vast underground city sprawled throughout the man-made tunnels and caverns, including offices and barracks and a hospital. It was to that hospital Brandan was taken first. After a thorough examination, he was issued a uniform and shoes and even a new watch. Then he was taken to the massive mess hall, where he was offered a hot meal and coffee. *Real* coffee. From there he was escorted to the Military Liaison Office of the American consulate and handed a comprehensive questionnaire.

He was exhausted by the time he'd written every detail he could recall, from the day his plane was shot down to the moment he arrived at the Rock. Putting it on paper seemed to make him live it all over again. He remembered his crew and could only wonder, for now, at their fate, as he had all these many months. He pictured the faces of the men and women who'd played a part in his survival and finally his escape. Some of them were probably dead by this time, if not at the hands of the Nazis, then from starvation or the elements. He especially wondered about Pierre. Had the old man made it back to his home and his family? He prayed to God he had.

When Brandan turned in the completed questionnaire, he asked, "Sir, when can I send word to my family that I'm alive?"

"You may send a brief cable to them now, but remember, you may not reveal where you are or where you've been all this time. Nothing at all."

"Understood, sir."

Half an hour later, he gave the message to be sent to a clerk.

DEAR MOM AND DAD AND BROTHERS ALL OKAY HERE GIVE MY LOVE TO EVERYONE HOPE TO BE WITH YOU SOON LOVE BRANDAN GALLAGHER

An hour beyond that, he slept soundly in a bed, warm and safe for the first time in what seemed like forever.

Chapter 70

PRESENT DAY–MARCH

Daisy awakened with a start. In her dream, Brandan had been safe at last and coming home. She'd remembered the unraveling of a lie. She'd recalled the truth that was yet to be revealed. She'd felt the return of shame. And she'd feared that a new and fragile love was in danger of vanishing like a wisp of smoke. A dream, yes, but the reality of her life at the time.

"'Therefore there is now no condemnation for those who are in Christ Jesus,'" she whispered, letting the truth of that verse begin to calm her racing heart, as it had so often throughout her life.

Daisy had read in a devotional that it was an aspect of grace to regret one's sins. Not to regret and be paralyzed by it, but to regret and, therefore, make better choices. To choose not to return to sin. To press on in Christ.

"'Not that I have already obtained it or have already become perfect, but I press on so that I may lay hold of that for which also I was laid hold of by Christ Jesus.'"

Her pulse returned, at last, to normal.

"'Lay hold of it.'" She released a breath.

How many years had it been since the events of her dream? More than seventy-five. How many more? She counted on her wrinkled fingers. Seventy-eight. Was it truly so many years? She counted again. Yes. Yes, it had been.

"Have I run a good race, Lord? Am I finishing well?"

A line from a movie popped into her head, a quote from Eric Liddell. *"God made me fast. And when I run, I feel His pleasure."*

Daisy had never been fast on her feet and certainly wasn't these days. But God had made her for a purpose, and she did know what it was like to feel His pleasure. She felt it now, and the trepidation and regrets brought on by her dreams slipped away.

She reached for her Bible and pulled it onto her lap. When she placed it on its spine, it fell open to 1 Thessalonians. A familiar passage—underscored and highlighted—drew her gaze. She read it aloud. "'Rejoice always; pray without ceasing; in everything give thanks; for this is God's will for you in Christ Jesus.'"

This was her purpose. This was her race for the time that was left to her. To pray without ceasing and in everything to give thanks.

She bowed her head and began, "Lord, I pray for Brianna . . ."

Chapter 71

SATURDAY, JANUARY 1, 1944

The sun was well up by the time Lillian opened her eyes on New Year's Day. A new year—1944—but the same war continued. Would it never be over?

Men at the base said there was no doubt the Allies would be victorious. They said Germany and Japan might fight on for a while, but they wouldn't and couldn't win in the end. The Allies would defeat them. Perhaps this year. Maybe the next. But they would be defeated.

Lillian wanted to believe it. She *did* believe it, most of the time. But she couldn't help but wonder how many of those same young men from Gowen Field, the ones she flirted with, the ones who said victory was nigh, would be killed or maimed in battle before the end came.

Too many of them.

Eyes closed again, she thought of Brandan. She didn't like to think about him. It was rare that she did. But for some reason a fresh new year brought him to mind. Was there even the slightest chance he remained alive? His parents wanted to believe it. When she saw them at church, even if they didn't mention his name, she saw the truth on their faces. They held onto hope, even after more than a year without a word.

Would she be like the Gallaghers if she and Brandan had married? Would she still hold onto hope after all this time? If they'd married in 1942, she would be like a widow in 1944 and yet not a widow. A wife and yet not a wife. No, it was better they hadn't married. She was better off. He'd been right about that, even if it had left her hurt and angry. Bitter even.

For some reason, Daisy came to mind next.

It was absolutely sickening to be around her younger sister. It had been bad enough seeing Daisy go all goo-goo eyes over her infant son. One would think Bobby Kinnear had invented learning to roll over, learning to sit up, learning to crawl. But lately, there seemed to be an inner glow about Daisy, one that had nothing to do with her son. Even when tired, even when stressed, Daisy seemed . . . joyful.

And it was as annoying as all get out.

After all, what did Daisy have to be joyful about? She was married to a man who was classified 4-F, a gimp who didn't always hear everything a person said if that person was on the wrong side of him. The ordinary type of guy who went unnoticed in a crowd. A husband who ran a boring business, whether that was canning fruit in the old days or making compasses in the present. Daisy was twenty years old and stuck with a baby and housework and no excitement. She never went out to have fun, never went dancing, never hung out with other girls her age.

"I'm glad it's not me." Lillian tossed aside the blankets and sat up on the side of her bed.

She let the words linger in her thoughts, then nodded to affirm them. She *was* glad it wasn't her. She *was* glad she wasn't stuck at home with a baby and laundry and dirty dishes. Unlike her sister, she was still having fun, despite the war.

No. She preferred the life she had, and she meant to live it to the full.

Daisy snuggled closer to Todd's right side, seeking his warmth in the chilly bedroom. It was a rare winter morning when he wasn't up and out of the house before daylight. And to make this moment even sweeter, Bobby had gone back to sleep after his early-morning feeding. The house remained cloaked in silence, except for Todd's gentle breathing.

Why have you blessed me thus, Father?

It was not the first time she'd asked God that simple question or that she'd marveled over His mercy and grace. But it was fully meant, as much now as the first time.

The intimacies of the marriage bed had surprised her when they happened at last. Her one brief and clumsy experience with sexual relations—the one that had left her pregnant with Bobby—hadn't prepared her for the pleasures to be found with her rightful husband. Todd was a caring and tender lover, and even in her innocence, she recognized what a gift that was.

I love him, Lord. I didn't expect it to happen, but I do love him. So why haven't I said the words? He's said them to me, and he's shown me his love in countless ways.

She drew in a deep breath as she pressed her cheek against his shoulder. *It's because I'm afraid to tell him. I don't deserve to be this happy. And what if I'm wrong? I thought I loved Brandan, and look what happened. That's why I'm afraid to say the words.* She inhaled again and released it.

No one should be afraid to love or to say they love someone.

Pulling back her head, she looked at Todd in the pale light that spilled from beneath the drawn curtains. He wasn't completely deaf in his right ear, but soft sounds were still difficult for him to hear. "I love you," she whispered.

There. That wasn't so hard.

He stirred and opened his eyes. Catching her watching him, he smiled. "Good morning." His voice was rough with sleep.

"Good morning."

"Our little guy still asleep?"

"Yes. He woke up at five but went right back to sleep after he ate."

Todd's right arm now around Daisy, he drew her close against him and closed his eyes. "Then let's not be in a rush to get up. I don't get many days off. I want to enjoy this one."

"You've barely taken a moment off since you got that government contract."

"Mmm."

"How can I spoil you today?"

He rolled his head on the pillow and cracked open one eye. Then he gave her what could only be described as a wicked grin. "I can think of a few things." He drew her closer and kissed her.

As if on cue, Bobby's voice rang to them from across the hall.

Todd chuckled. "I should have known."

Reluctantly, Daisy rolled away from her husband. "You stay in bed. I'll get Bobby and then start the coffee."

Before she could reach for her robe, Todd caught her hand.

"Don't go," he said.

Bobby squealed, not yet unhappy but getting there.

Todd sighed. "You start the coffee. I'll get Bobby."

After pulling on her robe and sliding her feet into her slippers, Daisy made her way out to the kitchen. They didn't indulge in coffee every morning, but New Year's Day seemed an appropriate occasion. She quickly filled the pot with water and added coffee grounds to the percolator before setting it on the stove.

She was about to head for the bathroom when a knock on the

back door stopped her. She glanced at the clock on the wall. It was after eight. Still, it seemed early for someone to come over on New Year's Day. Even members of her own family, which it surely was since they'd come to the back door.

When Daisy opened it, she found her mom on the porch, wearing a coat but with no hat on her head despite the frigid temperature. Her eyes were wide.

"Mom. What is it?"

"You won't believe it."

She pulled her mother into the house and closed the door behind her.

"It's Brandan Gallagher. He's alive."

Daisy fought to draw a breath. She reached for the nearest chair and sank onto it.

"It's true. Nancy and Andrew received a cable yesterday."

"From the war department?" Todd asked from the entrance to the kitchen.

Daisy looked up at him. He held Bobby on his hip.

"No. It was from Brandan himself."

Daisy's gaze was locked on her son. On the son who looked nothing like the man who held him, the man who loved him, the man who was his father in every way that mattered. "Where has he been? Was he a prisoner? Is he well?"

Her mom shook her head. "It said that he was okay and hoped to see them soon. That was all. No details. They've heard nothing from the war department. They have no clue when he'll come home."

Todd carried Bobby with him to the stove where he stood, back toward Daisy, seeming to stare at the coffeepot. As if that would prepare the coffee all the sooner.

"Your father and I are going over to see Elenore and Andrew later this morning."

"What about Lillian? Is she going with you?"

Her mom frowned. "I'm not sure. She's . . . confused. She's glad he's all right, of course, but she gave up on his return quite a while ago."

"When you see the Gallaghers, tell them Todd and I are happy for their good news."

"I will. Now I must go home. I need to help spread the word. We'll all be celebrating at church tomorrow. Oh, I can't believe it. It's a miracle."

"A miracle," Daisy echoed, even as uncertainty knotted her belly.

Todd turned from the stove to bid his mother-in-law goodbye. After Nancy was gone, he looked at Daisy. He wished he could tell what was going on inside that pretty head of hers. What was she thinking? What was she feeling? Only a short while before, he'd thought he knew. He'd almost seemed to hear her say she loved him.

What were her feelings now?

"He's alive," she said, almost too soft for Todd to hear. "He'll be coming home." Her gaze shifted to Bobby, who'd begun to squirm in Todd's arm.

"Soon, I imagine. Unless he's in a hospital."

"A hospital?"

"Hard to say what kind of shape he's in after all this time. The men I've heard about—the ones who've gone down in the war zone and then make it out—they get sent to England first. It could be weeks, even months, before he gets shipped back to the States."

Daisy rose from the chair and came to take Bobby from him. "Are you hungry again, sweetie?"

For a moment Todd couldn't release his hold on Bobby. *My son,* he thought as Daisy drew him away. And in that moment, he understood what he feared the most about Brandan Gallagher's survival and return—what would it mean for Bobby?

With surprising speed and efficiency, considering she now balanced a chubby baby on her hip, Daisy prepared Bobby's breakfast of infant cereal and pureed fruit. Then she set the boy in his high chair and sat down to feed him. Bobby's good humor was in full display as he swallowed spoonfuls of cereal and fruit. Between bites, he bounced his hands on the tray and babbled nonsense.

Sounds Todd had come to love.

He felt loss hit his chest like a sledgehammer. Another loss piled on top of too many other losses. He'd lost his ability to hear perfectly or to run at full speed. He'd lost his dad and then his mom. He'd lost the complete trust of the man who'd become a second father to him. And now? Would he lose his son too? Would he lose his wife?

"I need to do something in the garage." He grabbed his coat from the hook near the back door and rushed outside without waiting for Daisy's response. He tramped through the snow along the narrow sidewalk to the detached garage and went inside. After closing the door, he leaned his back against it.

"God, please . . ."

He drew a breath as he dropped to his knees.

"Bobby's my son. It doesn't matter that he isn't my blood. He's my *son*."

"For we know not how to pray as we ought; but the Spirit himself maketh intercession for us with groanings which cannot be uttered."

Before today, Todd hadn't fully comprehended that passage of Scripture, no matter how many times he'd read it or heard a sermon based upon it. But now he thought he understood. Hands clasped on his knees, head bowed, he released a low moan . . . and prayed the Spirit understood what he could not put into words.

Lillian sat on the sofa, between her mom and dad, listening to Elenore Gallagher as she read the cable they'd received for the second time in the last ten minutes, tears streaming down her cheeks even as she smiled.

Why on earth didn't I stay home? Or go to a movie. I could've gone to a movie.

The worst part was knowing that Brandan's mom expected her to be overwhelmed with emotions. She wasn't. She didn't know what she felt. The girl who'd loved Brandan didn't seem to exist anymore. That very same morning, she'd realized how thankful she was that she and Brandan hadn't married before he left for England. Was she now supposed to pretend to still love him after almost a year and a half? They hadn't parted on the best of terms, and his one and only letter from England a month later hadn't done much to fix that.

"Excuse me," she said softly as she rose from the sofa. "I need to use the bathroom."

Still smiling through tears, Elenore said, "Of course, dear. You know where it is."

Lillian did know. She'd been in the Gallagher home countless times after becoming Brandan's steady girl. Even while he was away at college and then in training in the Air Corps, she used to come to see the woman she'd expected to become her mother-in-law. But she'd only visited the Gallaghers one time after Brandan had been declared missing in action. It had seemed . . . pointless.

What do *you feel?* she silently asked her reflection in the bathroom mirror.

Naturally, she was glad Brandan had pulled through the crash and whatever had come after it. But would she want to be his girl again after he got home? She didn't think so. As much as she'd loved him—and she was sure she'd loved him—he hadn't been very good at putting her first. There'd always been something else that mattered. College. Training to be a pilot. The war. And she wanted a guy who would put her first, above everything else.

She supposed Brandan was some sort of hero, surviving all of those months under who knew what circumstances. There would be a lot of celebrating when he came back. They'd write about him in the newspaper. There might be a parade, and perhaps he would be decorated. It wouldn't be such a bad thing to be seen on his arm. Her girlfriends would be pea-green with envy, as Scarlett O'Hara liked to say.

With a sigh, Lillian reached over and flushed the toilet she hadn't used. Then she ran water in the sink and pretended to dry her hands on a towel. When she opened the bathroom door, she heard Elenore Gallagher say that it was almost more difficult to wait now than it had been after he was declared missing.

Lillian stopped, still not ready to rejoin the others. Instead, she turned to look at the photographs that filled this section of the hallway. Family photos. Elenore and Andrew on their wedding day. Their parents, looking stern and unbending. The three Gallagher boys, individually and all together. She paused to stare at one of them. Brandan, when he was little. Probably not even a year old. So adorable. When she'd looked at pictures of him in the past, she'd sometimes imagined what their kids would look like. Dark hair. Light eyes. Chubby cheeks. A lot like Bobby looked.

It was amazing. Why hadn't she realized how much her nephew looked like Brandan when he was the same age? Remarkable. She would almost think all little boys looked the same, only look how different William and Yancy were in their baby pictures. It was almost as if—

The air caught in her chest. What was she thinking? It wasn't possible.

"Lillian?" her mom called. "Are you all right?"

"Yes." Her voice broke on the word. After clearing her throat, she said, "Yes. I'm fine. Just looking at the photographs." Her eyes went back to the photo of Brandan. Or was it a photo of Bobby? It could be.

But surely that was a coincidence.

Chapter 72

SUNDAY, JANUARY 2, 1944

Daisy didn't go to church the next morning. She didn't feel well. It wasn't an excuse. Her head pounded, and her stomach churned. She'd spent the night in the chair in the living room, reliving her mistakes of the past and fearing the consequences that were still to come in her future.

I sinned. I don't deserve to be happy. I'm not worthy. God forgives, but there are consequences. I knew there would be consequences.

Her mom liked to quote the verse that said a person shouldn't be anxious for tomorrow because it would be anxious for itself. Daisy would like nothing more than to stop worrying, to stop the anxiety that churned in her stomach, but she didn't know how to do that. If only she could ask. But how could she without revealing the whole truth?

There was something else her mom liked to quote, the line from a poem by Sir Walter Scott: *"Oh, what a tangled web we weave, When first we practise to deceive!"*

It was true. So horribly, exactly true. Her sin had turned into a lie, and that lie had snowballed out of control. And now it was time to pay the piper.

Brandan Gallagher was alive. Brandan would be coming home. If he saw Bobby—*when* he saw Bobby—would he know the truth at once? Would he care? Would he want the world to know? Would he be proud he had a son or despise her for getting pregnant with a child he didn't want?

The Brandan Gallagher who'd taken her in the back seat of his Pontiac convertible hadn't been the man she'd wanted him to be, hadn't been the man she thought she'd loved since the age of fourteen. She hadn't known who he really was back then, so she didn't know what to expect from him now. And that frightened her.

The back door opened, and Todd entered the kitchen. He set his Bible on the counter before walking into the living room.

"How are you feeling?"

"Better," she lied.

So many lies.

His gaze lowered to Bobby, who sat on the floor near Daisy's feet. "Reverend Rubart shared the news about Brandan from the pulpit." He settled onto the sofa and then lifted Bobby onto his lap. "There was a lot of rejoicing and plenty of tears."

"We knew there would be."

"Yes."

She hated how stiff they'd both become since getting the news about Brandan. It was like a return to how they'd acted and spoken in the early months of their marriage. She'd thought they were past the awkwardness. They loved each other, even though she had yet to declare her feelings aloud. They loved each other, and they loved Bobby. They were a family. Brandan's return wouldn't change that.

Would it?

Of course it would. How could it not?

The back door opened a second time. This time to reveal Lillian, her eyes narrowed and her mouth pressed into a hard line as she stared at Bobby. Cold air swept past her and into the living room, and still she stood there, staring and silent.

"Lillian?" Daisy got to her feet.

As if awakened from a trance, her sister slammed the door behind her, her gaze shifting to Daisy. "Is it true? Tell me it isn't true."

"Is what true?"

Lillian looked at Bobby.

And Daisy knew the answer to her own question.

Lillian called her a foul name. A word that would have gotten her mouth washed out with soap if their mom had heard her use it when they were young.

Todd rose to stand beside Daisy.

"She slept with my boyfriend." Lillian almost spat the words as she glared at Todd. "Did you know that? Or did she trick you into marrying her?"

"She didn't need to trick me. I wanted to marry her."

"How long was it going on?" Lillian's gaze swept back to Daisy. "How often did he go to you when he should have been with me?"

Daisy felt her heart break. Shame seemed to burn her from the inside out. "Never. He never wanted to be with me, Lillian. Never. He wanted you."

Lillian's laugh was sharp and loud.

Startled by the harsh sound, Bobby started to whimper. Todd bounced the boy in his arms, attempting to soothe him.

The last thing in the world Daisy wanted to do was talk about her painful past, about her night with Brandan, especially not in front of Todd. But she had to try to explain to her sister. "Lillian, please. Sit down. Let me tell you what happened."

"Why should I? You'd only lie to me."

"I won't lie." Tears welled in her eyes. "I won't lie about this. I promise." She turned toward Todd.

He didn't need her to say anything. As was so often the way, he understood what she needed before she asked. "I'll take Bobby to his room and put him down for a nap."

The sisters stood looking at each other until they heard the bedroom door close.

"Does Brandan know about . . . about Bobby? Did you write to him in England?"

"No."

"Which question are you answering?"

"Both. He didn't know I was pregnant. He doesn't know I had a baby. And I never wrote to him. Not even once."

"You stole him from me. You always were jealous that he fell for me. I knew it, but I never thought you would sleep with him in order to take him from me. You're the reason he wouldn't get engaged to me after Pearl Harbor. You're the reason he wouldn't marry me before he went away."

Daisy took a step toward her sister. "That's not true. Even when . . . Even the one time it happened . . . he was thinking of you. He loved you. He probably still—"

Lillian slapped her. The crack reverberated in Daisy's ears as she pressed a hand to her stinging cheek.

"That's enough!" Todd stood in the hallway again, his gaze locked on Lillian.

"You're a fool, Todd Kinnear."

"I'm many things, Lillian, but a fool isn't one of them. This is my home. Daisy is my wife, and Bobby is our son. You have upset them both. It's time you left."

Lillian looked as if she wanted to slap him the same way she'd slapped Daisy. But she wisely turned and walked to the back door. Before opening it, she glanced over her shoulder at Daisy. "You'll be sorry for what you've done to me."

"I'm already sorry."

"Not sorry enough." Lillian left, slamming the door a second time.

"She'll never forgive me," Daisy whispered.

"She will. Eventually."

"Do you believe that?"

He sighed, then shrugged. "I don't know. I hope she will, but it's up to her. You can't *make* her forgive you."

She turned toward him. "What do you think she'll do now?"

He came to her and took hold of her hands. "Whatever it is, we'll get through it. We'll get through all of it together."

Will we? she wondered as he drew her to him. *Will we get through it?*

Chapter 73

PRESENT DAY–MARCH

During the night, the wind whistled around the corner of the condo. Lights from the parking lot cast dancing shadows against the closed window blinds, adding to the eerie feeling.

Brianna lay in the bed, the blankets pulled tight beneath her chin, listening to every unfamiliar sound and wishing she was at home in her own bed. At one point, she even found herself fighting tears. Why? She wasn't sure. Perhaps it was the weather. Perhaps it was knowing Greg was on the other side of that wall.

The evening had been pleasant. Even fun. At first. She and Greg had snuggled in front of the fire for a time. They'd prepared dinner together. Greg had volunteered to wash the dishes while she dried them. Afterward, they'd returned to the sofa and the fire and a movie on the TV. He'd kissed her. She'd kissed him back. He hadn't done anything he shouldn't have done, and yet . . . Yet she'd begun to feel vulnerable, exposed, unsure. She'd had the feeling that he was barely restrained from doing far more than she would want. That he was growing impatient with her. His hands had begun to roam, and she'd stopped him. He'd complied, but there'd been something in his eyes that had sparked fear in her chest.

Why was I afraid? Why am I still afraid?

She glanced toward the door, then got out of bed, went to it, and turned the lock in the center of the knob.

I'm being silly.

She scurried back to bed and huddled under the warm comforter.

"But examine everything carefully; hold fast to that which is good; abstain from every form of evil." As those verses from the Bible entered her mind, so did something Hannah had said about them during one of their Sunday lunches. *"'Form' in that verse means 'appearance.' Avoid even the appearance of evil."*

"Shut up, Hannah." Brianna covered her face with a pillow. Letting shadows on the blinds make her nervous and afraid was one thing. Imagining her friend lecturing to her in the middle of the night was something else.

A sound caught her attention. She pulled the pillow from her face. There it was again. Holding her breath, she looked toward the door. There wasn't enough light to see, but it sounded as if someone had tried to turn the knob. And there was only one other *someone* in the unit besides Brianna.

Don't wait. Act now. Go!

Quietly, as if she, too, might make an unwelcome sound, she reached for her phone on the nightstand.

Chapter 74

MONDAY, JANUARY 17, 1944

Walking beside his father-in-law, Todd leaned into the icy wind coming from the west. It was too cold to talk, too cold to do anything but hunch down in his coat, his collar pulled up and his hat pulled low. Eager to get to the warmth of their own homes, they walked with long, quick strides.

More than two weeks had passed since Lillian's confrontation with Daisy, and his sister-in-law hadn't shared the facts with her parents. At least not yet. If she'd told them, Carl would have said something to Todd, or Nancy would have said something to Daisy. So far, nothing. Somehow, that made it even worse. Lillian's parting threat seemed to hang over their heads. What would she do? Whom would she tell? What would she say?

Todd worried about Daisy. She wasn't sleeping much at all and wasn't eating either. As in those early months of her pregnancy, she'd lost weight, and shadows had returned beneath her eyes. He felt as hopeless to fix things now as he had then. Perhaps more so.

It didn't help that Nancy had shared what news she heard about Brandan with Daisy, beginning with the official Western Union cablegram from the Office of the Adjutant General to Brandan's parents stating that their son was returned to duty on the twenty-first of December. An odd way to phrase it. What did "was returned to duty" mean after a man had been missing in action for so long?

"He'll spend time in England first," one of the men at church had said to Todd. "If he's hurt, he'll recover in one of the military hospitals there. And they'll debrief him. That won't be fun. All those months in enemy territory. They'll want to know how he survived and how he escaped. They'll want to know who helped him."

It took effort not to wish the British would keep Brandan on their island forever. But Todd knew that wasn't the answer. He needed to pray for Brandan. He needed to pray for Lillian and Daisy and Bobby. He needed to pray for God's will to be done.

Help us, God. Please help us.

The two men stopped, as they normally did, by the sidewalk leading to Todd's front door.

"See you in the morning," Carl said, still tucked into his coat like a tortoise into its shell.

"In the morning."

"Hug that grandson of mine."

"I will."

With a nod, Carl moved on toward his house.

Todd followed the walk to the front door. Opening it, he called, "I'm home!"

As he closed it behind him, Daisy appeared from the hallway. Her hair was pulled back into a ponytail, her preferred style since becoming a mother. She offered a quick smile, but it did nothing to hide the strain written on her face.

"How was your day?" he asked.

"I think Bobby's getting a cold."

Todd shucked off his coat and put it away. "Is he running a fever?"

"No. Just a runny nose. He doesn't act sick."

"Does he need to see Dr. Hamilton?"

"It's only a cold." She drew in a breath. "But, actually, we did go to see the doctor today."

"But you said he—"

"I needed to see him."

Todd moved toward her. "What's wrong?" He clasped her shoulders with his hands. "I know you're not sleeping or eating enough. But I thought—"

"I'm pregnant, Todd."

Surprise shot through him. It hadn't occurred to him that she might get pregnant. Even though they'd shared a bed for the past three months, for some reason he'd never considered she would have *his* baby.

She looked up at him with wide eyes. "Are you . . . are you happy about it?"

"'Happy'?" Surprise drained from him and elation took its place. "'Happy'?" He picked her up and spun her around. When she squealed, he stopped and set her down. "Sorry. I shouldn't have done that. Are you all right? What did Dr. Hamilton have to say?"

"He said Bobby will have a new brother or sister by the end of August." She gave him a little smile. "And I'm fine. A little underweight, like last time, but I'm fine."

"I thought . . . I was afraid you were . . . that you were worrying yourself sick. About . . . Lillian." He paused, then added, "And Brandan."

Her smile faded. "I thought the same at first. I was worried and sleepless, and I wasn't hungry. But then I realized I was late." She reached up and touched his cheek. "It is something to be happy about. Another baby. Isn't it?"

"Yes. It sure is. I'd spin you around again to prove it, but I don't want to make you dizzy. Or sick."

She took his face between her hands and drew his head down

so she could kiss him. He accepted the kiss like a drowning man gulps in air when he breaks the water's surface. There'd been such a distance between the two of them since they'd heard the news about Brandan. They hadn't kissed since that day. They hadn't made love again. And in this moment, he realized his fears had gone far deeper than he'd known.

When the kiss ended, he drew her into his embrace and rested his cheek on the top of her head. "I love you, Daisy Kinnear. We're going to be an even better family when there are four of us than we are with three."

Her voice muffled against his chest, she said something he couldn't make out.

"What?"

She pulled her head back and looked at him. "We've never talked about what size family we want."

"No." He chuckled. "I guess we haven't. I suppose as many as God chooses to give us."

There was love in her eyes as she looked at him. He saw it, recognized it, understood it. But he longed for her to say the words out loud. Loud enough that he could hear it in his bad ear. Loud enough for others to hear it too.

Loud enough for Brandan Gallagher to hear it.

Todd drew Daisy close again. Did she know that he was jealous of what she'd once felt for Brandan? He hoped not. He didn't want her to see that side of him. "When do you plan to tell your parents?"

"I don't know."

"It'll be hard for me to keep it a secret, walking to and from work with your dad."

"I know. But maybe now isn't a good time."

"Because of Lillian?"

She nodded as she withdrew once again. "She's so angry. I don't blame her. I did something terrible. I broke trust with her. I've had over a year to seek God's forgiveness, but I couldn't ask for hers without telling the truth about—" She broke off abruptly.

But once again, he understood. "Without telling the truth about Bobby."

"Yes."

"We'll wait awhile to say anything. We've got time. I've kept other secrets. I can keep this one."

Chapter 75

SATURDAY, FEBRUARY 5, 1944

The official document Brandan had to sign while still in England stated that he would never reveal to anyone the details of his many months in France because those details might be useful to the enemy and could be a danger to other servicemen. He couldn't disclose the names of those who'd helped him or the different ways he'd evaded the enemy or the route he'd followed to escape from occupied territories or any other facts regarding his experiences. Everything about his life from October 9, 1942, until December 21, 1943, was classified and would remain that way. It was as if a red-inked, all-in-caps *SECRET* had been stamped across his forehead.

What that oath of secrecy meant didn't fully hit him until the transport plane landed on the Gowen Field runway just after dawn on that Saturday in early February. During his debriefing, he'd answered every question posed to him, but from now on, he couldn't answer anything, no matter who asked. He couldn't tell his parents or his brothers what had happened to him. He couldn't praise the men and women who'd saved him, at least not with specifics. He couldn't tell Lillian what had kept him away from her all this time.

Lillian.

He'd thought about her often during his journey back to America and especially throughout the final leg of his trip to Idaho. Would she be glad to see him again? Would she be there, waiting for him as she'd promised?

His time in France had changed him, probably in more ways than he understood himself. He'd believed in God before he left for the war, but his faith was something deeper now. He saw the world through a transformed lens. Would the woman he loved see the difference in him? Would she be glad for the changes?

He remembered the two letters he'd written to her from England. He'd asked her to forgive him. Of course, he'd let her think it was because they'd had a rough time his last week on leave, but he'd needed forgiveness for a lot more than that.

Had Daisy told Lillian what happened between them? He'd asked her not to in the letter he'd sent through Jack. Had his friend given the letter to Daisy? Had Jack even received it? Plenty of letters went missing in wartime. What would Brandan find waiting for him now that he was home again?

He didn't know if he was ready to find out.

Daisy's mom bounced Bobby on her knee as she and Daisy sat at the dining-room table, cups of tea before them. Daisy's dad was working today, along with Todd, and Lillian was at the movies again. Which meant when her mom asked Daisy to bring the baby over it had been easy to agree. There was no chance of running into her sister's hostility.

"Bobby's so strong," her mom said, her grandson now standing on her lap. "Look at him. He'll be walking before you know it."

"He already walks while holding onto the furniture."

"I hope you've moved anything dangerous or breakable to spots out of his reach. You were the worst. My goodness. The moment you could crawl, you were into all sorts of mischief."

Daisy smiled. Her mom did that a lot when they were together. She would comment on Bobby, then her thoughts would go back in time to when her daughters were little, and she would share stories about them. But there was one thing Mom never mentioned. She and Dad never spoke of Bobby's early arrival date. Sometimes, in those first weeks after his birth, disappointment had been obvious in their expressions, but they hadn't censured Daisy or Todd, and they'd never loved Bobby any less. But how would they feel if they knew the *whole* truth? If they knew Bobby wasn't Todd's son. What would change then?

Her left hand lowered to her stomach and stayed there. At ten weeks along, there was a new roundness to her belly. It had happened much sooner than with Bobby. She didn't need maternity clothes yet, but she felt the changes happening in her body. She and Todd would need to tell her parents before too long.

The doorbell rang, and her mom started to rise with Bobby in her arms.

"I'll get it," Daisy said. "And you can put him down if your arms are tired."

A moment later, she pulled open the door and felt the world come crashing to a halt.

"Hi, Daisy." Brandan stood on the porch.

Despite his coat and hat, she could tell how much thinner he was. A shocking change from the robust man she remembered. His cheeks were gaunt, and there was a deep weariness in his eyes. A white scar marred his chin.

"May I come in?"

"Yes. Of course. Yes. Come in." She took a couple of steps back. "Welcome home."

"Thanks." As he stepped into the house, he asked, "Is Lillian here?"

Daisy shook her head.

"Brandan." Her mom now stood right behind Daisy. "How good it is to see you."

"Thanks, Mrs. Abbott. Good to see you too." His gaze went to the stairway as he removed his hat. "So, Lillian isn't here?"

"No," Mom answered. "But she should be back before long. She went to the movies with some friends. Please come in and wait for her."

"Who's this?" he asked, curiosity filling his eyes.

Daisy didn't have to look to know who he meant.

"This is my grandson, Bobby. Daisy's little boy."

His gaze returned to her. "You got married?"

She nodded.

"My folks didn't tell me that. Who's the lucky guy?"

"Todd."

His eyes widened with surprise. "Todd Kinnear?"

She nodded again.

"Wow. Wouldn't have guessed that about you two. But congratulations."

Daisy turned and took Bobby from her mom's arms. "I think we should go home. Bobby needs his nap, and Lillian won't want us in the way when she sees Brandan."

"Wait. Don't you—" her mom began.

But Daisy was already halfway to the dining room. She wanted to flee without a backward glance, but she forced herself to pause and turn. "It really is wonderful that you're back, Brandan. Your parents never gave up hope that you were alive and would return to them."

"Thanks, Daisy." But his eyes were on Bobby, and a frown creased his forehead.

Grabbing her coat and the baby's blanket, she made her escape.

Lillian paused on the front porch and waved goodbye to June Olson before June and the two GIs pulled away from the curb.

She knew that when she went inside, her mother would want to know everything about *The Song of Bernadette*. Her mom rarely went to the movies, but she wanted others to tell her about what they'd seen. What could Lillian say about this movie? It was dramatic and Jennifer Jones was amazing, although her character was a bit too religious for Lillian's liking.

She opened the door, calling, "Mom, I'm—" The rest of her words died in her throat as Brandan rose from a chair, like a ghost from her past.

"Hello, Lillian."

She closed the door. "Brandan."

Her mom got up from the sofa. "I have some things to see to in the kitchen." Then she hurried from the living room.

Lillian couldn't think. She didn't know what to feel. She'd believed Brandan dead for a long time. For even longer, she'd been angry at him for leaving her behind, for not marrying her or at least getting engaged. And then there'd been the fury when she learned about Daisy and Bobby. Lillian had loved Brandan for years, and then she'd tried to forget him while she dated other guys. Seeing him now, her world felt upside down and inside out.

"When did you get back?" Did her voice sound normal? She wanted to sound normal.

"Early this morning. I went home to see the folks first thing. They didn't know I was back in the States. I didn't know for sure how or when I'd be in Idaho, so I didn't try to alert them. I came to see you as soon as I could get away."

She went to the sofa and sank onto it. "Have you been waiting for me long?"

"Not quite an hour." He sat on the edge of the easy chair. "Daisy was here when I arrived."

Lillian stiffened, and her jaw clenched. Fury flared in her belly at the sound of her sister's name on his lips.

"I couldn't believe it when she told me she and Todd got married. And they have a kid already."

Truly, did he not know? Maybe he hadn't seen Bobby. Then again, look how many months had gone by before Lillian saw what was right before her eyes.

"I guess I was gone longer than I thought I was," Brandan added.

"It felt like an eternity for everybody who cared about you."

"It felt like an eternity to me too."

Her heart pinched, and her bitterness lessened. Brandan might be wearing a crisp, new uniform, but he looked like he'd been through hell. He was way too thin, and his jacket hung off his shoulders. He was still handsome, but in a sad kind of way. And he looked older than his actual years. He would turn twenty-five in another week or so, but he looked much older.

"Lill, the last time I saw you . . . Listen. I know I hurt you, but I . . . I loved you. I still do."

"You do?" The anger started to churn inside of her again.

"Yes. But there are things we need to work through. I'm not . . . I'm not the same guy who left Boise back in forty-two."

"'Things to work through.'" She clenched her hands in her lap, fighting against the facts she wanted to throw in his face. But why fight them? Didn't he deserve anything she said to him? Didn't Daisy deserve it too? She leaned forward, her voice low. "Do you mean things like sleeping with my sister and getting her pregnant?"

He drew back as if she'd slapped him, and the shock on his face almost made her sorry she'd said it. Almost.

"Did you see him?" she demanded in a near whisper. "Did you see Bobby?"

Brandan nodded.

"And you didn't know at once that you're his father? He looks just like you in your baby pictures."

His head bowed now, he ran the fingers of one hand through his hair. Was he ignoring her question? Or maybe he was trying to think up another lie to tell her.

"Do you still want to tell me you loved me back then?"

"I did love you." He looked up, meeting her gaze. "And I love you now. I'd like to say more, but I don't think you're ready to hear it." He stood. "I'd better go. I hope . . . I hope we can see each other again soon. I hope we can talk about the past."

She wanted to throw something at him. She wished she could crack his skull open.

He went to the door. Stopping with his hand on the knob, he asked, "What did Daisy tell you about that night?"

That night? Did he want her to believe it was only one time, the same way Daisy did? Had he and Daisy made up some sort of story together?

He looked back at her, waiting.

"She hasn't told me anything except that the baby's yours. What more is there to say?"

"A lot more, Lillian. A lot more." He opened the door and left the house.

She shot to her feet, pillow in hand, and threw it at the door, releasing a cry of frustration at the same time.

Her mom came out of the kitchen. "Lillian, what's wrong?" She looked around. "Where's Brandan?"

"He's gone!" She ran for the stairs. "And I don't care if he never comes back."

Chapter 76

PRESENT DAY—MARCH

The clock on the nightstand read 7:02 a.m. when Brianna got the text.

We're here.

Drawing a relieved breath, she rose from the side of the bed. She was dressed. She'd been dressed for the past couple of hours, but she hadn't left the bedroom, and the door remained locked. Her bags were packed, and as far as she knew, her skis, boots, and poles were still against the wall by the main door to the unit. If possible, she'd like to leave without seeing Greg. She'd written a note to leave behind. Could she be that lucky?

The bedroom door opened without a creak. With a bag in each hand, she crossed the living room, arriving at the front door just as a soft knock sounded. She opened it at once. Tears flooded her eyes at the sight of Adam and Hannah standing on the walkway.

"Are you all right?" Adam asked, his voice low.

She nodded.

"What the—"

Before Brianna could turn toward the sound of Greg's voice, Adam stepped past her. "We came to take Brianna home."

"Brianna?"

She faced him.

He wore a baggy T-shirt and a loose-fitting pair of shorts. His feet were bare, and his hair was disheveled. Still, he was unbelievably good looking.

"I'm sorry, Greg. I . . . shouldn't be here."

He held out a hand as if inviting her to come to him. The look in his eyes beckoned her. It seemed sweet and tender. But it wasn't. Not really. There was danger there. A danger she hadn't fully understood before. Danger she'd barely sidestepped. If she hadn't locked her door last night . . .

A shudder passed through her.

Hannah touched Brianna's shoulder. "Let's go."

Greg's expression hardened. "Nobody forced you to go on this trip, you know. You *wanted* to come with me. You could hardly wait to come with me. You were begging for it."

"I know." She tilted her chin in a show of bravado. "The mistake was mine. The bigger mistake would be if I stayed."

"I should have known you'd turn coward. You church girls. What a waste."

Brianna saw Adam's right hand ball into a fist, and she reached out to take hold of his arm. "It's all right. Let's go."

"You got everything?" Adam asked without looking at her.

"Yes. I just need my ski stuff. I've packed everything else."

Adam took a step forward, escaping Brianna's hold. "What do you do, Truman? Troll young-adult groups at churches for girls you can deceive?"

Greg huffed as if Adam wasn't worth answering. But Brianna saw the truth written on his face even as GeeGee's questions repeated in her memory once again. *"What sort of man is he? What is his character?"*

Shame washed over her. She'd been charmed by Greg's handsome face and his smile. She hadn't bothered to find out who he was. Not really. A couple of visits to church didn't make someone a Christian. It wouldn't have taken much effort on her part to learn that about him. She'd *wanted* him to be the perfect guy, and she'd ignored all the signs. The signs Hannah had seen and warned against. The signs her great-grandmother had wished she would look for.

"Come on, Brianna," Adam said.

She turned her back on Greg, glad to leave and thankful she'd had the good sense to text Adam in the wee hours of the night.

Chapter 77

SUNDAY, FEBRUARY 6, 1944

Todd watched as Daisy bundled Bobby into his coat. He noticed how her hands shook, and his concern increased. "We don't have to go to church." He didn't know if he wanted to stay home more for her sake or his own.

"We should be there today." She looked up at him. "It would be wrong to miss the celebration. My mother's right. It is a miracle he's back. It will look . . . odd . . . if we aren't there. Our families are friends."

Todd knew she was right. That wouldn't make it any easier to see Brandan, to wonder what he might say or do. Did Brandan know by now that Bobby was his natural son? And if he did, had he figured it out on his own, or had Lillian told him?

But Bobby isn't really his son. He's my *son. He's* our *son. Daisy's and mine.*

That was true. That was all true. But if Brandan Gallagher wanted to lay claim to the boy, what then? What would that mean? Brandan was a soldier home from the war. No doubt a decorated or soon-to-be decorated soldier. A hero. Sympathy would be on Brandan's side, and with a few words, he could ruin Daisy's reputation, perhaps forever.

Some people would judge her. Supposed friends might shun her. And what if some of that spilled over onto Bobby? Daisy would find that unbearable. So would Todd.

A discreet couple of questions to an acquaintance who'd trained in the law had calmed some of Todd's fears about Brandan's return. Todd was Bobby's legal father, and that would not change. He had been married to Daisy at the time of their son's birth, and his name was on the birth certificate. Nothing would change that. But there was still damage that Brandan or Lillian—or the two of them together—could do if they chose. Families were at stake. His own. The Abbotts. The Gallaghers. So many people could still be hurt.

The walk to their house of worship felt more like a walk to the gallows. Neither he nor Daisy said a single word from the moment he closed the front door until they arrived at the entrance to the narthex of the church. Only then did he say, "Ready?" She nodded, and they went up the steps together, Todd with his hand under her elbow as she carried Bobby in both arms.

"Oh, Daisy. Have you heard?" Patty Dickson grabbed Daisy's upper arm. "He's back. But of course you've heard. Lillian would have told you." Patty released Daisy's arm and patted Bobby's cheek. "Where is Lillian? I haven't seen her yet."

"I don't know. My parents aren't here yet either?"

"Not yet. But the Gallaghers are in the sanctuary. You can't get close enough to say boo. There's so many there before you, wanting to congratulate him and welcome him home." Patty lowered her voice. "He looks dreadful, really. Like he hasn't slept or eaten in months."

Daisy answered with a nod.

Todd leaned toward Patty. "We'd better go in. The service will begin soon."

"Yes. You're right. Maybe we'll talk later." Patty went on her way.

"Are you all right?" he asked Daisy.

"Yes."

They moved together toward the stairs off to the right. A few Sundays ago, Daisy had decided she preferred to sit in the balcony with Todd and Bobby rather than take the baby to the nursery. She hadn't explained why, but Todd thought he knew. It had to do with Brandan being found alive. She'd felt the need to keep her son close at all times. Todd understood. He felt the same way.

He was glad they'd made the change before today. It wouldn't look odd that they chose not to be in the main sanctuary. He wanted distance between himself and Brandan.

No. Not the complete truth. He wanted distance between Bobby and Brandan. He was afraid of what Bobby's natural father might say or do.

Todd helped Daisy settle into the front pew of the balcony. After he sat beside her, he took Bobby onto his lap and removed the boy's coat. Only after that did he allow himself to look down at the sanctuary.

He saw the Gallaghers—both parents and all three of their sons—moving into their usual pew. The comments from Daisy last night and from Patty Dickson a short while ago hadn't prepared him for Brandan's changed appearance. It wasn't only the weight loss, although that was striking. There was something about the way he moved, as if he was in pain or as if he didn't trust where he was or who he was with. At least six or seven weeks had passed since Brandan had escaped or been rescued, and those weeks with the Allies had doubtlessly improved his condition, which made what Todd could see seem even more alarming.

He's been through hell.

He glanced at his wife, then down at Bobby. While he and his little family had made some sacrifices in this time of war—rationed coffee, sugar, and meat, gasoline in short supply, tires nonexistent—they'd never gone hungry, never been cold because they couldn't heat their home, never been forced into hiding because of enemy soldiers wishing them dead. He had a great deal to be thankful for, and no excuse for wishing any ill on a man miraculously returned to his loved ones.

I don't wish him ill. I just wish him far away from Daisy and Bobby.

His gaze shifted to the Abbotts. Carl and Nancy had arrived, but Lillian wasn't with them. He wondered what that meant. Or if it meant anything at all other than she hadn't come to church.

Father God, how do we walk through this minefield?

As the congregation rose to sing, Todd wondered, *Would I have done anything differently if I'd known how things would be today?* The answer came to him in an instant. No, he wouldn't change anything. He would still have offered to marry Daisy when he learned of her pregnancy. He would still have fallen in love with her. And he would still be Bobby's true father.

All he could do now was try to live honorably before God and do the best he could by his family.

Chapter 78

WEDNESDAY, FEBRUARY 9, 1944

Daisy carried Bobby from his bedroom into the kitchen where she opened the freezer door and withdrew the cold cloth that had been dipped in chamomile tea earlier.

"Here, sweetheart. Suck on this. It'll make your gums feel better."

He fussed and flailed his arms at her, and when she tried to put the cloth in his mouth, he turned his head away in a snit.

"Oh, please, Bobby. Please. Mommy's tired, and the day's hardly begun. It will help if you'll just suck on it awhile. Remember how it helps?"

She thought of the young mother with the teething infant in the drugstore all those months ago. Another lifetime ago. She remembered thinking that woman could be her someday. And here she was. It *was* her. She loved being Bobby's mother. But at this moment . . .

Tears filled her eyes as she carried Bobby and the cold cloth to the living room. She was about to sink onto the sofa when a knock on the door stopped her. It was tempting to ignore it, but Bobby's sudden shriek of complaint could be heard by someone half a block away, let alone someone standing on the front porch. With a sigh, she went to answer it.

Her heart plummeted at the sight of Brandan, in uniform, standing beyond the doorway.

"Daisy." His gaze shifted to Bobby, then back to her. "Could we talk?"

She wanted to refuse. She wanted to slam the door in his face. Instead, she took a step back. "Come in."

The one good thing was that Bobby quieted, his aching gums forgotten with the arrival of a stranger. A stranger who wasn't a stranger. Not to his mommy.

Brandan entered the house, looked around, then walked across the room, putting distance between them. As much as the room allowed.

Daisy closed the door. Her mouth was dry, but even without that, it would have been hard to speak while memories assaulted her. Memories that burned, made her sick, reminded her of the most shameful moment of her life.

Again, Brandan looked at Bobby. "Lillian told me about . . . him."

Daisy's breath caught, and she moved to the sofa and sat before she could fall down. Only when Bobby complained did she realize how tightly she held him against her chest. She allowed him to wriggle free from her arms and to slip down to the floor.

"May I?" Brandan pointed to a chair.

She nodded.

He removed his hat before sitting, and he watched as Bobby walked unsteadily while holding onto the edge of the sofa, the little boy staring back at him. It alarmed her, the similarities between the two.

"Why have you come?" she asked at last.

He met her gaze. "Not to cause you trouble, if that's what you thought."

That was exactly what she'd thought, and his words didn't reassure her.

"There's a lot I can't tell you. A lot I can't tell anyone, for security reasons. The military required that I swear myself to secrecy about what happened from the time my plane went down until I reached safety over a year later. I may not ever be able to tell. Not ever."

"Whatever you went through, it must have been awful."

He continued as if she hadn't spoken. "But what I can tell you is this. God dealt with me about what I did to you. I didn't know—" Again he looked at Bobby. Again he returned his gaze to her. "I didn't know I left you to face a . . . a pregnancy on your own. I was already ashamed that I . . . took advantage of you. I stole your innocence, Daisy, and then I thought I could avoid any consequences, the way I usually did. I thought if I kept it a secret, no one would know and Lillian and I would . . . would be okay. We'd go back to the way things were. I didn't realize then how much I believed things would always go my way."

He closed his eyes for a moment. "I was selfish and arrogant, and I didn't see it." He looked at her again. "Even when I asked God to forgive me after . . . after that night, even when I promised God that I would live a better way, I thought I could go on doing things my way, under my own power, and I wouldn't have to truly face what I'd done." He paused again, then added, "'Pride goeth before a fall.'"

Daisy saw something on his face, something in his eyes, that told her he was a different man than he'd been before. It wasn't the physical change in him. This went deeper. But why should she be surprised? She was a far different woman than the girl who'd driven his convertible into the foothills, even while knowing it was wrong to do so.

"Brandan, I—"

He put up a hand. "Wait. Let me finish. Please."

She nodded her compliance before helping Bobby climb back

into her lap. On his own, he picked up the cool cloth—not nearly as cold as it had been—and put it in his mouth, as if wanting to be quiet with her.

"After I was shot down over France, I met a man whose faith went deeper than anybody I've ever known. There he was—in danger, hungry, suffering losses few of us in America can imagine—and he was able to trust and praise God without reservation. His English wasn't perfect, but it was good enough that I was able to learn from him in the time we were together. He saved my life more than once." Brandan leaned forward, his eyes searching hers. "But more than that, he helped save my soul. He helped me truly repent in my heart and my mind."

"You *have* changed," Daisy said softly.

The corners of his mouth tipped up, a hint of that devastating smile he'd used so often when around members of the opposite sex. And yet it, too, was different. She saw humility in that small smile rather than a swaggering confidence.

His gaze lowered to Bobby. "Someday I'd like to know more about . . . about what happened while I was away. Not today. Not yet. But someday." He was silent a short while. Then, "Are you happy, Daisy?"

"Yes. I'm happy."

"Todd's a good husband? A good father?"

"Yes. He is good. Very good. Good to both of us. He loves Bobby, and he loves me."

"I'm glad." He glanced in the direction of the house next door. "Do you think Lillian will ever let me explain? Not excuse myself. Just explain."

"I don't know, Brandan. She isn't talking to me. Not for over a month."

His expression fell. "I take it that's my fault too."

"She's hurt and angry. She didn't know about Bobby until . . .

until after word came you'd been found, and she didn't believe me when I told her that you and I . . . that we hadn't been . . . that we hadn't been seeing each other behind her back."

"I heard she's been seeing other guys. Made new friends. Going out a lot."

Daisy nodded.

"Guess I can't blame her. But I'd like her to know that thoughts of her helped keep me going. She's one reason I fought so hard to survive."

"I'll tell her, if I get the chance."

Brandan nodded, then rose from the chair. "I'd better go."

As Daisy began to rise, a sharp cramp stole her breath. She fell back onto the sofa with a cry.

"Daisy?"

She shook her head. "It's all right. I—" Another pain silenced her.

"What can I do?"

"Get my mother," she managed to say as another cramp tightened her belly and something warm turned her skirt bright red.

Brandan bolted from the house without further encouragement.

Chapter 79

WEDNESDAY, FEBRUARY 9, 1944

Todd was down on the factory floor, talking to one of his newer employees, when he heard his secretary call his name. Irritation crept into his voice as he turned around. "Yes?"

"Mr. Kinnear. You have a call, sir."

"Can you take a number and tell them I'll call back?" He'd given the girl those instructions more than once since hiring her. When he wasn't in his office, when he was dealing with matters in the factory, he didn't want to be disturbed. Just take a message.

"It's your mother-in-law, Mr. Kinnear. Something about your wife going to the hospital."

"What?" He took off running. It felt like an eternity before he held the receiver to his ear. "Nancy? What's happened?"

"Todd, I'm sorry. I think she's having a miscarriage. There was so much blood. I've got Bobby. Brandan took her to the hospital."

Brandan? The name reverberated in his chest. *Why Brandan?* He shook off the question. "Which hospital?"

"St. Luke's."

He put down the receiver and turned around. His father-in-law stood in the doorway.

"It's Daisy. She's been taken to the hospital. I'm going now." He wished his car was in the parking lot, but it wasn't. He would have to walk to the hospital. Run was more like it. What was it? Ten blocks? More?

"Go," Carl said. "I've got things covered."

Todd grabbed his coat and shot by his father-in-law, too worried to say anything else.

Midweek in the late morning, the sidewalks were mostly empty. A few businessmen and a few shoppers were out, but not so many that it impeded Todd's mad dash from Kinnear Canning to St. Luke's Hospital. Even his bad leg couldn't slow him down too much. He would pay for the exertion later, but that didn't matter to him now.

"Your wife was admitted," the woman behind a desk informed him.

She gave him a room number. Todd hurried in the direction she pointed, fear pounding in his ears. But his heart seemed to stop when he saw Brandan Gallagher standing in the hallway outside the room he sought.

Brandan's worried expression eased slightly when he saw Todd's approach. "Thank God you're here."

Were those bloodstains on his jacket?

"You can go in," Brandan added.

As if Todd needed his permission.

There were two beds inside the room, but the second bed was empty. In the first, Daisy lay with her eyes closed. Her face was nearly as white as the bleached sheet beneath her.

Todd stepped to the side of the bed and took hold of her hand. "Daisy?"

She opened her eyes, and tears fell across her temples and into her hair.

"I got here as fast as I could."

"I . . . I lost the baby," she choked out.

He nodded.

She looked at him, eyes pleading. "Why?"

"I don't know. It doesn't—"

"Am I being punished?"

"Punished?" He shook his head as he leaned closer. "No."

But even as he answered her, he wondered about the man beyond the door. Why was it Brandan who'd rushed Todd's wife to the hospital? Was that the reason she feared she was being punished? Now that Brandan was back, did she want to leave Todd? Did she want to be with Brandan again? Were they—

"Our baby," she whispered as she closed her eyes. "I'm sorry, Todd. I'm so sorry." She rolled her head on the pillow, her face now turned away from him.

He stayed until her tears stopped trickling from the corners of her eyes and her breathing became even. Exhaustion had, at last, put her to sleep. Only then did he release his hold on her hand and move away from the bed. He wanted answers. First from a doctor and then from Brandan.

But he wouldn't get answers from Brandan. He was no longer waiting in the hospital corridor beyond the doorway. Todd's questions for him would have to wait.

Hours later, Todd left the hospital. Because of Daisy's excessive blood loss during the miscarriage, the doctor felt it best for her to remain under observation for twenty-four hours, but he assured Todd she wasn't in any real danger.

"Go home and get some sleep," the physician had added. "And don't worry, Mr. Kinnear. I see no reason why your wife shouldn't be able to carry a baby to full term in the future."

Head bent into the winter wind, the darkness of evening already blanketing the city, Todd made his way toward home. He didn't run this time. There was no urgency.

Remembering the last words the doctor had said to him, he wondered if there would be another pregnancy. Daisy had never said she loved him. He'd imagined it in so many things she said and did, but he'd never heard her say the actual words. Maybe if Brandan hadn't survived the plane crash. Maybe if there was still a baby on the way, a baby that was his and Daisy's.

He felt a prick of guilt. He and Daisy did have a child. They had Bobby. And he didn't wish Brandan dead. Gone, maybe, but not dead.

He went straight to the Abbott home and knocked on the front door, then let himself in. The family was at the dinner table, Bobby in a high chair between his grandparents. Lillian sat across from her mother but didn't look up from her plate when he entered the house.

Nancy rose from her chair and came toward him. "How is she?"

"Exhausted. Sad. She'll be all right. Staying overnight was more of a precaution."

"We didn't know she was expecting."

"She wanted to wait for a special occasion to announce it."

Lillian made a soft grunting sound but still didn't look up.

Nancy took hold of his arm and drew him toward the dining room. "Sit down and have something to eat."

"I'm not hungry. I should—"

"Eat anyway." She helped him out of his coat, then urged him onto a chair. "You need to keep up your strength. It's important in times of stress."

Arguing with her would be a losing battle. "All right."

"Good. We have pork chops tonight and mashed potatoes with gravy and peas. Bobby loves the peas. His grandpa smashed them for him." There was a green stain around Bobby's mouth, proving his grandmother's words.

Todd smiled at his son and his heart constricted with dread of the unknown.

"It was a miracle that Brandan was there when it happened." Nancy set a plate of food on the table before him. "His car was here, and he was able to drive Daisy straight to the hospital. Otherwise, we would have had to call for an ambulance."

He'd had no appetite before. Now the idea of eating made him feel sick.

Lillian lifted her gaze at last. "Why *was* Brandan at your house, Todd?" Her words were tinged with bitterness.

Fear not. He felt those words whispering in his heart, and something stilled inside of him. He couldn't explain it. The future remained uncertain. Yet he felt steadied for now.

"I don't know, Lillian. Does it matter? He may have saved my wife's life."

To Reverend Rubart's credit, he hadn't asked what was wrong when Brandan arrived at the church after leaving the hospital.

"I need to think and to pray," Brandan had told him.

The pastor had motioned toward the sanctuary. "Stay as long as you need. I'll lock up after you're gone."

Brandan wasn't sure how much time passed—several hours, at least—while he sat in the sanctuary, praying, talking to God about the people he'd hurt, trying to figure out a way to undo his sins of the past. But he couldn't undo sin. He could be forgiven. He could get a second chance. But he couldn't undo what he'd done. That would be like trying to put autumn leaves back onto a tree after they'd fallen. Nature didn't work like that. Neither did life.

Eighteen months. He'd been gone from Idaho for eighteen months. A year and a half. Not such a very long time. And yet everything seemed to have changed. The ground beneath him felt uneven, uncertain.

Memories of Lillian had helped keep him alive during those awful months in Nazi-occupied France. But now she wouldn't talk to him, wouldn't see him, wouldn't let him apologize again. Could he blame her? From what little he'd ascertained, she hadn't known about his night with Daisy until recently. So the news was a fresh shock to her. She hadn't had many months to think about it, as he had.

On the other hand, she seemed to have moved on after his plane went down. He'd heard from others, including one of his brothers, that over the past year Lillian had gone out with quite a few of the guys from the base where she worked. So even if she'd never learned about Brandan and Daisy, perhaps she wouldn't have wanted anything to do with him. Her love hadn't lasted.

He was a different man than the one who'd been shipped overseas. Could he expect Lillian to be the same woman he'd left behind? No, because circumstances, experiences, had changed her too.

Then there was Daisy. He'd taken her innocence without a thought. He wanted to blame the whiskey, but he couldn't. With or without the alcohol, he'd been selfish enough to take advantage because he was angry with her sister. And then he'd written her that letter from England. He didn't remember the exact words he'd used, but he knew he'd told her he didn't care about her, that he loved her sister, that their night together hadn't meant anything to him.

It was all just one big mistake.

Daisy had thought she loved him, or that night in the foothills never would have happened. Brandan had known she was infatuated with him. She'd thought she hid it, but he'd known. He'd liked knowing it. And he'd taken advantage of her feelings, then left her in a mess. He'd left her pregnant, and she'd had to find a way to live with that reality. Her solution had been to marry Todd Kinnear.

He recalled the expression on Todd's face as he'd hurried toward

Brandan down the hospital corridor. Todd loved Daisy. That had been clear as day. And the two of them had been expecting a baby together.

That brought Brandan's thoughts to the boy. The little boy who looked so much like him. Bobby was cute and healthy and loved. That, too, was obvious.

What would Brandan have done if he'd still been stateside when Daisy discovered she was pregnant? Would he have stepped up to the plate? Would he have done the right thing, offered to marry her? His gut told him the answer was no. He would have looked for a way out. And it wouldn't have been because of Lillian. Not completely. It would have been because he wasn't ready to be tied down, because he was focused on a career as a pilot, because he was too blasted selfish to marry a girl he'd used so abominably.

"So, how do I make things right, God?" His voice echoed in the empty sanctuary. "I can't change the past. How do I do the right thing now? How do I make the future better for the people I care about?"

He left the church without an answer but trusting that God would show him what to do when the time was right.

Chapter 80

PRESENT DAY–MARCH

From a corner table in a favorite restaurant, Brianna saw Adam enter through the main doors. He spoke to the hostess, then his gaze swept the room until he found her. He nodded, said something more to the hostess, then started in Brianna's direction.

The palms of her hands felt moist, and she wiped them on her pant legs. It had been hard enough to admit to her parents the danger she'd put herself in, to confess her willfulness and selfishness and the lies she'd told along the way. Telling GeeGee hadn't been easy either, and she knew they would be having more conversations in the future about her poor choices. But somehow, talking to Adam about it would be the most difficult of all. She wasn't even sure why.

The drive home from McCall three days before had been made in tense silence. Anger had emanated from Adam, his white-knuckled hands clenching the steering wheel. At the time she'd wondered if he was mad at her or only at Greg. When she'd asked Hannah later, all her friend had said was, "You need to ask him."

That time had come.

Adam slid onto the booth's bench opposite her. "I'm glad you texted me. How are you?"

"I'm okay. I've had some hard talks with Mom and Dad. GeeGee too."

"I imagine."

"Adam." She looked down at the paper napkin she'd begun to shred. "I'm sorry."

"For what?"

"For not listening better to God. Or to my friends."

Something about him seemed to relax. She felt it more than saw it.

"GeeGee told me once that unbelievers don't have to justify their sinful choices, but when a Christian chooses to sin, they will either repent or they will find excuses for their actions." Heat rose in her cheeks, but Brianna forced herself to keep eye contact with Adam. "I won't make excuses. I chose to go where I shouldn't. At the time, I made excuses to myself and to the people I care about. I didn't know Greg was playing me, but that doesn't really matter. I'm not responsible for his actions. Only for mine. And I'm truly sorry."

Adam leaned back, and the slightest of smiles turned the corners of his mouth. "You're different."

Her heart fluttered, pleased that he'd seen what she felt. "I hope so."

It wasn't only that she'd been frightened up in that condo in McCall. It wasn't only that she'd seen her foolish mistakes that had put her in that situation. It went deeper than that. God had been at work within her, even as she'd tried to ignore Him. And the wisdom GeeGee had shared with her, the stories from the past, the snippets of Scripture—those had all played a part in a transformation in her spirit, a transformation she hadn't recognized until this week. Somehow, over the past few days, as she'd humbled herself before God, she'd begun to see what He'd wanted to change within her heart, what He'd been changing.

Once again, her great-grandmother's voice asked those questions in her memory: *"What sort of man is he? What is his character? Who is he at his core?"*

Brianna hadn't been able to answer about Greg, but she could answer about Adam. He knew Jesus and loved to serve God. He cared about other people, and he cared about her.

"Thank you," she whispered. "For being a true friend."

He leaned forward, reaching across the table to cover one of her hands with his own. "I'd like to be more than a friend, Brianna, and I think you know that."

Something fluttered in her chest. "I know." Perhaps it was the departure of fear or the arrival of faith. Whatever the cause, she knew she wanted more with Adam too.

Chapter 81

THURSDAY, FEBRUARY 10, 1944

Silence filled the car on the drive home from the hospital the following afternoon. For Daisy, staring out the passenger window, the entire world seemed cloaked in gloom. Something beyond the gray from the cloudy skies. Her mind felt clouded as well. It was too difficult to hold a thought longer than a moment, so she didn't bother to think at all.

Rather than driving to the garage via the alley, Todd parked the car at the front curb. He got out and hurried around to open her door. At first she didn't move. It was as if she didn't know that's what he wanted her to do, even after he held out his hand to help her.

"Daisy?"

At last she let him draw her out of the car. With one hand gripping her beneath the elbow and his other arm around her back, they slowly walked toward the front door. But before they reached it, panic assailed her. Beyond that door was the memory of pain and blood and loss. Beyond that door lay the reminder that God had finally punished her for her sin.

"I can't go in there," she whispered.

"It's all right. You can go straight to bed."

"No." She pulled back. "I can't go in there. I can't."

"But, sweetheart, you have to go in. You need to rest. We're home now."

She looked toward her parents' house. "Take me there. Let me go home to my mother." She turned her face toward Todd. Even in her panic, she recognized the hurt she'd caused him with her request. But she couldn't help it. She couldn't. "Please."

"All right." He swept her feet off the ground and carried her back to the main sidewalk and over to her parents' front door. Daisy hid her face against his chest, breathing in the familiar scent of him, thankful for the strength of his arms.

Todd didn't knock. Somehow he managed to open the door while holding her in his arms. She felt the warmer air of the house wash over her. It seemed to bring a sense of security with it, and she relaxed.

"Todd?" she heard her mother say.

Daisy didn't lift her head. She couldn't bear to look around.

"She said she couldn't go into our house," Todd explained.

"Oh. Of course. Well, take her upstairs to her old bedroom. It's the door on the left."

Todd didn't reply, but a moment later, he began the climb.

Daisy tightened her grasp around his neck. He took each step with his right foot first, making the journey feel extra slow. Only then did she realize how much more pronounced his limp was today. She couldn't summon the energy to ask why.

Todd placed her on the bed. The bed she'd slept in right up until she married him. She rolled toward the wall and began to weep. Silent tears filled with shame and pain and regret. She'd lost her baby. *Their* baby. The one conceived in love. And it was her fault.

A blanket was drawn over her shoulders. The creak of the door told her when her husband left her alone. She wanted him with her but didn't have the strength to call him back.

O God, did You have to discipline me this way?

Nancy and Carl stood together in the living room, arms around each other, when Todd descended the stairs. Nearby, Bobby played on the floor with some big wooden blocks.

Todd looked at his mother-in-law. "You should go up. She needs you."

Nancy stepped forward and hugged him, whispering, "She needs you too."

He nodded but couldn't quite believe her.

Nancy moved on toward the stairs.

"Sit down, Todd," Carl said. "You look done in."

It was a fair assessment. Physically. Emotionally. Spiritually. He was spent, done in, worn out.

He lifted Bobby from the floor and held him close, needing the touch of him, the smell of him, the sound of him. Bobby didn't seem to need the same from his dad. He wriggled and protested until Todd put him back on the floor with his blocks. Then Todd sat on the sofa.

Carl took the easy chair opposite him. "She's going to be fine, son."

Will she? Will we?

"Losing a baby is a hard thing for a woman to go through. I remember how it was for my own mother. She miscarried twice between me and my younger brother. I was maybe eight or nine that second time. I remember how melancholy she was. I expect it was hard for my father, too, but men don't show it the same way. At least that's how it was for my father and how it's been for me."

Before Bobby's "early" arrival into this world, Todd had brought many questions to Carl Abbott. Whether a problem was big or small, he hadn't hesitated to ask the man for his advice. Carl had been a surrogate father, a man he respected and trusted. But after Bobby was born less than nine months after the elopement, things hadn't been quite the same between the two of them. He'd never regretted that change more than he did now. He could use Carl's advice.

Maybe if his father-in-law knew the whole truth, maybe if he knew Todd hadn't taken Daisy into his bed until they'd been married a full year, maybe if . . .

But no. He couldn't be the one to tell Carl. If it ever came out at all, it wouldn't be Todd who told him about his grandson's conception. It would have to be Daisy who did the telling.

With his elbows on his thighs, Todd put his face in his hands and prayed. *Help us, Lord.*

A moment later, Carl's hand landed on Todd's shoulder. "God will see you through this."

"It's more than just the baby." His voice broke.

"I know."

Did he know? Todd looked up, but Carl's head was turned toward the stairs. Todd followed his gaze to see Nancy coming down the steps.

"She's asleep," she said. "Let her stay for the night, Todd. I think she'll be able to face things better tomorrow."

"If you think that's best." He stood. "It's time we went home."

"Let Bobby stay too," Nancy said before Todd could reach for his son. "Please. I think it might help her if she can be with him."

Weariness washed over Todd. Or was it hopelessness? He hadn't the strength to argue or to even know if the decision was right or wrong. "All right." He looked at Carl. "I don't think I'll go into the factory tomorrow. Can you take care of things for me?"

"Of course. Don't give work another thought."

He wouldn't give it a thought. He knew Carl could manage without him. Probably better than Todd at the moment. All he cared about was Daisy. Daisy and Bobby.

He entered his house a short while later. It felt cold, dark, and empty. He flipped the light switch on, and shadows seemed to scurry into the corners and under the furniture. The faint fragrance of whatever Nancy had used to clean the house the previous day lingered in the air, a reminder of what must have happened. Daisy in pain and starting to miscarry. Brandan lifting her up and carrying her to his car to drive her to the hospital. Nancy staying behind with Bobby, cleaning up the blood from the sofa and floor.

Todd had only those few facts. Speculation pushed in to fill the empty spaces.

Strange, wasn't it? Last night, he'd felt more at peace when Daisy was still in the hospital. God had told him not to be afraid, and the fear had left him. He'd brought Bobby home, put him to bed, then had fallen into bed himself. Now his wife and son were sleeping next door, and a hundred questions tried to pummel him and keep him from ever sleeping again.

"Why was Brandan at your house, Todd?" the memory of Lillian's words taunted him.

"Why was he here?" he asked aloud, wanting the answer even without his sister-in-law's taunting.

Why had Brandan been with Daisy?

What had been the purpose of his visit to Todd's home?

Had Brandan done something that caused Daisy to miscarry?

It was Daisy's voice he heard in his memory now. *"Am I being punished?"*

When she'd asked that question yesterday, he'd told her no. It wasn't punishment. But was it tit for tat? Todd had Brandan's son, so Brandan somehow caused Daisy to lose Todd's unborn child. Was that possible?

A groan escaped him as he made his way into Bobby's bedroom. The spare bed was still there. The bed where Daisy had slept for a year. The cradle was gone from the room, returned to the garage months ago, too small for the fast-growing boy.

Todd went to the crib and picked up a soft blanket. Time and again, he'd watched Daisy brush her cheek with one of Bobby's blankets. Now he mimicked her, but instead of sliding, the fabric snagged on the stubble of his beard. He'd forgotten to shave that morning in his rush to return to the hospital.

Taking a few steps backward, he sat on the bed. *God, help me. Help us.* He dropped Bobby's blanket onto the floor and covered his face with his hands. *Please don't take Daisy and Bobby from me. They're my family.*

Chapter 82

FRIDAY, FEBRUARY 11, 1944

Daisy opened her eyes at the soft creak of her bedroom door. She expected to see her mom bringing Bobby back after feeding him his breakfast and seeing her dad off to work. Instead it was Lillian who stepped into the room. Daisy pushed the hair away from her face as she sat up.

"Have you left him?" her sister asked, that now familiar harsh edge in her voice.

"Sorry?"

"Have you left Todd? Are you back home for good?"

The question surprised Daisy. It shouldn't have but it did. "No."

Lillian took a step toward the bed. "But you can't leave Brandan alone, can you?"

"Lill—"

"Don't try to tell me otherwise. It's obvious or he wouldn't have been there when . . . when it happened."

"I didn't go to see Brandan. He came to see me. He had something to tell me." Daisy lowered her legs over the side of the bed. The room swam for a moment, then righted itself. Again, she pushed her hair away from her face. "I'm sorry."

"You're sorry?" Lillian's voice rose.

"Please sit down. Please let me explain." Her head seemed stuffed with cotton, making it hard to think straight. Still, she needed to try. She and Lillian hadn't spoken to each other in more than a month. They'd barely seen each other since that dreadful Sunday. "Please, sis. You need to know. You need to understand."

"Oh, all right." Lillian plopped onto the chair.

A memory flashed in Daisy's head. The morning after Daisy had been with Brandan in the foothills, Lillian had come into this same room and sat in that same chair, looking for advice. *"Don't you get it, Lillian,"* Daisy had snapped at her. *"Brandan could die, and all you can think about is getting a ring on your finger."* She'd said those words and much more. But she'd spoken out of guilt, not love.

Lillian's expression remained hard. "I'm sorry you lost your baby."

"Thank you," Daisy whispered.

"Are you . . . Are you okay?"

"Yes." Daisy drew a breath and released it. "Yes, I'm all right. Tired but all right."

"Good, then. Lucky you."

"Lillian, I want to ask a favor."

Anger sparked in her sister's eyes. "A favor? *You* want a favor from *me*?"

"Yes. I want to ask you to listen without interrupting. I want you to hear everything I have to say. You may do with it as you please after I'm done. You can believe me or not. You can stay angry or let us be friends again. I hope you'll come to a place of forgiving me."

Lillian snorted but kept her lips pressed together.

Daisy waited for a more definite objection but none came. After drawing another deep breath, she began. "You were right when you said I was jealous of you and Brandan. I lost my heart to him when I was still fourteen. I thought what I felt for him was love. It wasn't. Not really. But I believed it at the time."

Lillian crossed her arms over her chest and stared hard in Daisy's direction.

"I never told him how I felt. I never told anyone how I felt. I didn't know you'd guessed my . . . my feelings. And Brandan never let on to me that he'd noticed. Besides, I was just your kid sister. He only cared about you."

"And flying," Lillian said bitterly.

Daisy offered the slightest of smiles. Both in agreement with the comment and in tolerance of the interruption.

"Sorry. Go on."

"What happened—" Daisy broke off, swallowed, then made herself keep looking at Lillian as she continued. "Only Brandan can tell you why he was at the Starlite on that Friday night. He'd been drinking. A lot, I think."

"Brandan doesn't drink."

"He did that night. And when I saw him, I only meant to help him outside for some fresh air." She held up a hand to stop another protest. "That's all I meant to do. Just help him outside. Maybe drive him home since he wasn't in a fit state to drive himself. But things . . . things went all wrong after that."

Now she had to lower her gaze. She couldn't look at Lillian as she shared what had happened that night in Brandan's convertible. The shame she'd felt, especially when she realized Brandan hadn't wanted her, hadn't thought of her, and had been eager to be away from her when his senses returned.

"I never . . . I didn't see him again after he let me out of his car in the alley on that Saturday morning. Not until I saw him last week when I was with Mom. He didn't know about Bobby, and we left right away. That was it until he came to see me on Wednesday."

"Why? Why did he go to see you?"

Daisy lifted her eyes at last. "Because he's a different man than the one who left for England. He isn't focused only on what he wants. He's grown up, and he's grown closer to God. He wanted to tell me he's sorry for what he did to me and ask my forgiveness. And he wanted me to tell you that thoughts of you kept him going while he was in France. He wanted to get home to you."

Lillian leaned forward at the waist, her crossed arms lowering, hands now on her knees. "He told you that?"

"Yes."

Lillian straightened again. "Well, if he thinks that'll make me forgive him, he's got another think coming."

Do I believe God withholds His forgiveness in the same way Lillian's doing now?

The question shimmered through Daisy, stealing her breath away. She heard it in her own voice, and yet it felt as if another, greater voice spoke the words. In the hospital she'd wondered if she was being punished for her sins. Last night, she'd asked God why He'd disciplined her in such a way.

Now she wondered if, when she'd confessed her sins and asked Him for forgiveness, she'd believed that God responded, *"You've got another think coming."* Because why else would she expect Him to withhold forgiveness and punish her by taking her unborn baby? That wasn't the loving Father she knew. That wasn't the Lord she served.

A week or two ago, she'd read a verse in Philippians, and she recalled it now. Paul wrote about forgetting what was behind and laying hold of what was before. She realized now that God had tried to show her the truth even before she lost the baby. He'd tried to prepare her for that moment. She must forget what was behind and stretch forward to the things that were before her. She couldn't change her past. It was done. But she could trust God while reaching for her future, a future that God in His mercy had provided for her. She could trust Him to work all things together for her good.

Even this.

She sucked in a breath as she realized she wasn't afraid to go home. To go home to Todd. To face the loss of their baby together. She understood, as she hadn't before, that while God had forgiven her, she'd clung to her guilt. Now she could let it go, must let it go. She had to put her past, all of her past, at the foot of the cross and leave it there.

She stood and reached for the clothes she'd removed last night. "I'm sorry, Lillian. I need to get Bobby. We need to go home."

"Now?" Lillian got to her feet.

Daisy stilled. "I love you, sis. You may not believe it, but I do. I will always be sorry for hurting you. But I'm not going to live in the guilt of it any longer. When I confessed my sins, Jesus washed me white as snow. I'm going to live like I believe it."

Lillian stared at her as if she'd grown another head.

Impulsively, Daisy stepped forward, took her sister by the shoulders, and kissed her cheek. "I'll pray that you find happiness, Lillian. I don't know what that looks like for you, but I'm going to pray for that often." She whirled away and began to dress.

Jupiter rose from his bed and padded across the kitchen, toenails tapping on the linoleum floor. Arriving at his master's chair, the dog placed his muzzle on Todd's thigh and looked up at him with doleful eyes, as if to ask, *When will they come home?*

"I don't know." Todd put his elbows on the table, then rested his forehead on the heels of his hands. "I don't know."

Jupiter whimpered.

"I don't know!"

At Todd's angry tone, the dog backed away.

Todd straightened and held out a hand. But before he could say anything, the back door opened. "Daisy?" He stood, his gaze flicking to Bobby in her arms, then back to Daisy's face.

"I'm sorry," she said.

"For what?"

"For so many things."

She closed the door behind her before unwrapping Bobby from his blanket and setting him on the floor. With a squeal of delight, he crawled to Todd and, holding onto Todd's trousers, pulled himself up.

My son. He lifted the little boy into his arms. He'd felt Bobby's absence from the house throughout the night, and the last thing he wanted to do was let go of him again. But Bobby had said hello and was ready to move on. He demanded to be put down, and once he was on the floor, he crawled out of the kitchen to where a box of toys sat within easy reach. Both Todd and Daisy followed him to the living room.

Daisy removed her coat and placed it across the arm of the sofa. Then she turned to face him.

My wife. He couldn't imagine life without her. She'd filled all of the empty places in his heart, some that he hadn't known were empty until the moment she filled them. When they'd married, he'd known she loved Brandan—a man lost over war-torn France—but he'd believed friendship between them would be enough. And it had been for a time. But then he'd fallen in love with her and had begun to hope for more. He'd hoped and he'd believed. They'd made a new life. They'd shared a love for Bobby, and there'd been another baby—

He closed his eyes, at the same time closing off that thought.

"Todd."

He looked at her, heart aching.

"I don't love Brandan. The silly girl I used to be was infatuated with him for a long time, and I made mistakes because of it. Big mistakes. But I . . . I'm not that girl any longer."

What was she saying? What did she mean?

"Brandan came to see me only to say he's sorry for what he did. He's changed too. And he doesn't want to make trouble for us. He knows that I love you and that Bobby is our son."

"What?"

Twin tears traced paths down her cheeks. "I love you. And Bobby is *our* son."

"But you've never said—"

"I didn't know how to say it. After such a long time, I didn't know how. I was afraid."

"Afraid of what?"

"I'm not sure. Afraid I'd be wrong again, I suppose. No. That wasn't it. I was afraid I didn't deserve to be happy after what I'd done. I'd sinned, but despite it, I had a husband who loved me and who loved my baby. A husband who'd taken my shame upon himself and protected me from gossip. I felt guilty for what I'd done, but I also felt guilty for being so content and happy in my new life. And my guilt made me afraid that I could lose it all, that it would be taken from me."

Todd took a step toward her, lifting a hand at the same time to touch her cheek, to wipe away a tear. "I didn't understand. I should have, but I didn't."

"I didn't understand either." She pressed her cheek into the palm of his hand. "Not really. Not until this morning. Not until a little while ago. It was as if God drove out all the confusion and uncertainty and fear in a flash. He showed me the truth." A smile blossomed as she met his gaze. "And the moment I saw the truth, I ran home. To you."

He pulled her into his arms, needing the feel of her against him, wanting to know that what she'd said was real, to know that she was real, to know his little family was real. "You ran home to me," he whispered.

"Yes." When she leaned her head back to look up at him, there were more tears in her eyes and on her cheeks. She smiled through them.

He kissed her then, his heart full of joy and thanksgiving.

Daisy Kinnear was truly home at last.

Chapter 83

PRESENT DAY–APRIL

Brianna sat on the floor in GeeGee's bedroom. Her phone remained in her jean's pocket. She wouldn't record what her great-grandmother had to say. Not this time. She hadn't come to glean information that would improve or add to her history assignment. She was here to listen and take the words to heart.

"Brianna." GeeGee leaned forward in her chair. "I know it can become a cliché, but Romans 8:28 is true. For those who love God, for those who walk in His purposes for them, He does make *all* things work for good in their lives. I have experienced it myself, time and again." She drew a breath as she leaned back in her chair. "Let me tell you the parts of the story that I've left out. Remember when I said I'd told lies, that I'd lived a lie? That's the part of my story I'm going to tell you now."

Brianna listened to her great-grandmother, sometimes surprised, sometimes disbelieving. In some ways it felt as if GeeGee was talking about a different person from the one Brianna knew. That younger Daisy had loved a different guy before she'd loved Brianna's great-grandfather. And Brianna's own grandfather hadn't been a Kinnear. Not by blood anyway.

"Did your sister ever forgive you?" she asked when GeeGee fell silent at last.

"In time. But it was never the same between us."

"Who else knew about Grandpa?"

A pensive smile curved GeeGee's mouth, and her eyes held a faraway look. "Only those who mattered. I learned the difference between lying to cover my sin and simply keeping my own counsel out of wisdom." She nodded as if to affirm her words. "After Lillian and Brandan, eventually my parents were told the truth, and before Bobby turned three, we told Brandan's parents as well. The Gallaghers became an integral part of my children's lives after that. Both Bobby and Elizabeth. They became the grandparents they couldn't have from Todd since his parents had passed on. And finally, when they were old enough in turn to understand, Bobby and Elizabeth were told."

"How did Grandpa take it?"

"Knowing how much Todd loved him and how much Todd loved me made the biggest difference, I believe. And I suppose it helped that Brandan wasn't a complete stranger. Brandan moved away after he got married, but he and his wife came to visit his parents and brothers every year. So every summer there were barbecues and such where the families were together. The Kinnears and the Abbotts and the Gallaghers, just like it was when I was in high school."

GeeGee released a soft breath. "Brandan told me once that he'd asked God how he could make things right. He found a way by becoming a friend to Bobby, a mentor of sorts. And by never trying to be Bobby's dad. He never tried to replace Todd in Bobby's eyes. Todd was Bobby's dad, from the moment Todd married me to the moment he stepped into eternity."

"You've had a good life, haven't you? Despite messing up royally when you were my age."

GeeGee laughed. "Yes, dear. I have. A very good life. Sometimes a hard one. Life is full of hard things, even when it isn't us who have, as you put it, messed up royally. But when we walk with God, life is always good, because He is."

"Romans 8:28," Brianna said softly.

"Indeed."

Chapter 84

SATURDAY, MAY 26, 1945

That Saturday afternoon in May, nearly three weeks after VE Day, was warmer than normal for Boise. Trees sported pink and white blossoms and sweetened the air as Daisy and Todd walked from the parking lot toward the entrance of the church, Daisy cradling their eight-weeks-old daughter, Elizabeth, and Todd carrying two-year-old Bobby. Just inside the doors, they saw her parents, deep in conversation with the Gallaghers.

"Oh, look at that darling girl." Elenore Gallagher leaned closer. "She looks just like Bobby did at that age."

It wasn't true, of course. Elizabeth had a different shape to her nose and mouth and was much fairer in coloring. But Daisy only smiled in answer.

"We'd better find our seats." As he spoke, Todd put a hand beneath her elbow.

Elenore nodded. "Yes, do go on. We'll have time to talk at the reception afterward."

They walked to the entrance to the sanctuary where they were met by an usher. He had the look of an airman or soldier about him. A friend of Brandan's, no doubt.

"Bride or groom?"

A ridiculous question since the bride was from England.

Todd answered anyway. "Groom. And keep us at the back." He jerked his head toward Bobby. "In case this one gets restless."

The usher nodded and took them to the back row on the right side of the church.

As they settled into the pew, Daisy said, "I've never seen Mrs. Gallagher look as happy as she does today."

"Brandan found himself a really nice girl."

Even as Daisy agreed, she felt a wave of sadness for her sister. Lillian wouldn't be at the church today. She and one of her friends from the base had moved to Portland the previous summer, and she hadn't been back to Boise since. Daisy had written to her at least once a month since the move, but Lillian's replies were brief and cool. Daisy couldn't help wondering what she thought about Brandan getting married.

To the soft strains of a violin, an usher and Elenore Gallagher walked past them, followed by Brandan's dad. A short while after they were seated, Brandan and his two brothers stepped into view at the front of the church.

Happiness washed over Daisy. Happiness for a friend. After many months of serving his country in Washington, D.C., where he'd met and fallen in love with the lovely Jocelyn Bottomley, Brandan looked healthy and strong. Not only physically strong but emotionally and spiritually, too, if a person had the eyes to see those things. Daisy wished her sister could have recognized the man he'd become, but she'd never given him a chance.

Please, Father, help her learn to forgive. Set her free from the bitterness that binds her still.

The music changed as the bride came down the aisle. Jocelyn's gown was simple, but her appearance was radiant. And the look on

Brandan's face as he watched his bride walk toward him told Daisy everything that was in his heart.

Todd leaned closer to her. "Do you wish you'd had a wedding like this instead of an elopement?"

She considered the question. Did she wish it? That her family and friends might have been present? That she might have had a lovely wedding gown? As she tried to imagine such an event, she realized that if it had happened that way, it most likely wouldn't have been Todd standing beside her as they spoke their vows. And she didn't want a husband other than the one she had. Her choices, both good and bad, had brought her to the place where she was now. If she had made another choice at the start of the war, she would have followed a different path.

She looked at Bobby seated on his dad's lap. She looked down at the infant girl sleeping in her arms. Returning her gaze to Todd, she answered, "God causes all things to work together for the good of those called to His purpose, to those who love Him."

Joy blossomed within her. The truth of that promise had never been so real to her as it was now. God had not only forgiven her, but as she'd trusted Him more and more, He'd turned even her worst choice into good.

Oh, how His love and mercy amazed her.

Epilogue

PRESENT DAY–JUNE

Daisy pressed the open Bible to her breast and repeated two verses from the Psalms. "'Make glad the soul of Your servant, for to You, O Lord, I lift up my soul. For You, Lord, are good, and ready to forgive, and abundant in lovingkindness to all who call upon You.'"

Brianna and Adam had been by a short while before. Gracious, Daisy liked that young man. He reminded her a little of Todd. Not in looks but in essence. He wasn't the flashy sort. Solid, steady, faithful. It pleased her that Brianna seemed to understand those things about him as well, and Daisy had delighted as she'd watched the romance bloom between them over the past couple of months.

During their visit, Daisy and Brianna had talked of things past and present, about the 1930s and 1940s—even though Brianna's college assignment was long since finished—and about the world as it was today. Even more important, they'd talked about the Lord.

Alone in her room now, Daisy whispered, "Brianna's come into a new place with You, Jesus." As the words faded into silence, she allowed her thoughts to drift back in time. She, too, had once wanted what she couldn't have—or at least shouldn't have—and in time she'd taken what wasn't hers to take. She'd made her bed of sin and shame and thought she would have to lie in it forever. At first, she hadn't understood unmerited grace, not even when it had been poured out upon her. But time with the Lord had helped her to see.

Happiness washed over her, as it was wont to do, and she closed her eyes, prayerfully taking members of her family—one by one—before the throne of grace, asking God to complete the good work that He'd begun in them. As her heart filled with gratitude, she knew His love and mercy would continue to amaze her until she drew her final breath and stepped into eternity. The lyrics of a favorite song from long ago came to mind, and with the words came the memory of the loved ones who awaited her in heaven: Todd . . . her parents . . . Lillian . . . Bobby . . . and so many others who had gone before.

"I'll be seeing you," she whispered with certainty, a contented smile bowing her mouth, "for great is His faithfulness."

A Note from the Author

Dear Friends:

As a teenager, I sometimes dreamed that I fought with the French Resistance. I have no idea why. Did I see a movie that first planted that idea? I can't say for certain. But I do know I've always been drawn to stories set during World War II. I have an affinity for the clothes and hairstyles of the era as well as the music and dances. And yes, the movies—both those that were made in the late 1930s and early 1940s and those made about World War II.

When the idea for *I'll Be Seeing You* first came to me, I intended to write a historical novel about two sisters and the man they both loved, set on the home front. But books sometimes take unexpected journeys. That was definitely true for this novel. And so I met a willful college student, circa 2022, who had her own story to tell, and suddenly Daisy had a great-granddaughter who needed her particular wisdom.

During the writing of this novel, research gave me a new admiration and respect for the boys who flew the B-24 bombers (and other planes). For one thing, I didn't know there wasn't any heat. They almost froze to death up there! Next time I'm in a commercial airplane, I'm going to thank God for the heating and cooling system in it.

Researching is one of my favorite parts of writing a novel. An author never knows what she will discover that she didn't know before. Naturally, I hope my research lends reality to fiction and increases a reader's enjoyment.

As I write this note, I am deep into my next novel, but it's too soon for any hints. To stay up-to-date on what's new and what's coming, I hope you'll visit my website (address below). Be sure to sign up for my newsletter while you're there. I always enjoy hearing from readers. You make every book worth the journey.

In the grip of His grace,
Robin

https://robinleehatcher.com

Acknowledgments

Every book needs a lot of help to get from the author's brain into the hands of readers.

Many thanks to the amazing fiction team at HarperCollins Christian Publishing and to the sales reps who get my books into all of the different sales outlets.

I'm continually grateful to my agent of almost thirty-three years, Natasha Kern. Oh, what a journey this has been, my friend.

An enormous thank-you to Susan Meissner, who gave me the encouragement I needed when I was feeling unable to do what was required.

God has blessed me with so many wonderful writer friends over the course of my long career. Their wisdom, their humor, their faith have made my life so rich.

Thanks to the women in the At His Feet Life Group for praying for me and this (among other) books. How sweet it is to have sisters in Christ.

And, of course, my thanks to my readers. Your emails and messages and comments on social media mean a great deal to me. So often, a word will come at just the moment when I need some encouragement. Maybe you don't know how much that means, but I hope you do.

Discussion Questions

1. Was there a scene in the book that you found particularly meaningful? What was it and why?
2. On the night Daisy met Brandan at the Starlite, she made a decision that would alter the course of her life. What choice(s) have you made that changed your course? Was it for better or for worse?
3. Romans 8:28 can feel like a cliché, but Daisy learned how true it is. God did work out all things for her good because she loved Him. Can you look back and see a circumstance that God turned to good in your life, even though it felt disastrous at the time?
4. At the dinner table, Adam asked a question that resulted in a rousing conversation: "Is telling a lie always wrong?" What do you think of the answers he received? Do you agree or disagree?
5. Despite her great-grandmother urging her to learn more about Greg, Brianna fell for what could be called a "wolf in sheep's clothing." What are the dangers of taking people (or situations) at face value without looking deeper? How can you avoid those dangers?

6. While in an empty sanctuary, Brandan asked God how he could make things right when he couldn't undo the past. If he asked you that question, how would you answer him?
7. When Lillian said that Brandan had "another think coming," meaning she would withhold her forgiveness from him, Daisy realized she'd acted as if God said the same thing to her. Have you ever believed God was withholding forgiveness from you?
8. Daisy learned there was a difference between lying to cover her sin and keeping her own counsel. Have you struggled with telling others either too little or too much?

From the Publisher

GREAT BOOKS

ARE EVEN BETTER WHEN THEY'RE SHARED!

Help other readers find this one:

- Post a review at your favorite online bookseller
- Post a picture on a social media account and share why you enjoyed it
- Send a note to a friend who would also love it—or better yet, give them a copy

Thanks for reading!

About the Author

Robin Lee Hatcher is the author of over eighty novels and novellas with over six million copies of her books in print. She is known for her heartwarming and emotionally charged stories of faith, courage, and love. Her numerous awards include the RITA Award, the Carol Award, the Christy Award, the HOLT Medallion, the National Reader's Choice Award, and the Faith, Hope & Love Reader's Choice Award. Robin is also the recipient of prestigious Lifetime Achievement Awards from both American Christian Fiction Writers and Romance Writers of America. When not writing, she enjoys being with her family, spending time in the beautiful Idaho outdoors, Bible art journaling, reading books that make her cry, watching romantic movies, and decorative planning. Robin makes her home on the outskirts of Boise, sharing it with a demanding Papillon dog and a persnickety tuxedo cat.